Influential

AMARA SAGE

faber

First published in the UK in 2023
by Faber & Faber Limited
Bloomsbury House, 74–77 Great Russell Street
London, WC1B 3DA
faber.co.uk

Typeset by MRules
Printed and bound by CPI Group (UK) Ltd, Croydon, CR0 4YY

A CIP record for this book
is available from the British Library

ISBN 978–0–571– 37734–3

Printed and bound in the UK on FSC paper in line with our continuing commitment to ethical business practices, sustainability and the environment.
For further information see faber.co.uk/environmental-policy

2 4 6 8 10 9 7 5 3 1

For Connie & Lesley,

I did it! Thank you for always telling me I could.

I love you and miss you dearly.

July

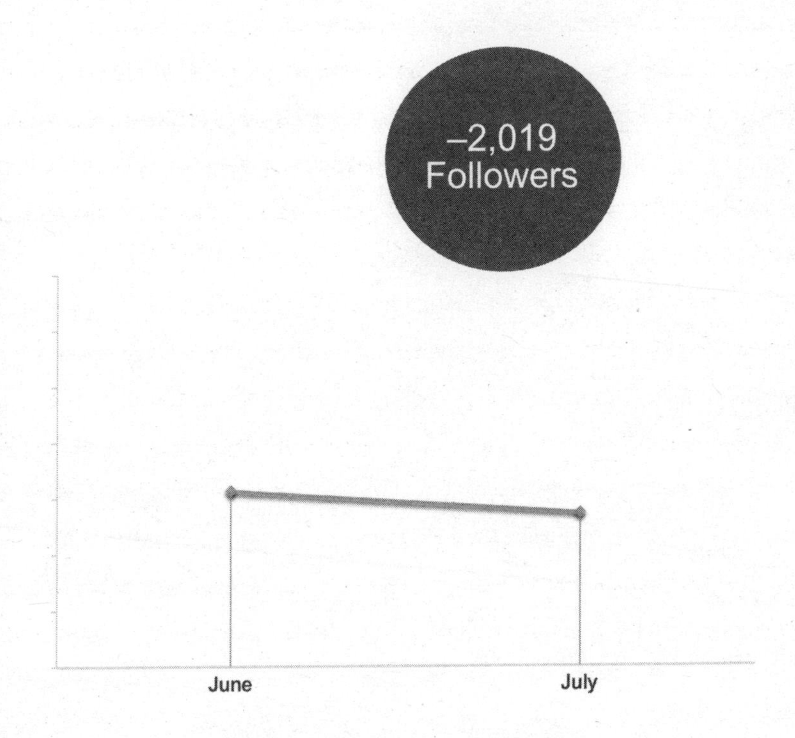

1

thereal_almondbrown

1079 **3.5M** **98**

Posts Followers Following

ALMOND BROWN

Public Figure
Vegan living | Cruelty-free beauty
Contact: Spencer@bigstarpr.com
Follow @evefairchild for more

I go to Settings. Account. Delete my profile.

When the end credits for *Unsolved Mysteries* are done rolling,

Netflix asks me if I'm still watching. I sigh, my breath shuddery from crying. The question seems passive aggressive, or maybe Netflix is just reflecting my own self-judgement back at me because *I know* it's bad that I've spent the entire week since school ended in bed, alone, bingeing shows. That I've woken up, written off the day, and decided to pick up right where I left off last night.

The black screen shows my reflection: low-angled, double-chinned, matted curls piled on top of my head. My brown skin that would usually be naturally sun-glowed a darker shade this far into July looks blotchy and blanched from staying inside.

Every atom of me looks entirely different to the girl in the first photo at the top of my Instagram, angelically smiling out from a spotlit vanity mirror, poised with the pads of her fingers massaging a pea-sized pearl of cream into her face, her chin up, hair falling in perfect ringlets down her back. Next to her is Eve Fairchild – or Mum, as I call her – roller-balling moisture across her forehead, one hand daintily reaching for the product in centre focus, its VeGlow label face out. The direction was 'mother-daughter pamper sesh', though I felt the farthest thing from relaxed.

When we came home from that two-day shoot in London, Dad had finally moved all his stuff out, taking Honey with him. Mum must've known because she'd had the house cleaned, the stinging smell of bleach stripping away the sniffs of my dog that clung between the sofa cushions, her hairs wiped clean from the skirting boards.

Everything shit seemed to happen at once. With Dad leaving and school ending, taking the pretence of any friendships I had left with it, I just haven't been able to post anything since. I can't be pushing vitamin-D supplements when I haven't absorbed a single milligram of sun all week, or share my OOTDs when I'm on day six of wearing the same bra and never change out of my pyjamas.

I've hated being an 'influencer' for years, but I could at least grin and bear it when we were simply *bending* the truth of our lives. Now that truth has snapped and shattered into jagged shards of hurt and blame, it's getting harder to catwalk my way over them like Mum expects me to.

I close the lid of the laptop because no, Netflix, I *haven't* been watching. For the last twenty minutes I've been doing this little thing I like to do at least three times a week called having an existential crisis.

I go back to my phone.

Do you want to permanently delete
thereal_almondbrown?
Yes No

My thumb hovers over the screen, the words a blur, my body heaving with that desperate, gaspy breathing that always comes after the kind of crying that empties your head, leaving an ache at your temples. Since Mum gave up knocking on my door a while ago and I heard her leave for London without me, I sit up, drawing my knees under my chin.

Big day today. Spencer set up a meeting with VeGlow at noon to discuss our product collaboration with them, and then we've been invited to the Skwimmy's launch at five – this new shapewear/swimwear hybrid brand we've been promoting. I pick at the crusted edge of a scab on my leg, wondering what story Mum'll make up about why I'm missing both.

If I press Yes now and permanently delete my account, I won't be thought of as a prospective business deal ever again. I won't have another ad campaign like VeGlow's to miss meetings for, or followers zizzing like mosquitoes behind the glass screen of my phone, or a launch party with a beachwear dress code to worry about when my skin's torn to shreds. Everywhere bubbling with people and people and people. Strangers who know me by name.

But no ad campaign means no money.

And I have life-alteringly important plans for this money.

I can't stay here while everyone else from school is getting government grants for university courses I didn't qualify for, and proper jobs with HR departments that would advise against hiring me after googling my name. VeGlow's advance is paying for connecting plane tickets to somewhere far, far away from here, to a country outside my demographic where I'll be irrelevant to ad companies. Somewhere hot enough I can breeze about sun-dazed, cocktail in hand, too unwound to care that I don't have a 'next step'. That advance is also paying for my first meal in the departures lounge that I can eat while it's still hot without taking a photo of it first, that I can choose without having to check the carbs, the calories, the saturated fat.

I'd come back home eventually, when the algorithm had churned me out of its memory and even Mum would have to admit my irrelevancy; I'd have been replaced by one of the thousands of other girls tagging their selfies with #digitalinfluencer or #fitspo, #styleblogger, #midsizefashion.

My eyes flick between the Yes and the No.

But can I wait until the contract's signed? And then however long after till the bank transfer comes through. After Eve&AlmondXVeGlow gets released to the public and I'm thrown into interviews, meet and greets, Q&As, and the endless 'Can I get a selfie with you?'s.

My God, no, just fucking delete it already, delete everything.

I sigh, throwing myself back onto the bed, because of course I can't; I'm contractually shackled to my socials for at least another six weeks.

Miserably resigned, I go to the internet, click history.

Today

10:19 Sad songs playlist

10:17 Medically induced coma. optional

10:15 Can you cry yourself to death

10:09 Why can't I stop crying

10:01 Sertraline 100mg side-effects crying

Clear browsing data: last hour

My phone screen dims and I let it.

2

The next morning's a Friday morning. Probably the last time I'll see Mum till Sunday night.

Her tit's about to go in her coffee. I slather my toast with butter, one eye on the breast pocket of Mum's Stella McCartney shirt as she hovers over her mug, phone in hand. I don't say anything, but loudly turn the page of the magazine in my lap.

'Light's not ideal here,' she mutters as she leans further over the marble table on tiptoes, holding her phone overhead, drone-like, to capture her breakfast flat lay. Her neck strains as she checks the shot lines up on her screen, the movement gathering skin at her collarbone like fine folds of ribbon, so delicate compared to her taut, fillered face.

My stomach groans into the fidgeting silence as Mum microadjusts the food. I don't tell her I'm starving because I skipped dinner last night, huddled away in my bedroom cocoon; I just watch her eyes flicking from phone screen to breakfast spread, which, I have to give it to her, does look good. I'd definitely double-tap. I nibble my lip looking at the cashew butter crumpets, *cubed* avocado, fresh organic fruit, and overnight oats that were #gifted to us by a brand called Oatsy who now own the rights to our breakfasts for the next few weeks. Mum stretches forward even further to nudge a satsuma wedge centimetres to the left, and that does it. Black coffee bleeds into her white silk blouse.

'Ow, fuckety, ow, that hurt.'

'Can I eat now?' I say, reaching for the plate of mushy, geometrical avocado and grabbing a triangle of toast.

Mum scowls at her camera roll. 'One more.'

It's actually three more. She sits down, already pinching and zooming with her thumb and finger, swiping through filters. After a few minutes of silence, she sighs and snicks the screen lock.

'You okay?' I say, not looking up from pretending to read Mum's article in *Women's Weekly* about 'Fabulous foods that boost your metabolism'. I can feel her staring at me, so I prompt her to start talking about her favourite topic. Her. 'How did the Skwimmy's launch go last night?'

'Mmhmm. Fine, it was fine.'

'Okay.' I know something's up because: a) she's not vlogging, and b) usually she'd be launching into the prosecco-fuelled antics that her and some noughties *Big Brother* contestant or footballer's ex-wife got up to last night. Silence means scandal. Maybe she fell out of a taxi? Got papped leaving a club with some Tik-Tok boy? 'What is it, Mum?' I ask, before I lose ten minutes of my life catastrophising about the possibility of being introduced to a new twenty-year-old twerking stepdad.

'Oh nothing. Just thinking,' she says. I blow at a loose curl falling over my face and look at my Mum, perfectly made-up and ironed out at seven forty-five in the morning, bar the coffee stain, trying her best to be nonchalant about whatever it is she's about to tell me. 'It's just Celeste Shawcross was telling me they've turned St Bart's into a wellness centre now. Sounds very *you*.'

Oh? As she babbles on about the old church renovations by the Downs, her tidy, nip-tucked chin bobs against her interlaced fingers, her white skin faux-freckled and fake-tanned. She's gone for a mid-part today after hearing that the side-part's officially dead, her blonde hair scraped back into a low bun.

I taste a spoonful from the bowl of Oatsy, positioned centre stage in the flat lay, as Mum lifts the lid of her Mac, tapping at the keys for a second before tilting the screen towards me. Turns out Oatsy's just another brand of bland, regular old oats, if a little artificially sweet, but it doesn't matter – I've already got my review typed up in my Notes and approved by their marketing team. I take another tentative bite, unlocking my phone as my teeth scrape the spoon, skim reading what I'm supposed to like about this gloop.

So, Oatsy helped me start my day off ✧just right✧ today guys, with a bowl full of creamy, sunbaked, golden oats, topped with fresh fruit and agave. Check out my latest morning routine video for a how-to! Use my code Almond20 for 20% off your first box of Oatsy today!

I go back to my avo toast, realising Mum's expecting me to be interested in the new website for the church Gramma used to go to before she moved to the retirement village, though I haven't been listening properly. Chewing, I blink at a homepage that's all pastel pinks and greens with words like 'Cleanse', 'Horizons', and 'Friendships' in big, bold fonts.

'Yeah, nice. Looks ... holy.' I shrug.

'I've signed you up.'

'What?' I say, spraying crumbs.

'I have signed you up for some classes—'

'What classes? We're not religious.'

'It's a wellness centre now – *listen,* darling. They have all kinds of classes. If you just have a look there might be something else you'd like to sign up for. Hot yoga? Ooh, tai chi?' I slide the laptop back towards Mum and cross my arms. She sighs again, finger massaging the space between her eyebrows. 'Look, it's six sessions, Almond, that's it. I've signed you up for six little sessions with this organisation called Tranquillity. First one's today at five—'

'Today!? Are you for real?'

'Yes, I'm *for real,*' Mum says. 'It'll be good for you, it's – you know – self-help, group therapy, counselling,' she says, flippantly rolling her wrist as she talks. 'You'll be with other kids your age with *problems.*'

'I just finished three months of CBT with Dr Wallace. You think I need more?' I rub at the rough patch of skin on the back of my neck, already knowing the answer.

'Quite frankly, yes, I do,' she says, peeling off her coffee-stained shirt and sitting perfectly chill at the dining room table in just her bra.

'What about Dr Wallace?'

'What about him, darling? Who do you think wrote your referral? This programme isn't just for any old kid who cries depression on the internet' – Jesus *fucking* Christ, Mum – 'it's exclusively for young people already receiving treatment. Dr Wallace thinks a group environment is what's best for you right now.' I feel my nails dig sharp little crescent moons into my palm, imagining Mum having whispered phone conversations about me, with *my* doctor, making plans and predictions like managing my mental health is nothing but a business strategy. Though I guess to her, it is. 'Your followers are falling.' See. 'You never come out of that room – I hardly see you. It's summer, darling – where are your friends? What's happened with Callie? I haven't seen her in ages.'

I swallow, my throat Sahara-dry at the mention of her.

Before the pandemic when everything got so corporate and calculated, before everyone got forced inside and hungrily dependent on the only human connection they could legally access through their phones, before vegan banana-bread baking, mother-daughter at-home yoga classes, and the endless live Fri-yay quizzes had found me a million followers, me and Callie wouldn't go as much as twenty-four hours without seeing each other.

Things are different now, pressurised.

The last time I saw her was three Fridays ago. I had a rare evening off after some high-up PR person decided that their

'Invisiboost Bra' wasn't age appropriate to be promoted by under-eighteens. I was officially uninvited to their Booby Banquet launch – think muffins, tarts, and other round, squishy sugared foods with buttercream nipples piped onto them – so, instead, I just showed up at Callie's house like I always have done.

Dressed in an oversized Care Bears t-shirt and joggers, my backpack bearing peace offering Pop-Tarts and those cheapo fruity facemasks we've ritualistically applied at every single sleepover since we were seven, I walked into a gathering of kids I didn't know were a part of our friend group now, crammed into Callie's garage that her dad had midlife-crisised into a home bar with a pool table during lockdown three. Steph Halls, wing attack to Callie's goal attack in the school's netball team, drew herself up to her full height, hands gripped around a pool cue as she murder-glanced at me, before turning to Callie and mouthing, *what the fuck?*

What a welcome. Turns out, during the height of lockdown while I was holed up being the internet's bestie, Steph was busy stealing mine. As 2020 raged on and our follower count spiralled into the millions, Mum had me on a coronavirus content-making schedule while Callie and Steph were having daily FaceTimes, watch parties, and taking part in the same bums-and-tums livestreams together. And years later, despite the world adjusting to its new normal, Callie and me just can't seem to find ours. Too much has changed.

That night, Callie stayed offish at first, acting like she didn't even notice me interrupt her party, squidged into her nineties inflatable armchair, on the lap of this boy she eventually told me was named Theo. Later, when her love for me had been loosened by liquor, we sat hip to hip in the jelly chair as Callie told me she was *in* love with him. She knew the passcode to his phone and everything, which she sloppily thumbed in while he went to the bathroom to show me selfies of them together.

'Oh shit, too far.'

One accidental swipe scrolled all the way back to last July in his camera roll, and there, in the thumbnail, was me on my knees in the sand, screenshotted from an Insta post of me being an #ad for that year's Urban Outfitters' beachwear collection. Quick to enlarge it, Callie gasped, flicking through different shots of me wearing bikinis in ochre, khaki and apricot.

Mum's nostrils flare, waiting for my answer.

I screw my eyes tight, feeling the way I felt that night watching Callie's face crumple with disgust and hurt as she slapped the phone into my palm. She'd ripped herself away from me so fast, her stiletto-shaped nail had pierced the chair's plastic, leaving me to deflate down to the ground. Apparently, my pictures ending up in his screenshots was entirely my fault for *'baiting myself out'* and worth seventeen years of our friendship.

'What *about* Callie?' I say.

'Well, you say the two of you are fine, but I haven't seen her since ... well, I can't remember the last time I saw her to be honest.'

Because, even if we were *talking right now, you make it so I never have time to see her any more,* I don't say.

Mum scrapes her chair back and strides over to the new Liberty's mirror Spencer bought 'the house' after we closed the Serenity deal with VeGlow – gold, gilded and nearly covering the whole wall where our family photo gallery used to be, any photos with Dad in them bubble-wrapped and stacked away in the attic.

Standing in front of the mirror in a nude bra, wide-leg black trousers and fake snakeskin heels, Mum looks back at me through the mirror's reflection, unfastening the white-gold hoops from her ears.

'You and Callie used to be inseparable, darling. She was here so much I should've been charging her rent, for God's sake. It's obvious you've had a falling out, and with everything going on with your dad and I—'

'Mum, please. Can we not talk about all this right now? It's seven a.m.' I wince as I pick off a strip of skin from the corner of my mouth.

'It's eight,' Mum says distractedly, her mouth falling open as she fiddles with the clasp on her earring.

She marches off into the back of the house, shaking her head and muttering something about today not being a hoop-earring kind of day. Tears prick at my eyes and I flake off a scab behind my ear, my brain flickering with that Zippo sensation of release. Aflame, then gone. I wipe my eyes though I'm not crying, I'm *watering*. Dr Wallace laughed when I called it that but I wasn't trying to be funny, it's just what happens when I'm late for something, or I have to book my own doctor's appointment, or I'm being told off by a teacher. Dr Wallace says it's a stress reaction, same as my skin picking, or excoriation as he diagnosed it.

'See, what are you doing right now?' says Mum, having done a loop around the ground floor, striding back into the dining room through the open plan kitchen.

She's buttoning herself into a new shirt. It's champagne chiffon with a jabot collar, classy, a shirt with places to be. I look down at myself slouched in one of Dad's old basketball jerseys and flannel pyjama bottoms as an itch flares up my forearm, my fingers curling to scratch it.

'Why are you picking at yourself? Don't *do* that.'

'I'm not,' I lie, feigning dusting toast crumbs off myself. One of Honey's spiky, golden hairs floats onto my empty plate and I get an idea. 'Fine, if I go today, to these classes . . . can Honey come back and live with us? I've been thinking—'

'Almond, we've been over this.' Mum's eyes flick to mine in the mirror, wide with warning, before she throws her hands up and turns to face me. 'This house just isn't a good home for her any more, surely you can understand that after what happened? Don't you remember how sick she got?'

Of course I do, I want to scream.

How could I forget coming home to a noiseless house, no paws tearing up my uniform, no sloppy welcome home kisses. After fifteen minutes of frantic searching, I found her behind the door that was supposed to remain closed at all times, in the *post office*, which is what Mum calls the spare room where she stores all our PR packages. Honey was flopped down on her side in pools of her own vomit, the ivory carpet smeared brown with chocolate and diarrhoea. Turns out the new cleaner Mum had hired had left the door open and Honey had eaten her way through two baskets of leftover gifted Easter eggs. One sleepless night, a thousand-pound vet bill, and a lost brand deal later, a baby gate was put across the stairs and Honey was left to sleep on the cold, hard floor of the kitchen, howling to be curled up in my bed where she belonged.

'I know you love her, I do too—'

'No, you don't, you never did,' I say.

Mum smooths her hands over her helmet of hairspray. 'I do, darling. I can't believe it, but I do miss her. I miss them both.' Our eyes meet and mine fill with tears. She swallows, her voice low and quilted. 'But I think this is what's best for *everybody*, right now. I think your dad could do with the company.'

'But—'

'No, actually,' she says softly. 'No buts. Honey is still going to be in your life, just not here. You'll see her all the time at your dad's new place.'

'Okay,' I mumble, blinking before peering up to the ceiling. 'Don't want Dad to be alone, I guess.'

'Exactly. And Almond?' Mum walks over to me, the echo of her heels bouncing off the high ceiling. She goes to kneel at the side of my chair, but I see her think better of it in her outfit. She stands over me instead, her perfume chokingly strong. 'I know this is all such a big adjustment for you and I'm sorry you're hurting, but we've got a huge, huge opportunity coming up and I need you to be with me on this one, okay?' She cups my face, her thumb catching my tear in its track. 'Our Serenity ad with VeGlow goes live *tomorrow* and then if they want to keep us on as ambassadors, we'll have to do all sorts of press events before the official release date. Meet and greets, interviews, maybe TV.'

I scratch at the sore skin on my thigh through my pyjama bottoms, feeling panic prickle over me as Mum confirms what I knew already. So basically, if this elusive Serenity product we're slapping our names onto sells (spoiler alert, it's a vegan and cruelty-free *corrective* cream that neither me nor Mum had any creative control over) and VeGlow sign us up to do a whole catalogue of ad campaigns, I won't just be famous inside a phone any more. We're talking ads everywhere, out there in the real-life world. I won't just be Almond Filter Face to Callie and Steph any more, I'll be Almond Billboard Face, Bus-Shelter Face, Side-of-the-Fucking-Building Face.

My head's shaking *No*, but Mum keeps on talking and talking, her eyes shining, pupils dilated. Now Dad's not around to deflect her materialism into home renovations, or her rapacity into impromptu family holidays, it's obvious 'work' is all Mum's ever cared about: money, ads, and #spon, obsessing over numbers and stats, always competing with other influencers to try and secure the highest-paying brands.

'You know I mentioned Celeste Shawcross?' I take a deep breath, stare blankly. 'You know her, she's just hit five million, has a daughter your age. Well, even before last night, we've been DMing, me and her – Spence put us in touch. And *she* told me she's sending her daughter, Imogen, on the *exact* same Tranquillity course this summer because Immy's got a case of the boohoos as well. So, you'll have a little therapy friend. Won't that be fun?'

I breathe in deeply again and count to five like Dr Wallace tells me to do, focusing on the walls of my chest expanding, oxygen settling in my sinews with the exhale. Mum tuts, picking out the crud from under her acrylic nails.

'I don't have time for this,' she says, checking her phone. 'I need you, Almond. In forty-seven minutes the Serenity ad goes live on my profile and I need you to be promoting, promoting, promoting! You've been absent on stories and livestreams lately. Spencer and I think you need to get some interaction going, something like those would-you-rather questions Electra Lyons has started doing every night.'

Because of course, if Electra Lyons is doing it, then why aren't we? Mum's not wrong though – I used to be like Electra, replying nice things to followers, wishing someone's nan a happy birthday.

Two weeks ago, I got tagged in a selfie I don't remember posing for, where I'm smiling but dead behind the eyes. I was waiting for an Uber outside Dad's new flat, after he'd humbly shown me around all five hundred and fifty square foot of it, and I'd left its empty shell echo realising that this was all actually happening, Dad was moving out and he'd never be coming home to us again. The girl who posted the selfie was nervous, I remember, not sure she should be asking me for a photo but doing it anyway.

Later, I read the long caption she'd written about our twenty second interaction, numb and empty, my eyes glazing over the words riddled with heart-eyed emojis and prayer hands. All I did was breathe next to her. It made me feel strange, like someone I'm not. Hollow. A hologram of a girl. Because I'm not brave or empowering, or whatever else she says I am. I'm not beautiful. That girl didn't know me, but the selfies, the vlogs and the get-ready-with-me sessions, along with their carefully curated captions, made her think she did.

She didn't know that right then, as she approached me on that crumbling wall outside Dad's flat, I was screaming inside.

Mum's mouth's been moving, but I haven't been listening again.

'The brief says we need five-hundred-thousand likes to get signed for VeGlow's autumn/winter season,' she's saying. 'Five hundred thousand people like the ad, and Paisley Parker says she wants me and you as the faces for VeGlow UK. I'm telling you, this correcty cream stuff's just the start, darling.'

I cough bile, gritty and acidic at the back of my throat.

'Do you know how much they're paying us?' I manage to ask, licking my finger and dotting up the toast crumbs from my plate. *One, two, three, four, five,* I count over and over. I catch Mum in my peripheral, gazing into her front-facing camera, lips slightly parted.

'Big money.'

'And they're paying *me* this time, yeah?' I clear my throat, trying not to sound too hopeful, so she won't suspect I have my own ideas for this Big Money after I turn eighteen on the twentieth of August. 'Like into my bank account? I'm nearly eighteen now—'

I'm cut off by the chiming of Mum's phone, which always

gives me heart palpitations because her ringtone's the same as my old alarm sound. She refuses to change it because 'Crystals' sounds the most *ethereal*.

'Look, I've gotta go,' she says, her mouth closing in a tight pout like a drawstring purse. 'Talk later, darling.' Mum leaves the room with her phone clamped to her ear, putting on the posh, gooey, toddler voice she uses to speak to any kind of management. 'Spencer, darling, everything good to go?' Without a goodbye, the door slams and I hear her crunching across the gravel outside, loud laughter clattering out of her mouth.

She sounds happier than she has all morning.

3

Review Appointment – Follow Up

Percy Wallace <p.wallace@dermamind.com> Jul 21, 16:07

to: Almond Brown <almond-h.brown@gmail.com>

Dear Almond,

I hope this email finds you well and that you are enjoying your summer holidays. I notice you haven't rescheduled our CBT review appointment yet . . . Almond, even though your treatment with us is coming to the end of its course, I highly recommend that you attend, as it gives us a chance to assess the outcome that talking therapy has had on your anxiety-related itching and excoriation. I also felt there was a shift in your overall mood during some of our later sessions that we didn't have time to address, which gives me cause for concern.

In the meantime, I wanted to wish you good luck with your group sessions. I've referred previous young patients to this programme who speak very highly of its success. I think being told that you're not alone in how you feel really resonates with a person when they hear it from people their own age, not just some old dinosaur like me.

Very best wishes,

Percy Wallace, MD
Consultant Psychodermatologist
DermaMind Clinic
619 The Drive, SWINDON
SN64 8YA

4

I send off a reply to Dr Wallace, promising to call and book in for my review soon, but I don't know. I don't see the point. I don't think any of this is *working*.

Reading his email conjures up the cradling comfort I felt sitting in the corner of his chesterfield sofa, Dr Wallace sitting opposite me, one leg crossed over his knee so his day-of-the-week socks were showing, hands folded under his chin, his constant nodding and *mmmhmming* fluttering his salt-and-pepper hair. Kind-eyed and carefully spoken, he'd clean his half-moon glasses with the hem of his shirt, giving off cottage-core, granddad vibes. For the last two months he'd offered me a feeling of safety as he encouraged me to talk, though I could never carry any of that safety with me outside of those four walls.

My phone clatters into the sink and I'm back at St Bart's – I mean, *Tranquillity* – staring myself down in the bathroom mirror.

Up until its renovation, Dad still joined Gramma here every

few Sundays but I haven't been here since I was twelve, wearing a #gifted fitted pantsuit to my granddad's funeral. Being here makes me feel just the same as I did back then; small and insignificant, too small for all the grown-up pain being housed inside these cold, reverent walls.

My make-up looks claggy from the cycle over; highlight moistened into sluggy smears of Vaseline on my cheeks, the foundation at my hairline slicked off by sweat. But I had to ride here. Mum was elusively busy, Dad doesn't *do* therapy or communicating, so he doesn't know about any of this, and there was no way I was giving Spencer the satisfaction of escorting me. So I biked it, bumping into Imogen Shawcross climbing out of some Uber Exec out front as I chained my bike to the railings.

'Hi.'

'Hey.'

Reluctantly, we walked in together, our first face-to-face intro awkward, stunted by the encyclopedic wealth of information we already have on each other from being mutual content creators and subjected to years of family vlogging. Like, why do I get to know that Imogen nearly died of appendicitis when she was eight, but not what A levels she studied? We follow each other but we're not friends. I watch her, she watches me, and we have an unspoken relationship of likes, comments and shares webbed between us. A pair of clumsy intimate strangers.

In the mirror, I dab at my face with powder, overline my lips a little bigger, and check for foundation creases under my eyes. Hesitantly, I slide open my front camera, nervous to break my brief social media hiatus since my only friends decided to throw a post-A-level party I wasn't invited to on the same weekend my dad left and I had to mute everything. The theme was British pop icons, which was meant to be the theme for the joint eighteenth birthday party Callie and I had been planning in the back of our Maths textbooks for years.

Though we're both born in August, me on the twentieth and Callie on the twenty-third, Callie's yaya, a sundried, card-reading hunch of a woman who performs party palmistry for a living, says our souls got so intertwined in the ether, our star signs got attached to the wrong baby at birth. She always said I was too dependent and introverted to bear the greatness of the Leo, and Callie much too prideful for the humbleness of the Virgo. I should've known our unravelling would mean we wouldn't be entering adulthood together, that by the time our eighteenths came around, we'd only be tethered by an old, frayed thread.

For the first hour or two of the party I obsessively checked everyone's stories, watching Freddie Mercury in drag, Queen Liz, and about six different Baby Spices stumbling through Steph's house, drunk and overly hug-happy. After crying myself into a headache, I deleted my whole school year and silently slipped out the backdoor exit of the internet.

Now that I think about it, I always expected this from Steph. She's low-key hated me ever since she fell in friend-love with Callie across the netball pitch and over post-match milkshakes. The jealousy radiating off her whenever my Gramma would pick Callie and me up from school, or when we lapsed into a childhood memory, was real. It was okay when we were eleven, but the more work obligations have made me miss out on sleepovers, house parties, and whole relationships that Callie's had, the closer Steph's crept, whispering petty poisons about me into my best friend's ear.

I scrutinise my make-up, camera already open. Nearly a whole two weeks offline is like a *lifetime* for an influencer. I'm probably a day away from conspiracy comments suspecting I've been kidnapped, urging me to wear something yellow in my next post if I'm in danger. I need to throw up a selfie or something, if only just to get Mum and Spencer off my back.

'Hey, I'm taking a selfie, want in?' I call to Imogen out of polite influencer etiquette. 'I'll tag you and whatever.'

'Um, thanks but no thanks.' The toilet paper dispenser clanks and shuffles in a cubicle behind me. 'Maybe we shouldn't be seen together . . . here?' she says from behind the door. 'Wouldn't want to scare off any sponsors.'

'Good point,' I say, my eyes somersaulting in their sockets.

I can't wrench my mouth into a smile right now so I duck my head, making my curls fall in front of my face. I suck in a deep breath, then scoop my lower back in so my butt sticks out, pulling my shoulders up and in, so my boobs look bigger than they are too. I take some pictures, take a couple more in varying positions, pick the best out of a bad bunch, then on autopilot, I go through the pre-upload process. Editing, filtering, @ing. I tag every part of my outfit with the appropriate brand handle, except my black opaque tights, denier 100, that have had to become a wardrobe staple of mine in the last few swelteringly hot weeks. It's not like I can @ Clifton Village Pharmacy, the only place I could find selling tights thick enough to cover the worst of my scars in the middle of summer without having to order them to the house. No wonder this make-up is *melting* off me. I can't let anyone see how bad things have got though, how much of myself I've ruined since home descended into shouting and slammed doors, eating dinner in different rooms and crying under the covers. How lonely this all is.

'You okay in there?' I ask Imogen. She's been a while and I haven't heard the tell-tale Velcro of a pad being unwrapped, so she could be in need. 'You need a tampon or something?'

'No, I'm good. You go in without me, I'll be out in a sec.'

Okay then. I scroll through my emails and copy and paste the pre-approved caption VeGlow marketing exec, Paisley Parker, sent over to be included under every one of my posts leading up to the Serenity launch.

100% Vegan. 100% Plastic free. 100% Glowing. I'm a #VeGlowGirl, are you? It's time to Glow up.

Head bent over my phone, I shove my way out of the bathroom door, glancing up to follow the signs to the Circle Space, which is where the confirmation email Mum forwarded to me earlier says group sessions take place. I skim through the comments already pinging up under my picture.

adele-bumhole123 Absolutely stunning as always

bradtanner.fitness Damn girl. hot!! Can't see no face though wtf?

jennathevegan96 I assume 100% vegan means no animal testing . . .? #greenwashing

images_of_imogen You're so pretty I hate you it's not fair xxxxx

ethereal.moon_fairy Always been a @veglowofficial fan, welcome Almond. Namaste.

zoweh.squarepants1 Soooo cute where's your skirt from????

electralyonslives This mirror selfie's giving me 2000's Mean Girls vibes and I am here for it💕

Wait, *what!?* Electra Lyons is up here handing out compliments referencing noughties pop culture in *my* comment section. I reply instantly, a pulse in my thumbs like this magnetic urge for her to like me.

thereal_almondbrown You mean this isn't the ugliest effin skirt you've ever seen? #sofetch

She likes my comment right back, as do a bunch of other people, and within thirty seconds someone's replied #friendshipgoals under the thread, despite this being mine and Electra's only interaction. Electra Lyons is everything you'd think somebody with the name Electra Lyons would be. A twenty-year-old LA party girl whose parents *cashed in* on the city's celebrity swirl of bohemian energy and sex, drugs and pool parties, who have job titles like Tantric Sex Therapist and Holistic Apothecary. She's basically gold incarnate, with her sandy, sun-toned hair and a perma-tan. Follower count in double-million-digits. One of those elite influencer types who's slinked into the circles of actors and artists, and now gets papped yachting with the Hadid sisters.

Loitering outside the door to the Circle Space, I tap into Electra's profile. 28M followers, only 107 following, and I check to see if I'm one of them now. And I am, she is. Electra Lyons follows *me*. And then the singed, cynical part of my brain, longing for normalcy says, *So!?* instantly extinguishing my fangirl fire.

''Scuse?'

'Sorry.' I step aside to let someone go through, looking up from my phone for the first time as they disappear. Figures move behind the door's frosted glass; there's a raised hand hello from the person I just let pass, muffled small talk, introductions.

A stress tear quivers loose and rolls down my cheek. I thumb it away quickly, my heart scudding against my chest the way it always does when I'm about to *meet* new people. Because I'm here and it's happening right now; there aren't any oceans, airports, or infinite cyberspace between me and the people behind that door like there is with Electra. IRL there's no autocorrect, no button to tell me I'm liked, no grainy, low-contrast filter to hide behind. I take a deep breath and go in.

Inside, the room's half empty, with only three out of ten chairs taken. I peel off a sticky label from the roll on the welcome table by the door, next to the obligatory plate of cookies and jug of orange squash. Quickly scrawling my name, I sit opposite a boy picking at a blistered patch of acne round his mouth. I'm reading the sticker plastered onto the middle of his t-shirt – Hi! My name is: Liam – when he notices me, so I cobble my teeth together in a smile. Instantly, his brow crumples and he gets out his phone.

I wonder if he's following me. He definitely won't be following Mum. He's wearing an E-Sports t-shirt with a snapback, and he doesn't exactly look like he's into yoga, clean eating or wellness retreats. But the way he's looking at me, kind of like how you look at a toilet seat when it's hung up in a gallery and called art, makes me think he must've seen me somewhere online. Probably a glitch in the algorithm, my pictures getting thrown up on his explore page like posed, soft-blur vomit.

Liam looks down at his phone just as a tall, laidback, loping man arrives – all loose ponytail, baggy clothes, hanging-open satchel – carrying a bunch of papers and a fresh roll of sticky labels.

'So, hey guys,' he says, beaming around the circle. 'How're we all doing today?'

Silence. Everyone's staring at screens. I smile at him, though it's more of a shrug with my mouth, and take my own phone out of my pocket to check it's on silent just as Imogen arrives and takes the seat next to me, eyes instantly cast down at her phone too. Cool, I guess? I could do without the struggle of small talk anyway: the name-dropping, brand-flexing, the thinly veiled hints at a collab to boost her smaller following. We were never going to be besties but still, the aloofness of stealing herself away inside her phone leaves me cold and lonely. It might've been nice to have a friend here.

My phone vibrates with a notification, taking me away from this very real renovated church space where nobody wants to talk to me, to the unreal depths of cyberspace where hundreds of people are trying to be heard by me.

n8hartmannn, nicstagram_71 and 138 others liked your post

woolandwateringcans Blimey aren't you hot in those tights!? It's nearly thirty degrees outside!

almondxxbrownxxfanaccount Love love love!!!! pleeease check out my page. I'm almost at 50k xxxxx

Scrolling then stopping randomly, I like a few comments for 'interaction', replying to a few with cutesy emoji spam, like 🖤✿ ❀ or 🌷💕☆, ignoring any that are about my tights. Already, drama-hungry people are speculating that I've illegally got a tattoo, but before my attention gets dragged down the rabbit hole of a comment thread dissecting what kind of satanic symbol I may have gotten inked onto my thigh, I get a message notification from Electra.

electralyonslives

I noticed you did the old swing the hair in front of the face trick in that pic ☺ I pulled that one for about a month straight after my last breakup. Hope everything's okay with you girl x

I don't know why I'm shocked to hear that sometimes Electra doesn't feel like showing her face too, that some of her smiles might be forced and behind them she could be feeling the same way I do, but I read and reread her message, finally feeling *seen.*

I'm not about to scare her off by trauma-dumping on her though, so I just say I'm fine.

thereal_almondbrown

When you know you know!

I'm all good, thanks for asking. I just have a pimple lol x

We're still waiting on a few more people to arrive so I switch to my *personal* account, @emerald.a.brown, to scroll through some stuff I'm actually interested in. My gramma let me borrow her name so I could make a private Instagram to follow conspiracy theory pages, true crime accounts and the staffydoglover hashtag. Incognito. When I log in though, I see I've got five new message requests which is weird. Unless I'm about to receive a meme from Mark Zuckerberg, surely nobody could've linked this account to me. Brown is the sixth most popular surname in the UK, and I signed up to this account with my spam email address too, with no identifying info included.

I decline the requests, skimming over the message previews, my thumb moving on autopilot as I look up to see three girls walking in. I stare as they giggle, like a sound effect from TV, their heads bent over the one in the middle's phone like flowers to the sun. Something pangs beneath my belly button, missing Callie, even Steph, and the togetherness of walking down school corridors, my arms linked with theirs. As the girls sit down, I comb my hair over my shoulder so it's covering my nametag. Still, I catch that little squint of recognition in one of the girls' eyes, her gaze like thousands of ants' legs walking over my skin.

A few minutes later, my gut plummets as a camera flash flares in my peripheral. Beside me, Imogen sits up a little straighter.

'Shit. Flash was on,' I hear one of the girls whisper. She tucks her phone inside her sleeve as the last members of our group wander in, her eyes roaming up, then down, at the floor, at her nails. Anywhere but at me.

The counsellor sees all this, pointedly sliding the filing cabinet door closed. He clears his throat, shuffling to a stop in the middle of the circle. 'Might I remind you all that we have a strict confidentiality policy here at Tranquillity. Okay? Phones away.' I'm paranoid as hell right now but I swear his eyes slink my way. Did Mum *tell* him who I am? Like we're anybody important in the first place? Oh, God.

He plops himself down onto the last empty seat in the circle, scribbles something on a sticky label, then pastes it onto his chest with both hands. 'Alrighty everybody, let's put a name to all your lovely, smiling faces, shall we? I'm Oliver,' he says, jabbing at his nametag with the lid of his pen.

While Oliver explains the ground rules for group sessions, I glance around the circle, locking eyes with a boy two seats to the left of me, holding the fullest and flakiest croissant I've ever seen. He's rugged-pretty, sturdy with a strong nose, full lips, and tousled curtains of hair that drape at his temples and fall over his face as he looks down to dust crumbs off a faded corduroy shirt. Blinking back up at me, he takes a big bite of his pastry, that curves in a plump smile in front of his face, grinning at me as he chews. His eyes are moodily beautiful, the colour of rainclouds. I smile back, my stomach rumbling loudly over Oliver's introductory speech. The boy raises his eyebrows at me, mouthing, *Hungry?* and laughs to himself as he licks powdered sugar off his fingers, giving me a one-sided smile that runs a pulse through my underwear.

I look away, out of practice, feeling vulnerable and so far from flirty, checking my phone one last time to distract myself.

What the hell? There's *another* message request to my personal account. Same creepy, dark-webby username as before.

anRkey_InCel47 would like to send you a message.

Accept Decline

My head snaps up, stupidly looking around the room for whoever keeps trying to send me shit on my very non-public Instagram, eyes narrowed as if some shady balaclava-clad man in dark glasses, tapping away at his phone, will be here at Tranquillity, waiting to offload his trauma like the rest of us. But this is the internet – it could be anyone, any*where*. I jab my thumb into Decline.

I can't think about this now so I put my phone away, finding myself leaning forward in my chair again, looking for Pastry Boy and those stormy eyes of his. My heart drops when I see him deep in conversation with the girl sitting next to him, doing some wide-eyed, big-handed whispering like they've known each other for years. I take in her thick thighs in fishnet tights, spilling over the sides of her plastic chair, her body thrown back with laughter, oozing confidence that takes up its deserved space. Pastry Boy slaps her arm with the back of his free hand and they crack up laughing again. I stare, wishing I could capture just an ounce of her loud, colourful conviction, but instead compensate the only way I know how, instinctively sucking in my gut and jutting out my chin like I've been told to do to look pretty since I was ten years old.

'So, now that we've made sure this room will be a safe space for *every*one' – his eyes quick-cut at me again, so I know Mum's definitely pulled the do-you-know-who-I-am? card, for fuck's sake – 'let's see who I'll have the pleasure of getting to know this summer,' Oliver says, running his pen down the register. 'Lex?'

'Here.'

'Joss?'

'Here,' Pastry Boy answers. *Joss.*

'Almond?'

My fingers curl around the edge of my seat, anticipating the stares. I'm not being a bighead either; I know there are thousands of us making money off their millions of followers and every day the list of Z-list celebrities gets a little grander and glitterier, but Bristol's a busy-nosed city and *Almond* isn't exactly in the book of popular baby names.

My skin rips into flames. What if they go raking for dirt on my Wikipedia page to figure out what's wrong with me before I've even shared anything? I allow myself one harsh swipe of my nails against the side of my neck.

'Yes,' I say, lips barely moving.

My eyes flick around the circle. Liam's still sneaking looks at his phone. Joss takes a nonchalant bite of his croissant. But the girls stare back at me with snarls and sniggers and slivers of hatred. Or else they're beaming at me, pleading with me, dragging fingers through hair, trying to trap me with bright, scary smiles that know me too well.

I flinch at the shutter sound of another phone camera going off.

'Guys, I will ban phones from even coming inside the Circle Space if this carries on. Safe. Space. Remember? Might I remind you of the confidentiality agreement you or your parents all signed. Anyway, welcome, Almond,' Oliver smoothly sails through. 'Samantha?'

Someone answers across the circle, but I don't see who; all my attention's prickled at my peripheral where I'm in a slanted staring match with the girl in the fishnet tights, sitting next to Joss. She bites her lip, chewing me over, forehead furrowed as she scans the back of her brain for the piece of internet she recognises me from. Maybe she remembers watching a video of me making Halloween crafts or getting a cast put on my arm or something else intimately inappropriate. My whole life's up on Mum's YouTube channel. From potty training to period-pad buying.

I try to tell my mouth to smile at the girl, to transform my face into the way she must be used to seeing me online, but it won't, so she breaks eye contact, looking down at her knees and flipping her purply-black fringe off her face.

To my right, I see Imogen's sitting pretty and coy, picking invisible lint off her top and bouncing her foot. When her name's called out, she answers in her Disney sing-song voice, waving daintily as if from a float in a parade.

'Yes, I'm here, hello.' She steels her smile at the circle of blank expressions.

Where I'd be revelling in the bubble of privacy her smaller social-media presence has granted her, I know that she's politely seething with the knowledge that she's unrecognisable here, her teeth fixed in place, lashes blinking overtime.

'Now.' Oliver's reached the end of his clipboard, hands folded in his lap, all mentally unstable adolescents accounted for. 'Before we begin, I want to make it clear that these sessions will only give you the Lego bricks, and . . . and the *instruction manual* to start building your happy head spaces.' You can tell he's super proud of that one; he actually pauses for the half-hearted pitter-patter of laughter that goes around the room. 'But it's *you* who has to do all the fiddly, diddly bits and the fitting it all together, alright? And as a bit of an ice breaker, I thought we could all share one thing that makes us smile in the morning. Could be a song, a person, what you eat for breakfast?' Oliver says, giving very much millennial-Ned-Flanders-after-a-cold-brew energy. 'Heather, why don't we start with you?'

It's the girl with the fishnets. 'My rabbit,' she deadpans, despite the red blotches flowering along her collarbone. She doesn't look like a Heather. She's got hair like the outside of an aubergine, slick and shiny, with milk-bottle skin and brightly mismatched clothes. 'Yeah, I'd have to say my rabbit,' she says again, and it's like her laughter piles into the back of her teeth, sputtering out at the corners. Composing herself, Heather looks me in the eye, and I think she wants me to find what she's about to say funny. 'Yeah, it – sorry he – always *comes* to my rescue on the dark days.'

Heather and Joss let out that wheezy, old man kind of laugh that only happens when you're not supposed to be laughing, like school assembly sniggering. They *must* already know each other.

'Your rabbit – that's lovely,' says Oliver, totally oblivious to Heather's vibrator joke. 'Pets can be an endless source of comfort, can't they? What's your rabbit's name, Heather?'

'Um . . . Buzz?'

Now *that's* pretty funny, but I suck my cheeks in to hide my smile anyway. I'm feeling sweaty and insecure, and not ready to give any of my real self away to these people yet.

'Cute, like *Toy Story*.' Oliver really puts his neck into his nodding. 'I like it. How about you, Joss?'

He smooths a hand over his shirt, neatening the crinkles in his corduroy.

'Hanging out with my dog, Dudley.'

Oliver snuggles his chin into his neck, smiling. 'I see a common theme here, guys,' he says. 'Comforting pets, great. Who's next? What makes you smile – what makes you want to get out of bed in the mornings?'

Imogen raises her hand. 'My morning skin routine.'

As I try to block out Imogen's in-depth description of the importance of applying her no-paraben-vitamin-C-enriched-SPF-50-mango moisturising balm in small circles, I think of what used to make me smile in the mornings and the pit of my belly hollows.

It makes me miss waking up to the velvet of her ear pressed against my chin, her soft snores hot on my neck. How she'd stay like that, curled into me for as long as I needed her, buried in blankets until the shouting stopped. But then Mum sent her away.

'Almond?' Eyes cast down, I try to focus on Oliver's hairy toes peeking out of his sandals, so the tears wobbling on my lashes don't fall. 'Tell us what makes you smile in the mornings?' he says.

'My dog, Honey,' I say, my voice thick and swampy in my throat.

When I look up, Joss is smiling that sad kind of smile at me that isn't really a smile at all, the kind that comes with an 'I'm sorry for your loss', or 'that's too bad'. But he nods knowingly, and I can tell Joss loves his dog Dudley the same life-support-machine way I love Honey.

5

Our allotted hour's almost over when Oliver starts handing out our homework assignments; a printout of a generic mood-tracking chart with activity boxes to fill in for *every* hour of the day and space to mark how each activity makes us feel out of ten. He filled out a mock one with us earlier, using his own weekly activities as an example. Work, Pilates and brunch with his mum. Simple, wholesome. I cringe imagining what my chart's going to be filled with. Photoshoot, eyebrow threading, being filmed by my mum while I take out the bins. Riveting.

'Oh, how is that an hour already?' Oliver says, tutting. 'Time just, you know – whoosh! Right, remember to fill in your charts, okay guys? Stay safe. Stay mindful. And have a nice weekend,' he calls into the scuffle of kids at the back wall getting their stuff.

I stay seated, busying myself with overly neatly folding up my sheets and putting them in my bag, recoiling from a girl called Varsha's lingering, pick-me stare, phone clutched determinedly in her hand, concealer touched up and selfie-ready. As if now, while I'm still sniffing and my eyes are all red, my heart's still raw and I'm feeling vulnerable from crying in front of these people, is any kind of appropriate time for a selfie.

'Bye! Good luck with the VeGlow post. Looks like you're gonna make half a mil,' Imogen chirrups as she hitches her bag over her shoulder, her eyes on her phone.

'Yeah, Spencer's been bombing my phone with analytics this whole time.'

'Spencer seems like *such* a babe – you're so lucky to have him as management.'

'Yeah, I guess.' I swallow the dry knot of desperation tied at my throat. 'Hey, what're you doing now? Do you maybe want to get a coffee?' I smile, inwardly cringing at my own last-ditch attempt to make a friend. 'I know a place not far from here.'

Her eyes flick up from the screen. 'Sorry, can't, I'm off caffeine and I've gotta run anyway. I'm promoting this new meal-replacement shake – disgusting, by the way – and the contract's asked for live weigh-ins on the daily, so . . .' She shrugs, already turning away, as if anything she just said might come off as a casual excuse. 'See you next week.'

'Oh right, yeah, see you.'

So much for our mums' idea of Therapy Friends Forever. It's so obvious Imogen's only humouring any kind of relationship with me for the sake of their interfering anyway. Even the possibility of a couple of hundred extra followers couldn't get her in the vicinity of a selfie with me, let alone to grab a coffee with me.

As the room empties, I unlock my phone to tackle the six missed calls and twenty-two messages from Mum, decidedly leaving Spencer on read. I scroll through the notifications, anxiety like an electronic whisk whirring my insides into batter.

Mum

Approaching 350k likes now . . .

Paisley and the big boss just liked!!!

OMG Aren't you excited!?!?

I *am* excited, but not for the same reasons as Mum. Like she said, being signed by VeGlow for a whole season of ads means Big Money. Even if I don't intend to appear in any of those ads in person, in real time. If they get all lawyered up after I disappear, they one thousand per cent have my permission to deepfake me into existence for their ads.

Ever since I was little it's always been hush-hush over how much money my endorsements have actually made me all together. Mum's always saying, 'I've been keeping it safe. Don't worry, I'm sitting on a little nest egg for you,' so the dolla must've been more than trickling in over the entire seventeen years I've been an influencer. Brands have been throwing cash at us for years, even before they had a name for what this job is. I've gone from modelling biodegradable nappies at three to promoting organic moon cups at thirteen.

I just hope VeGlow's payment is enough to get me out of

here, enough that the other money Mum's been keeping from me doesn't matter, so I won't have to ask her for any of it and she won't know a thing about me leaving before it's too late. I'll be gone – on a plane to Argentina, or Puerto Rico, or Morocco before she can try and stop me. Somewhere no one will know who I am.

I type out a reply to her.

Almond

More nervous than excited I guess

I pocket my phone and go to leave without saying anything to Oliver because, if I'm honest, I don't know if I can do this all over again next week. The staring, the overshares, the bare-ass-naked *feelings* talk. God, I sound like Dad. I'm just not used to ever telling anyone the truth of how I feel; my feelings are usually moulded out of my mouth by businessy hands to fit the next ad brief, or tweaked and twinged out of my face by Photoshop. Then again, maybe I won't even be here next week. Maybe VeGlow will want to snap us up officially and get us to sign a contract ASAP. I could be sipping sangria in Andalusia by next Friday.

'Hey. Cashew, is it?'

I turn around – slack-jawed and still savouring that imaginary cocktail of blood orange and wine on my tongue – to see Joss smiling at me, like proper smiling, with eye crinkles and cheek dimples. Like I'm the only person he ever wants to talk to again. Heather stands slightly behind him, bag resting on her thigh as she scrambles through it.

'Hi?' I stutter.

Up close I scrutinise Joss's appearance, eyes feathering over every detail of his face in about five seconds, the way my mind's been trained to home in on every blemish, every flaw, when I'm looking at myself in the mirror. The sleeves of his shirt are bunched up at his elbows, freckles mapping up his pale arms that he keeps crossing and uncrossing. There's a dozen dusted across his nose too. He runs a hand through his longish brown hair and smiles at me with chapped lips, his face close. As he laughs, I smell buttery cinnamon on his breath, his tongue slipping out to wet his lips as he's about to speak to me again, eyes never leaving mine.

'Cashew? Ha. Ha. So original. Excuse me.' I cut in before he can speak, because nobody ever wants to *just* talk to me. Especially someone this untryingly beautiful. I smell an ulterior motive.

I try to step past him, knowing he'll put a hand on my arm to stop me if he *really* wants to talk to me, and he does, his touch stirring something warm and fluttering in me, like my underwear's filled with butterfly wings. His stormy eyes sweep me into him, charging the air between us, making me feel heady, like there's coming rain. He won't ask me for a picture, I just know he won't, but I find I'm tensed up, waiting for him to say he follows me. Or for him to ask me what it's like being on the red carpet, how tall I am exactly, or how much money I get paid per post. But he doesn't. The moment's gone and he's not letting me go.

'Hey, don't leave.' He holds his hands up, splaying ten knobbly, boy fingers at me. 'Bad joke, okay? Sorry. It's Almond, right? Hev here was just telling me you're famous apparently.' *Apparently*. So, he doesn't know me? 'She's your biggest fan—'

'I am not, don't say that,' Heather says, all vowels as she reapplies her lipstick.

She snaps her purple pocket mirror shut and smiles at me, her lips plump and pursed, but not unkind. My fingers go to my own lips and I rub the softness there, still not sure if Joss and Heather are here to be nice or not. Dr Wallace says my body instinctively touches itself like this for comfort, soothing itself to trigger the release of oxytocin.

'Don't lie, Hev.' Joss taps my shoulder with the back of his hand. *Oxytocin, oxytocin.* 'She told me she used to have posters of you all over her bedroom you know, even kept a little Almond doll under her pillow and everything.'

'You're not funny, Joss.' She smiles at me properly, rolling her eyes so the dark, smoky kohl smudged over her lids makes them look like full moons, and I find myself smiling back. 'I followed you for a bit a year or two ago. Had to unfollow though – the *hey guys!* shit and all the ads were getting a bit much. You're not as annoying in person though. No offence.'

'Surprisingly, none taken.'

Joss isn't listening, his eyes down as he flicks through his phone.

My shoulders slump. Am I so uninteresting or unattractive that he needs to check his timelines mid-conversation? Probably. I have to remind myself that I'm not the girl whose picture gets drowned in digital love, the girl who's #bodygoals, #beautyqueen.

She's not real. And as Joss scrolls down with his finger, a vile little worm of insecurity starts taking bites out of me. *Not pretty enough* – chomp – *he's seen everything there is to see of you already, online* – crunch – *he only dates white girls* – gulp. I can't believe I'm actually jealous of that chunk of technology he's holding in his hand.

I'm about to do eyebrows at Heather but then she pulls out her phone too.

'Anyway,' I say in a sigh. 'I'd better go.'

'Look,' Joss says, leaning into me so I can see his screen. His shoulder bumps against mine and I get a whiff of his *smell*, you know how everyone carries their own house smell around on their clothes. His is like mown grass, torn bread, and sleepy dog. I feel his skin against mine. Oxytocin. Oxytocin. 'Here's our Dud. Wait, wait, look at this part.'

In the video Joss is showing me, he's sitting on the ground with his dog, Dudley, and sharing a melty ice cream cone with him. He rewinds the video a bit so I can see the part when Dudley flicks ice cream up into his face with his long, meaty tongue. We look up at the same time, laughing.

'I love him already,' I say. 'Frenchies are my second favourite dog.'

'Blasphemy,' he says, shaking his head. 'What have you got?'

'A staffy. Look, this is Honey.'

I hold my phone up to show Joss my lock screen photo of Honey sunbathing in the bay window, but I accidentally pull down my notifications screen, so black blocks of missed calls from Mum and the previews of her messages get in the way of the picture.

Mum

Haven't heard from you all day???

Almond call me back. Nearly 425k!

Are you still at your tranquil meeting!?

Have you put Do Not Disturb on again? We talked about this Almond.

I try to unlock my phone, but my hands are clammy and I can't hold it steady. It doesn't recognise me.

'Hang on.' I type in the passcode as Joss moves away from me, the moment skewered by awkwardness. Our eyes meet, and he gives me that same soggy smile he gave me earlier in group. Oh God, he feels sorry for me. 'Here she is,' I mumble, holding my phone out flat this time.

I smile too, looking at Honey's wet nose pressed against the window, her eyes closed to the warm sun on her face.

'What a beauty,' he says, really meaning it.

It's obvious Joss saw the notifications, but I'm glad he's pretending he hasn't, and I beam at him, happy to be sharing something as simple as a love of dogs with somebody.

'Hey, sorry to interrupt your meet-cute or whatever, but are you called something different on Facebook, like, for privacy?' Heather flicks her purply fringe out of her eyes. 'I can't find you.'

I lock my phone, the screen going black between us. What the hell's a meet-cute? I'll google it later. They laugh though, so I guess it's a joke and I laugh too.

'Uh, no.'

'Seriously though, you undercover or something?' Heather says.

So she wasn't just scrolling through her socials then, she was looking for the real me – not almondhazelbrown™, Mum's version of me.

'No,' I say, clearing my throat. 'I just don't have Facebook.'

'Good call, I've been thinking about deactivating for a while. It's soul crushing. All these dicks I don't talk to any more from school, spouting all this sexist, racist, transphobic shit.' Her nostrils flare, eyes wide with internet-activist fury, her mascaraed lashes like stiff little spider's legs. Heather shakes her head, shrugs. 'I stay for the memes, though. What's your Twitter?'

'Don't have Twitter either. I mean, technically I do but my manager controls it – I don't use it. I'm just thereal_almondbrown on Instagram. I'm not on anything else.' A lie. I also have my @emerald.a.brown account but I don't go giving that out to people I've only known five minutes. 'I don't really use social media, apart from' – I swallow – 'for work.' Half a lie. I don't *post* on social media unless it's for work.

There's a pause that makes me remember why I brace myself for bitterness when I call social media my *work*, mentally preparing myself for the eye-rolling, the argument that being an influencer isn't a real job, that it's just, 'Pictcha takin' and pretending to like 'tings', as Gramma Em puts it. But that judgement doesn't come.

Instead, Heather jerks her thumb at Joss. 'My God, we've got another one. Tinfoil head over here isn't online either.'

'Nope, and that's fine by me,' he says. 'It's getting insane, Hev.'

She groans. '*It's* not getting insane, mate. You are.'

'How about this then? The other day all I said was, "this sofa's hurting my back", except no, I didn't say that, I said, "my back's fucked from this sofa", and Mum was sat with me on her iPad, yeah?' His eyes narrow into slits as he leans into me conspiratorially. 'Next thing, she's showing me all these ads for lumbar support pillows and chiropractors coming up on her Facebook. They're always listening in, I'm telling you. Technology knows how we talk – it's the government's way of—'

'Oh my *God*,' Heather says. 'Have a day off, Joss? Bush did 9/11, Epstein didn't kill himself, and the royals are lizard people.' She dead-eyes me.

I laugh as Joss shrugs his shoulders. 'Don't come crying to me when the global elite—'

'I believe you,' I rush out, watching one side of Joss's mouth creep up into a smile.

'Can everyone stop interrupting me?' He laughs.

I look around because Mum says being into conspiracy theories and true crime isn't part of our image, but everyone's gone now except for Oliver. 'The towers collapsed from the bottom, like it was–'

'A timed detonation, right?' Joss finishes. I feel myself bobbleheading.

'You guys are sickeningly perfect for each other.' Heather smirks, one eyebrow raised. 'Anyway, at least you have a phone. We need a group chat.'

I hand her my phone so she can swap all our numbers.

'Nice to see you're making friends,' Oliver says, nodding as he passes us on a lap of the chair circle. 'It's good to have a support network outside of the group too. Awesome stuff, guys.' Picking from a bunch of fluff gathered in his arms, Oliver's walking around, placing stuffed animals on each of the seats. Right now, he's weighing up whether a penguin in a police hat or a koala in felt Ray-Bans gets the last spot. He sees us looking over and says, 'We've got a Tots Tranquillity session starting in about fifteen minutes.'

'Oh cool, toddler therapy, how 2020s,' Heather says. 'Well, uh, we'll be getting out of here. See you next week, Oliver.'

'I'd go with the koala by the way,' says Joss, inspecting a fluffy Pomeranian toy sitting very obediently on the chair nearest him. 'Make sure the kids get to see what one looks like before they're extinct.'

'God, out of everything we've heard today, I think that's the most depressing,' I say.

'Nah, I think koalas going extinct is on a *par* with that girl Imogen's hour-long skin routine on the depressing scale,' Heather says. 'Who's got time for that shit?'

I laugh, then feel bad about it, because I know Imogen's probably had that skin routine drilled into her by her mum since she sprouted her very first blackhead. Oliver waves us off with a dolphin plushie tucked under his arm, and I start thinking that maybe this therapy thing won't be so bad after all. What's six sessions of nodding, mmhmming, and filling out primary-school-esque activity sheets to me, really?

'Hey, Eve fucking Fairchild – sorry, I mean *your mum*, is calling you,' Heather says, and before I can stop her, she slides the screen across to answer the call, placing the phone to my ear.

Walking through the archway of the renovated church and down the steps, I take the phone, feeling something heavy settle over my shoulders like putting on a wet coat, its sopping faux fur cold and clammy at your neck.

'Hello . . .'

'500k, darling, we did it. Did you get my texts? VeGlow want *us*, Almond. Oh my God.'

'That's . . . great, Mum,' I say, lingering at the bottom of the steps, letting the others walk a little ahead of me. 'But what about—'

'And, and . . . I just got off the phone with Paisley, darling. She wants to run the ad in Piccadilly Circus. Can you believe it! Me and you together, ten feet tall.' More like fifty feet. I take in a breath, about to ask how much money they're offering, but Mum interrupts me with a squeal. 'Ooh, that's Spencer calling now, actually. See you later, darling.' The line cuts dead.

I take the phone away from my ear, staring at it like I've just made telecommunication with Mars. *Piccadilly Circus?* I swallow, looking at my reflection in the black screen.

As I catch up to Joss and Heather, a beat-up black Mazda with a red passenger-side door rattles to a halt in front of us. Heather steps off the kerb, placing a hand on the roof of the car as the guy behind the wheel shuffles over into the passenger seat.

'Well, this is me. My brother's teaching me how to drive because proper lessons are *expensive.* As is group therapy, but needs must. Anyway, Almond, *like OMG, it was so totes amaze to meet you.*' Heather flaps a hand in front of her face, pretending to fangirl before laughing it off and grinning at me, goofily genuine. 'Seriously though, it was cool meeting you. And I'll see you probably every night in the corner of Rich's computer screen, Joss.'

'No, not every night.' He laughs, ruffling a handful of unbrushed hair at the back of his head. 'Dick.'

'*We* were friends first, right, from college,' Heather says to me. 'But then one day Joss comes over and meets my brother, Rich. I leave them playing X-Box for *one* hour. Fucking, boom, the bromance was born. Speaking of, I'd better go – Rich's already regretting agreeing to this,' she says, as he reaches over to the wheel, giving two quick toots on the horn. A litter of crushed Coke cans pour out onto the kerb when Heather yanks open the driver's-side door, heavy metal music crashing out of the car. 'Shit,' she says, staring at the ground then over at her brother.

'Just go, I'll get it,' Joss says, shooing her into the car. 'Good luck.'

'Thanks. Bye!'

'I meant to Rich.'

'Idiot.' Heather slams the door, flipping him off.

'Bye!' I call, coughing as black smoke pours out of the car's exhaust.

I drag out watching the car drive off for as long as I can, till it dusts round the corner and I'm left standing awkwardly with Joss. I'm not even going to entertain the idea that he's attracted to me too, but I do let myself wonder if this friendship is going to be a purely *scheduled* kind of friendship, you know, the kind that only consists of hollow small talk and bored text exchanges about meet-ups outside of your allotted time together that never happen. Guess I'd better find out.

I clear my throat. 'It must be nice, like, already knowing someone in group.' I gesture limply towards the direction Heather drove off in.

'Yeah, it's actually kind of messed up we ended up here at the same time.'

'Yeah?'

'Yeah, I mean I was on the NHS waiting list for *any* kind of CBT for months after referring myself, just waiting to hear from somebody. Then, because they found out my mum gets some kind of fancy health insurance with her work, I got offered this six-week placement here at the exact same time Hev gets an urgent referral for, uh— You know what, I shouldn't have said that – it's not my story to tell. But yeah, it's nice we get to do this together.' I nod overenthusiastically and Joss smiles at me over his shoulder, gathering the Coke cans up from the gutter. Our eyes meet as he walks past me to the recycling bin nestled between the church's clothes and toys donation bins. 'So, do you live around here?' he asks.

‘Yeah, not far. I mostly live with my mum in, uh,’ I falter, my eyes roving over Joss’s faded shirt, spying a moth-hole bitten into the shoulder; I don’t want him to think I’m a posh twat, but I don’t want to lie either. ‘Clifton,’ I say, deciding to milk my new status as a co-parented child. ‘But my dad’s just got a new flat in St Paul’s, so yeah, I get to go there at the weekends now, shared custody and all that . . . What about you, where d’you live?’

‘Sorry about your parents – that must suck. But yeah, I’m not far from you. Redland actually. It’s just me and Mum at home. Sometimes my sister too, but she mostly spends her time shagging back and forth from here and London, where she’s meant to be at uni.’

‘Is that a bad thing?’ I say, about to verbally whip his ass for slut shaming.

‘Only because her bedroom’s right next door to mine. She can do what she wants,’ he says, pausing for a second. ‘I don’t think she’s happy though.’

‘Oh,’ I say, not sure how to respond. ‘I hope she’s okay. What’s she studying?’ As soon as I ask, I cringe, remembering the stack of uni prospectuses I never bothered to read collecting dust on my bedside table.

‘Law. She was just telling me about this criminology module she gets to take next year.’

‘No way! That’s sick.’

‘Tell me about it. I was meant to be joining her there this year too, but my student loan wouldn’t have even covered my rent up there. So, I’m taking a year out to work and save.’

'What'd you do?' I ask, way too quickly.

'Make cold calls for some big IT software company, which is as dead as it sounds.' Joss pinches the bridge of his nose, head shaking. 'I hate it, so fucking much. But I gotta have at least a few grand behind me before I can quit.' He sighs. 'Sorry, this is boring.'

'No, no. That's rough,' I say, brain desperately trying to compute something to say to keep the conversation going but only coming up with error messages.

Joss chews on his lip. 'Hey, we should watch some documentaries together some time, if you're into conspiracies and all that. They just put all the old episodes of *Cold Case Files* on Netflix.'

'Wait, are you actually asking me over to Netflix and chill?' I tease.

'*No*. No, no.' His face looks slapped with embarrassment, a bright red sting to his cheeks, as I try to hide my disappointment at how fiercely he just denied any sexual innuendo there. 'I don't even have a TV in my room, or a laptop,' he goes on. 'So, unless you'd like to ... *do stuff* ... in the company of my mum and my very hyperactive dog' – I notice new red blotches flowering on the tip of his nose and his chin and can't help but smile – 'I'm thinking we stick to just the Netflix and hold the chill for now?'

I can't help it, a laugh bursts out of my clamped lips, spit spraying in his face.

'I'm sorry,' I say, actually laughing, like from my belly. 'We'll hold the chill. But I'm totally up for just Netflix.'

‘For now.’ He laughs too, dragging a hand through his thick hair, his face beetroot red.

For now. Meaning at some point he wants me to come over and watch Netflix ... without watching Netflix? That fluttering in my underwear is back, but it’s hotter, a pulsing, like how I have to cross my legs when there’s a sex scene on a TV show – not the quaint under-the-covers kind, but when it’s all tanned limbs and sweaty thrusting.

‘So, I’ll text you.’

‘Yeah, text me,’ I say, glancing down at my phone.

Mum

6 Unread Messages.

6

As Joss walks away, I go to Safari and type, 'define meet cute' into the search bar and the first result releases a flurry of birdwings in my chest. I wind one of my curls round my finger, looking off down the street in the direction he went.

Apparently, in a film or on TV, a meet-cute is described as two characters sharing an endearingly funny encounter that leads to a romantic relationship developing between them. 'It all began with a meet-cute in a quiet café,' the example reads.

I bite my bottom lip, imagining how ours would read in the script.

It all began with a meet-cute in a group therapy session.

7

I see snippets of Mum through the venetian blinds, watching me as I wheel my bike down the driveway, the pink-tinged summer sky swimming with curdled clouds, still warm for seven o'clock. The electric gate glides silently over the gravel, then clunks shut behind me, closing me in.

As expected, Mum crowds me the second I open the front door.

'Darling, there you are.'

'Yep. Here I am,' I sigh.

She looks different than she did this morning. And I'm not even talking, like, in a foundation shade or new haircut kind of way, I mean in a *bone structure* way. Every day it's like she's morphing further away from the person who gave birth to me. It's like opening the door to one of those bots from that old *Stepford Wives* movie, except this one's been upgraded with veneers and a smartphone soldered to her hand. It's Mum's turn to sigh now, staring at my sweated-off ghost of full glam, the mascara smudged into my eyebags, the flyaway hairs at my temples. She even glares glittery, like she's trying to subliminally sell me charcoal teeth whitener or something.

'Well, I thought you'd be whizzing home on your little bike after I called with the VeGlow news.' She grips my shoulders, meaning to draw me in closer, pour some of her excitement into me, but her acrylics dig hard into my shoulder blades. 'I still can't believe it! Isn't this magical, darling?' she says. A strand of her blonde hair sticks to her glossy lips, like a fly on ointment. She lets go of me to pick at it without breaking eye contact. 'Come in, hurry. We've been waiting hours, Almond.'

'Who's we?' I say, knowing exactly the kind of people she means by *we*. Their names might be different, their clothes and colour schemes altered slightly, but the only people who come to visit us now are all the same. Lifeless, empty vessels. Walking advertisements.

Influencers.

'Oh, you know, just some *friends*, come to celebrate our good news! How was the therapy thingy? Celeste Shawcross is here.' Her eyes flare electrically wide. 'She'll want to hear all about how much fun you and Immy had, I'm sure.'

Yes, because crying in front of ten total strangers is just so *fun*, isn't it?

'It was okay,' I say, toeing off my Converse.

'Good, good. I want you to tell us all about it later. But come, look at this gorgeous spread I've put on for the girls. I want me and you to have a nice night together before your first weekend away at your dad's tomorrow.'

I take a breath, about to remind her that *she* has weekends away from *me* all the time, but decide it's not worth it, especially with a room full of influencers in earshot.

'Come say hi. Come on, come on.'

I flinch as Mum laces her fingers through mine, the cool metal of her chunky, silver rings between us, so our palms aren't quite touching. I look down at her fingers, plated with topaz, amethyst and rose quartz that her life coach says are for protection, clarity and earth magic, and fight the urge to pull my hand away.

Mum waggles her fingers through the beaded curtain to the living room, like she's doing party magician magic, then shuffles me towards the women sat around her new Japanese chabudai table. Before I can even open my mouth to tell her I want to shower first, Mum slips her hand out of mine and scampers off, shrieking, *'Hydration, ladies!'*, leaving me standing in front of two women determined not to interact with anything existing outside of cyberspace, silent except for the clacking of their acrylic nails against their phone screens.

'Look girls,' says Mum, the beads chittering as she comes back through to top up their glasses with ice water. She's got her TV voice on, a BBC English accent dripping with artificial sweetener. 'My little Almond's finally home.'

'Hello.' I change my own voice up too, airy and iridescent, like a silvery soap bubble.

'Wait, wait, come back in. I want to get your genuine reaction to seeing us and all this lovely food,' one of the women says. She finally turns and I recognise her as Celeste Shawcross from posed mother-daughter shots on Imogen's Instagram. I hesitate, *really* hoping she's joking because once you decide to press record on a relived moment, how real can your reaction be anyway. I've never been able to pull off a convincing surprised face. 'Oh, never mind, I've got your mum's anyway. Hi there, sweetie.' Her eyes rove up and down my body. 'I've read so much about you. You're much taller in person aren't you.'

'Yeah, I guess.'

My muscles twitch and tighten, tucking in the soft parts of me, my feet inching a little wider so there's a gap between my thighs. She looks older in person than she does on the grid; her cheeks are puffed and shiny, tight like when you paint PVA glue onto your palm as a kid and let it dry. I can just about make out the shape of Imogen somewhere underneath her padded layers of face.

'I'm Celeste,' she says finally, as if we haven't heard of each other. She rises, careful not to snag the leather of the *giant* Louis Vuitton bag positioned between her feet with her matching heels, and kisses me on both cheeks.

As she pulls back, I twist my mouth into a smile, wondering if you peeled off a layer of Celeste's skin, would it flake off in curls the way PVA glue does, like see-through wallpaper.

'Nice to meet you,' I lie.

'How was our little Immy today then? Being a moody bitch as usual?' Celeste cackles, eyes blaring up at Mum, who stutters to join in with the cackling too.

'Nice,' I mumble, though no one seems to hear me over the laughing.

Towering above them all, the tiny table, tiny chairs, tiny women, I reach for a falafel and Mum bats at my hand as if I were a fly.

'No. Not yet,' says Mum. She gestures to the other woman at the table, dark-skinned, bold and curvy with a strong scowl, bent over her phone.

I've never seen her before, not even on socials. Are we just up and inviting strangers into our house now if they have a high enough follower count? Or I wonder if this woman's been hand-picked to be here because of her skin colour? Sinister, but I've seen a few heavily thumbed-up comments on Mum's recent posts pointing out that she never collabs with any influencers of colour, and I'm her own daughter so I don't count. But surely she wouldn't stoop so low as to pick somebody at random to fill a quota. Our management, Spencer, though ...? Yeah, he definitely would.

'This is *Nevaeh*, Almond,' Mum coos. 'Her name's Heaven backwards, darling. Isn't it lovely?'

Nevaeh lifts her head, her chemically straightened hair stiff with hairspray to hide any afro whisps.

'Hi babe. Ohmygod are those your natural curls? Love it.' The words tumble from her mouth, charmingly fake.

'Hey, Nevaeh.' I wave. 'Can I sit down now, Mum?'

'As if you have to ask,' Mum says, joining in with the choral cackle. 'Yes, sit, sit. Ooh, actually.' My eyes close heavily, mid-squat above the chair. 'Actually no, before you do, darling, shall we …' She makes a little rectangle with her fingers and thumbs and mimes pressing the shutter button on a camera, her laugh tinkling out of her, high to low, like fingers running down piano keys. 'Well, it's not going to photograph itself, is it! Seems a shame to let all this food go to waste.'

Her hand flourishes over the spread; stuffed pimento olives, baked artichoke hearts, buffalo cauliflower bites, and a dozen other dishes of vegan tapas. Mum's arranged the food in a colour coordinated, immaculate flat-lay so it looks more like a flower arrangement than a meal, and I know she'll say in her Instagram post that it was all homemade, but I bet if I go and look in the bin right now, I'll see a ready meal plastic graveyard.

'Oh, right,' I say, getting up again, my kneecaps bumping hard against the table. 'Yep, let's take some photos—'

'You're not just taking them, darling, I said we were waiting for you, didn't I. The girls want a photo *with* you too, you know. Sharing is caring.' She leans close, whispers the next part in my ear. 'Your account could do with a few new twenty-and-up followers, you know, darling – you're nearly eighteen now and we'll have to be updating your content to appeal to an older demographic soon.'

'Right,' I say, self-consciousness sliming down my hunched shoulders. She makes it sound like I can just remodel my interests and personality traits as simply as installing the new iPhone update.

I start hanging up light reflectors that look like flattened disco balls, opening up foil umbrella lights and sticking them on tripods, then flicking to the settings on Mum's DSLR camera that emulate natural sunlight the best.

We get mine out of the way first – me in the middle stood with Celeste and Nevaeh, their arms around my waist, my long legs, wrapped in their layers of nylon, crossed at the ankles.

'I love how noughties fashion's making a comeback,' Nevaeh says, pinching my tights and stretching the material out into a little translucent tent.

I laugh noncommittally, checking for snags as Mum hurries over and nibbles the daintiest little bite mark out of a falafel and gets me to pinch it between my thumb and finger in front of my open mouth. Smile, click, flash.

'Perfect,' Mum says. 'One more for luck, though.'

I hold my freeze-framed face for one more camera flash and then I'm free. Now it's my turn to play photographer. Their shoot takes forever though because they all gather around the camera to discuss the photo's pros and cons after every single *fucking* shot. So I wait, watching as they hollow their cheeks, bloat their mouths and vacuum pack themselves into poses for the next one. And the next.

Placing my eye to the viewfinder for the eighty-fifth thousandth time, a pressure builds at my temples and my throat strains, like I'm going to start crying. Could be from tiredness, the mental strain of today, the fact that I can't just go and take a shower and chill in my pj's, or at seeing these strangers in my house on a Friday night, while Dad and Honey are on the other side of town living out of boxes. I swallow back a sob, count to five in my head, and take one last photo.

I pull back. 'That's it, Mum, I'm not doing any more. I'm hungry,' I say, not looking her in the eye. 'You look … nice. There's at least three there you'll like, okay.'

'Fine,' she says, pouting. 'Someone's grumpy. Eat some super-green salad, darling.'

Ah yes, the answer to all life's problems: super-green salad.

The three of them hurry past me to look through the playback as I slump onto the stool by the window. I pick at the food, but it's all soggy from sitting out untouched for hours, swirling in congealed oil.

'Almond?'

I lift my head, see Mum's stepped away from the girls and is leaning towards me.

'Yeah?'

'Thank you.' Her voice tones down a few octaves and for a second, she looks skittish and drained as she delicately rubs her eyes with the back of her wrist, suppressing a yawn. She smiles at me wearily, a flickering lightbulb. But just as quick she's turning back to Celeste and Nevaeh, fully masked up again, beaming open-mouthed. 'Okay, *girlssss*, is it time for bubbles?'

I raise a half-eaten piece of flatbread in response to her 'thank you'. I want her to notice the tears threatening to spill, to ask me what's wrong, to be here for me, present right now, but she looks away, doesn't see. She's bent over the camera, puffing out her cheeks and doing the whole self-deprecation routine a lot of us feel compelled to act out whenever we're confronted with a picture of ourselves. The three of them laugh, feeling delightfully acknowledged by their shared insecurities.

I screw the whole piece of flatbread into my mouth and chew on it viciously, only noticing Celeste eyeing me over the top of the tripod as the ball of stodge slides down my throat.

'Ooh, that's a lot of carbs, honey! Are you sure?'

Oh, fuck you.

It's getting near ten and they're still here. I just want to crawl upstairs and sleep everything away, but Mum says I need to stay and smile for people's stories. More exposure, more connections. So I'm stuck here, feeling as background as the artificial potted plants.

As I rip one of my nails off with my teeth, my phone vibrates.

Dad

Hey baby, hope u all good. Can't wait to see you for our first weekend in the new flat tomorrow . . . Honeygirl is gassssed!! I swear she knows you're coming. Got me running round in circles tryna calm her 😂 Anyway your Gramma's here n she's buggin me to ask your mum if she's still coming to celebrate her big 7-0 next week? Her and Doreen doing the food order tomorrow.

I should've known this was coming. Dad's too sensitive and Mum's too reactive for them to be talking right now, when this whole new normal is still fresh out of the box, bubble-wrapped with no return receipt. But what can I do?

Might as well add Official Parental Liaison Officer to my Insta bio.

'Mum?' I say on the down low. She's listening to Nevaeh recounting the time she slept with one of Beyoncé's backing dancers, eyes wide with A-list adjacent jealousy. I clear my throat. 'Mum? Mum—'

'Yes, Almond. What?' she hisses.

'Dad wants to know if you're still coming to Gramma's party.'

'When is it again?'

'Next Saturday.' *Don't you remember?* 'July twenty-ninth.'

She gasps, her fingers pressing against her mouth. 'Oh, nooo,' she whispers, eyes straying back to Nevaeh as she describes cumming with her ear pressed against a cleaning cupboard door while Beyoncé sang 'Halo' a few feet away from her. 'I'm sorry, I completely forgot about Emerald's party – I can't. I've been asked to cut the ribbon at this new yogic spa. Oh, Almond, you'd love it—'

I cut her off, not needing to hear the excuse. 'Okay. I'll tell them you're not coming.'

It's not like I thought Mum and Dad would get back together after a couple of rum punches and a shared slice of hummingbird cake, but I'd be lying if I said I hadn't been imagining us there as *a three* again. I reply back, letting Dad down as gently as I can, not sure if he'll be relieved or disappointed but knowing that whichever it is, he'll feel it in a big way. I hit send, just as I get a notification from a group chat called 'Tranks' that I'm apparently a part of now.

Heather

Sup bitches

I break into a smile, remembering Heather mentioning a group chat. My eyes flick up to Mum and her friends but none of them are paying any attention to me as they cheers, cheers and cheers again with their flutes of pink bubbly. Then they cheers one more time to make sure everyone's managed to get a good boomerang clip, arms swooping in time, the pale band of soft white skin I notice around Mum's wedding finger making me turn back to my phone.

Heather

How're my fellow tranquil teens feeling tonight???

Joss

Ground rules: No harmful language. Please be aware, be mindful

This is a safe space.

Heather

Namaste bitch. Almond you there?

I drop my fork, let it clatter into Mum's handcrafted tapas bowl. Talk has turned to ad revenue now and Celeste is flexing hard, telling some story about being sponsored by this American organic dog-food brand. I touch my phone screen, lighting up the conversation between Joss and Heather again. The fact that they're asking after me melts through me like I've just taken a bite of warm, buttery toast.

Joss

Yo, Macadamia. You there?

Almond

Yeah here.

Give me a break with the nuts. What kind of a wanky name is Joss anyway?

Thought he was trying to say Josh with a lisp

Heather

Ollie looks like he should have a lisp, right?

Almond

Ollie is it? On nickname terms already?

Joss

Ahaha, Heather's already signed up for extra Saturday sessions

Also, Josh is the most NPC name on the planet. Come on

Almond

Lol. What's NPC??

My ears tune back into Mum's conversation at the mention of my name. I look up and she's staring at me, a forkful of kimchi poised in the air.

'Celeste was just saying, darling, how lucky you are to have such a scrummy natural colour.'

'Yes, you should feel so privileged,' Celeste says, pushing an untouched edamame and bean-sprout salad around her plate. 'No faffing about with fake tan – you were just born brown. Honestly, you have no idea how lucky you are.'

Silently stunned, I listen to Celeste launch into a TED Talk about how us brown people are the lucky ones because being tan looks so healthy and – thanks to the Kardashians – is just so *in* at the moment. She explains the painstaking efforts beauty brands are now going to to be inclusive. Wow. I guess I *should* be grateful that I can wear just about any colour except brown – her actual words. Fuck, I guess slavery sure was worth the sacrifice now that Estée Lauder's Double Wear comes in Espresso, Mocha and Mahogany shades. I wonder if she thinks people of colour are *lucky* they get to experience all the racial profiling, unequal job opportunities and police brutality that comes with our skin tones too.

'Really?' I manage. 'You actually think that?'

This whole time Nevaeh's been silently chewing her food, a chopstick hovering in one hand, the other scrolling through comments too quickly to read, having completely given up any amicable pretence now that the pictures are done, the handles are tagged.

'I don't do politics,' she says robotically without looking up, probably feeling my stare burning into her. I'd say from the rage-grip she has on her phone and the snarled set of her lips that she most definitely does *do politics*, just doesn't want to be seen doing them.

'Like, I'm so jealous.' Celeste reaches out her claws and lays a hand on my forearm, as if trying to telekinetically tell me she didn't mean any of that in a racist sort of way.

'Yeah, thanks?' I mumble, getting the message that we're not getting into this tonight, and not about to waste my energy educating a forty-year-old woman who *exists* in this world anyway. A woman who has access to the internet and all its resources and voices that can explain to her why what she just said was so wrong and ignorant and just so . . . *not it*. But I'll leave her to do that work herself, or else she can carry on and get herself cancelled one day.

At this point, I think it's a choice to stay ignorant.

As Celeste seamlessly switches the topic to Imogen's meal-replacement deal, my skin sears with the anxiety of confrontation, even if it was all in my head. I curl my hands into fists, nails biting into my palms to try and distract myself from the itch crawling up my leg like I've just swished through a field of nettles.

I pick up my phone with both hands for something to wrap my fingers around, scrolling through the group chat messages before pouring myself some lukewarm tea from the pot on the table.

Heather

NPC = Non-player character = Joss is a nerd. Also I do not fancy Mr Pube Toes.

OLIVER looks like Santa's shaved his beard, sacked off the North Pole, and gone to study psychology at Durham. I would never.

I elephant spray a mouthful of jasmine tea across the table, mostly drenching Celeste and extinguishing their conversation as laughter dribbles from my mouth. Oh, shit. Mum closes one eye, then the other, like when you turn one of those real-life, poops-and-cries baby dolls upside down. The room goes silent, though I swear I can see Nevaeh's shoulders shaking with silent little laughs, right as a dumpling speared by Celeste's chopstick slides off and straight into her enormous LV bag.

'Balls,' Celeste says, hauling the bag onto her lap. 'Chi-Chi has *totally* irritable bowels. If he eats one of these, he'll diarrhoea in the Uber. Are they gluten-free? Please, Eve, tell me they're gluten-free?'

'Who the hell is Chi-Chi?' I say, laughing harder at Chi-Chi who *so totes* has IBS.

'He's my purebred, Italian Greyhound,' Celeste snaps as Chi-Chi's bony little head peers out of what I now realise is a designer dog carrier. 'How do you not know?'

A dog? Mum's mouth swells into two fat witchetty grubs as she presses her lips together, daring me to say it – the source of so many screaming matches. So, I do.

'I thought dogs weren't allowed in the house any more.'

'Well, Almond.' Her tongue slices out the L in my name so rigidly. 'Chi-Chi is Celeste's support dog and was only ever going to be here for a couple of hours, and it's very important – *very* important – for Celeste's wellbeing that she has Chi-Chi present at all times.'

She lays her chopsticks neatly side by side on her napkin. I stare at them, wanting to snap them in half and chafe their splinters against my skin.

'Yeah, well Honey's *my* support dog,' I shout across the table. Why do I let her do this to me? I was laughing a second ago. 'You've never been there for me the way she has, and she's a *dog*. And anyway – support dog for fucking what?'

Mum gasps. 'Almond!'

'I have narcolepsy and postural orthostatic tachycardia syndrome,' Celeste says, gathering Chi-Chi in her arms like I'm some rabid rottweiler about to death-shake her tiny little dog in my jaws. She clambers up from the table, tottering in her pinprick heels.

As the complicated words of her diagnosis sink in, it feels like the room and everything in it shrinks, except for Celeste – five-million-follower-strong Celeste – clutching Chi-Chi. Oh God, I didn't mean to be an asshole, I swear. I thought Mum was making up an excuse, setting double standards for me and allowances for her impressive friends. It wouldn't be the first time. I was challenging *her*, not Celeste.

Guilt squeezes my guts in its fists.

The room stays silent except for keyboard clicks and acrylic on glass as Nevaeh taps away to her millions. Please don't let her be live tweeting.

Okay, deep breath. I can fix this. I meant to be mad, but I never meant to be intolerant.

'I didn't mean it like that; I totally get why you need a support dog with your condition. And no one gets to demand an explanation from you – I can't believe I did that. I just miss my own dog, is all. I didn't mean to direct my anger at you.' My eyes flicker over Mum as my voice snags on the sharp emotions in my throat. 'I'm sorry. Chi-Chi's really cute.'

Celeste sniffs once really hard. 'I know he is.' She eyes me, her thumb pecking at her phone. 'Apology . . . being considered. But I think we'll be going now, Eve. My people will be in touch with your people.'

Mum scrambles to her feet, knocking into the chabudai table and sending bowls of health foods skittering across the floor. I hear her following Celeste out to the damn driveway, dripping out apologies in her sweetest, sugary voice. It sounds desperate though, like when you're at the bottom of a bottle of syrup and it wheezes out empty.

'Am I a bad person?' I say to Nevaeh, numb to the tears sliding down my face.

'Honestly?' She looks me dead in the eye for the first time all night. 'Babe, I don't give a flying fuck what you are – Lewis from last year's *Love Island* just liked my photo.'

8

Ting, ting, ting, ting, ting.

'*Ommmmmm.*'

Shzhshshhzzhs, ting, ting, ting.

Is that . . . maracas?

A vague memory of Mum unboxing a load of percussion instruments floats into my half-consciousness, to be used in a sound bath for her next Self-Soothe Saturday livestream.

'*Ommmmmmmmm.*'

My hand spiders around on the bedside table looking for my phone. I squint at the screen, yawning. It's eight, and the last time I checked the time before falling asleep it was three thirty-something. I couldn't sleep, the image of Celeste snatching her tiny little dog away from me replaying over and over again in my head, until my mind had morphed me into something monstrous, and words with claws and teeth came out of my mouth that I knew I never said or thought.

'Narcolepsy isn't a real disorder.'

'People with support dogs are just attention-seeking.'

Because it didn't matter what I actually said or meant, if Celeste wanted to cram those words into my mouth and then into a 280-character tweet, she could, and the internet would wild out with it.

I check Twitter now for cancellation confirmation but my name's still only being mentioned in the same old confusing curdle of superfan love and slut-shaming, so maybe Celeste's finished considering my apology and it's been accepted.

I drift in and out of sleep for an hour, lulled by the reverberating hum of a singing bowl seeping through the floorboards.

When I'm properly awake, I scroll through the rest of the conversation I missed on the Tranks chat last night, mostly reaction gifs and plans for the weekend. I can't believe I didn't even think about checking my phone after Chi-Chi-gate last night. I guess, besides Callie and sometimes Steph, I'm not used to having people from real life in my messages who *actually* want to talk to me. Usually if I know someone personally who's trying to message me, it's just people I sat next to in Geography four years ago pretending we were besties in school in exchange for shout-outs and freebies.

The time ticks over to nine thirty and I throw the duvet off me, wincing away from the bedsheet freckled with brown dots of dried blood, and as I stand I notice fresh red-raw scrapes up and down my shins. Last night while my brain was consumed by anxious catastrophising, I must've done this to myself without even realising. All the drama and anxiety of being a person on the internet is making my skin thing worse. I need to leave.

I scan the patchwork quilt of crumpled clothes on the floor that are too clean for the wash basket and too dirty for the wardrobe. Stuffing jeans and a jumper into my bag, I get dressed in my comfys – my uniform of leggings and a hoodie that I wear whenever I'm with Dad or Gramma and I know there's no danger of a camera being turned on me while I eat a meal or take a fucking breath.

God, I need some trash TV, delivery pizza, and blanket time with my dog. My phone vibrates as I'm already reaching to pick it up, rattling the pills in my pillbox. Seeing it's Joss melts the warmest smile across my face, especially when I realise he's messaged *only* me, not the group chat, his virtual presence calming my heart rate and the anxiety I felt a moment ago. I sink back down onto the bed.

Joss

How's my favourite little child killer today?

Almond

Wtf??

Joss

Killer like, a nut allergy? Almond = nut.

Almond

Oh I knew what you meant, it just wasn't funny

And thanks for clarifying that an almond is in fact a nut!

Joss

Damn, I might be wasting my time trying to get a laugh out of you

My comedy genius is wasted.

Almond

Depends what you're trying to invest your time in lol

Joss

You.

Holding my phone to my chest, I lie back on the bed and allow the fire that ignites in the low soft of my belly to follow a hot oil trail through my middle, igniting my heart with an undiscovered feeling I don't know what to do with. Even though I've never had a proper boyfriend before, I know how *liking* someone feels – that jittery, sherbet feeling of having a crush. *This* feeling is bigger than that, less fidgety. Wholesome.

I sit up, my smile fading a little bit as reality rains over me. I mean, we met yesterday – how do I know he's not some sociopathic stalker, or a blogger worming his way under my skin to get to the good dirt for his WordPress, or just a *mean* boy, a fuckboy, a softboy, a boy who's going to ghost me after summer's over. I'll reply to him later, after said Honey cuddles, pizza, and two to three episodes of *Love Is Blind*.

I throw my antidepressants into my backpack along with my phone charger and sling it over my shoulder, inadvertently catching sight of those *fucking* prospectuses beside my bed. As if I need to be reminded that I've definitely failed two of my A-levels and might not have been able to scrape a C in Communication and Culture, the one subject I cared anything about. Psychology and Sociology proved a little too close to the bone.

When you're the face of whatever-the-fuck beauty brand it is this month, they kind of *need your face* for photoshoots and PR events, which means as well as all the fun stuff outside of school like house parties and prom-dress shopping, you miss a lot of the necessary stuff too like free study periods and revision sessions. And revising on set is near impossible to do when you've got a whole horsetail of makeup brushes swishing at your face from every angle. Imagine trying to read while you're being told, 'Chin this way', 'Blink, honey, blink', 'Look up, now down, now over to the corner'. While everyone was learning how to sell themselves to universities in their personal statements and CVs, I was learning how to sell eyebag elixir to people who don't need it.

The most I can say about Mum's reaction to my predicted grades is that she was … underwhelmed, but assured me she would pay for all my resits next year. Dad seeing my final school report was actually the catalyst for The End, when he'd finally had enough of sleeping on the sofa and watching Mum whisk me out of school. He'd always wanted me to go to university; I'd be the first in the family, and it pains me that I don't get to give him that pride any more. Not that I even got as far as narrowing down my choices to the ones I wanted to apply to. I guess when you've essentially peaked at seventeen, university doesn't seem so important.

I text Mum goodbye so I don't interrupt her livestream, then cycle down from Clifton, through the main part of the city and arrive at the Bearpit, an underpass tattooed with graffiti and neon posters leading to St Paul's where Dad lives now.

A minute later I'm bumping along a pot-holed high street, lined with a bunch of depressed-looking shops, most of the shutters pulled halfway down like rusted eyelids. The streets are grotty, littered, falling into disrepair. But at least people smile at you on the street here, and there are more people with big hair or burqas. Google Maps says I'm seven minutes away as I hop off my bike at a zebra crossing, and flinch at a hand on my shoulder.

'Almond?'

No, no, no, I know that voice. What if she wants to try and talk everything over? Except Callie isn't exactly the type to *talk* things over. In five seconds she could be screaming, and in another five seconds someone could be livestreaming. Fuck, not here, not now. I blink back the sting of stress tears, my mouth wrestling itself into a confused smile as I take out my AirPods, spin around and – there's Callie, her face cracking into a sort-of smile too.

I feel my shoulders loosen with muscle memory as I'm flooded with the sweet easiness that comes when you're around someone who knows your *everything*. Your pizza order, your bra size, your first animated Disney crush, your first period story, how you drink your tea. Because *she* was my everything.

Callie hitches her bag strap higher up her shoulder, narrowing her eyes at me, guarded as she crosses her arms, definitely regretting starting this conversation.

'I thought that was you,' she says eventually. 'You alright?'

'Hey, yeah. I'm – I'm okay. How are you? How'd you do in exams – think you'll get your predicted grades?' I hear the harsh R's and the deep vowels of the Bristolian accent I'm always trying to hide in videos roll right back into my voice, sitting comfy on my tongue as I forget the last three weeks of being left on read, falling back into Callie's familiar closeness.

'Hopefully. Need three Bs to get into Goldsmiths,' she says, all reluctant with it like she wasn't the one to come over and start talking to me. 'And you?'

'Well, good luck, I'm sure you did okay,' I say, ignoring her question because we both know I won't be passing these exams, let alone be qualified enough to go off to uni in London. Our eyes meet, and in a sudden surge of lonely desperation to get back to us, I decide to say it, to have The Conversation. 'Where have you been, Cal? I texted once, after we . . . after that night in your garage. Didn't you see it?'

She scoffs. 'Where have *you* been, Almond? For the past two years?' she says, slashing at the prissy little ribbons of our small talk, tongue scissored.

'Working. I'm always . . . working—'

'Oh yeah, because missing my sixteenth to fly to Rome for the weekend must've been such hard work. You must be exhausted.'

'Yes,' I say, shoving my bike a little too forcefully against the crossing post. I'm a big hand-talker when I get mad. 'I am. Why're you even bringing that up again? You *know* they moved the photoshoot dates last-minute because of a weather warning – you saw the emails, you saw the *legally binding contract* with my name on it, didn't you?' My chest heaves, adrenalin stirring up nausea in my stomach as people pause in my peripheral, wanting to watch the drama unfold. Callie clamps her lips and pops her eyes wide, tucking her crossed arms even snugger as she waits for me to carry on. 'And it wasn't all just pizza and proseccos over there, you know? We're talking hanging around on set for twelve hours with only a bottle of water and pineapple rings to eat so I didn't bloat for the photos, and—'

'Okay, so what about my—'

'Let me talk!'

'*So, what about my* seventeenth birthday? Where were you then? Or when you begged me to partner with you for that *Othello* presentation that I did all the prep for, that you then *missed*. Or when I called and called you that time after I met my dad's new girlfriend? Who he's engaged to now, by the way, which you'd know if you ever asked me about my life.'

I press the base of my palms to my eyes, fingers clawing at my hairline in frustration.

'I don't know what to say, Cal.' Sobs snatch at the breath I draw in, threatening to break like waves in my throat, drowning my words. I count to five. 'I do care about your life, about you.

Dad told me about the engagement ... I meant to ask if you were okay, I wanted to talk to you about it in person but there wasn't ... there's never any time. I'm sorry, I am, but I've not been' – *I've been depressed* – 'feeling like myself lately.'

'Oh, yeah? Could've fooled me. You look like you're doing just fine in all them slutty pics you post on Insta ...' *Slutty!?* Her mouth stalls, tongue running along the inside of her gums like she can taste the charred rot that word left in her mouth. Instead of backing down though, finally getting that out of her system only fuels her hatred, and what she says next spits straight lighter fluid on it. 'And ... and it's getting worse, you know – you look so desperate, man. Everyone's talking about how you're basically naked in that VeGlow post. Don't you have any respect for yourself? Do you actually *like* having old men wank over your pictures?'

'Oh my God, seriously? *This* is what we're talking about. Surely you can see that it hasn't got a thing to do with me whether some boy you're talking to has a picture of me saved on their phone from a year ago.' We're shouting now and I feel squirmy from the stares people are giving us. 'That doesn't mean he doesn't like you now.' I remember her face again that night, sinking with confusion, and even though I know it wasn't my fault, I hate that I'm a part of that hurt. I exhale softly, like I'm blowing on hot food, hoping my voice comes out a little cooler. 'What was his name, Leo—'

'*Theo*,' she says through her teeth.

'Shit, Theo. Theo. Sorry. Either way, he's some boy you're not speaking to now. Some boy you chose over me.'

'Fuck you.' Her cognac-coloured eyes brim. 'I thought he liked me.'

Blinking her long, curled lashes, a tear slips down her cheek, inky with mascara. Great, *she* calls me a slut and now I'm the one feeling bad for making her cry. And why can't she just look ugly doing it? Her tears track lines in her foundation, the exact match of her mixed skin, blended with the Greek olive tones from her dad and the warm brown of her Caucasian and Trinidadian mum. As she studies the cracks in the pavement, she tugs her fingers through the knotted ends of her loose waves.

This Theo kid must be dumb.

'Oh, Cal.'

I reach out to hold her, but she jerks her shoulder away.

Stressing with not knowing what to do, what to say, if I should leave, I wring my hands together like twisting old rope into knots, my skin burning. *Slutty.* How could she say that? I'm slutty now? And who the fuck is this 'everybody' that's talking about me? Besides the 'everybody' of the internet. I think of Callie and Steph, hanging out without me in the den in Callie's garage, talking about me, passing a phone between them with pictures of me on it, Steph sitting in the beanbag that used to be mine, and feel the itch inflame the rest of my body.

Callie eyes what I'm doing to my hands, my skin chafing in red raw patches, and I see her jaw go slack. Her hand twitches at her side, like she wants to reach out and stop me from doing it, but she doesn't; we're both breathing heavy and jittery with adrenalin.

I groan, shoving my hands in my pockets, clenched. 'Look,

it's not me wanting to post stuff like that, I'm not the one making all the decisions. I mean, obviously I'm in the pictures. But I just show up at the shoots and they tell me how they want me to look. It's my job. You wouldn't understand—'

'Fuck it, I don't want to understand. I don't care any more.'

'I didn't mean it like that. And *who's everybody*?'

Behind me, the walk/don't walk man bleeps, flashing green, and people start to cross.

'Um, the whole school?' Callie throws her arms out, shaking her head as she turns and walks away from me, hair splaying over her shoulder. 'I'll see you around, Almond,' she shouts over her shoulder.

I don't even bother calling after her. I just stand there as the crossing turns red, then green again, watching people with happy, normal lives go about their business. My skin sears and I don't want to be in it. I look over at a family sat at one of the tables on the pavement outside Jemima's Jerk Café, a hazy, reggae rhythm winding out from the open window as the family share bites of their food with each other off wooden forks. Then at a group of girls gaggled around the table behind them, picking at a plate of chips, laughing loud.

'Ooh, that looks nasty, are you alright?'

'Huh?'

An elderly lady clucks at me, her eyes, swimmy with concern, staring down at my hands, while she clutches her handbag tighter.

I look down at my hands like they're not my own, just as shocked as the old lady is when I see blood dripping down the inside of my wrist.

9

Almond

Callie wtf just happened. I hate us fighting, can't we just go back to the way things were? I miss you so ducking much! And there's so many things I want to tell you . . . and so many things I want you to tell me. Look, I'm sorry about Theo, I really am girl, but he was the one who saved those pictures of me on HIS phone. You think I like that? That I wanted him to? That I like knowing that. I don't even know his last name. But you deserve better. So for all the things you're mad at me for, I'm sorry. Please reply.

Love you x

Message Not Sent

This person isn't receiving messages at this time

She blocked me.

10

I take a detour on the last stretch of high street before I get to the concrete offshoots of residential streets where the red pin on my phone says Dad's flat is. Ducking into a chemist, I grab a pack of plasters, then buy a peppermint tea from the café next door to use their bathroom to change out of my hoodie, the cuff blotched with blood. At the table, I sip my tea, checking to see if Callie's blocked me on all her socials too. My shoulders sag as I realise she has, the search bar coming up empty when I type in her name.

When Google Maps tells me I've arrived, I slow-drift to a stop, the spokes of my bike tick-tick-ticking underneath me as I take in the entirely square house in front of me, squat and split into two flats. My wheel bumps into the wall of number one where Dad lives, at the end of a terrace of identical red brick houses. As I lock my bike, I smile to myself, though it's weighted down a little with loss, realising that Dad's going to be happier here. Windows are flung wide along the street, curtains billowing cooking smells and radio shows on the breeze. I can see into the garden three doors down where kids screech with laughter as they *pew-pew* each other with plastic water pistols. Dad always felt confined back in Clifton, with everyone hiding behind intercoms and doorbell cams, driveways jammed with four-by-fours and wrought-iron gates.

Takeaway leaflets and junk mail crinkle under my feet as I go through the unlocked front door, down the hallway he shares with his upstairs neighbour, and push open the door to 1A.

'Dad?'

Our eyes meet through the dingy dark, my head peeking round the door. He's on the sofa, his arm suspended in the air, smoke trailing away from his fingers.

What?

'Hey, baby,' he says through a solemn cloud of grey, smoke curling its clutches around him, the nicotine hit shining in the whites of his eyes.

I stumble as Honey jumps at me, my feet unrooted, unsteady by seeing Dad smoking again, and I sink to the floor, sucking in my lips as she licks kisses all over my face with her sandpaper tongue.

'Hey, Honey, hey,' I murmur into her fur.

Her head whips between Dad and me, like she can't believe I'm really here. I guess she hasn't got used to living without me either yet. Her tail wags so hard it moves her whole butt from side to side which makes me start laugh-crying, proving that seeing Dad silently smoking and my encounter with Callie has all been way too much. I nuzzle my face into her neck to wipe away the tears so Dad will think I'm fine, even if he clearly isn't. I take a deep breath and count to five.

'Dad, what . . .' I stare at the pack of cigarettes that he worked so hard to never have to buy again. 'You're smoking?'

Forcefully, he stubs it out into a pint glass filled with bottle caps, wheezing like an old car exhaust into his other hand, my skin being pricked all over by long, glinting needles of panic. My fingers twitch.

'No, not smok*ing*, just a smoke. Just the one. Baby, what you doing here?' Dad moves like he's in slow motion across the part of the room where the sofas are pushed into an L shape, framing his massive TV that's way too big for a flat like this. He flings the curtains wide, opens the window. I'd call it the living room but Dad's flat only has one room that doesn't have a bed or a bath in it, so it's also the kitchen and where we eat, making it more like the everything room. 'What time is it?' he says. 'I thought you'd be here for lunch, like we said last week.'

'Yeah, I woke up early and . . . I just wanted to see you . . . I can go if you want?'

'*No.* No, I never want that. Baby, don't scratch.' *Am I?* Reaching me in two strides, he pulls my frantic hand away from the inside of my wrist and holds it in his, my nails thankfully not prying enough to have started the bleeding again. 'You okay?' he says, his voice all low and gravelly.

'Yep, I'm fine. I just really missed you guys.' I let Dad wrap me in a hug, both of us burying our unhappiness on the other one's shoulder. It *is* fine, *I'm* fine. I have all day and all night here with Dad and Honey, even if Dad's not quite keeping it together. He will for this weekend, for me. And *forget* Callie, I don't need her. 'Are *you* ok?'

'Uh.' He runs a hand through the short fuzz on his head. 'Yeah. I'm good. Better now I get to spend the day with my girls. Sorry about the mess.'

I have to look away from his sad, trying eyes. Because the trying doesn't seem to be enough, his lids shrouded by bruises of tiredness. He looks lost, surrounded by boxes of our old life yet to be unpacked.

'You had breakfast yet?' I ask, needing to busy my brain, motion my hands into doing something other than giving in to the anxious itch and tearing at my skin like it's wrapping paper.

Dad just shakes his head, eyes glassy as he finds something for his own hands to do, gathering up the mugs and dirty dishes around the room.

The first kitchen cupboard is bare except for some half-empty bottles of spirits, and the second one's home to a money spider and a sad tin of kidney beans. *Why doesn't he have any food?* My hand snakes up my sleeve and I twist a scab off my elbow, raised like a bottle cap, staring at Dad's empty kitchen. I press the gifted faux cashmere of my jumper to the wound, stemming and hiding the bleeding with its maroon material. I look in the third cupboard where I find plain flour, and spot two browning bananas on the worktop next to the sugar jar. I get an idea.

'My girl's fixing me something goood,' Dad says when he hears me clicking on the gas, his mood lifted a little by the sunshine streaming through the window, warming us both as he hooks his phone up to the speaker and shuffles through our Kitchen Dancing playlist.

He hums along to the happy, bumblebee opening of 'Little Bitty Pretty One' which splits my face into a smile as I'm mixing pancake batter. My phone vibrates in my pocket and I pull it out with sticky fingers. It's an email from EscapeAways.com inviting me to *Dip my toe into their eleventh-hour summer holiday deals*, a banner above the text boasting the beaches of Bora Bora, Cape Town, and the Seychelles all fading into one another. I forgot I signed up to their mailing list the other night in bed, mapping out a trip across Southeast Asia and making a mental note of the costs and connecting flights, while Mum filmed a 'Lies People Tell You About Your Forties' video with a former *X-Factor*-finalist-turned-Mumfluencer downstairs.

'Ow!' A screwed-up ball of parcel tape bounces off my forehead as Dad mimes a slam dunk, smacking his chest and stomping his feet like LeBron James celebrating. 'Oh, is it now? Let me show you *how*,' I say, balling up the tape even tighter, then sending it soaring through the top of the swing bin.

Dad chuckles, going back to his unpacking and singing the wrong lyrics to Gwen Guthrie's 'Ain't Nothin' Goin' on but the Rent' under his breath as I wonder if I could really leave this clown, even for Bora Bora beaches.

My phone goes off again and I'm fully expecting to have to scroll through an essay from Mum on why I need to take up livestreaming on Saturday mornings, with accompanying screenshots of today's engagement analytics. But it's not Mum. Leaning my elbows on the kitchen counter, I stare at Joss's name on the screen, realising I still haven't replied to him from earlier.

You, he'd said.

He's trying to invest his time in me.

'What you smiling at that phone for, hmm? You got some boy hanging around that I need to know about?' says Dad, coming over to half pretend he's peering over my shoulder.

'No, nothing, shut up,' I say, even though it feels like my heart is beating in my damn throat. I look at Joss's messages and bite my lip.

Joss

You okay? Sorry if that was too much . . . I'm just trying to say that I like you, that's all

There's a yearning tug from somewhere below my belly button as I type out the words I want to say back, waiting with my thumb hovering over 'Send'. Because once I press that, then it's out there, another piece of me given away to a stranger.

But it's weird – even though I just met him, Joss doesn't feel like a stranger to me, he's not just data, or some little red heart, or talking to me in 280-characters or less. And he's not like the boys I knew at school, always wanting to play trashy games like Never Have I Ever or Spin the Bottle, their hands always on my thigh, my butt, or trying to get into my pants. Never just holding my hand because they wanted to, but because they wanted *to be seen* holding my hand, hoping to hold on to everything that might come with it. Followers, freebies, fame.

Of course I've got trust issues.

But Joss doesn't seem to buy into all that, the constant posing and flexing, baiting for likes – he doesn't even have an old pre-teen Facebook I can stalk. He's a luddite in the only way you can be as a nineteen-year-old in the 2020s, still using a smartphone but not at all trusting or happy about it. And in his unconventionality, he's the most beautiful person I've ever seen, because I *haven't* seen a million and one copies of him on my explore page. Messy, freckly. Rough hands and dark, dirty-blue eyes, sea-tossed and depthless. That rare kind of beautiful that's almost strange-looking.

He's real and he makes me feel real too. So I press send.

Almond

I like you too

Saturday 11:42

Joss

So like what level of fame do you have to reach before the illuminati approach you for membership? Is 3.5mil enough, are you there yet?? Can I get in on this?

Almond

I reckon you gotta be at least half way to Beyonce before you're on their radar. They don't just let in anyone you know, and I gotta say, I'm not sure you'd make the cut . . . I'll put in a good word for you when my time comes though. And I thought you didn't do social media! How do you know how many followers I've got?? You been stalking me?

Joss

I wouldn't say stalking no. I'm part of a covert mission sent to gather intelligence on how the influencer industry uses pretty girls to brainwash millions –

I've said too much.

Almond

Hahahah ffs

A snore rumbles in the back of Dad's throat, his big body passed out and folded into the sinking spot in the middle of the sofa. The room smells like fried sugar and oil and I'm warm from Honey's head in my lap, warm on the inside too. We're all sprawled on the two lumpy sofas, with some mindless movie about supercars and guns on low volume in the background. It's three in the afternoon and it's sunny outside but I don't mind that we're just watching TV. I'm contentedly cocooned.

I get out my phone, remembering what Mum said about

follower interactivity. Better throw something up on stories. I cross my legs over and flex my calf muscles to make them look slim, as if I actually *do* the yoga classes I'm always promoting for Mum's channel. I take a picture of Honey lying by my side, her head in my lap, and fix it with a sunshiny filter, captioning it, 'My happy place', before uploading it to my story. I know Mum'll see it and I know it'll sting, but I don't mean it to.

It's just the truth.

I flip my phone face down, ignore the heart-eyed reactions already pouring in.

My skin blisters at the attention, but I don't scratch this time. I bury my hand into the softest part of Honey's fur instead. My phone *bzzzses* in three short bumblebee bursts and it makes us both jump, neither of us used to the personalised text alert I've set up for Joss so I can differentiate his messages from Mum and Spencer's.

We've been texting on and off all day, about anything and everything. Conspiracy theories, TV shows, parents, university. Sex. Not in a Tinder way, or how it was with boys at school, prying and overly eager, just about our own experiences and how everyone's addicted to porn these days. Even though Joss turned nineteen last month, I learned he's only ever had one serious relationship – one more than me – and a string of one-night stands after they broke up last year, my imagination tangling me with him in one of those scenarios.

Also, a May birthday makes him a Gemini to my Leo and makes *me* a firm believer in all Yaya's astrology now. Ninety per cent compatibility rate, baby.

I open Joss's latest message and draw my phone in closer to my chest, even though Dad's dead asleep. It's a video of him walking towards the bathroom door, shirtless, wet hair slicked back, droplets of water jewelled across his shoulders. He flips the camera and I watch him tug on the handle, revealing his dog, Dudley, who immediately stops pawing at the carpet below the closed door when he sees Joss, tail wagging.

Joss

Thought I'd introduce you to my little stalker. He can't leave me alone for 5 minutes

he's written underneath.

Almond

So cute

I should send something back. I swipe up and open my front camera, instinctively sticking out my jaw to get rid of my double chin as I adjust the brightness and hold my phone up at a high angle, so the camera's looking down on me. Tugging the neckline of my t-shirt down, I draw my shoulders up and in, so my boobs give me that little capital M of cleavage. I take the picture, looking up through my lashes with a bit of a pick-me smile, lots of boob, and Honey's sleepy head in my lap. Then I take it again because my lip's stuck to my tooth in the last one. I take one more, thumb out a reply and press send, throwing my phone onto the beanbag by the TV with a mini squeal.

Almond

Here's me and my girl. We're just chilling today

As soon as the phone lands though, there's the incessant scrunching noise of Joss's text alert going off against the beanbag. I crawl across the carpet to my phone and stare at the back of the case, biting my lip in a grin, wanting and desperately not-wanting to know what he's replied to my PG-13 tit pic. Unlock.

Except it's not Joss. My phone's shuddering with message after message.

anRkey_InCel47

Your legs are soooo fat. U make me sick.

Your happy place is McDonalds. Fat cow.

They're responses to the picture I just uploaded to my story. I stare at the words till they blur, blinking away tears as another message comes in.

anRkey_InCel47

I fucking hate you so much I wish you would just die already. Fat ugly bitch

You think your so much better than everyone else don't you!? Just fucking kys. Go on

Kill yourself.

My heart hammers, chipping away at my ribcage. I don't know why *this* hater out of the gazillion messages I receive like this on the daily is getting to me but it is. Is it the new meds? Or maybe just the fact that this has come when I finally felt something good.

I wipe my eyes, patting the spot on the carpet next to me, making Honey peel one eye open. She sees that she's needed and trots over to be a good friend. I stroke her, staring at my phone. Usually I can predict which posts are going to attract hate or not. Wearing a sleeveless top? Bullying. 'Bingo wings.' Is it tight fitting, low cut? Rape threats. 'Show-off little slut.' A close-up selfie? More bullying. 'Ew, you have pores? Is that a blackhead?' Wearing a full face of make-up!? 'Whore. Clown. Cakeface. Try-hard bitch.' Tons of abuse. Any photos with Dad or Gramma Em in them? Racial abuse. 'Monkeys. Go back home.'

A scurrying little mole of unease tunnels down through my insides. I've seen that name before, I swear. But I can't scroll up any further; today is the first time they've contacted me. Wait, no – today is the first time they've contacted @thereal_almondbrown, but there were those message requests I got yesterday on my first day at Tranks, sent to my private account. My *secret* account that only has two followers, my dad and Callie. Is it just a coincidence that I start receiving targeted hate the day I let myself be vulnerable in front of a room full of strangers? Paranoia floods my brain in gunky black, parasiting itself to my memories of meeting Imogen for the first time, Joss and Heather, that boy with the sneer, Liam, the giggling girls, Varsha, Lex.

With shaking hands, I reply.

thereal_almondbrown

Leave me alone. Please

I throw my phone down, suddenly feeling like there's a million black bugs crawling around inside of it, about to worm their way out through the screen and under my skin. I'm shaking all over as I climb onto the sofa and lie down, Honey following, curling into me as my phone vibrates on the floor with another message. I peer over the worn leather sofa cushion.

anRkey_InCel47

Just fucking kill yourself already.

11

Somehow I managed to keep it together for the rest of the weekend at Dad's, thankful for the boxes to unpack and the empty spaces to decorate, throwing myself into warming the place up into something close to homely. My hands were always too busy taping, folding, or stacking to be wandering towards my phone, my mind too hopeful to dwell on those vile messages.

When I arrived back at the house in Clifton, Mum had arranged a home cinema night with a professionally decorated concession stand complete with a popcorn maker in the living room. A projector flickered the first *Bridget Jones* film onto the wall, our old favourite, and as I dropped my bag onto the floor, she looked up at me with genuine relief that I was home. I knew she'd had help and that I'd be seeing the accompanying ad on Instagram for whatever 'date night at home' brand she'd collabed with. But at least she's trying.

On Monday the distractions were over. Dad works every day

from six till six and Mum's had to be on site to be filmed learning about the factory process of how Oatsy oats are sorted and packaged most days. So I've been home alone all week. With my phone. It sits on the bedside table and I jump every time it vibrates. It's this Anarchy troll; they won't leave me alone, messaging me anywhere from once to a hundred times a day. About my teeth, my pores, my weight, my height, my nailbeds, hairline, hip dips, the way I eat, drink, smile, talk. Breathe.

anRkey_InCel51

I wish you would just STOP breathing. Like pls

Who tf sold you a vest-top. Ugly bingo-winged bitch

I found your other account btw. Your lucky it's clean

Hahaha, you're a ducking female Hagrid with that hair

I hope u choke on that detox tea whore

Whenever I block them, they just make a new account.

An anRkey_InCel48 spawns, then a 49, a 50.

Just now, they've tagged me in the comments under a picture of a white marble coffin.

anRkey_InCel51 This would be perfect for you bestie

Prayer hands emoji. Simpson-coloured, winky tongue emoji. Kissy lips.

Why has this comment got *nine likes?* Are there nine other people who seriously wish I would kill myself too? Anxiety boils through my blood, simmering just under my skin like it has all week, so I'm never not itchy.

Underneath Anarchy's comment, someone's replied.

sunderland.til.i.die Can't stand the half-breed slut.

I hunch myself over, the racism winding me like it always does whenever I see it, though Spencer vets the worst of the hate after a post's initial upload. I cringe inward as the word slut slithers into my ear wearing Callie's voice, till it sheds its skin, becoming louder, a thousand voices spitting the N-word at me too, shaming my body in every way possible. Eyes squeezed shut, my phone goes off again and I recoil, curling into myself further.

It'll be Anarchy. The group chat's died out because, well, why wouldn't it? After only one meeting, me, Heather and Joss don't really have a lot to talk about yet; no memories to regurgitate, no gossip gleaned from common friends. And Joss never did reply to my ... *slutty?* high-angled, softcore boob pic. Is it slutty, though? Didn't he send me his nips in 4K first? Do I think it's slutty, or do I *think* I should think it's slutty?

My phone goes off and I stare at the screen, trying to convince myself it'll be Callie. She always instantly dismissed any hate I got, belittling the commenter into insignificance through screenshots of their bios, usually something like, 'Michael🖕 Flat Earth Atheist 👽DON'T BELIEVE THE LIE👽 Blew up mum's vajayjay 💣02/10/88' and dissections of their usernames. When I got alerted to my first hate forum by a 'concerned fan' who wanted me to know what was being said about me on one of those gossip sites any influencer knows they should never, ever go searching for their name on, Callie built me a blanket fort and cocooned herself in there with me all weekend after I succumbed to the morbid curiosity and read pages and pages of its pure venom.

My phone goes off *again*. Maybe it'll be Dad. But if it's not Anarchy, it's usually Mum though. Or Spencer-dickface-Dorsey telling me the gifs I used in my daily scheduled story aren't aesthetic enough.

But this time it's none of them. A smile ghosts across my lips.

Heather

Hey, you coming to Tranks today??

I take in my dingy, depression-dirtied room, the sheets blotched with blood, my nails crusted with skin and dirt, the tremble in my hands as I type out a reply.

Almond

Yeah, I'll be there. Save me a seat

About to be late for group, I powerwalk into the building, following the sound of Oliver's voice chittering down the hall. Head down, hood up, wearing sunglasses to hide the puffy bags under my eyes, I inch myself into the room and beeline for the last empty seat between Imogen and Heather, with Joss on Heather's other side, tilting himself forward on his chair's front legs when he sees me. He opens his mouth—

'Hey hun,' Imogen whispers, snatching my attention, kiss-kissying her eyelashes at me.

'Hi.'

'Hey, you.' Heather nudges into me. 'What's with the shades? Get hounded by paps on your way in?'

Laughter tickles in my chest though it doesn't reach my lips. I nudge her back, shushing her as Oliver clears his throat. His placid face lingers on each of us in turn as he stands in front of a whiteboard in his elephant-patterned harem pants, eyes balmy, looking like he's blinked straight out of a meditative state.

When there's silence, he says, 'Welcome. Today's focus is all about Unrooting. Seeing if we can dig down into the soil of ourselves with both hands to pull up our problems by the root.' Across the circle, I see Liam roll his eyes, scudding the heel of his trainer against the floor impatiently. 'For our first exercise, I'm going to give you a minute of quiet reflection time to think of *one word* that best describes the reason you're here. If you're not feeling ready to open up today, that's okay. It can be as obscure as you like, and likewise if you feel comfortable sharing more of your story in this session, I'm going to be inviting you to explore your chosen word with us, okay?' He nods, his topknot bouncing back and forth. 'Okay, reflection time starting . . . now.'

I glance around at everybody, trying to gauge the shared level of trust in this room and how deep I want my word to be. Watched? Divorce? Lost – or fucking found? Anxious, sad? Heather swerves her body into my eyeline, trying to get my attention.

'You okay?' she whispers. I nod. Barely.

'Heather?' Oliver says, trapping her with a painfully hopeful smile. 'You done?' Shit, am I next? *What's my word?* 'Can you tell us your word, the root that's been sprouting the bad-feelings weeds that brought you here.'

'Shame,' she says, no hesitation, eyes straight ahead.

The black marker squeaks against the whiteboard, the word somehow less imposing in Oliver's elegantly looped lettering.

'And if you feel comfortable, would you mind detangling those roots a little bit? Tell us why "shame" comes to mind?'

Heather's lips peel apart, sticky with plum-coloured gloss, moving over unformed words as she tries to figure out what to say, her fingers spinning the rusted silver skull ring on her thumb. 'Shame like . . . fat-shaming,' she says, hiking her chin up. 'Shame about my scars. My whole life it's like everyone's always been telling me I should hate my body. My mum's a group leader for this thing called SlimIt, one of those toxic weight-loss programmes that gives you a gold star for starving yourself all week, and my grandma, my aunties, every single one of my cousins is perfectly proportioned, like, they'd come up on those body-type quizzes as hourglass, banana, pear, or whatever. And then there's me. The . . . watermelon.' Heather shrugs, throwing her hands down at her sides. 'But I never really gave a fuck about them because, well *because*. Fuck them, I didn't— *don't* care what they think. If they really love me, they should want me to love me. Right?'

I touch my knee to hers. *Right.*

'So, at what point do you think their views started to make you feel shame?' Oliver says with a head tilt, his bun toppling to the side.

Heather sighs, eyeing me as her face gets stirred up with emotions: embarrassment, disgust, amusement ... *jealousy?* A self-deprecating smirk settles on her lips. '*They* didn't. But I had a really bad break-up. Turns out he was a misogynistic narcissist who started posting my photos on those cancerous threads for pick-up artists and red pill, blue pill incels. Once those *assholes* get in their head that, God forbid, a fat girl might find herself attractive and, oh no, other people might be attracted to her, it becomes too much for their tiny, roid-raged brains.

'I don't know why – because the *last* thing I want is their approval – but they did it. They broke me. They made me think that my family were right to force their diet advice down my throat all those years. That I was ugly. Unlovable. No matter what I did I couldn't get their words out of my head – still can't. But I show up for myself every day, I wear the bodycon dress, I don't "dress for my size" even though it's hard sometimes, because I am *not* about to let those limp dicks win.'

'Oh, Hev,' I whisper, resting my head on her shoulder, 'you are so beautiful.'

'I'm sorry that happened to you, Heather,' Oliver says, his hands in prayer at his chest. He rocks his wrists to emphasise every word, his fingers steepled toward her. 'You didn't deserve that. Thank you for being the first to share today, that was very—'

'Don't call me brave.' She winces. 'Please.'

'Okay,' Oliver says, soft as peach fuzz.

Joss hooks his arm around Heather's neck, planting a fierce kiss on her temple, which she swipes off dramatically, though she softly knocks him on the arm.

'Thanks, mate,' she mumbles.

By five forty-five, Shame, Guilt, Bingeing, Sister, Minecraft, Consent, Weed and Anxiety are listed down the whiteboard in shiny black ink, their severity dressed up in silk by Oliver's delicate strokes and curlicues. When it comes to my turn all I can manage to say is, 'Pretending,' shaking my head when Oliver asks if I want to elaborate. I want to, I want to shatter this skin that the influence industry has papier-mâchéd over me my whole life, year by year encasing the old me behind a new layer of lies. But I don't feel ready to crack out of the mould they've fitted me into yet, let out the dark echo of my own voice.

It's lonely in here, but it's safe.

'Not today? That's okay. Thanks for sharing, Almond. I hope that next week when we come to ask those who did grapple and tend to those roots today – too much metaphor? It is, isn't it? Maybe hearing how it made those who shared feel, a week on, will encourage more of you to open up with us. Right, who haven't we done . . .' Oliver peers down at the clipboard on his chair. 'Joss? We haven't heard from you. What's your word?'

'Uh.' He scratches the back of his head, then pulls his hair that sits choppily on his shoulders into a fist at the nape of his neck. 'I don't know,' he says, tipping his chair back to look at the ceiling.

'When you look back at making the decision to get help, do you remember the kind of things you were doing, who you were with, what emotions you remember feeling?'

'Dissociated,' Joss says with sudden clarity, his chair thudding to the floor. Oliver nods low, his forehead crinkled, prompting Joss to go on. He takes a deep breath, then sighs out his words. 'With the world, and a lot of the people in it. The government. It all started in 2020 with the first lockdown. That constant cycle of dread they call the news, and the constant barrage of social justice that at first outraged me and spurred me on to want to make the world a better place, but later fucking drowned me, made me feel insignificant. Scared. So, I disengaged completely, deleted everything. And now I hardly talk to anyone.'

Oliver takes a breath, probably about to ask him to unpack some of what he said but Joss cuts in front, not unkind but weary with finality.

'That's it, I'm done.'

As we spill out onto the steps in front of Tranquility, I thank Heather for texting me earlier and inadvertently forcing me out of bed to come to group, because I *do* feel better now. We mill about by the bins with some of the other kids, my eyes always finding Joss in the quiet crowd. He looks burrowed away in himself, hands balled in his pockets, shoulders hunched, like sharing in group had the opposite effect that Oliver made us imagine. I want to reach out to him, take his hand, but I'm guessing he's processing right now and I don't want to overstep it, which I might already have.

Selfishly, I feel a sore sting of embarrassment remembering that there's an unreplied-to photo of me on his phone, with my tits sandwiched together so tightly the filling's about to burst out. I shuffle out of the circle, away from him and my cringe, watching everybody from the outskirts.

Imogen hovers close by texting on her phone, pretending she's not listening to everyone's conversations, probably desperate for a chance to get to talk normally for once and not about her body-fat percentage or stool quality as she's been collabing with that meal-replacement brand, Fast-Off, and all she eats is sewage-coloured sludge. I peer over, not too suss, to see what she's supposedly transfixed by – YouTube's featured page, boasting a bunch of clickbaity thumbnails for toxic tea channels and eight-year-old kids being made to film toy reviews. I mean, if you're going to fake-scroll, at least go to Instagram.

Heather's talking to a girl called Samantha, who's shuffling gravel under her feet, occasionally glancing around at everyone with a shy smile. The group's other boy is stood with us too, eyeing up Heather's tattoos. Thanks to today's session, I now know that his name is Marius, and that Marius huffs glue when he hears his parents arguing at night.

And Joss's still staring at the floor, kicking up dust, so tensed that a vein's wormed to the surface of his skin, sticking out down the length of his forearm.

That's all of us, everyone else has gone home to their Friday nights.

'Sooo, does anyone wanna do something now?' says Heather, shielding her eyes from the sun. I nod, not wanting to go back to my room where Anarchy's words crawl the walls at night, closing me in. 'We could go to the Greyhound? My brother's behind the bar so he'll definitely serve us.'

'Sure. Will there be boys there?' Imogen starts fussing with herself, using her front camera as a mirror and curling back her eyelashes with a finger.

Heather swivels her eyes up to the sky for a second, lolling her tongue out like she's dead. 'Uh, if by boys you mean gross, old men? Then yeah.'

'Oh, God,' Imogen says, rummaging around in her bag. I watch with recognised horror as she slathers on another layer of liquid lipstick.

'You look *fine*,' I whisper-smile.

'I'm in. Day's too nice to go home yet anyway,' Marius says, though I get the feeling he wouldn't want to go home even if we were stood in a downpour of torrential rain.

'I'll come,' I say, my guts already twisting.

I'm supposed to be browsing launch-night outfits with Mum later – she's been gifted a complimentary personal shopping experience at Harvey Nick's. I pull out my phone as the six of us start walking and send her a let-down text.

Almond

Sorry can we go shopping another time? I'm going out with some friends from group for a bit. X

Immediately the little grey dots that mean she's typing start to bounce on my screen, and before I can overthink it, I switch off my phone. I can't be bothered to argue with her – and the launch night's not for another two weeks anyway. I shove it in my pocket and feel Joss's arm graze against mine as he falls into step with me.

'You been to the Greyhound before?' he asks. My nerves are a wreck now that I'm alone with Joss, and the toll of having Anarchy tear down every aspect of my appearance for a week straight entangles with the insecurity of having my picture left on read, until I find I can only shake my head. 'Great pub, shit dog,' says Joss, nudging into me this time.

'I like greyhounds,' I manage.

'Nah, they're too bony.' He fake-coughs into a fist, awkward. 'Can't imagine they're very comfy when they lie on you. Dudley's always doing that.'

We walk on in silence for a bit, everyone else a little way ahead of us on the pavement, chatting buzzily, while I keep rereading Anarchy's latest comments inside my head. Still, Joss stays by my side. I look down at his scuffed white Vans, the hems of faded loose jeans turned up, a gaping hole in the knee that I can guess wasn't there when he bought them.

'You shouldn't scratch,' he says gently, pulling my hand away from scraping at the inside of my wrist. I didn't realise I was. Joss doesn't let go and threads his fingers through mine, his face ducking into my eyeline and coaxing my eyes up to meet his. 'I think it's great that you shared today by the way, and I'm sorry I've been distant this week. It was a bit of a bad one for me.' He taps the side of his head and I stay quiet, listening, gripping his hand tighter. 'I felt depressed as shit – you know that whole cold to your bone, dead tired, can't get out of bed feeling, right around the same time work offered me a bunch of double shifts I couldn't turn down.'

'Why?' I ask, cringing at my ignorance as soon as the question's out of my mouth. *Why*, says the girl who's paid thousands of pounds to pull facial expressions in front of a camera.

He shrugs. 'I need the money.' Joss stops dead on the pavement, swinging me round to face him. 'But I meant what I said before. I like you, Almond.' When I don't respond to his kind and careful words with anything more than wriggling the puzzle pieces of our fingers closer together, he leans in even closer, so I feel his breath hot in my ear. 'Oh, and you looked fucking hot in that picture you sent me, by the way.'

Oh. My hips steer me closer to him, my body making decisions all on its own. I bite my lip, wanting so bad just to kiss him.

Breathless, I say, 'You know, I think that's the first time you've ever called me Almond and not some other dumb nut.'

He grins.

'You're right, my bad. Sorry, Pistachio.'

12

Liked by **evefairchild**, **spencey_dorsey** and 338 others

thereal_almondbrown Today feels like a good day ☀ what do you feel grateful for today? For me it's the summer sun (and all the glorious vitamin D it's giving me!!), good vibes and new beginnings . . . talk to me in the comments x x x x

[Image description: Two shadows are holding hands as they ignore the 'Do Not Walk on Grass' sign, and walk the heck across that grass on a sunny Friday afternoon anyway]

13

I stare at myself in the Greyhound's cracked bathroom mirror, my reflection jaggedly split from crown to clavicle. I wet my thumb and finger, try to tame some of the frizz that my curls have unravelled into, tie my hair up, take it down again, tuck it behind my ears, then untuck it. Sighing, I turn away from myself, getting out my phone to switch it to Do Not Disturb as reactions to my latest post *buzz* and buzz like a swarm in my pocket. But before I do, a message from Electra Lyons catches my eye, her words like a sweet salve slathered over the one sting of hate I accidentally sighted just by unlocking the screen.

electralyonslives

You sound happy, girl. I love this. And I demand to know who you're holding hands with. Spill!!!! (or don't, I'm just playing) 😇

electralyonslives

P.s I'm feeling grateful for the opportunities this life has given me. Hate to be one of THOSE influencers but I have got big big news to announce very soon. Stay tuned angel

thereal_almondbrown

You tease!! Is this real life big or business big?? And girl, you know you are being nothing BUT one of those influencers rn

thereal_almondbrown

You are not a movie!! Do not hit me up with the teaser trailer

Typing ... appears underneath my last message and I wait, my smile cosy as I entertain the thought of blowing my VeGlow money on America and visiting Electra – not in LA, home of the green-juice goddesses and the call-the-paparazzi-on-yourself pariahs, God no – but maybe we could meet somewhere busy and bustling on the East Coast.

electralyonslives

All will be revealed👀

thereal_almondbrown

Booooo. But ok gl🔥

Since I'm here, I do a quick swipe through comments, hearting a few for engagement, about to mentally check out of the internet for the night when my self-sabotaging subconscious picks out a familiar username from the comment crowd.

anRkey_InCel51 Who's this in the pic then!?Obviously someone blind or planning to pump and dump you once they've rinsed you for a couple free pr trips

In an instant my heart rate's fuelling that palpable adrenalin rush round my body that internet conflict ignites, breaking my resolve not to respond to Anarchy as I decide to DM them.

thereal_almondbrown

Fuck off asshole. Go live YOUR OWN LIFE. Stay out of mine.

Do Not Disturb firmly on, I bang out of the grubby bathroom door to find the others, off getting a table in the beer garden, determined not to let that evil little *fuckhead* ruin my night.

It's practically empty outside apart from the oddballs I'm here with, laughing and crowded round a wooden table, all bright hair, inked skin and loud clothes. As I get closer, I recognise the guy in a black shirt and loose tie handing out a tray of pints as the guy who picked Heather up last week.

'This is my brother, Rich,' Heather says, when she sees me coming over. 'He's kindly agreed to give us table service all night, haven't you, mate?' I laugh, nod a little Hello to Rich. 'See, Almond, the Greyhound's a classy place – don't listen to the bad press.'

'Run along, Jeeves.' Joss claps his hands together, shifting over for me to sit down. 'Chop-chop.'

Bumping the empty tray down on Joss's head, Rich laughs and pushes his glasses further up the bridge of his nose.

'This ain't happening every time you place an order, mind,' he says in a very Bristolian accent.

Foam moustachioed, Heather takes another gulp of her pint, shooing him off. 'Okay, thank you, goodbye Rich.'

The atmosphere stales as Rich walks away and I notice Heather cut her eyes at Imogen before she and Joss glance sharply at each other.

'What's this?' I ask, craning my neck to see what Sam, Marius and Imogen are laughing about at the other end of the table, their heads close together, watching something on a phone screen.

'Guys.' Joss doesn't look up from folding his beermat smaller and smaller, an edge to his voice.

Heather takes a long swig of her pint, sliding one over towards me, a quick shrug-smile lifting her lips. And then I hear *her* voice. Mum's camera voice.

'I think that's Joe back from the shops now. Let's see what he's forgotten this time, shall we, Apples?'

My grip tightens round my pint, cold condensation against my clammy fingers. *Her Apples*, the ridiculous pet name Mum gave to subscribers of her YouTube channel, equally ridiculously named, the Garden of Eve. Why're they watching one of her vlogs? My fingers slip, slopping the beer, the amber bubbles tornadoing up towards the foam as I realise which one they're watching.

'Turn it off,' I say automatically.

'Oh my God, guys, can you believe this. Average Joe's only gone and—'

Under the table, my nails curl piercingly into my palm.

Average Joe, the name Mum's followers thought up to belittle my dad in her comment sections where viewers wittered words of marital advice, complained about the amount of time he spent at work, or hinted at harmful racial stereotypes about black fathers. As if they could know anything about him as a person, or us and our family dynamic, from watching a week in our lives told in scissored clips, the way a celebrity's 'Best Bits' are after they're kicked off the reality show. Seven whole days of deciding what's for dinner, hanging wet washing, and arguments as trivial as Dad not screwing the cap back on the toothpaste, gets edited down so the audience only ever gets to see the polished plate of polenta chips, the eight-minute segment of Mum contractually gushing about the planet-friendly laundry detergent she's on the payroll of, and the whispered one-sided recap of their ridiculous toothpaste argument from Mum as she performs her updated 'getting unready' routine.

I can't stand the normal domesticity of our life getting cut into thirty minutes of context-lacking content to ensure the video gets lumbered with at least three ad rolls.

'Aw, Almond.' Imogen pouts, leaning over and thrusting her phone at me. Mum's sneering face fills the screen corner to corner as she whispers conspiratorially to the lens. *'He's a waste of space guys – only joking!'*

'Don't be moody. Marius was asking what kind of content it is we make and well, it's just your mum's so funny in this one. It's the perfect example of family vlogging. So, it's like reality TV,' she says to Marius, 'just real life with all the gritty, realistic bits left in like this. Literally, Almond, your mum's face when your dad brings home chia seeds instead of flaxseed, I just *can't*.' Imogen giggles. 'She's fuming, and she's got this big vein on her forehead. I can't believe she kept this in.'

'Yeah, me neither.' I try a self-deprecating smile. 'Can you turn it off though please?'

'I can't believe that's your *mum*?' Marius slurps the foam off his pint, shaking his head. 'She is *fit*. Is she the one off that boujee sofa advert?'

'Yes.' The word grinds out through my teeth. I scrape my elbow against the table's rough wooden surface, filing away at myself.

Joss squeezes my knee under the table but I'm numb to it. I can't take my eyes off my parents arguing in the palm of Imogen's hand with the pause button in the corner of the screen, like this only happened for entertainment and not in real life. I was so happy half an hour ago, holding hands with Joss as we walked, tilting my face up to the shimmering warmth of the sun, smiling at snippets of conversation drifting back to me. All of that feels forever-ago and far away as my consciousness drains back into the phone in Imogen's hand, the ever-black presence of my digital life vortexing me in.

'If only you paid attention to me, Joe.'

'Are her tits fake?' says Marius. 'Sorry, I know that's your mum but, come on.'

'Really, man?' I know having Joss by my side should make me feel better, less alone, but I can't breathe, like I'm wrapped in clingfilm, something invisible and suffocating between us. 'Seriously, stop being assholes,' he says. 'Watch this shit in your own time.'

'Okay then, Apples, I guess I'll have to show you this protein shake recipe without *the flaxseed, thanks to someone.'*

Sam reaches up and tightens her ponytail, her eyes flicking between me and the screen. 'Your poor dad—'

'Aw my God, look there's Honey. She's like a puppy here.' Imogen holds the phone out to Joss this time. He just stares her down, his eyes not straying anywhere near the screen as he sips his drink, his arm so stiff it's almost mechanical. 'What was she here, like six months?'

Imogen directs the question at me, but I'm all the way spaced out with the realisation that anyone could find out the answer to that with a quick google. I shrug, wanting to snatch Imogen's phone up and tuck the memory of my puppy away, to have baby Honey just for me to remember, snuggled away in family photo albums, but I can't because . . .

. . . my life is not my own.

'What did you say?' Joss swoops his head low, ear near my lips.

'Nothing.'

Did I say that out loud? I look down and realise I've drained half of my pint already.

'Honestly, guys, you have to work *at a marriage. Comment down below if you know what I mean—'*

'Shut up!' I scream, reaching across the table and smacking the phone out of Imogen's hand. There's a crunching of glass as it lands in the gravel, my mum's voice broken and tinny, scattering shards of my old life into the dirt.

I take deep, raggedy breaths as I scour my nails against my arm, triggering pain receptors that tremble messages up my arm and blanket my brain in serotonin, blunting everything else going on.

'I'm ... so sorry,' Imogen says, staring at her face-down phone. She clears her throat, fluttering her false lashes up at me. 'Are you okay? You're not okay, of course you're not.' Her eyes glance back at her shattered phone. 'I didn't mean to be a total bitch, I'm such a fan honestly. I just didn't think— Oh my God, I didn't think at all. That was super inappropriate of me, wasn't it? I guess I just haven't gotten over getting to be your friend yet.' She swallows, fingers dithering across her clavicle. 'I grew up watching you and your family.'

'Yeah, sick friend,' Joss says gruffly. 'She's so lucky to have you.'

Friends? We're not friends. Does she think *this* is what friendship is?

'I'll go,' she says, jittery as she slips on her cardigan, her bottom lashes wet with unspilled tears.

Suddenly all my adrenalin's swirling away, my plug pulled. 'No, don't. I'm sorry,' I say, ignoring Heather's mouth as it drops open. I slump over the table, drained.

'*You* have nothing to apologise for,' she says, clicking the stud in her tongue along her teeth and glaring at Imogen, sharpening that glare as she aims it at Marius.

She's right, but I'm done with this now. Let's fake nice and move on.

'It's fine. Seriously though, Imogen, I'm sorry about your phone,' I say. 'Is it broken? My, uh, manager can get you a new one.'

I chug two mouthfuls of my pint, picturing Spencer's face when I ask him to replace Imogen Shawcross's phone because I smashed it to the ground. Relevant, #relatable, e-girl Imogen with her preppy, pastel edits. Polka-dot background, cherry blossom outfit, hands on hips, feet turned in. Pink and white everything. Spencer'll be livid.

She picks up the phone, looks it over and shrugs as I lean over to see it for myself. Oh God. Dozens of hairline cracks splinter down from the top right corner of the screen in a dainty glass spiderweb.

'It's just the screen protector,' Imogen says, pinning a smile to her face. 'Ugh, I'm such a bitch.'

'You're not,' I say, bland and monotone, sighing before taking another huge gulp of beer. Joss's hand rests on my thigh, his thumb tracing small circles. 'I get weird seeing other people watch me or my mum online, that's all.'

Marius forces a laugh. 'Yeah, no shit.'

'I can't explain it.'

'And you don't have to,' Heather says, using her pinkie finger to draw a dick into the condensation on her pint glass and scowling over at Marius.

Actually, I can explain it. Maybe it's because in 0.46 seconds, absolutely anyone can get access to the pixelated archive of my literal entire life. Maybe it's because the whole world can pause, rewind, and rewatch those intimately mundane snippets of what used to be my family. Or maybe it's because I'm right fucking here, *Imogen*. I watch her brushing up her lashes with a mascara wand and realise I'm so over wanting to hang out with her now, or with anyone for that matter. I just want to go home.

I down the dregs of my pint, swallowing the peaty dribble that's left.

'There'll be other pints,' Joss says, his voice crackly soft in my ear.

'Actually, it's okay,' I say, unpeeling myself from him and sidling out from the table, my vision a little swimmy as I stand too fast, only now remembering Dr Wallace's warning about mixing alcohol with my antidepressants. 'I think I'm gonna go now.'

'Oh no, don't go. Please don't go because of me.' Imogen's desperation springs tears to my eyes and I can't tell if they've sprung from stress hormones or if I'm actually crying. *What am I talking about?* Of course I'm crying. Why'd she just do that? Show my parents arguing in a vlog like it's a KUWTK highlight? 'I'm such an idiot,' she says.

'I'll come with you,' Joss says, looking up at me.

'No, stay, it's fine,' I say, sipping shallow breaths and thinking up an excuse to be alone that's not rude or anxiety-inducing. Um. 'I have this thing with my mum tonight anyway. I wasn't planning on staying long.'

Wait, this *was* actually true. I turn my phone off Do Not Disturb mode, waiting for it to blow up with missed calls and voicemails because I cancelled on Mum last minute. But amongst the notifications still spewing in from Instagram, there's only one message, and sadness shivers through me as I read it. She's actually being nice, supportive even. I reread her text, my emotions giving me a hundred and ten per cent right now.

Mum

Ok darling, another time. How exciting, have fun with your new friends! I'm out tonight now – last minute cocktail tasting sesh woohoo!! but in case I don't see you before your grandma's party tomorrow, I've left her present from me on your bed❤️

Love & hugs xox

It chokes me up knowing that Mum still got Gramma a present. Maybe because *this* Mum seems so sweet, stripped back from the self-aggrandising drama queen stirring up our family's business that I just witnessed her playing up to be on camera.

A few notifications down, I self-destructively take in what Anarchy's been spamming me with since I uploaded that picture of mine and Joss's shadows holding hands.

anRkey_InCel51

So glad you have time to tan when there are so many other people literally DYING to be in your position.

‘Want me to walk you back to your bike, then?’ Joss says.

anRkey_InCel51

You entitled thankless bitch. Kys.

With panicked hands, I jam my phone back in my pocket as Joss starts to get up.

My eyes linger on him, and for a second, I want to say yes, but then I notice his rolled-up sleeves, gathered at the elbows of his tanned, freckly arms as he squints up at me through the sun on his face. I remember what he said about this week being tough for him, that he’s been working twelve-hour shifts surrounded by screens and ringing phones, and now that he’s here I don’t want to drag him away from this, from talking and tipsiness in the evening sun, *in*to my unhappiness.

‘No, really. You should stay, I’m *fine*. I’ll see you all next week. Have a good night,’ I say, my fingers trailing across the back of his neck as I take my hand away from his shoulder. ‘I’ll text you.’

I walk away, clutching my phone as it shudders with hate.

14

'Oh, how very ... urban.' Spencer jerks up the handbrake of his massive, big-dick SUV in front of Dad's flat, craning round to peer over the top of his Ray-Bans at me in the back seat. 'Is it always this loud?'

'No? It's a birthday party.' *You dick.*

My own gramma's birthday party that I'm four hours late to thanks to the impromptu Q&A we had to film this morning. Promo disguised as 'content' before the Serenity launch, despite VeGlow only briefing us on it at nine-thirty last night, demanding Mum put teasers like, 'Another baby?', 'Online dating?' and 'Regretting the divorce?' in the title for clickbait.

Trauma sells, I guess.

The engine rumbles idly as Spencer fiddles with the radio in my peripheral, checking his mirrors, ready to pull out.

'Thanks for the lift, Spencer.'

'No probs. And hey, remember what we talked about,

okay – I need to see more of you on stories. Gimme updates, gimme anything – ooh something fun, you're at a party, so use it. A quick boomerang of you dancing or something, whatever, but I do need a selfie to stories at 11 p.m. though, that okay? Paisley's requested more interaction during peak time for socials in New York. You've got your portable ring light?' I nod once, military style. 'No background clutter, absolutely *no* alcohol anywhere near the shot, and no guest appearances, okay. Just you.'

'Fine.' How sad is it that all I'm allowed to show my followers is perfectly poised unreality? Not the loud, sloppy, unplanned fun that's happening right here on the other side of the street. 'Bye, Spencer.'

The heavy door clunks shut and Spencer tinkles his fingers at me before he roars off down the narrow, car-lined street, doing thirty in a twenty zone. Just as he's about to swerve out of sight, I thrust my middle finger out at the boot of his car, wishing I didn't care about him dropping Mum as a client and that I could just shove my *fuck you* right in his smarmy plastic face.

I cross the road and linger at the gate, staring at the sprawl of people in the tiny front garden outside Dad's flat, all here for Gramma Em's birthday. Doesn't make sense at all to invite fifty-something people here, but the retirement village where Gramma lives now doesn't allow gatherings, loud music, or fun in general, so of course she brought the party to us. I scan the garden for any sign of Callie or her family, who've been invited to every one of my family gatherings since literally before I can remember. Callie's family moved into the council flat next to Gramma's when we were babies, and with Gramma being the block's resident babysitter, we were bound to end up highchair-to-highchair being spoon-fed mashed carrots in front of the *Teletubbies*. Bound to end up best friends.

A hand slaps my upper arm. 'Aight?'

I frown, turning to see Shaquille, the son of one of Dad's friends, who's so obviously stoned, with eyes like sundried tomatoes.

'Hey,' I say, trying to keep the judgement out of my voice.

'Shit, if I showed up this late to my nanna's birthday party, she'd beat my ass,' he says, kissing his teeth.

'Well remind me to stay the hell away from your nanna.'

'She's over there.' He points with his can of Red Stripe to a lady with smooth brown skin and a tightly sprayed weave, bumping her hips to the music so hard her cane's starting to dig down into the grass.

We look back and splutter laughter at each other, and it's a nice moment before I see his eyes travel down and up my body, openly and with confidence, daring me to even try to tell him off. He probably thinks he's entitled to because he's seen it all before on my Instagram. Shaquille tilts his can toward me as an offer, for a sip of his drink and something else too, I think.

I lift my chin. 'No thanks, I'll get my own. You seen my dad? Or my dog?'

Shaquille sniggers, upending his can and crunching it in his fist. I raise an eyebrow.

'He *was* out back with mans. Ya know.' I roll my eyes as he mimes putting a smoke to his lips. 'I ain't seen your dog though.'

'Thanks. 'Scuse me,' I say, not waiting for a reply before shouldering through the mess of people stood in the doorway.

I swipe a can of something off the side, noticing Callie and Steph sitting on top of the kitchen worktops, all jerked necks and raised eyebrows. I crack the can, huffing out a fake-nonchalant laugh that I hope she hears as Callie pops a bubble of gum on the end of her tongue. *Why* is that girl's attitude laid on so thick? Since our fight in the street the other day, I get that she's upset about everything else that came before Theo now, the sorry-can't-make-its and my phone being out of service in another country when she needed me. This isn't just over some boy. But can't she see that I never wanted any of this either?

We stare at each other, all the years of late-night phone calls, dumb in-jokes, and borrowed clothes stretching between us like the frayed piece of string we used to use to play telephone when we were little kids. Me on the balcony at Gramma's old flat, Callie squished up against the railings on her own balcony full of clothes horses and old baby toys. This was before it was normal for kids to have iPhones and Androids, when we still had to pretend with plastic cups, like the one I know she's sipping cheap, sugary orange juice and vodka from now, the only alcoholic drink she can stomach.

Neither of us looks away and it's like the air fills with the static buzz of all the things we left unsaid.

A wet heat trickles in my palm.

I tear my eyes away from hers, look down. I've picked a gash on my wrist.

In the hush between one song finishing and the next one starting, I hear a glass shatter on the concrete outside, a toddler bawling its eyes out and a roar of grown-men laughter. I don't think the three are related but it's too much in here; too much loud, liveable, real life that I don't know what to do with. And the one person I want to talk to is looking at me like she doesn't know me.

I make moves for the bedroom, quick, grabbing a sheet of kitchen roll on my way and pressing it to the dripping blood at my wrist. I say *the* bedroom 'cuz Dad couldn't afford a two-bedroom flat, so I don't have a room of my own here to hide in, just my sunflower bedding stretched over Dad's old mattress while he takes the sofa every weekend. So I slip away from Callie and Steph into what I think will have been made up into my bedroom for the weekend and close the door behind me, falling back against it. Eyes closed, I sink to the ground, the bass in the speakers thumping through me, reverberating my bones.

Are we really out here celebrating seventy-three this hard?

'Baby, you're here.'

My eyes fly open. Dad's sitting wide-legged at the end of his bed, elbows resting on his knees, wearing his Chicago Bulls jersey and baggy shorts. Why he's still dressing like a twenty-year-old from the nineties, I do not know. What I *do* know is that all I want to do right now is curl up in his arms and for him to hush the world away.

'What you doing in here for?' he says, straining a smile through his voice as he tries to convince the both of us that he's sober. 'Does Gramma know you're here?'

I note the slur in his voice and how he put about five extra Ms in the word Gramma, the carpet of dirty clothes, the cigarette stink, my sunflower sheets still folded at the end of his unmade bed and the closed curtains. In a count of five, I sigh out my breath, holding Dad's dazed, watery eyes. I count to five *again*, which is obviously a bullshit technique because my voice still comes out switchblade sharp when I speak.

'Why are you always so surprised to see me?'

'Huh?'

'Always asking me why I'm here. *What you doing here, baby*?' I mock his deep, mahogany voice, knowing this hurt was meant for Callie and not Dad . . . but none of what I'm saying's untrue. I drink a few mouthfuls from my can. Full mouthfuls like it's water and I'm parched. 'I'm here 'cuz you're here. And I'm here right now in this room because I felt bad I couldn't find you.' And then in a mousy soft voice, I say what I've been thinking since he left. 'Don't you want to see me?'

'Woah, woah, woah, slow down.' He goes to get up off the bed, to come comfort me like I want him to, but he's clumsy-drunk and sags back down, putting a hand to his temple. 'It's not like that, okay? I mean, it is but . . .'

Holding his stare, I clench the kitchen roll tighter in my fist, waiting for him to continue.

'I *was* waiting for you to get here, you know. I had our Kitchen Dancing playlist on and everything. I even helped cook callaloo just for you. But you said you had filming stuff and then the boys got here and . . .' He trails off, looks down at his feet.

‘Oh,’ I say quietly.

He doesn’t need to finish, I know what he’s not saying, that I took too long getting here, so he chose *the boys* – a huddle of tattoos and smoke – over me. He probably thinks filming Q&As is fun for me, that I really wanted to spend four hours answering questions like, ‘If you were an ice cream flavour, which would you be?’ but felt I *had* to come here.

‘Dad, I really wanted to be here earlier, I just couldn’t, I—’

‘It’s OK, I get it. You got your own stuff going on.’ He sighs. ‘My baby’s all grown now. Speaking of, since when do you drink Red Stripe? Who gave you that?’

For a second I feel guilty that Dad doesn’t know he should be telling me not to drink this. It was left to me to tell him about the antidepressants myself, but I haven’t got around to it, bottled it, when I remembered the instant defensiveness that came over him when I told him I was seeing a therapist, his face wrinkled with injured pride. And not a mention of it since.

I googled it anyway, and the NHS says I’m less likely to experience side-effects when you’re on the kind of pills I’m on, and right now, feeling the way I do, it seems worth the risk.

‘Nobody. I took it.’

A smile tugs at the corners of his mouth. I try to fight it from catching on to mine too. Me and Dad have always found it hard to stay mad at each other for more than five minutes. I *believe* he wanted to spend time with me – sober, dancing-to-golden-oldies time, not mopey, hidden away, sitting-in-the-dark time – and I can’t stay mad at him for thinking I’d bailed out on him for a video. Again.

I sigh. 'I'm sorry, Dad.'

'Nuh-uh. None of that.' He holds up a hand, his pinkish palm dry and blistered from work. I remember pretending to read his palm as a kid, giggling because the cracked lines under his littlest finger said he would have a bajillion babies, but he ended up with just me.

'Almond.' He looks me dead in the eye now, his voice catching at the back of his throat. 'It's me that should be sorry. I haven't lived in a place by myself since I was nineteen years old. And that only lasted like, what, six months before I met your mum.' He starts scuffing his shoe against the carpet, the eye contact faltering. 'This being here and living without you, without you both, is hard for me and it's kinda scary and overwhelming, baby. So, I'm sorry if I'm not . . . adjusting too fast. What you said earlier . . . I don't mean to sound *surprised* to see you, I'm happy to see you, always. I'm just realising now that maybe I'm not so happy for you to see me. Like this.'

'Oh.' It's all I can say around the lump in my throat.

'But I'm gonna try harder, okay. I promise. Now let's go have a boogie, yeah?' He claps his hands, muscling up a smile that doesn't quite reach his eyes. 'This is meant to be a party.'

'A boogie,' I say, sniggering and sniffling at the same time.

Dad bundles me through the everything room, and with his heavy arm around my shoulders it's like I'm shielded from the mess of noise and people that was all too much earlier. From the corner of my eye, I see Callie and Steph getting shooed off the kitchen worktops, an older lady whipping the backs of their bare legs with a swirled-up tea towel, which makes me suck in a smile.

'G'wan, get,' I hear her Barbadian tongue cluck after them.

My head whips around. *Gramma Em.* I haven't even said Happy Birthday yet.

'Almond, baby!' Gramma cries, catching Dad about to slip us out the back door towards the tinkling of calypso music from the speaker set up outside. ''As it really been mi birthday fuh ova thirteen hours and am still waiting for a hug off mi only grandchild? Tsk.'

'Happy birthday, Gramma,' I say, as she reaches out for me and I bury myself in her puddingy arms.

'Mmm, thank you, thank you.' Gramma follows us outside, fanning herself with a napkin. 'Ooh, I love this song,' she says, singing the wrong lyrics to 'Work' along with Rihanna.

Kissing out her lips, she winds her hips over to me, shimmying between two of Dad's mates, and I giggle as she bounces her big bum.

'Oh my God, Gramma,' I say, my cheeks hotting up, even though I'm laughing and joining in too. Honey jumps up on her hind legs and licks kisses all over my face as I hold her paws in my hands. 'Work, work, work, work, work, work,' I sing, trying not to let the fact that I can see Dad lingering around Shaquille as he lights up a spliff ruin this moment.

Gramma sees too, her lips pursing judgingly as she twists me and Honey away from them, enveloping me in her soft, earthy-sweet smell of coconut oil and shea butter as she loosens up her voice, lapsing into patois with Rihanna at the song's bridge, and dances me into something close to happy.

The party's in wind-down mode by ten. While Dad's snoozing on the sofa through the clean-up, Gramma's friend, Doreen, fusses about the kitchenette putting pots in the sink to soak, and gathering up dirty dishes. Gramma Em's sitting next to me on the sofa, all loose and jiggly, a party hat hanging lopsided off her perm as she peers down her roll of chins at a birthday card. Go Gramma.

Callie and Steph slurrily screeched their thanks and goodbyes about an hour ago, with me having to clamp my lips shut, ironing out any hint of amusement from my face as Callie sang along to 'Dancing Queen', replacing the lyrics to make Gramma still young and sweet at seventy-three. They left with Shaquille in search of a free rave, and as the door closed, I downed the rest of my drink, swallowing its soothing scorch of relief. Yeah, I'd managed to avoid them all night, but I'd be lying if I said my ears weren't pricked every time Callie's laugh snorted into a honk, wondering what Steph had said to make her laugh so hard.

I'd be lying if I said I didn't miss her like crazy.

I nurse my fourth – no, fifth? – tumbler of rum, fighting the syrupy heaviness of my eyelids. Because it's not 6 p.m. in New York yet, and I have to stay up late to give my transatlantic fans the selfie VeGlow thinks they so desperately crave. Actually, you know what ... I scroll through my backlog of selfies stored for occasions exactly like this, or if I've spilled sauce down my outfit, or my hair's looking windswept, and schedule one to go up at the appointed time. There, done. Why didn't I think of this earlier?

'Here, let me help you,' I say, waving Doreen away from the side table next to me, about to enact my one good clean-up deed before going to bed. I get up and gather a bunch of glasses between my thumb and fingers, swaying as I carry them to the sink. God, I need some air. 'I'm gonna see if there's anything else to bring in from outside,' I mutter to nobody in particular.

In the hallway, I peel myself along the wall for support, suddenly woozy and heavy-bellied, clammy hot. Lurching myself out the front door, I stagger onto the lawn, gasping in the cool night air which only prickles sweat across my brow, dizzier still. *Oh no.* I bend over, hands on my knees, as the liquor burns through my empty stomach, stings up my throat and gushes from my mouth.

'Fuck.' I spit the taste from my mouth. 'That was vile.'

'Fuck. That was vile.'

My head whips up at the tinny echo of my own voice. My eyes search the front of the house, gloomy with long-stretched shadows, but nobody's there. I check my phone, reassured that it's still locked and I haven't accidentally recorded myself.

As the recording of my voice loops back around, there's a snort of laughter. I smell nicotine wrapped in a synthetic watermelon mist dizzying on the breeze towards me. A puff of thin, grey clouds lifts up into the sky from a side alley.

'Chunder!' I hear Callie as I round the corner, her Bristolian accent clomping over the vowels when she talks. Steph's horsey burr of a laugh echoes just behind. What are they still doing here? I saw them leave with Shaquille over an hour ago.

'Alright, babe?' Steph says, speaking around the lip of her vape.

'Alright,' I say, blanking Steph, my eyes fixed on Callie's, hers trained on the video of me puking, replaying over and over on Steph's phone. 'What the hell, Cal?'

Callie's frowny lips peel apart but Steph cuts her off.

'So, what happened?' She blows her rotted fruity breath right in my face. 'You a bit drunk? Or did you finally see yourself in the mirror and realise what you *actually* look like, and that all your pictures are airbrushed and fake as fuck? I'd be sick an' all. Wouldn't want any of your sponsors seeing this, I s'pose.'

Anxiety lurches in the pit of my belly at the threat of exposure, public humiliation.

'I'm not talking to you,' I say, swallowing down the panic over something that hasn't happened yet. If I can just *talk* to Callie, I can stop them posting the video. 'Why are you being like this, Cal? Is this really still about Theo? You're just saying goodbye to seventeen years of friendship over some boy you were talking to for like, five minutes? And all the other stuff, missing birthdays, all the big stuff, whatever I did – no, *didn't* do. I can make it up to you. I don't want to do it any more, the whole Instagram thing.' The silky river of liquor flowing through my brain makes me reach out to twist a lock of Callie's hair around my finger, and for a second it's just us two, little again at my gramma's old flat, giggling as we learn to braid each other's hair. 'Can you delete the video, please?'

She wrenches her shoulder away from me, her hair slipping out of my fingers.

'Nah, you don't get to do that. And why you even bringing him up for? I told you, this is about more than *Theo*. I told him he can have you if he's still obsessing over your pictures while he's talking to me. Wasteman.' She pops her gum, trying to be hard, but I notice the quiver in her lip.

'Cal,' I say. 'This isn't you.'

This isn't the girl who cried for an hour straight after we bleached our girl-stashes for the first time in year seven. The girl who keeps a framed picture of *my* dog on her bedroom wall.

Our eyes lock, my head shaking the tiniest bit, and as I listen to my desperate recorded retches heaving out of Steph's phone, it's almost as if I can hear the hate comments already.

What a bad role model, how could anyone look up to this.

Obviously she isn't handling the divorce very well.

What terrible parenting.

'Can you turn that shit off?' I hiss at Steph as I hear the front door flung wide, lulled laughter and sleepy-slurry goodbyes pouring out into the night. I turn, looking for Gramma, hoping it's not her leaving so I can still say goodbye.

'Annnnd . . .' My head whips back, Steph's finger poised over her screen. '. . . post.' Her black, Sharpied-on eyebrows disappear into her fringe as she shrugs playfully, batting her lashes at me.

I sway back on my heels a little, place a hand on the wall of the house to a) steady myself and b) so I don't clench it into a fist and smack Steph clean off her feet.

She takes a deep drag from her vape before saying, 'I tagged you in it of course – wouldn't want your followers to miss this.'

Beads of sweat dot across my forehead, my stomach swirling hot with anxiety and rum.

'For real?' Callie snatches the phone out of Steph's hand, the wild shock on her face illuminated by the light of the screen. 'You actually posted it?'

Somewhere beneath the lightning strike of panic that jolts through my chest, I realise Callie was never going to post it. She must still care . . .

And yet there's the hint of a sour, self-satisfied smile that twitches at Callie's lips. 'You actually posted it,' she says, clearly conflicted.

'Yeah? And?' Steph exhales a long plume of smoke into my face.

As my phone vibrates with the tag notification my skin ignites as if someone's struck a match against my bones and set alight the alcohol in my bloodstream, burning me up from the inside out. I close my eyes against Callie and Steph's bickering as they wrestle with the phone.

'Almond, stop.' Callie yanks my arm out from where it's crept up under my top. She closes my hand into a fist, my nails crusted with blood and skin. 'Look at what you're doing to yourself. She'll delete it – you'll delete it, won't you, Steph?'

'Don't,' I say, my voice shuddering out of me. 'Don't pretend like you're not enjoying this.'

'I'm actually not.' While Steph's distracted with checking her vape cartridge, Callie snatches the phone out of her hands. 'There.

It's deleted. So, you can stop crying about it now,' she says.

'It'll be too late. But thanks,' I say, spitting every last bit of betrayal I feel into my sarcasm, knowing Callie had a part in this. '*Really.*' I walk away from them, watching my phone for the inevitable reupload notification, realising that there's too much toxicity between us for me and Callie to ever go back to the way things were.

My hands stay gripped around the phone, just waiting. Nothing yet, but there will be. It can't have been up for more than thirty seconds, I know, but those thirty seconds stretch through different countries, cultures and time zones, notifying the phones of the early-riser followers checking their emails in bed; the night owls who said they were going to sleep ten TikToks ago; hospital staff scrolling socials on break; a parent squinting at their screen during a night feed to stay awake; Paisley Parker awaiting her peak-timed selfie; Spencer raking through the explore page for microinfluencers with potential that he can prune and pimp for profit; my mum hoping her daughter's doing her job properly.

Somebody saw it.

And, of course, one of those somebodys had to be Anarchy. They've sent a particularly rough zoomed-in screenshot of me bent double, mouth hanging open, a string of bile suspended by my front teeth.

anRkey_InCel51

How does anyone look up to you!? Like???? How is your life even worth living??

anRkey_InCel51

Obviously I've screen recorded it

Now what to do . . . what will I do with this exclusive first look at The Real Almond Brown

Bzzt-bzzt.

But it doesn't matter what Anarchy decides to do with it, because someone else *has* already decided. I tap into the latest post I've been tagged in.

Liked by **frooot.looop**, **oliviajadeyy.hart07** and 46 others

teafortwo.xo Uh-oh! Looks like @thereal_almondbrown's had too much of an (illegally!) good time. At seventeen, the healthy lifestyle influencer is still underage to legally purchase or consume alcohol unless accompanied by an adult🔞!!! And with Almond's audience analytics confiming that two thirds of her audience is under legal drinking age, we're not so sure @veglowofficial should be giving her an even bigger platform to showcase her bad behaviour on! What do you think Tea Sippers!? Tell us in the comments, should Almond be cut from VeGlow's Serenity campaign?

My phone shakes into a continuous rumble, notification after notification crashing in, anxiety breaking over me in waves.

Who *are* the people running these accounts? That scour the internet for mere moments of misery and slivers of scandal to spoon-feed to their audience with a side of misplaced social justice. I'm a human girl who's seventeen and still figuring it out. Aren't we all? Haven't the people running this account ever got too drunk and thrown up? When Electra posted a story on New Year with her pupils dilated into black holes and her mouth running rabid, fans flocked to her comment sections armed to the teeth with heart emojis and inspirational quotes, concerned she was relapsing again after a stint in rehab. Not even a typoed hint of cancellation. Is there a set number of followers you have to scrape in to reach untouchable status? Or are we so far removed from the hate itself, desensitised and separated from screen to screen, that it's become less about the target and their individual circumstances, and more about the pure schadenfreude urge to destroy.

Yeah, I did A-level Psychology.

How am I supposed to get the algorithm of being a girl just right when the rules keep changing?

15

esme.r.d_10 Omg ew!!! Hope @thereal_almondbrown is ok!!? ❤

alice_june.inlondon Aw this is so sad, poor Almond☹ She must feel so humiliated xx

iamlevi_lewis This is toooooo funny😂😂😂😂😂😂

anRkey_InCel51 Hahaha. This is the best thing I've ever seen. DISGUSTING

anRkey_InCel51 So glad someone else caught this. Nothing can ever be deleted lololol

riannagrace-reads Um, the question is does she even know this has been uploaded . . .?

shaquilletheillest Nah fam. That is next level disrespect init. U can't upload this shit

zalfie5everxx Underage drinking? I'm so disappointed in you. You're not the girl I thought you were ☹

anRkey_InCel51 @veglowofficial Hey what's your next campaign gonna be ✨#Jaundice✨

mollyb_productions You sweet baby angel, we all still love you 💖💖💖

anRkey_InCel51 Do VeGlow really still wanna be associated with this low life alchy tho???

mummyofthree_isme Maybe wait til you're a bit older hun? Ur poor liver lol xo

ellisxxleigh Who would film this anyway?? Is she ok? X

fuck.politeness1988 Lmfao lightweiiiight . . .

djdaneversssson Wtf is this. Get this off my page!! Fucking vile mate who is she

rhys.Jones999 Oh my dayyyzz. How pathetic are u

anRkey_InCel51 Alcoholic at 17, literally what is the point of going on. Kys.

georgia1995patricia @kelsiii.bb567 you last night 😂😂

16

Blurry-eyed, staring at the direct messages from Anarchy racking up since Tea for Two posted the video, I clutch my phone in one hand, trying to quietly close Dad's front door with the other.

'There you are.'

Already on *the edge* of the edge, every one of my muscles jumps up under my skin. I strain to see across the everything room, lit only by a string of fairy lights and the buzzy streetlamp outside, making out Dad's hulking frame hunched on the sofa.

'Dad,' I hiccup. 'You scared the shit out of me. I thought you were asleep.'

I don't know how long I sat on the wall outside for, refreshing and refreshing that video, watching as 418 people individually *liked* seeing me retch my guts up on camera. Without taking my eyes off the screen, I mumbled goodbyes to the party stragglers as they hugged, called cabs, or searched the road for the number plate of their Uber driver, only looking up when Gramma's fat, costume-jewellery-clad finger jabbed at my phone.

'You okay in 'dere, child?' With the screen's ghostly glare on my face, I hoped it wouldn't light up my rampant, irrational fear for Gramma to see. She has enough real-world problems going on, with her high blood pressure and trying to keep on top of the property she owns back in Barbados, for me to introduce her to the petty internet drama I'm mixed up in. 'Mi worry about you, yuh know. Hmmm.' She nodded, considering her intuition before crushing me up into a hug. 'Come 'ere. Gramma always be 'ere.'

Her dressed-up scent of coconut oil spritzed with Chanel No. 5 lingers in the flat now. Tearing my eyes away from another new message from Anarchy, demanding I reply to them in all caps, I drop into the sunken spot on the sofa next to Dad, scuffing at some dried rice and peas that have been trod into the carpet. He sits back and stretches his arm around me, wrapping me in his stalwart stature, shrinking the world away to just this room. Here I can convince myself I don't exist on the internet, sitting in comfy silence in the low lamplight, listening to the snuffled breaths of my dog sleeping belly-up at my feet, the air coated musky and warm by cooking smells of allspice and ginger, comforted by my dad's laugh-lined face and heavy-lidded eyes.

'Love you, Dad,' I whisper.

'Uh, I love you too, baby, but ...' Flaring his nostrils wide, Dad sniffs at my curls, my clothes, even his own armpit, before leaning close to catch a whiff of my breath. 'Damn, I thought that was turpentine I could smell, but turns out it's just my baby girl's *breath*. How much'd you drink tonight?' he says, smoothing my hair back.

'I don't know,' I groan. 'Too much rum.'

'Rookie. Now, I don't want to get all preachy on you, 'cuz who am I to talk when it comes to drinking. But what I lack in judgement, I do make up for in experience, and all's I can say is that when I was your age and I drank too much, I had some *stupid* experiences. And I'm talking *stupid*,' he says, as if he knows about my vomit splashing across hundreds of people's timelines as we speak. 'Still, ain't gonna tell you not to drink 'cuz those experiences made me the man I am today. All I'm gonna say is, be *careful*. Don't you ever do something you don't want to do, just 'cuz somebody else is doing it, okay? Also, you're in for one hell of a hangover tomorrow, so enjoy,' he says, drawing me closer.

'Nah, I won't – only old people get hangovers,' I tease, plucking at one of his grey beard hairs.

'Watch yourself, girl,' he says, his laugh draining away as he stretches his arms above his head, stifling a yawn. 'Anyway, it's been a long day – I'm gonna try and get some shut-eye.'

I check the time on my phone – 23.22, headed above an onslaught of DMs from my number one fan. Anarchy's slamming my notifications with a mix of comments on the safely scheduled selfie that went up as planned, comments on Tea for Two's reupload of Vomitgate, and an onslaught of DMs. As I scroll down, Anarchy's usual buzzwords grab my attention – slut, whore, bitch, slag – but my eyes widen as I skim too fast over a string of numbers next to a whole bunch of exclamation marks. What *fresh hell*?

I feel Dad eyeing me from the side, so I peel my eyes away from the screen in case he asks me what I'm looking at. Like Gramma, Dad's got enough going on in real life. And even though I haven't seen him smoking since I caught him last Saturday, that twenty-pack of cigarettes on the coffee table is down to the last two, assuming that's even the same pack. Our talk earlier when I found him hiding out in the bedroom tells me he doesn't need any more stress.

'It's only half eleven,' I say.

Scrunching up his beard with both hands, he says, 'Only? This is late for an old man like me.'

'But I'm not tired yet. Wanna watch *Bad Boys II*?'

'Yeah, go on then,' he says, though I can see he's already fighting sleep as he relaxes back against the sofa cushions.

I crawl over to the TV, pop the DVD out of its case and feed it into the DVD player, sitting back on my heels to watch the menu load up. Old school.

'Ready, Dad?' I ask, slouching down next to him.

But his head's lolled back already, his mouth hanging open. And I'm alone.

Almost, Honey reminds me with a snore.

I unlock my phone, eyes flicking up as dated CGI fire explodes across the screen. I go straight to YouTube, trying to ignore the notifications from Anarchy that keep sliding down from the top of the screen as my heart climbs ever higher up my throat. On autopilot, I search for the 'Garden of Eve' YouTube channel and scroll through Mum's archive of videos.

Look, I'm lonely and nostalgic, and watching Mum's vlogs feels like clutching a withered scrap of security blanket. Stopping when I get to a playlist from years ago, I find the thumbnail I'm looking for – fuzzy-haired, five-year-old me, freeze-framed crossing a finish line. Staring at my little self, I think of all the millennial mums creating parenting content now, opting to edit the baby emoji, or a heart, a star over their baby's face, protecting their identity, even withholding their name sometimes, preserving their modesty in case this someday adult doesn't want the learning curve of their entire toddlerhood on the internet for all their future partners and employers to be able to access. Not to mention the sinister threat of predators being able to find out their school from a name and a hint of a uniform these days. How I wish this level of foresight and protection was as widespread in the noughties as it is now, and that I grew up with the *choice* to remove the emoji if I wanted to.

Casting 'Almond's First Sports Day!' onto Dad's prized forty-nine-inch smart TV, I fold my arms, sink deeper into the sofa cushions, and swallow that bittersweet spoonful of nostalgia. Maybe I spend too much time watching these old vlogs, I dunno. But shouldn't I get to enjoy the only upside to having your whole childhood broadcast across the internet?

A mid-roll advert cuts through Mum's vlog and I distractedly skip it, knowing my favourite part's coming up. Mum holds the camera high over our heads as the three of us roll about laughing on the ground, and I blame it on the alcohol as tears spill down my cheeks.

As quiet as I can, I let myself cry over our old life.

I cry till my face hurts and the tears have dried in salty streaks down my cheeks. It leaves me tired and husky, face hurting. I need to go to bed. When I go to disconnect my phone from the TV though, I see that messages from Anarchy are *still* piling up.

They're not going to stop until I acknowledge them, so I take a deep breath, holding it in my chest as I open up my DMs.

anRkey_InCel51

STOP IGNORING ME. STOP IGNORING ME. STOP IGNORING ME.

TOO GOOD TO EVEN ANSWER MESSAGES FROM FANS NOW ARE WE

YOU FUCKING ENTITLED LITTLE BITCH!! ANSWER ME!!!!!

FINE I'LL JUST KEEP SPAMMING YOU UNTIL YOU DO

💀

💀

💀

💀

💀

I CAN DO THIS ALL NIGHT

thereal_almondbrown

What do you want?

anRkey_InCel51

Scroll up. I'm not repeating myself.

So I do, the screen a blur of insults until my thumb flicks to a stop, hovering over a big chunk of text, the one that caught my attention when I was talking to Dad. The one with the numbers and exclamation points.

anRkey_InCel51

That video of you being sick ain't nothing on what I've got on you. That tea for 2 bullshit can keep it

Send £500 to anarchyanderson@protonmail.com. Use PayPal. £500 BY TOMORROW NOON. If you tell anyone about this, I'll know. If you go to the police, I'll know. Just send me the money and I'll leave you alone.

thereal_almondbrown

And what if I don't?

I reply with shaking hands, leaning away from Dad on the sofa as I try to calm the tremors crashing through me, quaking my earth. Right away, those little dots start bouncing as Anarchy types out a reply.

anRkey_InCel51

If you don't. I'll make everyone else see you for the slut I know you really are.

[Image loading . . .]

Is that a picture of me? *What am I—*

My cheeks bulge as I catch a stomach-full of throw up in my mouth, running to the bathroom with my phone in my hand before I heave myself over the toilet. I slump to the tiled floor, my phone convulsing with messages. I smear the sick off my chin, make myself raise the phone to my face and smother the cry that escapes my lips when I see the picture properly. Tears torrent down my cheeks.

The shot's taken from up high, looking down through a black forest of wiry chest hairs at a forearm-thick, erect penis looming over a girl's face. Only it's *my* face. I haul my head over the toilet bowl again as bile dribbles from my mouth. How the hell has Anarchy made it look like that ugly, veiny, *rolling pin* is about to go off in my face!? Anger surges through me and I kick out hard, denting the side of the bath.

It didn't happen, it can't be my face, because *this* is my face. I stare open-mouthed at the me that isn't me, mirroring my expression in the picture. How can it be me and not be me at the same time? I mean, I *know* it's not me, but she has my same chocolate-coloured curls tucked behind both ears, ears that I notice have the same double-studded piercings as mine, the same two front teeth, slightly stuck out from years of thumb sucking. She's me.

Three dots jump up. As Anarchy types I hear Dad stir in the

next room, his voice, gruff with sleep, calling out my name. His knuckles rap softly on the door.

'Are you crying? What's up?'

Stumbling as I get up too fast, I twist the lock on the bathroom door, trying to calm my breathing down before I speak.

'Not crying,' I gabble, clasping the phone to my chest like I'm afraid Dad'll pick up on some of the sick hate radiating out of it. 'Just not feeling well.'

'Oh yeah?' he chuckles. 'Where's miss *only old people get hangovers* now, huh?'

anRkey_InCel51

I'm waiting.

I manage a quick *hmm-hm* of a laugh before Dad walks away. Sinking to the floor, I peel off my jeans, desperate to feel something other than hurt and confusion. Something I can control. Driving my nails deep into the fleshy part of my thigh, I scratch and tear, pain receptors prickling signals to my brain to flood it with serotonin. Dr Wallace told me that. Nerve cells send a little text to your brain that something hurts and the brain starts releasing happy chemicals as a distraction. I curl into myself, head on my knees as I hear Dad move up close to the door again.

'Well, the bed's all made up for you in there now. I've left a glass of water and some painkillers on the windowsill. Hope you feel better soon, baby. Night.'

I snatch in a breath. 'Night,' I say, watching blood run in rivulets down my legs.

17

Damage Control

Spencer Dorsey <dorsey.spencer@bigstarpr.com> Jul 30, 00:37

to: Almond Brown <almond-h.brown@gmail.com>

cc: Eve Fairchild <eve.s.fairchild@gmail.com>

Almond, hi.

I'll skip pleasantries. Obviously, we know what I'm here to discuss. I've seen the video.

Am I disappointed you've threatened our image this close to our biggest brand collab to date? Yes. Will it be the end of the ad campaign? Highly doubt it.

As I'm sure you'll have been tracking as closely as I have, your follower count is actually increasing. Probably not with genuine fans, more just cancel-culture vultures here to watch the show, but still, increasing. And with Tea for Two's video nearing the 10k view mark in just a couple of hours, I'm sure engagement will only be on the up until this story peaks and drops off tomorrow evening. Not to mention the level of traffic coming through Eve's page too. Accidentally, well done.

Now, if I know marketing directors like Paisley – and I do – she'll take this in her stride as a no publicity is bad publicity thing and be glad of the extra reach the Serenity ads will get. After all it's just a little bit of sick, it's not like you've been accused of sexting minors – product will not be mysteriously discontinued like you-know-who's little scandal played out.

But just to cover ourselves on all angles we're saying this was food poisoning, ok? From something home-cooked, spicy, we wouldn't want to burn bridges with any local businesses and potential clients. Food poisoning will also tie in nicely with a bit of a side endorsement I've landed you. Herbavive, here's their tagline: 'Herbalise your health revival'. How original. Essentially, it's an over the counter shot of vitamins and minerals that can combat headaches, sickness, colds etc. We can combine damage control for last night with this promotion. I'm thinking fresh-faced selfie, so, spritzed hair like you're just out the shower, only apply base layer make-up, no highlight, no mascara, we want to look as natural as possible. Back to basics. Hold the Herbavive bottle up to camera like you're about to take a sip. Job done. Caption something like: 'Whenever I'm feeling a little under the weather, like last night's tummy upset thanks to my own attempt at making wild mushroom enchiladas, I like to revive my body with a dose of nature's medicine,' bla bla bla. Send to me for approval before posting. And . . . relax.

If it weren't for all the stress you caused me tonight, I'd say I couldn't have planned this better myself.

Ta, Spence x

Spencer Dorsey
www.bigstarpr.com
Twitter: @spencerdorseydoesit

18

**** 6189 *VISA*

Recent Transactions

Patreon Membership	
On Mondays We Wear Murder	£4.20
Wine and Crimed	£5.99
Society-Schosmiety	£8.50
PayPal	
anarchyanderson@protonmail.com	£500.00
JustEat	
The Freezin' Vegan: Ice Cream & Sundries	£16.38

August

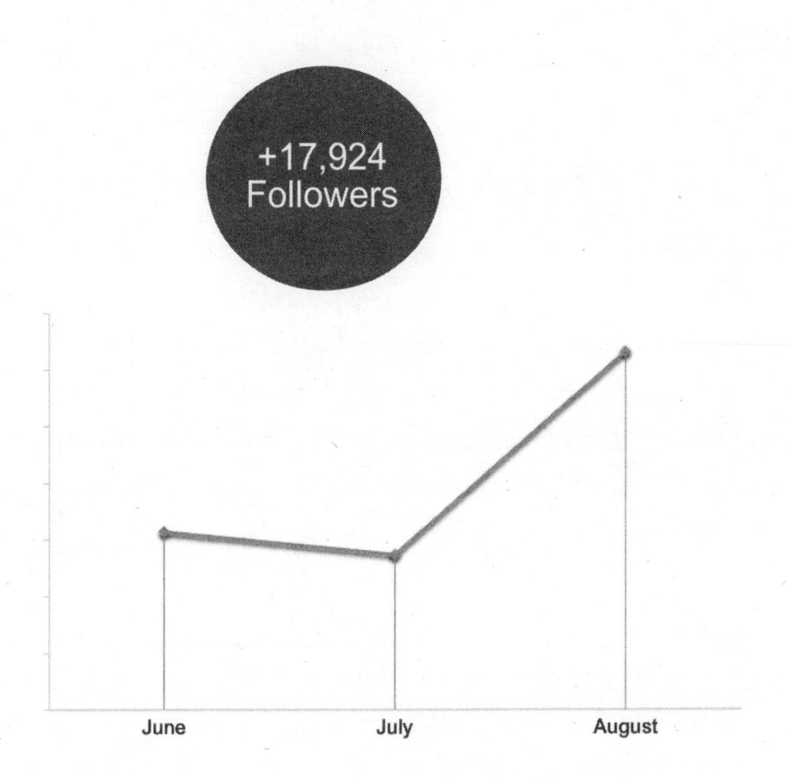

19

Friday 4 Aug 18:32

Heather

Hey, come outside😉

Almond

????????

Heather

Can you just come open the gate please?? It's raining!

We're outside, obv.

I key in the code for the gate from my phone, swiping past the missed calls and voicemails from Oliver, undoubtedly trying to find out why I skipped today's Tranquillity session, and open up the doorbell cam app to see who this 'we' is outside my house.

Heather and Joss, I'd assume, except she didn't put it on the group chat.

I'll listen to Oliver's voicemail later ... or maybe I won't. I already feel bad enough.

The grainy doorbell footage shows Heather and ... *Imogen?* at the end of our winding driveway. The world's most unlikely duo. I bet Heather's been holding back so hard she's bitten another hole through her tongue. Obviously, they've come straight from Tranks and are probably wondering why my chair was empty, but why are they at my house? *Why* is Imogen here? I let them in to find out.

My jaw tightens remembering that cutesy giggle of hers, ringing forced and false like a horror movie doll, that had bubbled out of her mouth as she played the video of my parents' marriage breaking down in front of everyone.

I zoom in on Heather with my thumb and forefinger, admiring her outfit as she walks up the gravel driveway; Doc Martens, holey fishnets and a denim dress. Slightly behind her, Imogen's striding in baby blue skinny jeans and a cream cotton jumper, pink leather bag in the crook of her arm, and ... what the hell is she holding a bunch of flowers for? Her eyes keep flicking up to the camera, shoulders lifting as she gives it a sheepish smile, like she knows I'm watching and she's sending subliminal 'forgive me' signals through the lens. This has to be what this is, right – an apology? The showing up unannounced? The flowers?

Trudging downstairs, still in the comfys I've been wearing all week, I sniff under my armpit, jerking my head away at the ripeness of stale deodorant and junk food sweat coming through my hoodie. Oh God, when did I last shower? Surely it can't have been five whole days since I tried to douse the hangover out of me in Dad's dribbly little shower? No, it's been four; I had a bath the night I got back to Mum's to calm the pulsing rawness of my legs after what I did to them on the night of Anarchy's tyrannical takeover of my phone.

I groan as I get to the door, dabbing at stress tears.

They're going to ask me why I didn't show up at Tranks today, and what do I tell them? My insides shrivel with shame at the thought of admitting I haven't left my bedroom since Sunday night because some stranger on the internet is blackmailing me with a deepfaked dirty video of me. Shame that my life is so out of my control that someone was *able* to do this to me. I shudder, seeing the image in flashback. Part of me wants to tell them but I can't deal with the drama of it all leaking into actuality, especially when I'm only just beginning to get a handle on my life *off*line. But I don't want Heather pitying me as I squirm under her questions about how that video made me feel, or to sit here speculating over the seven billion people Anarchy might be. I just want it all to go away.

I've paid the money, it's done. CTRL+ALT Delete.

'You live up a *big* hill,' Heather says as I open the door. 'Hey.'

Lingering in the doorway, I smell rain falling on concrete, the air hazy with droplets, the sweetness of the gardenia flowers Mum's had planted along the front of the house. Outside smells. I reach my hand down, touch the velvety soft of the gardenia petals, my face instantly lifting just being around other people, breathing in fresher air.

'Hey. Speaking of,' I say, peering over Heather's shoulder as the gate clunks shut. 'How d'you know where I live?'

Heather's eyes slide to the right as I pick up on the slight twitch of her head towards Imogen. Eyebrows shooting up, Heather starts criss-crossing and roving her eyes about in their sockets like crazy, till I have to splutter into a cough to cover up my laugh.

'These are for you.' Oblivious, Imogen thrusts the flowers under my nose, her cheeks blushing pink. 'For last Friday. I was being such a bitch playing that video in front of everyone. I bought them to group today but you didn't show.'

I nod slowly, taking the flowers from Imogen. With her glittery lips sparkling that rehearsed yet somehow endearing smile across her face, I almost laugh. She reminds me of a little lap dog. Tiny, sweet, and quiet, like their Italian Greyhound, Chi-Chi. Cruelly, I think of patting her on the head and telling her *Well done, you did a good job*, because that's so clearly what she needs, but has doubtlessly never heard from her mum. From the excruciating hours I spent with Celeste a couple of weeks ago, it's obvious she's an extreme micromanager like my mum, only if Mum's ego eclipsed the sun, she had a daily average screentime of thirteen hours, and she painstakingly took the time to write all her post captions L I K E T H I S.

I stick my head into the petals and sniff, deciding to make nice because even though what Imogen did was proper shady, we've still got to spend three more hours together at Tranks, and of course she'll be at the Serenity launch next week. Plus, I can't remember the last time I saw an apology play out like this in influencer land – usually it's scripted self-indulgence, crocodile tears, and barefaced blame shifting. Turns out face-to-face dialogue, eye contact, and thoughtfully kind gestures just might get you somewhere.

'Thank you. You didn't have to with the flowers,' I say, limply lifting them. 'I honestly forgot all about it. Thanks though.'

'They're black-eyed susans, marigolds, and dahlias,' Imogen chirps, bouncing up on her toes. 'I know you like—'

'Sunset colours,' we say at the same time, making Heather trill out the theme tune to *The Twilight Zone*. 'Take it you watched the Serenity Q&A then? They're lovely.' I let a silence fall between us that I hope has a finality about it, suddenly very conscious that I stink, the crown of my head is slicked with grease, and I haven't spoken to another person in real life for a whole forty-eight hours.

Mum won't be back from her *business* trip till tonight. And by business trip I mean she's gone to stay at some five-star country house hotel to try out a brand's new eyeshadow palette and film herself wearing it having dinner, drinks and massages with a dozen other identical women.

If she could *see* the state of me now.

'Aren't you gonna ask us in?' Heather asks bluntly. 'I got wet and sweaty for you walking all the way up here.' She runs her tongue across her teeth, making her voice go all low and sultry. 'And you didn't even buy me dinner.'

'Oh, for God's sake.' I laugh. 'Come in then.'

I'm about to ask them to take off their shoes when I remember that a) I actually don't give a fuck, and b) Mum's not even here to *pretend* to give a fuck, so instead I ask Heather, as casually as I can fake, how Joss seemed today.

We've been texting but my replies have been vacant and vanilla, not wanting to pretend to Joss like I do with everybody else that everything's okay, but also not wanting to scare off a conspiracy theorist technophobe with the knowledge that I'm being cyberstalked. I could lie, yeah, but it would be a big, fat *lie* lie to tell him everything's fine, face lit by my phone in the darkness, wrapped up in my fusty sheets, shrouded by depression filth. Pizza boxes, frayed cables, crumbs and crumbs and crumbs, sticky tissues, screwed-up paper, junk food slugging its way through my body. So, I've been distant.

Though I can't keep haunting his phone for much longer, semi-ghosting him like a vague, boring-ass poltergeist who only responds with GIFs, hearted message reacts, and a couple of 'Nm, you?'s. I miss him.

Heather shrugs. 'Seemed okay. Like, I definitely didn't see him smile the whole time we were there, but he didn't seem down in any which way in particular. Distracted, maybe.'

'I thought he looked *super* tired,' Imogen pipes up.

'Oh,' I say, swallowing self-indulgent guilt, wondering if he'd been up waiting for a reply. 'Want a drink?' I ask the girls over my shoulder as I walk into the kitchen and flick the kettle on. 'Actually, before I forget, you didn't tell me how the hell you knew where I lived?'

'Mum dropped us off?' Imogen says, barely suppressing a

duh??? 'What are these like?' She studies the label of a Herbavive sample I left lying on the table.

'Disgusting. Oh yeah, I forget she's been here. How's Chi-Chi?'

'Coffee, please. Black, two sugars,' says Heather, mooning over herself in Mum's massive mirror. 'Who's Chi-Chi? And hey, is this dress too short?' Facing her butt to the glass, she bends over and studies her reflection through the gap between her legs. 'Like, if I was going to tie my shoes, could you see my pants?'

'Yes, just a tad. Do you have any peppermint tea?' Imogen asks. I nod as she seats herself at the head of the dining table, fingering Mum's delicately fanned out collection of this week's gossip magazines. 'My dog, Chi-chi,' she tells Heather. 'He's *gooood* – bit of a dodgy tummy after Mum brought him here but he's doing fine now.'

I hand out our drinks, watching as Imogen wafts the minty steam up into her face.

'I'm so sorry about what happened when I met your mum, by the way. Did she tell you?' I ask, our eyes locking as she nods, moving the mug in front of her mouth. 'I'm always afraid what I say is going to get twisted, but your mum was cool about it. I hope she doesn't think I hate Chi-Chi now.' Imogen shakes her head, flinching as she sips her too-hot tea. I take the seat next to her. 'With influencers everything's just so *ahh!* all the time, you know? I fucking hate being on the internet.'

'How can you hate it? Look at this place!' Imogen waves a hand around at the gilded frames hung on the walls holding fine-lined expensive art, meaningless beauty industry awards, and glossy photographs of Mum with various unsmiling celebrities. Her eyes fix on a photo of Mum taking herself way too seriously, pouting next to a rigid Victoria Beckham. 'It's beautiful. I'd *kill* to live here,' Imogen says as Heather rolls her eyes. 'Not that I have it too shabby – or shabby at all, what am I saying?' Imogen tuts, banging her mug down too heavily on the table. I take a sip of my own tea, watching Heather clack her tongue stud along the backs of her teeth, getting the sense she's enjoying Imogen's flustered privilege check.

'I know what you mean,' I say, throwing Imogen a bone, observing these two people feeling their feelings.

I get it that Imogen might feel jealous, the same way I yearn sometimes for Electra's life of doorstep beaches in a thriving who's-who city she can get lost in, but at the same time I can also relate to Heather's frustration. From the outside it's impossibly hard to empathise with people who get paid some people's yearly salary to simply show up, pose and post.

'Anyway, if you weren't on the internet, where would you be?' Imogen asks.

'Happy,' I say, flatly.

'Deep,' Heather says in a stoner voice, nodding slow. 'I get it, though. Like, I don't think this,' she waves a hand around the room, 'would make it all worth it for me. Don't get me wrong, it's a beautiful house. I just couldn't handle that amount of info on me being out there. Like, you know you probably have a wikiFeet page, right? There's probably whole forums of creepy creeps out there who—'

'Can we not?' I say, flash-imagining the kind of kinks Anarchy could Photoshop up with images of my feet taken from pictures of me walking along the beach, vegan shoe brand ads, and countless videos from Mum's channel like, 'Mother & Daughter Mani/Pedi Package Vlog [AD]'. There's not an inch of my body not on the internet Anarchy couldn't non-consensually conjure up a kink with . . . well, except my genitals, and I literally mean the cracks and points. I've worn many a pair of low-riding jeans and triangle bikinis, and I'm sure it wouldn't be hard to deepfake someone else's sex parts onto me.

'Oh my—' Heather retches. 'You have one by the way, a wikiFeet. Listen to this: "Almond's long slender toes and pure soles – that's S O L E, by the way, not soul – represent true beauty." I want to laugh, but is this too fucking gross? Like, not in a kink-shame way but in a you're-seventeen-and-there's-clearly-people-wanking-over-your-feet way.'

Numb to this revelation, I just shrug. 'Nothing on the internet shocks me any more.'

'Do I have one?' Imogen asks, *hopefully!?*

'Uh . . . no. Congrats,' Heather says, showing Imogen the 'No Results Found' page under her name. 'I've reported your page, Almond. Way too many paedos talking about how they're waiting for you to turn eighteen on there.'

I nod, absentmindedly. 'Cool.'

If Heather knew about what Anarchy was threatening me with, would she think that I had asked for it? Dangling my body like bait over the internet for creeps to catch a hold of.

My stomach clenches and I instinctively flip my phone face down on the table. I imagine Anarchy sitting smugly at a computer, seeing my money come in – *my* money. Not the big bucks from jobs and ad campaigns that Mum's supposedly tucked away in an ISA somewhere, but money saved from birthdays, Christmases, and the tenners that Gramma Em slips me whenever I visit.

Money that I was saving up to get out of here.

'Hey!' Heather dings the side of her mug with the sugar spoon, reeling my mind back in from outer space. 'Did you hear me?'

'No, what? Sorry, you just got me thinking about upping all my security settings.'

'Always a good idea,' Imogen says, her phone buzzing on the table next to mine. 'Ugh, sorry, it's my mum, one sec.' Delicately sliding out from the table, she scurries out of the room, not answering the phone until she's out in the hall with the door shut. 'Hi, Mummy.'

'Did she just say *mummy?*' Heather draws her chair closer to me, mouth open to repeat whatever she just said, but then her breath catches. 'I'm worried about you.'

'Don't be.' I try to smile reassuringly, knowing it's weak, and then scald it down with hot tea instead.

'Well, I am. And not that it's any of my damn *business* whatever's going on between you and Joss, but anytime I'd look over his shoulder since we all met, he'd be texting you – the kid doesn't shut up about you. And now he's all mopey and you're not showing up for Tranks. Did something happen?'

Latching on to the downsized, more palatable picture of my problems – boy trouble – I tell Hev about how I'm worried the weight of my world might break Joss, that being with me will be too much, and how it's hard for me to trust people. I'm not lying, simply chopping up the truth and throwing out the worst bits, blackened and festering with mould.

'I know what'll cheer you up,' she says. '*And* get you together with Joss so you can actually talk, so close you can smell each other's breath—'

'Weird.'

'What are you doing tomorrow night?'

'Probably wallowing with a bit of *Unsolved Mysteries*, eating way too much pita and hummus—'

'Well, now you're not!' Heather says, taking a slurp of coffee, her eyes blinking moony-wide at me over the rim. 'My parents are away this weekend and Rich is throwing a party, so obviously I blackmailed him' – I wince at the word – 'into letting me invite some of my friends too, or else I'd livestream the whole thing to Mum on Facebook. See, I knew I still had that cesspool of an app for a good reason. Mums. Love. Facebook.'

I laugh, taking a sip of my tea. 'Joss is going?' I swill the rest around in my cup, not looking at Heather.

'Yep. He said no at first, but I lied and told him you were a hundred per cent going to be there, so of course he changed his mind.'

I can't help but smile for real, with all my teeth, making Heather's eyes roll up into her skull. She pokes her tongue out, faking a gag.

'You're both *so* annoying, honestly. Just get together already.'

I laugh, about to tell her to shut up, when Imogen blunders back into the room, her eyes red, mascara smeared to her temples where she's tried to hide her crying.

'Sorry. Have to go now,' she mutters, her lips barely moving.

'Oh, really?' I ask, scraping my chair back. 'What's wrong?'

Ignoring me, she gathers up her bag, shaking so much she drops it onto the floor, spilling what looks like the entire contents of Boots' cosmetics section under the dining table.

'Hey, what is it?' Heather says, sweeping a hand underneath and coming up with a fistful of glossy tubes in varying shades of pink.

'Nothing, nothing.' Sinking to her knees, Imogen's face glazes over for a second, staring vacantly at her scattered make-up, a tremble in her bottom lip, kittenish and distracted, before she starts hurriedly clawing it towards her. 'I'll see you next week.'

'Wait, so, are you not coming to the party?' Heather says. 'I gotta know, for numbers. I'm only allowed like, ten people.'

'Maybe.' Imogen sniffs, fidgeting with the straps of her handbag.

She's dawdling, making a show of rummaging through her bag now, checking she's got everything. I chew the fleshy inside of my lip, thinking about asking her if she'd like to stay over because even though she's a bit . . . shit, it seems like home is the last place she wants to go right now. And I know the bone-crushing weight of that feeling all too well. Heather rises from her chair, reaching out a hand.

'Immy ...'

As I say her name, she flinches back into herself. 'So, um. Bye, I guess. Bye.' She gives us a little frantic wave and turns on her heel, my mouth still hanging open as she propels herself out into the hall.

'Thanks again for the flowers!' I call as the front door slams.

We stare at each other, Heather's upper lip snarled up in disbelief.

'That girl is just ...' She splays all her fingers out, eyes blinking wide, as if mentally trying to take a step back. 'Wow. Should I be worried about her too? I mean, I know we all met in group therapy, but I'm sensing that is *not* enough for her.'

'We can't say that – we barely know her. Maybe that's just her way of coping. *We* barely know each other.' Which is true, though it doesn't feel like it. Evidently, because I feel safe enough to ask her, 'Can you stay for a bit? I don't want to be alone.'

I expect Hev to splurge out puke noises, fake gagging with her middle finger but she doesn't. She wobbles on one leg to stretch out and toe me with her boot.

'Not going anywhere.'

'Thanks,' I say, suddenly struck shy with the unfamiliarity of having a friend over. 'Wanna watch TV?'

'Sure, but can we watch you and your mum's episode of *Celebrity Pointless*?'

'Fuck off.' I laugh, pulling her with me out into the hall and through to the living room.

We flump down onto the chesterfield at the same time, and

I switch on the TV, clicking on to the next episode of *Unsolved Mysteries*.

'This place is mental,' Heather says, gazing around the room as she strokes the sofa's velvety arm. We watch the first five minutes in silence, though I'm not concentrating, my eyes flicking around the room and occasionally sideways at Heather, wondering if she feels like she's already been here before because Mum's exposed the whole inside of our house to the internet. 'So, what's it like?' she says, shifting sideways to face me.

'What's what like?'

'Being you. Being . . .' Holding up her hands, she dazzles her fingers out into a rainbow arc. '. . . *internet famous*,' she whispers, obviously taking the piss.

'You want the truth or the spiel I give TMZ?'

'Both, hit me with the lies first.'

A smile aches my face as I wring every last drop of enthusiasm I can muster out of it, straining it through my voice like pulpy orange juice. 'It's such a blessing to have a caring and engaging audience of millions to interact with and tackle daily life with, to get paid to document and share my likes and interests, my favourite vegan recipes, and promote slow fashion. But most of all, I'm so humbled and honoured to be able to open up my DMs and know I'll get to read such supportive, encouraging messages from people all over the world. And no matter what, I know I'm never alone.'

Heather slow claps, eyes gaping at the show. 'That was scary good. Now what's it really like? Give me the tea.'

I grab a cushion and crush it to my chest. 'It's fucking tiring. Being judged in the comments about *everything* I do, especially my diet and my body. It's terrifying, to be honest. To get death threats for promoting an sportswear brand *you had no idea* sources its stock from sweat shops.' Heather nods, lips pursed, knowing the scandal I'm talking about from two years back. 'I know I fucked up there. I should've done my own homework and not trusted Spencer to give one single shit about ethically sourced material, but still, do I deserve to die because of it?' My voice buckles with the weight of remembering that a small school of people took time out of their day to tell me to drink bleach for that. 'I get messages that make me feel fat, skinny, not white enough, not black enough, too made up, too natural. One minute I'm too ugly that I'm undeserving of all this shit, the next I'm too pretty which makes me a *self-obsessed little slut*. A quote. And all this is coming from literal children, or men older than my dad, or women my mum's age who tell me *I'm asking for it*. And the worst part is, no matter what, I know I'll never get to be alone.'

Heather launches herself across the sofa at me, cocooning me. 'Mate, I'm so sorry. Your life sucks.' I laugh into her shoulder, wiping my tears on her sleeve like a toddler. 'And to think there are little kids telling their teachers they want to be influencers when they grow up.'

'Don't,' I say, and then quieter, 'They have no idea. After this whole Serenity launch is over, I'm out. I'm not doing the whole influencer thing anymore.' I swallow, looking up from the ground.

'Now if you want to ask me any more, I'm gonna have to send you an invoice. What do you wanna watch?'

'Okay, interview over.' She grabs the remote and searches for something on Disney+, wrestling one foot out of her Doc Marten with the other hand.

Clouds part on the screen as we zoom into the city of Springfield, watching Homer swerve through the opening credits of *The Simpsons* in his pink car. Heather obnoxiously sings along to the theme tune and elbows me in the side to get me to join in until I lump a cushion into the side of her face. We chat through a few episodes, the anxiety that was tingling at my mind brushed back under my brain by how easy it is to laugh when I'm with Heather. I fall open slowly, comfortably apart, like the feathering pages of a book, as I tell Heather about my half plans of getting out of here, how I don't want to leave Bristol for another crammed city where people might still know me, and she nods as I flesh out my fantasy of living in a grass hut and rescuing tropical animals. Not once does she doubt that I'll get there, or try to hold me back, she just listens.

I miss this. I miss having a friend.

Later, Heather's scrolling through her explore page for me, because I find it fascinating and terrifying in equal parts how well the algorithm can get to know a user, when my latest post pops up.

I laugh bitterly. 'Joss must think I'm such a catfish.'

'No, you're not. You're the opposite of a catfish, you're like a . . . like a fishcat. You look *better* in real life. Even when you walked in last week all rehab chic with the sunglasses, he like, stopped talking and just stared at you – didn't you see his neck go all red? Why don't you just text him now, ask him to go on a dog walk?'

'Should I? Okay, okay,' I say, thumbs pitter-pattering out my text.

Almond

How about we take Dudley and Honey on their first date tomorrow before Hev's party? I thought maybe we could arrive together . . .?

Also tell Dudley that Hon likes chasing squirrels, peanut butter biscuits and long walks on the beach (basic bitch lol)

'He's probably at work,' Heather says, as my messages go undelivered, 'Phone's off.'

'Yeah,' I say, scratching at my collarbone, thinking that maybe my week of *Casper the Friendly Ghost*-ing him might've actually scared him off.

After a couple of hours of *The Simpsons* and snacks, Heather checks the time on her phone.

'Shit, it's almost eight-thirty. I should go. I wanna get food for the party tomorrow. And I don't care how old we are, there're only two types of people in this world. People who love a good sausage roll at a party. And liars. End of.' She wedges her feet back into her boots, bending to lace them up. 'Don't worry, I'll get some veggie – no *vegan* – bits for you as well.'

'Thanks,' I say, sliding my phone out of my pocket, weighing it in my hand as I gaze up at Heather. 'Wait. Before you go, sorry but can we get a selfie?'

'Oh, piss off.'

'Please? I haven't uploaded anything all week and my manager's right up my ass about it.'

Really, I couldn't give less of a shit about Spencer hounding me on the daily with WhatsApp's telling me to *Engage!* But I get the impression Heather's not usually one for selfies. And I don't know, it might be nice to remember this evening. To just take a picture with my friend, destined only for the camera roll, and not have to worry about having to make up a stupid poll to interact with followers, like *Are you snuggled indoors, or out splashing in puddles on a rainy day?* or some other utter bollocks.

She's still staring at me blankly, so I say, 'I'm putting a filter over it anyway, 'cuz look at me, I look like microwaved shit. We can choose one of the ones that makes it look like you have a whole different face. No one will know it's you.'

'Microwaved shit,' she repeats in a cackling laugh. 'Ugh, go on then. No filters though, you take me as I am, and you as you are, or I'm out.'

'Fine. But wait, look.' I bounce up next to her and hold my phone out at arm's length, swiping through a few filters until I find my go-to that smooths a blurred mask over your skin like digital foundation. The filter layers on tiny, mascaraed lashes too and gives the picture an overall glowy, gold glaze, like we're on some tropical beach and not just standing in my living room. 'Not feeling it?'

'*No*, I'm not. Almond' – she cups my chin, eyes pouring sincerity – 'you are enough.'

I swallow hard.

'Okay,' I whisper, willing myself to feel it, to know it. *I am enough.*

Pressed cheek-to-cheek with Heather, I smile open-mouthed, looking very much bed-headed-Netflix-binge kinda cute, like I've just got home after a sleepover. Heather bites her tongue, eyes squinted, giving raving, rainbow, fairy-punk, as I click the shutter button.

'There, that's your lot.'

'You don't wanna do one more?' I say, following her out into the hallway.

'No, I don't.' She smothers me in a hug, chuckling in my ear. 'So, I'll see you tomorrow, then. Come over at, like, seven. I'll text you my address.'

'Okay, cool,' I say, nerves fluttering in my stomach. A party where I don't have to mingle, network, cold-press out every drop of niceness within me, extracting every sugar-coated compliment. A party with people my own age. With Joss. 'Thanks for coming over. I didn't know how much I needed this.'

'Aww ... gross.' On the doorstep, she slaps my arm lightly. 'Kidding. It was nice hanging out with someone who doesn't think farts are funny and won't start crying if I so much as cough while we're watching a movie. And by that, I mean someone who isn't my brother or Joss.' She laughs. 'Anyway, bye. *Tomorrow*, okay, I'll see you tomorrow. Bye.'

'Yes, already. Tomorrow, got it.'

The front door closes and I'm alone again, but not lone*ly* like I was before. I pad back through to the living room, smiling down at my phone after deciding to upload the picture of me and Heather to my story unedited, when two notifications ping through.

My lips peel apart, jaw dropping in shock.

New upload from Celeste Shawcross

EXPOSING THE SNAKE IN THE GARDEN OF EVE . . .

Oh, fuck. Is this why Imogen whirlwinded her way out of here earlier? Because she knew this was coming. Not even three milliseconds later, there's a text from Mum. I flop down onto the sofa.

Mum

Have you seen Celeste's new video!? That bitch!!!!! I'm almost home. Spence is coming over. We need to talk come-back strategies x

Oh, fuuuuuck.

With shaking hands, I swipe to open the video, the thumbnail alone igniting my legs in a forest fire of an itch. There's Celeste in full glam, making a gasping expression, with a screenshot of me – bare-faced and puffy-eyed – taken from a day-in-the-life vlog after just waking up. My picture's been Photoshopped next to her with a fat, red X across my face, the words *Toxic Energy* written underneath.

Sinking my nails into my calf, I press play.

20

EXPOSING THE SNAKE IN THE GARDEN OF EVE – THE HONEST TRUTH ABOUT EVE FAIRCHILD AND ALMOND BROWN☕

265,071 views · Premiered on 4 Aug

Celeste Shawcross✓

3.78M subscribers

'Hello, my starlets, welcome back to my channel. I hope you're all feeling shining, shimmering and *serene* today. Now, as you can probably guess from the title of this video, today's content is going to be a little different from my usual uploads, one that I *never*, ever in a million years thought I was going to have to make . . .

'So recently, it's come to my attention that some members of the beauty community are hiding some pretty effed-up, discriminatory views. Now, as you know, Eve Fairchild and I have been online friends for *years*. And don't get me wrong, I still have *so*, so, so much love and respect for this woman . . . which is why I feel so let down by the way Eve has chosen to raise her daughter to view people with invisible disabilities. People like me, suffering with mild narcolepsy and postural orthostatic tachycardia syndrome, otherwise known as POTS. But I want to get this straight first – though Eve is definitely *part* of the problem, my main issue here concerns Almond, and Almond alone.

'Now here's the tea. A couple of weeks ago, I went over to Eve and Almond's house to celebrate their collaboration with VeGlow Beauty, a brand I have worked with *many* times in the past, but who I *won't* be working with ever again if they go through with this campaign of theirs, featuring Eve and Almond. Throughout the whole dinner that night, I could feel, like, this aura of *hatred* coming off Almond, like, she wouldn't look at me, wouldn't talk to me. Quite frankly, I found her rude – but whatever, I thought. The *issue* came later, when Almond realised my support dog, my precious, little Chi-Chi, who you guys all know and love, had been under the table the whole night. Starlets, she proceeded to *scream* at me for having my dog in the house. I felt *attacked* by this, this *bully*, like, I actually feared for mine and Chi-Chi's personal safety – and I just knew I had to get out of that house, like right then in that moment, I knew Chi-Chi and I were in danger. I think Almond is in a very unstable mental state at the moment and honestly, I get it, with Eve and Joe's divorce, I can see why she'd be stressed. I'm an *empath*. But I just don't think someone harbouring all that negativity towards someone like me, someone with an invisible illness, should be anyone's role model right now. Almond Brown, as far as I'm concerned, is cancelled . . .'

21

'Postural tacha ... tachycardia syndrome is an abnormal increase in heart rate that occurs after sitting up or standing,' Spencer reads off his phone. He scowls up through his lashes. 'Why would you make fun of something like that?'

'I *didn't*,' I say, jabbing Mum's phone screen and aggressively adding garlic sesame noodles to the Deliveroo order.

Isn't it bad enough that I have the whole world believing I'm now some anti-HIV, anti-neurodivergent, anti-everything-that-happens-on-the-inside, intolerant asshole, but now I have to fight to get my own manager to believe me? I mean this is a *reach*. Anyone who's met me for even five seconds could tell you I'd never, ever, in a million years, object to having a dog in the house. All seventeen minutes and forty-eight seconds of Celeste's video came straight out of her BBL.

'Have you chosen yet, darling? I'm starving.' Mum leans over the table and takes her phone out of my hands.

I take out my phone to look at the menu on my own screen then almost drop it. My stomach sweeps sick with nervous anticipation at the sight of her name.

Callie

Hey . . . I know you obviously know the whole internet's mad at you. Again. But I just wanted to let you know that I know you didn't attack Celeste Shawcross. And that you're not a 'D-list dicktease denying human decency to people with disabilities' in the words of Damo from s2 of Love Island

A true poet

I guess I just wanted you to know that there's someone out there that believes you x

Almond

D-list? Bit ambitious but I'll take it, thanks Damo. And thank you, Cal, for saying that. It actually means a lot

Especially coming from you x

Callie

You don't have to thank me. Not when I still owe you an apology for the other night

My grip around the phone softens as I melt a little closer to the screen.

Callie

I had no idea Steph would post that video, or why she even took it. I was pretty lit and just went along with it because I was still pissed at you x

Almond

And are you still mad now?

Callie

Honestly, yes. I don't want to be though

Almond

Can we just talk? Like about everything. I'll buy you dinner at Jemima's? I miss you

Callie

I'd like that. I can't tomorrow – I got a job now(!!) but how about next Saturday? The 12th?? I'm finishing early at 6 then

I miss you too☹

My whole body slumps forward over the table, flattened by the thought of telling her I can't make it, and the reason I can't. Callie's either forgotten or rightly hasn't paid attention to the Serenity launch date announcement that went up on my feed weeks ago. And I have to tell her, ruining this moment. I can't not explain, avoiding the fact that I'm choosing 'work' over her *again* by staying vague, when that's what we're fighting about in the first place. She'll see it all over the internet and think I binned her off for a better offer, I know how Callie thinks. I sigh, typing slow.

Almond

I'm so sorry but I can't next Saturday. It's the launch with VeGlow in London. And I can't just not be there 😩 Sunday??

Callie

Can't or won't?

Almond

Can't!!! I swear. Obviously I'd rather be hanging with you! I seriously don't want to go, I'm dreading it x

Callie

Out in London with bottomless champagne and eating those proper nice or-durve things. Must be torture 🙄

Almond

Sunday????

. . .

The dots in the bubble bounce then fade as I stare at our messages until the screen goes black. When the end result is nothing more than a pose and a picture, I get that it's hard to see a launch party as anything close to work, but it is. I have a call time, a uniform of sorts, the physical exertion of pinning my face up all night with fake smiles. I'd give anything to cancel and spend the night with Callie but I'm contractually obliged to take part in this forced fun. How can I make her understand? Maybe she just needs more time, and to actually see me as *she* knows me, distanced from all this, disowning the version of myself she knows is complete bullshit.

And she will ... once the launch is over.

At the head of the dining table, making my impending cancellation all about him, just as I predicted he would, Spencer leans back in his chair. He folds his hands behind his neck as he sighs, looking up to the ceiling, his too-tight periwinkle shirt shrinking up, untucking from his jeans so I can see a wisp of pubes, underarms ringed with yellowing dried sweat stains. #candid.

'I'm haaaaaving ... tempura. No. Curry.' Mum presses her lips together, scrolling through the menu, her pout souring. 'Actually, I'd better just have some wok-fried greens. Sad face,' she says, pulling one. 'The launch is coming up super soon. Are you sure you want noodles, Almond?' In a stage whisper she adds, 'Carbs.'

'Absolutely,' I say with certainty. You only get one life's worth of meals and am I fuck going to waste even one of those on a *salad*, even if it is wok-fried.

'How can you even be eating at a time like this? I'm this close to a nervous breakdown,' Spencer whines, pinching his thumb and forefinger together, a molecule of space between them.

Mum stops scrolling, batting her eyelashes at him in disbelief. 'I'm hungry, Spencer. That's how. Besides, why would I bother flooding my body with stress hormones when I have *you*, my little PR star, who's going to sort it all out for us.'

He goes quiet, slowly lowering his hands into his lap, Mum's harsh tone shrivelling him down like salt poured over a slug. And *nervous breakdown*? Is he for real? I'm sat here scrolling through a slew of detailed death threats, my skin looking like a slice of Swiss cheese, and *he's* having the breakdown.

Though Mum's clearly over it and the silence has been stewing for a few minutes, with a sharp intake of breath, Spencer gushes, 'You know what, you're totally right, I should get something too – add a miso to the order for me, thanks. I mean, you've got to keep your strength up at such a stressful time, haven't you. Like, nourish yourself?'

God, this guy's literally as spineless as the noodles I just ordered.

'Noodles do nourish the soul,' I simper back.

'Oh my God, you're *too* funny. Can you say that again for my story?' In a literal bright white flash, Spencer's phone is trained on me. 'Again.' He nods robotically.

'Uh, noodles nourish the soul.' I shrug, feeling all types of exposed. 'I guess.'

'Not as good.'

'I don't care.'

Spencer's eyes *cut* to me, and I bite back a smile. 'Better not put it up anyway,' he says. 'Remember right after David Davenport uploaded his apology video and got caught singing along to the radio in a McDonald's drive-thru? And everyone was all *how could you possibly be sorry when you're this happy!?*'

'Mmmm. True.' Mum nods.

I bet the real reason he's nervous about all this is because he's terrified of *Mum* getting officially cancelled too. Right now she's on the cusp simply by association. And what would Spencer do without reliable Eve Fairchild, his most solidly booked client? What would Mum do?

Suddenly – and so unexpectedly – I get an adrenalin shot of guilt to the heart, because as much as I resent my mum for, well, everything, she loves her work and she's *good* at what she does. She always shows up, at least half an hour early, comes bearing litres of charm, zen, and just general good vibes on tap, performs a smile or whatever, and always makes sure her Apples leave a like, a comment, and subscribe at the end of it. She's earned her likes. Because being liked isn't just a given any more. I'm the proof. Sure, you can pay to look like a Kardashian or for bots to jack up your follower count, but it's those little red hearts that sponsors are counting on. In influencer world, 'likes' are currency and my mum is one rich bitch.

'Done. Right, food's on the way,' Mum says, locking her phone. Propping her elbows on the table, she slats her fingers together, looking pointedly at me. 'Now, let's talk about hashtag Almond Brown is cancelled.'

I groan. 'There's a hashtag? Already?'

'Of course there is!' Spencer snips. 'When Celeste Shawcross accuses you of ableism to her five million followers, there's going to be a bloody hashtag. What's the time?' Flicking his wrist to read the gold Gucci watch Mum gifted him last Christmas, he tuts. 'Eight thirty-four. She said she'd call at eight thirty.'

'Will you calm the hell down?'

'No, Almond. I will not. Calm down,' he says. It's like his brain's cutting up his sentences with kid scissors. My eyes flick to him, his wrist now limp, palm to the ceiling like that Gucci gold is weighing him down. 'This brand deal was going to be the biggest break of my—' His jaw tightens. '*Our* careers, and now, because the community's been infiltrated by you gen-Z, trigger-happy, social-justice warriors, I can just wave goodbye to an invite to the NTAs, can't I.' He gasps down at his phone, standing up so abruptly his chair smacks to the floor. 'Hiiiiiii,' he sings, Cuban heels clacking against the wood floor as he exits stage left, walking out into the hall. God, have a day *off*, Spencer.

My phone vibrates and I snatch it up as soon as I see *that* username. Anarchy's sent a response to the picture of me and Heather I posted to my story earlier. Of course.

'What? What is it?' Mum asks without looking up, the sudden movement of me grabbing my phone just enough to draw her attention over to my vicinity. Clearly not enough to drag her eyes away from whatever's on her screen. It's like only half of her brain's in the real world, the other half numbed by the narcotic star space of the internet. 'Has someone else made a video about you now?'

'No,' I say. My knuckle cracking as I grip the phone tighter reading Anarchy's words.

anRkey_InCel51

My eyes! What ugly HAGS you both are!!

'Are you sure it's not more call-out crap?' Mum says. 'Because your face, darling, says otherwise. Let me see.' Glancing up, I see she's staring right at me now, her phone down on the table. We sit across from each other, her waiting for me to talk, me waiting for her to lose interest. *I win*. 'One min,' she says, as her phone goes off again, her thumbs already lashing out a fast reply, 'and I'll be all yours.'

All mine. Right.

I don't think I've been all yours since the womb, Mum.

Clearly in self-destruct mode, I reread Anarchy's messages while Mum's distracted.

I peer at her over the top of my phone. Should I tell her? Could I? I mean, this situation's gone beyond the trolling comments of a ride-or-die hater – it's verging on obsessive, *and* I'm being blackmailed now. If I tell her, maybe Mum can get Spencer to rope in BigStarPR's legal team and get me some kind of internet restraining order against this creep. Is that even a thing – can you do that? I know they'd tell me I was brainlessly naive to think Anarchy would stop after I'd sent that first £500 through. Because even I know now – and should've *always* known, what with the amount of true-crime content I consume – that there's always a next time. Anarchy couldn't even go a whole twenty-four hours without a DM to me, referring to their subreddit thesaurus of sexist slurs.

With only £192 in my account, and the VeGlow deal hanging

in the balance, my plan to run away to the other side of the world seems more and more impossible. And a budget flight to a cityscape like Paris or Berlin just won't cut it. According to analytics, nearly two thirds of my audience is European.

I scroll up our message thread to see the picture of me and Hev again and wonder if I even *want* to go any more, when I'm finally getting somewhere with sifting through the jumbled parts of my ordinary life that got mixed up and lost amongst all the Instagram unreality. How can I leave when I'm just starting to find the right puzzle pieces of me that slot together? Meeting Joss and Heather, going to therapy, getting out into the sunshine, being among real people – all these things fit perfectly into the bigger picture of how I want my life to be. I've felt happiness for the first time since the world began to fall apart—

anRkey_InCel51

Your friend's even fatter than you! Is that why you got in a photo with her, to feel better about yourself? Selfish skank. How shallow can you get.

But then I read Anarchy's last message and I'm ready to catch the next flight again. Their vile version of events grate into the memory of me taking that picture with Heather, my mind feeding it slowly into a shredder for me to pick apart. Did I subconsciously take that photo with her to make myself seem skinnier? I don't *think* so. Did I? *No.* I took it because I love Heather. We had a nice time together and I wanted to remember it. I'd give anything to be back in those quiet, lazy hours I spent with her. When I felt comfortably normal.

I skim through some other responses to the picture of me and Heather on my story, numb to the everyday sexism I get from my followers, telling me it's a crime I'm not wearing concealer, or that I look like a corpse. Vain, pasty, entitled – *lucky*. My heart's also deadened to the 'I love you's, the compliments calling me beautiful, peng, an inspiration, hot, jailbait, a worldie.

A certain type of message I get maybe once a week but have never seriously considered jumps out at me now. It's @ron_majors1961 asking if I'd like to be his 'Cross the pond sugarbaby' for a thousand dollars a week in exchange for pictures of my feet.

Interesting.

Well, Ron, I may just take you up on that offer if VeGlow do decide to drop us from the campaign. I can send you sandy feet pics from the beaches of Santorini all the way to Mexico if the money's good. I take a screenshot of Ron's proposition and send it to Heather.

'I can't stand this,' Mum says, making me jump. Though her eyes are trained on the wall of text I can see over the top of her screen, I notice they're filling with tears.

'What's up?' I say, instantly regretting faking ignorance when I see those tears spill over. Of course I know *what's up* – Mum's career's probably over, all because of me and my big mouth running rogue and speaking my big emotions out loud.

'What they're saying about you online.'

My lips part but no words come.

She's crying over me?

'It's just with how you ... *are* at the moment. I don't want any of this awful shit to make you worse, you know with your skin and your ...' She swallows, peering up to the ceiling. '... Depression. You were doing so well – making friends, leaving the house—'

Surprising us both, I scramble around the table, knocking the wind out of Mum with how hard I throw my arms around her. I bend myself over the back of her chair, resting my cheek on the top of her head and it's ... nice. I can't remember the last time we even touched each other without it being at the instruction of some photographer trying to capture 'real intimacy'.

'Oh,' she says, her hand tentatively reaching up to pat my forearm. It takes a few seconds, but I feel her squeeze tight around my wrist, like I'm a paper thing about to be torn away from her by the wind.

We break apart as Spencer makes his re-entrance, so high drama as he bursts through the door. He fixes us with a shit-eating stare, his lips ducky and smug as he closes the door behind him and falls back against it. I mirror his smugness, folding my arms.

'I've saved us,' he drawls. 'Paisley and I agreed, Celeste has just boosted our sales by about twenty-five per cent with all this exposure, the silly cow. Like I said with Chundergate, there's no such thing as bad publicity, ain't that right, my sweets?'

'Fucking fabbo!' Mum cries, doing that quick kind of pitter-patter clapping nobody does in real life. 'I'm *so* ready for this to be over. I was just saying to Almond that I'd hate for this little blip in the public's favour to undo all the *hard work* she's put in to sorting out what's going on in here.' She spider-fingers her hand over her head, like my mental health issues are merely a serious case of headlice. 'Celeste obviously concocted all of this to try to sabotage the launch. The timing's just *so* transparent.'

The launch! Got it. Can always count on Mum to come through with that ulterior motive. I shrink away from her, sucking my lips in so I don't kiss my teeth as I walk away. And just like that I decide I can't tell Mum about Anarchy, not when things are so fragile between us. Knowing how she is right now, so obsessed with pleasing the right people, I can't risk confiding in her only to have her downplay Anarchy's hate as 'just a normal part of the job.' Because if I hear her say something like that, I don't know how I'll ever be able to find my way back to her.

'The conniving little witch. You're right, it's so obvious. The launch is eight days away. Eight.' *Clap*. 'Days,' says Spencer.

'So, what's the plan?' Mum says, both of them happy for my problematic ass to fade into the background now.

'So, tomorrow Paisley's coming to us this time to discuss our clapback over dinner. She's made reservations for the four of us at—'

'But I can't do tomorrow night,' I whisper.

'Why not?'

'I'm going to a party.'

'Whose?' they say at the same time.

'My friend Heather's.' I attempt to catch Mum's eye, trying to subliminally remind her of how good she just said it was for me to have friends right now. 'From group. She's the one on my story.'

'Oh God, yeah, *her.* Please don't upload any more selfies with her. What is she, bo-po Wednesday Addams?' Spencer guffaws at his own joke, biting his bottom lip.

'Spencer! Oh, just ignore him, darling. I'm glad you asked her round. I only wish I'd got to meet her, get to know one of your new therapy friends.' Mum purses her lips, considering setting me free for one night. Sighing, she says, 'Is there any way we can do the meeting without Almond, Spence?'

His eyelids flutter down as he fans his fingers out in front of him, pretending to inspect his immaculate nails. I'm all tense with anticipation and my spine feels wound up like a jack-in-the-box's, waiting for a hard *No.*

'Yeah, you know what?' Spencer bats me on the shoulder. 'This could actually work in our favour. You're a bit unpredictable at the moment,' he says to me, not even bothering with the pretence of *No offence.* 'If it's just us and Paisley, Eve, we can have full control over how we handle this situation, maybe write Almond a little script of what we need her to say.' No joke, he says all this without a hint of irony, Mum bobble-heading along with it. 'So, you go have *fun* with your *friends*, and leave all the adulting to us.'

Strategising our next move at internet-drama chess is the least adult thing I can think of, but okay. I nod, already mentally checking out of this situation, fizzing with excitement for tomorrow, like I've just shot up my veins with lemonade. Stupidly,

I take a gulp of water before checking Heather's reply to Ron's offer to be my Foot Fetish Sugar Daddy.

Heather

Please send Ron my way.

My feet are primed and prepped. I can do flip-flops, crocs, pedicure, socked un-socked. My feet are v-e-r-s-a-t-i-l-e

Whatever the kink I am HERE for it. You can tell him I accept paypal, it's hevshairytoes@payme1000dollars.com

And, of course, water sprays out of my nose with laughter.

'See,' Spencer says. 'This is why you're not coming.'

22

It's later and I'm in bed. Warm. Biscuity. Digesting my garlic noodles while background-watching a YouTube documentary on MKUltra. Cosily content, my socials all muted while #almondbrowniscancelled rages on, I'm swiping through years of OOTD posts on my grid, trying to pick an outfit to wear to Heather's party tomorrow, when Joss's name finally appears at the top of my screen. I sink down further under my sheets, cradling his kindness close.

23:37

Joss

Missed you at Tranks earlier . . . I hope you're ok x

Would love to take the dogs out with you tomorrow but I took the early shift so I could make Rich/Hev's party ☹ Hopefully catch up with you there?

I'll be the one in the Thomas the Tank get up. #ootd #fashionblogger

23

'Can you slow down?' I say, sliding across the back seat of Spencer's car.

'No. I can't. We're late for the meeting with Paisley to clean up *your* problematic behaviour, Almond, so that we can drop you at your little party. I saw that.' He scowls, catching me practically *bowling* my eyes to the back of my head in the rear-view mirror. 'Uh, the Satnav says *this* is it?' Spencer actually recoils from the tinted window as he pulls up the handbrake.

Mum lowers her sunglasses. 'Didn't you say it was number . . .'

All three of us look at number twenty-three in an ugly terrace of sixties houses with slanted roofs. Knee-high lawn, yellowing net curtains, sofa on the driveway. The downstairs window's been flung wide open, filling the street with a screeching guitar solo.

'Yep,' I say, grinning when I see Spencer's mouth gape open. 'Twenty-three.'

'Super,' he says, tightening his slender fingers around the

wheel. I've just unclipped the seatbelt when he says, 'Wait, wait, before you go – a little advice? Keep your phone on you at all times, volume all the way up. I'm thinking Paisley will want to go down the public apology route for maximum damage control. Video, not written. But we might need you on hand in case we do go written, best to get our statement out there ASAP.'

'Mmhmm,' Mum agrees, nodding so her blow-dry bounces. 'Ooh, where are we meeting again? I'm parched.'

'Fresio's. Our reservation is in ... oh joy, nine minutes. Anyway, this apology: if Paisley wants tears, we give her the ocean, if she wants receipts, we make up a whole till roll of them, alright?' I sigh out the breath I was going to say goodbye with, letting go of the door handle and slumping back in my seat. I pull out my phone and like a few comments on my 'Get ready with me for a summer evening get-together' reel that I edited and uploaded on the way over here. 'And another thing, do *not* drink too much tonight. Not only as your manager but as a ... a friend. I don't want to see any more videos of your breakfast in rewind, alright, so maybe limit yourself to, like, a shandy or two.'

We are not friends. And I'm already thinking about how I'm going to drown out this whole interaction with a quadruple vodka coke.

'You're so *opinionated*,' he moans on, 'which is a dangerous thing to be when you're drunk and have a platform like yours.' I swallow, reminded of the *actually* important advice on the NHS website, warning that consuming alcohol while prescribed antidepressants may worsen the symptoms of depression.

Advice I wonder why Mum never thought to read up on. 'The last thing we need right now is for you to go on another rant about invisible disabilities to give Celeste more fodder to take us down—'

'Oh, Spence, darling, do shut up?' Mum says, causing my jaw to drop down to the Starby's cup crowded footwell of Spencer's car. 'There was no rant, I've told you already. Almond was upset about her own dog, Honey, not being allowed in the house. It had nothing to do with whether Celeste should or should not have her service dog with her. You know, I can't *stand* influencers.'

Mum just apologised ... to me. Maybe all the masqueraded mothering she's been having a go at lately isn't a mask at all. I thought she was just trying to keep me in line before the launch, but maybe the fact that I'm being prescribed antidepressants and have wound up in two forms of therapy in the space of a couple of months *is* bringing her back down to Earth, back to her genuine, feisty, no-fucks-given self.

I've forgotten what it's like to have Mum in my corner. I shuffle into the middle seat, leaning forward between them, satisfyingly giving Spencer the back of my head as I look into Mum's face, checking for sincerity. Spencer splutters a fuzz of my curls out of his mouth.

'Now, go on, you have *fun*, darling,' she says to me.

And with that, barely giving me time to close the car door, the SUV tears off down the street, Mum holding up one motionless hand out the window in a goodbye. I take a deep breath, watching the car turn left and out of sight at the end of the road.

'Got a light?' a bearded, ginormous boy asks as I approach the house, an entirely black cigarette sticking out the corner of his mouth.

'Sorry, no.'

He grunts in response, loping off down the alleyway separating Hev's garden from her neighbour's, towards the sound of crashing metal music.

Before following him, I pause to check over my reflection in Heather's smeary front window. I love this faux leather mini skirt. It makes my butt look big and snatches in my waist, though I have to wear risky tights with it – only denier thirty – because any darker clashes with the pleather. But this skirt had to be the one.

20:04

Joss

Just arrived. Hev's bevved already.

Why do I feel nervous about seeing you, what have you done to me, Walnut.

Reading this and knowing he's inside, I twiddle with a curl at my temple, nervous too.

I haven't been bare-legged or worn any hosiery that could be described as sheer since late June when my sessions with Dr Wallace were winding down and my excoriation had really started getting out of hand. Since then, I've never dared go out in anything less than 100 to matte opaque 70. But I figured it's a house party, it'll be crowded, stuffy, dim-lit, and it's already past eight so only an hour-ish left of daylight. The scars are there, imperceptibly so, but there.

I crack a can of pre-mixed posh gin sent by one of Mum's current sponsors that I slipped from the fridge earlier and throw back a gulp, washing down any hint of hesitation I felt in the car. I was fine last time . . . wasn't I? No, I was, the hangover just felt worse because of how the night ended. The rhubarb and ginger syrupiness goes down way too easily as I dawdle, fussing some more with my outfit, plucking at my leopard print bodysuit and fluffing up my freshly washed curls. I am *vibing* with Scary Spice. Shielding my eyes from the setting sun bouncing off the window, I notice a blur behind the reflection. My heart stutters as I squint to refocus. Perched on one of Heather's kitchen counters, Joss lifts a cup to his lips and raises a hand, my cautious feelings for him scuttling back from the corners of my heart, not giving a flying fuck about waiting to be ready to show my whole self to him.

'Party's inside.' He appears in the doorway, khaki shirt unbuttoned to just below the collarbone, hands thrust into the pockets of stonewashed denim cut-offs, his hair gathered back into an untidy bun at the nape of his neck because it's been so stiflingly hot today. 'Or are you just chill hanging out here by the bins?' he says.

'I was . . .' Ignoring the fluttering I feel as his gaze trips down my body, his jaw slacking slightly, I shrug. 'I haven't been to a party in a really long time, to be honest. Think I got a little too comfy after lockdown.'

'No?' He steps down onto the path, so we're nearly the same

height, my lips level with the space above his Adam's apple. 'I thought Almond Hazel Brown would be top of all the guestlists. What with all your secret illuminati connections.'

I scoff, swigging from my can. 'Work is different. I *have* to be there, posing, laughing, smiling on cue. I want to be here, but it's like I've forgotten how to just be.'

'You're being just fine to me.' The corner of his mouth wrinkles in a half-smile.

'Hey, man!' A hand claps down on Joss's shoulder and I turn to see the bulking body of the guy who asked me for a lighter earlier wedged into the doorframe.

'Bill! Alright?' Joss's hand gets swallowed whole by Bill's, doing the awkward handshake-hug thing. Joss backs up, making room for me in the conversation. 'This is Almond, Bill. Bill, Almond. Bill was in the year below me and Hev at school.'

The year *below!?* This guy's puberty game is strong.

'Hey, Bill,' I say. 'Found a light yet?'

From behind his ear, he pulls out a matchstick, strikes it against the brick wall to light his cigarette and grins. 'When in doubt, always check that one random drawer in the kitchen.'

Joss nods. 'We call it the junk drawer in our house.'

'Yeah, I don't think we have one of those,' I say.

While they catch up about people I don't know from their school, I zone out, nodding and laughing in all the right places, though my mind's in a scramble. *Call your feelings by their name, get up close and personal with them, work out what they want,* Oliver told us, but I can't keep up with them.

I'm thinking maybe it's too complicated. Us. Maybe me and Joss would be better off just friends. I realise it's not only about wanting to be real with him that's been holding me back, it's what he said when he shared for the first time in Tranks, about how invasive and all-consuming being online was for him, how the internet and its algorithms were always eating away at his anxiety, decoding his psyche into an anxious mess with bombardments of fake news and targeted advertising. How he had to switch off completely. Imagine we were together and suddenly the anxiety-inducing thing becomes me, his girlfriend, an embodiment of all the mistrust, the divisive clickbait headlines, and the 'buy-this-buy-that-buy-me' infiltration he was trying to stay away from. I'm a literal walking, talking advertisement for fuck's sake.

What if he decides he has to switch off from *me*?

'Anyway, catch you later, man.' Bill holds up his massive slab of palm as he mooches over to join the crowd of smokers by the bushes. 'Nice to meet you ... Chestnut?'

'Fuck sake.' I find myself laughing, despite the emotional cyclone swirling in my head.

'Hey, he told me to say that.' Bill chuckles, shrugging his shoulders in time with the thump of the bass, the music having now ramped up into frantic DnB. 'I don't know what it means.'

'I gathered. Nice meeting you.'

We sit down on the doorstep, and I tuck my legs to the side, the dusk not quite dwindling into the darkness yet.

'He's cool.' Joss clears his throat as his hand scuffles around in his oversized pocket, awkward again now that we're alone.

'Hey, I brought you something. 'Cuz I know I was distant and now it seems like you've got some stuff going on.' He sighs out, exasperated. 'And I've missed you, okay. For real, I mean it. I've never met anyone I want to talk to as much as you.' I stare into his eyes while my two ideas of Joss – platonic, safe, uncomplicated vs potential boyfriend – grapple with each other. 'I've missed our late-night debates about what the Americans are hiding in Area 51.' His smile breaks like early sunrays. 'Here,' he says, curling my fingers around a paper bag he pulled out of his pocket.

I peek inside and see a row of fluffy, powdered doughnuts.

'What?' I smile too, feeling it radiate its warmth deep within me. 'Thank you,' I say, 'this is so nice, but I probably can't eat them.' The bag of doughnuts looks unmarked, which means there's no chance of me checking an ingredients list to see if they have milk, butter, or eggs in them, which baked goods nearly always do.

'They're vegan,' he says, shocking the hell out of me.

'What? *No.*'

'As if I'd bring you a present you couldn't eat.'

I take a bite and it's like biting with my kid-sized, loose-toothed mouth. The crisp, golden batter takes me far from this moment, back to standing on the edge of the pier, eating beach-shack doughnuts with Mum and Dad, a salt sting on my face. It's so simple and sweet and it's been so long since anyone's given me something *just* to give me something, like there's usually a contractual obligation or mention-request behind the gesture.

'*Mmm*,' I groan. 'It's like the inside's made of God's pillow stuffing, or something.' I lick the white, powdery sugar off my fingers. 'That was good. Where'd you get these? And why doughnuts? This is so deliciously random. Can I have another one?'

'Course. And I just asked Hev what you liked, because she *knows you*,' he says, air quoting around the fact that Hev used to follow me, 'and she said you used to talk about this small vegan artisan bakery all the time but when I looked them up, turns out they had to shut down during the pandemic.'

'Friendly Frostings!' I say, deciding not to tell him those posts were paid for – totally honest but sponsored, nonetheless.

'So, I asked my mum to make some,' he says, stuffing a doughnut into his mouth.

'No way. These are like *Bake-Off*-final-three-good, tell her.' As I swallow my mouthful of sweetness, I swallow down all my mixed-up feelings too, trying to just enjoy being in Joss's company again, even if we do end up remaining friends now. *Be present*, Mum always says. *Enjoy the now*. Because after all, I've missed him too. 'How long's your mum been vegan?'

'Uh, she isn't.' There's the grainy sound of him scratching his hair. 'I asked her to make these special, for you. I think these were the fourth batch? She was not having a good time with whatever the hell aquafaba is.'

I stop chewing, my tongue feeling around amongst the mushed-up doughnut in my mouth for the right words to say.

'Joss.' I swallow, fixing him with a stare. I can't believe he told his mum about me. 'That's so thoughtful. Thank you. Is this the nicest thing anyone's ever done for me?' I wonder out loud. '*Please*, tell your mum I said thank you. And to apply for *Bake Off*.'

He laughs a little, shrugging red as my phone vibrates.

Heather

Girl, where tf are you?? We have a situation.

Almond

Sorry! I'm outside. Just got here. Where are you??

Heather

My bedroom. Get up here ASAP-Rocky.

'And with that, I must leave you, my doughnut-bearing friend. Heather needs me,' I say, peeling myself up from the doorstep. 'And stop looking at my ass.'

24

Saturday 5th Aug 20:38

Mum

Paisley in loo. She wants you to film apology vid. Expected. Spencer will write a script dw. She says Celeste was a DIVA on last ad campaign. Apar VeGlow were expecting response like this from her!!!😮

On another note, found out more deets abt launch party eek! VeGlow so hushhush 🙄 But it's at top of the SHARD. We've made it, darling! I'm so proud of us!

When I'm back we need to prep – outfit, shoes, makeup, hair, tan, CUE CARDS. We can't have any more slips like Chi-Chi-gate again😂 hope you're having a nice time w your therapy friends!

Oop, she coming back from bathroom!!!

Hve to go. B safe xxxxxxxxxxxxxx

25

Cool people dressed in black line the hallway inside, rollies dangling from their fingers, tossing cold looks my way. I see no recognition in their kohl-rimmed eyes, only mild contempt, probably at my full-face of contour and cut crease, the leopard print and hoop earrings.

Whatever, I know I'm a basic bitch, but I make it work.

I hold my breath as I'm pinballed between the crowd towards the living room, pasting myself against the wall just in time to avoid getting socked in the gut by a rogue tattooed fist. Flailing limbs and whipping hair strike out from the crush that's engulfed the room, skanking to the shuffling rhythm of jungle music. I scan the angry faces for anyone I recognise from Tranks as I inch my way along the wall, spotting Marius tangled up on one of the sofas pushed into a corner of the room with some green-haired girl.

Jesus, this party went from zero to a hundred *real* quick.

Upstairs on the landing, I hover outside the door that's

Blu-Tacked with gig tickets and festival wristbands, an inverted crucifix Sharpied down the middle and so obviously Heather's.

I knock twice, slowly twisting the doorknob. 'Can I come in?'

There's a grunted sigh of relief. 'Fuck yeah, thank *God* you're here.' Heather leans forward off the bed in her tiny box room and wrenches the door open, pulling me in. 'She was already pretty far gone when she got here, but now . . .'

Slumped next to Heather and bent over a washing-up bowl is a jelly-boned girl, arms and legs hanging at her sides. I crouch down to see underneath the sweat-matted hair that's fallen over her face.

'Imogen?'

'She's paralytic. *Paralytic*, look.' Heather holds up one of Imogen's arms then lets it go, her hand a dead weight.

'Woah,' I say, steadying Imogen back onto the bed as she teeters forward.

'Don't want her to die n'all but I've been stuck up here for the past hour. Is Marius still chatting to that girl with dreads?'

'Ummm. Didn't see much chatting going on to be honest,' I say, arching an eyebrow.

'Fucksaaake,' Heather moans. 'Who th'hell drinks vodka like this anyway?' She holds up a bottle with a glittery straw thrust down the neck, nearly three-quarters empty.

'Someone who wants to get out of their head, Hev,' I say quietly.

Heather nods, helping herself to a shot of Immy's vodka. 'Hashtag relatable.'

'Right,' I say, cracking another fancy gin. 'I'm not even tipsy yet, so why don't you go find Marius and get rid of green dreads. I'll look after Imogen. Maybe call her mum. Even though she's an absolute bitch,' I add in a whisper. 'Is that a shitty thing to do? I don't want to be a grass, but . . .' I guzzle from my can, swallowing down the bad feeling I get when I remember how weird and flighty Imogen was after that phone call with Celeste yesterday.

'Yep. It's shitty.' Heather staggers up off the bed, snapping a clothes hanger under her platformed feet. I take her place, wrapping an arm around Imogen's shoulders. 'Shitty, but sensible. Up to you, babes.'

'Okay, *babes*.' I laugh.

'Yeah, what am I on about? *Babes?* Whatever, I'm kinda drunk.' Heather cups her boobs and jiggles them at me in the mirror.

'Go!' I say, reaching forward to ping the waistband of her purple satin flares. 'Go get Marius.'

She does one short, sharp nod, then pauses with her hand on the doorknob, the other still fondling her boob. 'No, I don't think I will,' she says. 'He was literally azkin' me for nudes not even four – *four* – fucking hours ago and now he's getting off with basically a Poundland version of me. His loss innit. But I will go and check on my cat though. I've shut her in Mum's room and I bet she's scratched the shit out of everything.'

And with that Heather twerks her way out of the room, squinching my heart with love, pride and a pinch of prideful envy, wondering if I'll ever be able to exist as unapologetically myself as she does.

When the door clicks closed, I focus my attention on Imogen, gently lowering her down onto the bed. I brush her hair off her face, grab a tissue from Heather's bedside table and dab at the sick crusted in the corners of her mouth. It's surreal, like seeing Barbie wasted. I prop up Imogen's head with throw cushions so she's not lying flat on her back, flinching as her lopsided lashes flutter open.

'AlmondHazzzzel . . . Brown?' she slurs, smearing a clammy palm over my face. I hate when people use my full name. It just doesn't feel like *my* name any more, merely a username. 'Ohmygoodness? Why's you in my room?'

'Hey, yeah it's me, but we're not in your room, we're at Heather's house, remember? Her party? Listen, is there anyone I can call? I don't *really* want to talk to your mum right now, but I will if she'll come pick you up?'

'No, no, *no*. Do not call my – my mum. Don't do that, please.' The suddenly lucid snap of her voice shocks me, and that bad feeling I swallowed down earlier rots in my stomach, remembering the shake in her hands as she answered the phone, that pleading whiny tone. *Hi Mummy*. The itching suspicion that something isn't right about their relationship. Imogen's sloppy gaze tries to hold mine, before sliding up to the postered ceiling, her eyes filling with tears. 'Please don't call my mum.'

And it's seeing her like this, as inebriated and loose-limbed as she is, drinking herself out of her own body, that makes me realise why Immy's *always* irked me since before we met in the flesh; she's the warped funhouse mirror of everything I fear I could be. A puppet being danced by her mum's cold, conniving hands. I hated seeing her ooze with enthusiasm with every new sponsor, eager to please and easy to adore, because I couldn't deal with Mum wanting that from me. That's not who I am, who *we* are, Mum and me.

But now the strings have been cut and I've seen the real girl underneath, the girl who handed me a bunch of sunset sorrys and drowns out her pain through a glitter straw, I want to protect her from this greed-guzzling Geppetto that's bigger than Celeste.

We need to dismantle the puppet-master machine that churns out girls like us from the top. I just don't know how yet.

I grab her hand, squeezing it tight. 'Okay, not her. I won't call her, I promise. Just breathe.' Though I feel sick with palpitations, I know I need to speak calmly to her now. She's frightened. I shush her, brushing my fingertips along her hairline like I've seen Mum do in one of her Self-Soothe Saturday videos. 'Is there anyone else I can call?' I whisper.

Mumbling incoherently, she fights her closing eyelids. Then just when I think she's about to pass out on me, her head rolls sideways off the pillow, where she painfully throws up bile down the side of Heather's bed, straining like her body's got no more to give.

'Oh, Immy,' I say, rubbing her back.

''M sosorry, Almond Hazel Brown.'

'It's all okay. You're okay.' I bring the cup of water on the bedside table to her lips.

When she falls back down against the pillows, I sit a little closer, holding her hand until her raggedy breathing evens out and I know she's asleep. I search for a phone through her stuff, spilled out on the floor from her upturned bag. I know I promised not to call her mum, but she needs to go home. Maybe I'll find an anonymous older sibling in her contacts who doesn't subscribe to the influencer lifestyle, who'll come pick her up, but her phone's dead. My guts churn with guilt when I see the spiderweb of cracked glass across the screen, grateful Immy hasn't told her mum about it. Because believe me, Celeste would've died and gone to clickbait heaven if she knew.

Almond Brown PHYSICALLY ASSAULTED my daughter and damaged our property.

I unravel the emergency charger Spencer insists I keep in my bag at all times and bend to plug Immy's phone in for her, catching sight of our reflections in the mirrored wardrobe door. Her face looks gaunt and pale where the healthy glow of blush and bronzer combo has been smeared off against the pillow, her body thin and tiny like a child's. I throw a blanket over her.

Taking a *big* gulp of my drink, I pat around on the bed to find my phone as it vibrates.

Joss

I'm coming up. Your babysitting shifts over x

I instinctively move over to the mirror to scrutinise my face as there's a soft knock at the door. I turn to see Joss with Samantha hovering on the landing behind him. She's still barefaced with a slicked-back ponytail just as she looks every Friday afternoon in group, though I notice she's applied a thin layer of mascara and a swipe of Vaseline as she slips into the room after Joss.

'Hi Sam,' I say, clearing my throat. 'You look nice.'

I cringe as soon as I say it. Why does every compliment we're trained to give someone have to centre around appearance?

Clearly uncomfortable, she nods curtly, silently sinking onto the bed and fixing Imogen's pillows.

'Sam didn't look like she was having too good a time downstairs,' Joss says, tripping over one of Immy's abandoned slingbacks. 'So I thought … two birds.' His eyes linger on me. 'And you could come back to the party.'

I look between them. 'Are you sure? I don't wanna dump her on you. I guess she's my friend, or colleague, or whatever.'

Nodding intently, Sam shifts backwards, making herself comfy on Heather's bed as she digs for some earphones in her bag. 'Too loud,' she whispers, popping them in.

'Okay. Look after her,' I say, leaning over the bed to clumsily peck Imogen on the forehead, obviously more waved than I thought I was. 'Bye Immy.'

With that, Joss tumbles me out onto the landing and as we clomp down the stairs, trying not to fall, I store away all the little moments of stolen touches and flickers of eye contact for me to overthink about tomorrow.

'Ready?' he says, his hand on the doorknob to the living room as we huddle together in the small space at the bottom of the stairs.

I nod, and as soon as Joss twists the doorknob, it's wrenched open by the force of the even bigger and sweatier crowd of people crammed into Heather's living room, jagging their bodies and nutting their heads to a DnB remix of one of Gramma's favourite songs, Sister Nancy's, 'Bam Bam'. He slots his fingers through mine as we're dragged into the sea of skanking bodies, gin and adrenalin roller-coastering through my veins.

I can't see Heather anywhere, but then again, I can't see much of anything, people are packed together so tight in here. I'm too self-conscious to dance to this music, but I like the wild smiles on everyone's faces and the safeness of Joss's hand in mine.

'You okay?' His breath is hot against my neck as he shouts to be heard above the music.

I nod, looking down at our hands still clasped together, a zizz of electricity sparking up through my middle and perhaps frying my brain to a crisp, because with that I throw us both into the centre of the crush. I close my eyes as we're sandwiched by skin, battering person to person as the dark, rumbling bassline drops and for maybe half a minute I feel free, lost in the chaos.

I get snatches of his smile, his wolfish teeth, our fingers scrabbling as we're swallowed by strangers.

Breathless and bruised, baby hairs slicked to my forehead with sweat, I lock eyes with Joss over a couple of swishing heads after the crowd split us up, and mime that I'm thirsty, my hand holding an invisible cup. He bundles me out into the hall just in time to see Heather slamming the kitchen door. She thunders towards us holding a bottle of prosecco, lipstick smudged all over her chin like grape juice.

'There you are! Ugh, I'm so pissed off and horny, let's get some air,' she grumbles, linking her arm through mine.

Outside, we crunch over shards of smashed glass as Heather leads us through her front garden's knee-high grass, brittle and browning from the sun, and out onto the pavement.

'You know what parties are?' she says, uncorking the prosecco as we perch on the kerb, me in the middle. 'An absolute ball-ache, that's what.'

'You're stressing too much,' Joss says, leaning his elbows on his knees to look over at her. 'And this is only, like, ten per cent your party. What's up?'

Lifting the bottle to her lips again, Heather shakes her head, her eyes scrunching up as she faces away from us, the streetlamp illuminating tear tracks on her cheek.

'Hey,' I say, softly putting my hand under her chin and turning her back our way. 'What's the matter? Is it Marius?'

'No.' She hiccups. 'Okay, yes, but only a tiny micropenis of a bit.' On my left, Joss coughs over his laugh. 'But I hate myself for letting him make me feel like this. I mean,' she waves a hand over her body, 'I'm me, I don't cry over boys like him.'

'Don't,' I say. 'Don't hate yourself for being human. He made you think he felt some type of way about you when he didn't.'

A text message quakes against my hipbone where my phone's wrapped against my body so tight, squinched into my skirt pocket. With some effort, I pick myself up off the kerb, turning to see Heather upending the fizz into her mouth with one hand.

I catch Joss's gaze loitering on my thighs, my hips, before his eyes snap up to meet mine and he ducks his head, suddenly intensely focused on picking crumbles of tarmac off his palm. I *feel* his stare in the front of my underwear, turned on by his desire for me, *this* me.

I bet he'd never save an edited, filter-fucked picture of me to a wank bank on his phone.

I've lived my whole life measuring my worth in the number of likes I can rack up from strangers on the internet in exchange for big-lipped, doe-eyed selfies. Kind of like selling my body, the PG-13 way. Which *would* be sick empowering if I was choosing to do it just for me, but I'm not, never have been. First it was Mum when I was too young to understand words like exploitation and consent, then when things got business-serious it was Spencer, and now it's both of them, combined with the three and a half million pairs of eyes I've got following me. It's not me that's got the power. That's why it's so hot to see someone want all of me, especially when he's talked to me, laughed with me.

Swaying on the spot, I stare at Joss, red patches climbing the sides of his neck and up his jaw, happy, loving and loved, when my phone goes off again.

The screen lights up with a series of Anarchy's reactions to my story; a mini montage of my make-up look in double speed, a share of my getting ready reel, and a straight-faced selfie of me and Joss posing on Heather's landing, with those pixelated, flame-guy sunglasses edited over our eyes to disguise my drunkenness.

Anarchy's sent a gushing, green vomit emoji. A pig snout. A butcher's knife.

'You okay?'

A butcher's knife!?

I can't breathe so I sit back down. 'Not really.'

And it's that threat of violence disguised in squishy emoji format that hurtles the desensitisation of online hate into reality. What if this person's actually unhinged and so set on sabotaging my life that they find out where I live?

Knives are sharp and people bleed in the real world.

Laying my busted-up head on Joss's shoulder, I cry snotty and ugly, trying not to hyperventilate as my thoughts spiral, colliding all the out-of-control things happening in my life right now. Anarchy, my parents, my skin, the Serenity launch, Callie . . .

'Hey, it's okay. I love you, you're safe. Do your breathing thing,' Heather whispers.

'Okay.' I nod-nod-nod with her, remembering, reassuring myself I know how to do this.

I can breathe . . .

Onetwothreefourfive. Inhale. One-two-three-four-five. Exhale. One, two, three, four, five. Inhale. One . . . Two . . . Three . . . Four . . . Five . . . Exhale.

In the stretch of blank space that breathing slowly gives me, it dawns on me that for once I'm not scratching. I'm not okay, I'm panicking, but I'm not giving in to that mindless itch, trying to numb the pain I feel on the inside by inflicting pain on the outside.

Instead, I'm holding all the fragmented parts of pain in my head, cradled on Joss's shoulder.

Deep, as Heather would say.

Or is it *Growth*, like Oliver would insist it is.

Or am I just drunk? Extremely drunk. (Fuck you, Spencer.)

I sniff, telling Heather, 'I love you too,' when I've calmed down enough to speak again.

Joss hands me a scrunched-up tissue from his pocket. 'Trust me,' he says, when I turn up my nose. 'You look like a Picasso painting.'

'Ugh, do I? You know, I thought my drunk crying days were over,' I say, smearing his gross-ass used tissue across my face. 'Guess not.'

A crisp packet scuttles along on the breeze and I stare blankly at it, my bottom lip stuck out, the skin around my eyes tight and puffy. When it comes close, I stamp on the silver foil, my flimsy, thirty denier tights snagging on the kerb's chipped concrete. A hole ladders up the back of my calf.

'Fuck,' I say, scrabbling to tuck my leg underneath me.

'Oh no, whatdyado?' Heather slurs. 'Have some prossexy, it'll numb the pain.'

'I'm not hurt, I'm fine, I just ripped my tights.'

'You got scars under there? Is that why you're always wearing those tights? You don't have to hide your scars here,' she says. 'Come on, lessee.'

'No way. You're drunk,' I say, sweeping her sticky fringe off her forehead.

'So? So's you. Wanna see mine?'

'Hev . . .' Joss's half-hearted attempt to stop her falls away.

Heather shimmies her trousers down to mid-thigh, so she's sitting on the edge of the street with her lacy, lilac pants on show, the straps of a suspender belt hanging loose at her sides. Casual.

Splaying the thickest wodge of her legs apart, where they touch just below her underwear, she shows me criss-crosses of broken skin lacing up her inner thighs like corset strings. I choke down a gasp, taking in the thinly crusted newer cuts intersected with the raised leathery worms of old scars.

Joss swallows, folding himself inward, arms wrapping around his knees. 'You promised me you weren't doing that any more.'

'I know, and at the time, I wazzn't,' she says with an indignant hiccup. 'Look, the road to recovery is not a straight line, *Joss*. It's not the A1, alright? There's gonna be roundabouts and zebra crossings, and, and–'

'Toll booths.' I nod.

'Yeah.' Heather points just up the road, bug-eyed. 'Bollards as well, see, always in the way and shit.'

'Alright, I get it. Enough with the analogy.'

'And three-car pileups.' Heather smashes her body into mine so I topple over onto Joss, domino-style. 'So will you show me yours?' she muffles into my shoulder.

'Heather,' I start, before she sits up and squidges a finger against my lips.

'Shhh. I'm not gonna call them something lame, like battle scars.' She rolls her eyes. 'But life *is* a fucking battle. And they're a part'a you, reminders of what you went through. What you don't wanna go back to, that's how I see mine anyways.'

Joss dead-eyes me. 'Look, you don't have to show us anything – and I know what I'm about to say probably won't help, but I really think *you* care more about these scars than everybody else does.'

'Yeah, you're right. Doesn't help,' I say, Heather echoing my sentiments just a beat behind me.

'Shut up, Joss.'

'Wait, I didn't say it right before.' He scratches his head. 'I guess I mean that *I* don't care about them, and the people who . . . love you, they won't care about them either. Fuck anyone else's opinion.'

Heather splutters out the swig she just took. 'Shall I leave you two alone, or—?'

'Shut up, Hev,' Joss says, letting his hair fall over his face.

'Lol. Romeo's right though. So, come on, get 'em off. Get 'em off,' Heather chants, pinching at my tights. 'Get 'em off.'

'Fine! Fucking fine. Help me then,' I say, satisfyingly driving my nails through the hole I already made and tearing upward, a wicked smile twisting my lips. With every rip, I feel lighter, afloat with elated relief. I hate having to wear these things – they're hot and chafey, limit the outfits I want to wear, and I'm always having to yank them back in place. Not for the first time tonight, I recognise a sense of release. They're just another layer of pretend that those puppeteer people made me think I needed.

Heather joins in first, grabbing a fistful of nylon and stretching it till the elastic splinters apart, leaving a gaping hole at my knee. I flinch when Joss touches my calf, his eyes flicking up to meet mine.

'This okay?' he asks.

I nod as he gathers up the frayed fibres, tugging downwards, so the ladder bleeds open all the way up my thigh. And together we tear apart the tights, sending tatters of material skimming down the road, gathering like shadowy cobwebs in the gutter.

When it's done and I'm staring at my pocked legs under the scrutiny of the streetlamp, I sit stiff, my friends on either side of me, silent, probably taking in the damage.

My body, my ravaged planet.

Scratches rake across my shins like red rivers, open sores dot up my legs like craters dug down into the earth of me, like the terrible aftermath of a natural disaster I inflicted upon myself. Wildfires and sinkholes.

Joss scoops me up, shifting me onto his lap as I cry silently, Heather scooting closer, laying her head on my shoulder. I know I'll be okay here. Because after the white-hot ravaging of a wildfire, when the pain's all burned out, there's calm. The smoke lifts up into the blue sky.

And after, there's healing. Growth.

I feel a chill at my ankles, tickling up the back of my calf and the hollow of my knee; a naked, natural outside whispering that I haven't felt on my skin for the longest time.

'You're beautiful,' Joss says, as Heather kisses my cheek.

And for once, I think I might be beautiful too.

26

'You're not giving me enough teeth. Show me teeth, sweetie, molars, how are people going to know you're innocent unless you can give them a proper smile? *Molars.*'

It is 8.59 a.m. My temples sear from the light of the soft boxes, blinding me from either side as I try to keep my balance on a stool in front of a green screen in Mum's studio. But I don't care. I'm dazed, but my face is still lifted by a sleepy smile, hungover but happy. Last night was the most unmanufactured fun I've had in ages.

'Test!' Spencer yells as the camera flashes, eyeball-meltingly bright.

I unlock the iPad he's placed on my lap and scroll through the apology script Mum, Spencer and Paisley concocted last night, hunched over their pitcher of pisco sour and dry ice, like SATC witches. The sentence, 'I will not be bullied by a forty-four-year-old woman' jumps out at me. Cold. Paisley wants us out here bringing up birth certificates and shit. I don't know if I have it in me for this pettiness today. I'm still on a high from last night.

An undocumented, drama-free night. A whole moonful of cry-laughing and dancing under streetlamps. I bet if I checked my screen time, my total pickups from yesterday would be under a hundred – which is good for someone whose job it is to be on their phone. The Uber receipt says I left Heather's house around four in the morning, my camera roll confirming that Joss was with me for some of that journey and that we must've made a pitstop at McDonald's. I sent Joss this one photo where we're cross-eyed with two chips thrust up under our top lips like walrus tusks and—

'Darling?' I look up from the iPad, from the blurred wall of text I've been dopily gazing at with a grin on my face. Mum's beaming at me manically. 'We've got the thumbnail now, so whenever you're ready.'

'Uh-huh. Just trying to remember my lines. Can I have a glass of water?'

'Spence, would you?' She sighs. 'We told you not to drink too much, for God's sake, Almond, we need this apology video out there *yesterday*.'

'I know,' I mumble, offering her a genuine smile, wanting to get this over with so I can tell her about Joss and his sugary sweet doughnut gesture. My happiness crinkles the layers upon layers of concealer, foundation and powder I piled on top of my hangover earlier, determined not to let this toxic situation sour my mood. 'Sorry. It was such a good night though, Mum.'

Ice cubes clinking, cuban heels clacking, Spencer strides back into the room, holding a tall glass of water out at arm's length to me, the sound of his shoes ricocheting inside my head.

'Thanks.' I gulp the glass of water empty. 'Ready now,' I say, eyes still emptily blinking over the iPad, over what I'm supposed to say to utterly decimate Celeste's character.

After the requisite 'Hey guys,' that Spencer's instructed me to dampen down a bit, the script begins with my account of Chi-Chi-gate, opening with Celeste's comments about how *'privileged'* I am to *'get to be'* mixed-race. I glance up at Mum stalking off to peer through the viewfinder, and don't know how to feel about this addition to the script. Because on one hand, out of the screenwriters for this drama, only Mum was there that night, which means she *was* listening and knew all along that Celeste was spouting ignorance disguised as a backhanded compliment when she said she was jealous of my skin tone because I didn't have to apply fake tan. Though her lips expressed nothing but an encouraging smile, on the inside, Mum must've seen how uncomfortable I was and secretly condemned Celeste's racial insensitivity.

But why *secretly*, why wait? Wouldn't it have been better to have had this conversation in person, in the moment, for Celeste to be able to ask questions, to have heard my thoughts echoed by Mum and Nevaeh. She would've gone away and reflected on everything, learned and grown, and then maybe the video she uploaded would've been an admission of *not knowing* – God, maybe even an apology to me and everyone else she's ever hurt with her hot takes.

And 'hot' takes there are many. They've compiled a list of every example of her being politically incorrect, socially tone deaf, or exploiting her privilege on the internet from way back to her humble Blogspot beginnings. It's all on a #CelesteShawcrossIsOverParty scale 'cuz past Celeste was so unwoke she was in a coma, but still, it doesn't feel right. I flick through the screenshots Spencer's saved of her tweeting at one of her followers in 2010 to just 'fizz up a bath bomb babes, get your nails done, cheer up,' after they said they were feeling suicidal. Then I swipe to a transcript of an interview she did with Perez Hilton in 2011 where she said she didn't *get* feminism because she appreciates 'good dick' too much.

I mean, this is all next-level ignorant, but *still*, I can't help feeling sorry for her. We're all growing and learning all the time. Twitter's gonna eat her alive after this.

'Almond.' Deafening clap. 'Sweetie, don't you see the red light flashing? We're filming. Speak.'

So, I open my mouth and start talking in a voice that's not mine. 'Hey guys . . .'

Staring into the black, mirrored eye of the lens, I watch myself dissect the evening's events, exaggerating according to the script and adding in my own bitter recollections in places, like how Celeste made me feel insecure about my height, and totally ignored me until Mum was in the room. Behind the camera, Mum stares at the recording on the screen, hand clenching her jaw, her eyes unreadable, while Spencer nods like a power drill, mouthing *Yes* at me with wicked glee.

When we get to the *brown skin privilege* part, I veer off-script, explaining how her ignorance belittles the everyday prejudices you have to face as a person of colour. Every time me and Dad would get 'randomly selected' going through airport security while Mum would breeze through, then dealing with that confusing punch of shame as other passengers tutted and wondered what we'd done; every unwanted hair touch; every 'you're pretty for a mixed girl'; every time a security guard's hawk-eyed me around a shop; every time someone's seen one of my posts and taken the time to direct message me the N-word. Spelled out. Hard R.

I stress that Celeste could *never know* how that feels.

'But, yeah, I'm sure it's really hard for you to have to put on fake tan sometimes, Celeste.'

I breathe heavily, all the light and laughter leftover from last night suddenly dissipated and I'm riled with pent-up rage, spurring on to the next section of my response video, ready to tear apart some of Celeste's old tweets. I rattle through endless microaggressions, wondering how she's been able to get away with this behaviour for so long. I don't think there's an 'ism' out there she hasn't committed.

'In 2012, Celeste referred to her seven-year-old daughter, Imogen, as 'a sexy little gypo' when modelling a full-skirted maxi dress, uh–' In my mind kid Imogen twirls her skirt and collapses into the Imogen I saw last night, blackout and boneless, throwing back a whole bottle of vodka just for a couple of hours of not being her. Drifting through dazed anonymity. 'And um . . .'

'Keep going, we can cut.' Spencer waves me on. 'Doesn't have to be all one take.'

'So, yeah, not only is she sexualising her daughter ...' *Will there be boys there?* Imogen had asked before going into the Greyhound, that desperate, unconscious desire to be wanted always there because it's been instilled into her since she was a little girl. Since I was a little girl. And earlier, wearing its evolutional skin of diet pills and 'nothing tastes as good as skinny feels' culture since Celeste was a little girl. Since Mum. I've lost my place in the script and scramble to find the words. '... but she was also obviously, um, using an offensive slur towards Romani people.' *Eleven years ago.* I close my eyes against the blinding lights. 'Wait, stop.'

Evidently Celeste still has a beanstalk-size amount of growing to do, I know that. But won't dredging up the catalogue of every single mistake she's ever made just isolate her, make her lean even further into those ideas and into the online factions of people that are openly intolerant? They'll welcome her with open arms.

We need to bring her closer for anything to change.

'I don't want to do this,' I say. My eyes meet Mum's and I *know* she knows this is wrong too. 'I can't. I'm not doing it.'

'Exposing prejudice against gypsies is where you draw the line?' Spencer says. My mouth drops open. 'Come on, this is career-ending *gold*.'

'Exactly! Why do I want to end this woman's career? Yeah, she hurt me, yeah, she's categorically ignorant, and frankly she's a bit of a bitch. But she's also just a person.'

Mum pushes the button to stop recording. 'Almond . . .'

'I don't want this posted. I'm going, Mum.'

I rip off the mic clipped to my shirt and stalk out into the hallway, jamming my feet into my trainers. I can't believe I even wasted my morning entertaining being a part of this sick internet reality show. I pull out my phone, desperate to check in on Heather like I have been since the second I woke up. After what she said last night, what she showed us, I need to talk to her, to make sure she's okay, or that even if she isn't right now, she will be.

Almond

You awake yet? I'm coming over. Need to see you x

Heather

Haven't been to bed mate.Can you bring pizza???

I wrench open the front door as I hear a commotion coming from the studio, and turn to see Mum striding towards me. 'Almond, wait,' she says, creases of anger attempting to screw through her Botox. But I don't stop. I can't stick around to hear her side with Spencer, not this time, not about this.

At the end of the driveway, I glance back at Mum standing in the doorway as her hand drops to her side, the pages of the script scattering at her feet.

27

Sunday 6th Aug 18:41

Heather

Thanks for coming over today My heart is full of love and my belly is full of margherita. I will be ok though guys, please don't worry

Almond

Ok. Just know that you can always call us whenever you feel like hurting yourself is the only option. I will never not pick up xx

Joss

10000000%. Anytime Hev

Almond

Can't wait for our Wellness Wednesday btw😂 I've booked a table for 7:30 at Don Giavanni's

Heather

We are NOT calling it that

Don't even try to get me to do anything close to therapeutic. The only breathing exercise I'm going to be doing is inhaling my spaghetti off the damn plate

Almond

A joke, a joke!!! This is gonna be as low key as possible. Just three friends and some pasta

Heather

Joss

Sorry off topic but did I leave my my leftovers at yours? Need to know if I should run after this bus or not.

There were at least four slices in there💔

Heather

Ummm. Let's just say they're no longer 'leftover' . . .😇

Thanks for your contribution to the Heather Kellogg foundation

Almond

A generous donation indeed

Or should I say *in cheese

Joss

Terrible, Peanut

Tuesday 8th Aug 20:56

FaceTime/Call Ended

Joss

Sorry I couldn't answer. Only just got off work . . . What did I miss?

Almond

I was just checking in on Hev. seeing if she needed me to come over and impart some Oliver wisdom.

Also I was filling her in on the whole internet hating me thing

Heather

Which while I do appreciate your love and support, guys, I do want to stress that I am fine! Actually fine, like I'm not just saying that🩶

Joss

Got it, Hev x

Almond

Ok xxxx

Joss

So, are you still Facebook's public enemy number one then??

Heather

Facebook!? Ok boomer

Joss

I'm tired. Give me a break

Almond

I'm still in the top ten. But I think that girl on TikTok who said people wouldn't have to use food banks anymore if only they'd pre-order her cookbook from Amazon for a measly ✨£18.99✨ has taken the top spot this week

Joss

Wow. Couldn't hold off on the shameless self-promo for a full thirty seconds. Bad take

Heather

In the bin with her

Almond

I know. My manager's thrilled. The only good thing about all this is that I've been told to 'lay low' online. So when we go out for dinner tomorrow you won't have to watch me do a photoshoot with the breadsticks lol

Joss

Oh no, please do😁

Wednesday 10th Aug 19:22

Joss

Running a little late. Can you order for me? Arrabiata for main please. And does anyone want to share bruschetta??

Almond

I will!

Heather

Please don't go all Lady n the Tramp on me. I'm already third wheeling HARD here

Almond

Girl, it's bread

Heather

Wouldn't have stopped my man Tramp 😍

Joss

Take back those heart eyes immediately

Almond

😱I'm calling the police

Thursday 11th Aug 22:05

Heather

Will you be gracing us with your presence at Tranks tomorrow, Miss Brown??

Almond

Yesssss💗☀ this week has been golden. I'm feeling so much better. Wish I was being cancelled every week tbh

28

It's almost four on Friday afternoon and I'm wrapped in a towel, collapsed back on my bed getting my sheets damp, muscles aching.

Mum finally tempted me to try yoga again this afternoon because she thinks all the negative attention from being cancelled has blocked my solar plexus chakra. Off camera this time and out in the garden, so I said yes, though she did insist we film a downward dog clip for her story. It didn't actually make it *onto* her story but still. I replay it again now, phone inches from my nose. With the camera watching side-on, we hold down dog for a couple of seconds, Mum sending her left heel skywards into a three-legged dog, before my balance goes and I topple into her, landing on the grass where both of us glance at each other and laugh, the baby hairs at my temples gelled down with sweat, Mum's face ruddied and real-looking. Too real-looking for Mum to post.

But at least I get to keep this clumsy, happy, accidental moment for myself.

'Okay, so last week we focused on the process of how we might *independently* seek professional help,' Oliver says, his big eyes in his strong lenses sweeping around the circle, giving each person a few solid seconds of eye contact. He lingers a little longer on me, smiles knowingly. *Welcome back*, I think he's saying, *it's okay if you had to take a week off.* 'This might prove useful in the upcoming months because I know a lot of you are about to go off to uni this September.'

I swallow down the bitter taste of knowing I'm not one of them, scanning the circle of sixteen- to twenty-one-year-olds, guessing at subjects. Varsha gives me bossy vibes, so I go with business or fashion. Liam's gotta be game development or graphic design. Sam, maybe history, or art – no, history *of* art. Arms folded, I judge passively, loneliness dragging me further into my own head. It's not like I ever had a *plan*, a career I've been steering my studies towards, or a degree I wanted to work hard for. It's not that I'm begrudging them their whole university experience – I guess I'm just jealous that they've all got acceptance letters for what the next chapter of their life will be. Whereas degrees, apprenticeships and even strawberry picking in Australia stray way too far off the path I'm being pushed along.

'Because remember,' Oliver's saying, 'this is a lifelong journey. We're not just gonna get to the end of these six weeks and have a sexy Satnav voice tell you you've reached your ideal mental health destination. It doesn't work like that.' Heather leans over me, throwing a smug, told-you-so look at Joss, before mouthing *A1* and leaning back in her seat, arms crossed.

'So, today I want us to explore the benefits of having a routine,' Oliver says, pushing his glasses further up his nose. 'Because if an active, engaging, healthy routine is in place, it leaves less room for our minds to wander toward those quick fixes we identified in previous weeks – you know, recreational drugs, alcohol, endless scrolling. *Distractions* from what's really going on in here.' Instead of tapping the side of his head, Oliver places both his hands over his heart. 'Of course, having drinks with friends and following people that interest you online is all fine and good in moderation – we just don't want those behaviours to take over the structure of our days, because they leave us feeling . . . ?'

'Unfulfilled?' Imogen offers.

'Exactly.' Oliver claps. 'It's unfulfilling. Good, Imogen. We want to *fill* our precious hours to the brim.'

Imogen twinkles her teeth at him. She was already here when I arrived today, her make-up immaculate, like her face has been *varnished* on, hair ribboning out from a high ponytail, and in deep conversation with Sam. Since Heather's party, I can't help but think she's compensating for the way she feels on the inside. I've wanted to reach out all week, but I haven't known what to say, how much of the drunken splurge of fear she expressed towards her mum she'll remember. Given her latest post, captioned 'Summer lovin' with the Mama Bear @shawcrosscelestial✿', I'd say Celeste was behind her daughter's strategically timed photo dump of the two of them posing in various summer activities to garner sympathy from the yummy-mummies and rally Imogen's followers behind Celeste's smear campaign against me.

Not playing into Celeste's games, I liked the post. For Imogen, and some semblance of peace between us all, because followers notice these kinds of things. I don't want my followers picking sides, leaving hate on any of the Shawcrosses' stuff. As soon as I'd liked the images of Celeste and Imogen, arms intertwined as they ate fluffy tufts of Mr Whippy ice cream and lounged poolside, Immy messaged me.

images_of_imogen

I hope none of the drama with mummy will come between us, Almond

I asked her not to post but she said it was strictly business, nothing personal. I hope we can still be friends🖤🖤🖤🖤🖤

thereal_almondbrown

Of course, Immy x

None of it really means anything anyway does it. I hope things are ok with your mum?xx

No reply, and I'm guessing that's because things most definitely aren't okay with her mum, despite how hard Celeste's hoping they appear to be.

Hey, I mouth at Immy, uneasiness squirming in my stomach. Imogen tinkles her fingers back at me, flicking her ponytail over her shoulder, and I wish I knew what she was thinking. No matter what her text said, if Celeste can convince half her audience I'm an intolerant ableist, surely she can convince her own daughter. I feel like I need another six months of these sessions to get over my trust issues alone, what with the anxiety of internet drama eating way too ravenously into my everyday life.

The week I've spent digitally distanced from it all has been the happiest I've felt in months. I haven't thought about Anarchy once after silencing their constant commentary by muting everything though from the lack of daily harassment I saw when I checked back in earlier, dare I say that maybe Anarchy's been losing interest? I know I did the right thing ditching out on Spencer's retaliation video too, even though Paisley wasn't pleased; she was banking on the extra Serenity sales the prolonged attention an internet feud would send our way. Still, even without a response to Celeste, me and Mum are up a couple of thousand followers each and they can't argue with that when they were expecting major losses. The consensus among the VeGlow PR team is that Celeste's claims weren't as 'high-key problematic' as other recent scandals deserving of a mass unfollowing, though I'm not sure why we're pitting people's past mistakes against each other like some fucked-up pageant of public shaming. In the end VeGlow settled for the vague, non-committal Notes app statement Spencer released on my behalf on Wednesday.

Spencer Dorsey @spencerdorseydoesit · 2d A statement from Almond regarding recent events: 'At this time, I will not be engaging with false accusations of ignorance and attempts to undermine who I know myself to be as a person.' [1/2]

Spencer Dorsey @spencerdorseydoesit · 2d 'I think some reflection is needed by both myself and Celeste before making further comment. To my followers, thank you for sticking by me and knowing my truth.' [2/2]

That last line of added melodrama was all him.

The latest update I got from Spencer is that the overall outrage and disappointment has all but boiled down into a simmering bitterness being stirred by only a few long-time haters. And thanks to the #cookbookconversation having taken over most of social media, even they've got a new distraction. Someone else to rip to shreds.

'So, before we start sharing today, I have a blank activity tracker for you all to take home.' Oliver's voice strains as he pulls his moon-phase folder out from under his chair and slides a sheaf of papers out from one of its plastic wallets. 'This one's marked up for just one day, because with this first tracker I want you to conduct ... an experiment of sorts.' He hands the pile to Sam, nodding at her to take one and pass them along. 'You'll see there's a place for you to rate how each activity has affected your mood *and* how much of a sense of accomplishment it gave you.'

'Why?' Joss asks, snagging my pinkie finger with his in the gap between our chairs.

'Well, Joss, because you'll see that while eating a family-sized bar of Galaxy may make you feel ten out of ten initially, the sense of achievement you get from doing that may only be like, what? A two, or if it's an especially big bar, maybe a three.' Oliver chuckles. 'Totally not speaking from experience or anything.'

Kind of like how capturing a picture of myself holding a tree pose in yoga earlier lifted my mood to a nine out of ten because it showed I'd showered, exercised and got outside in the sunshine today, but the one hundred and forty-eight thousand likes I gained after Mum told me I should post it zonked the achievement I got out of it down to a one, because suddenly it wasn't about the strength my body was cultivating any more, it was about how it looked; the brand of activewear I had on, the bulge of a belly roll caught between the waistband of my leggings and my sports bra.

The sexualisation of my body.

gymgirl_gains Do you have to force your sluttiness on everyone even when you're exercising. Look at that camel toe!!!!

If I hadn't posted it, I think the mark for achievement would've been a ten.

When we get outside, the sky's pink and muffly hot, as if God's put a red t-shirt over the sun to make his room look all romantic and sexy.

Walking down the steps, Hev gets sucked into an apology from Imogen about replacing her puke-splashed bedding as the others disperse, giving Joss and I a second to ourselves. By the hand, he leads me under the cool shadow cast by the stone steps.

‘Hey,’ he says, his finger hooking through the belt loop on my skirt as he pulls me toward him.

‘Hey.’

‘So, what are you doing tomorrow? Are you around for some *Unsolved Mysteries* and chill? Remember that? Why does that feel like forever ago?’

Every inch of me groans in frustration.

Why couldn’t it be any other weekend than this one?

‘I can’t this weekend,’ I say. ‘It’s the Serenity launch.’ I’m not even the slightest bit mad he forgot; I don’t want this, him, the idea of us, to get corrupted by any commitments the manufactured version of me has to keep. ‘I’d give anything to be at home with you’ – *in your bedroom* – ‘instead of in a room full of egomaniacs I’m obliged to talk to, trust me. But my mum would literally malfunction if I didn’t show up.’

‘That’s rough. How about Sunday?’ Joss says, his arms clasped behind my butt, zipping me closer to him. ‘My mum’s leaving for London tonight, visiting my sister all weekend.’ He brushes my curls back, his voice a half-whisper, ashy and low. ‘We can watch Netflix in my bedroom, the living room . . . on the kitchen table.’

Fuck.

My hips dig in just below his, my fingers interlacing behind his neck, my lids closing, face tilting, mouth opening . . .

Over Joss’s shoulder, a cream-coloured Beetle purrs around the corner with the roof down, tooting.

‘Okay, Sunday. I’ll see you at—’

‘Literally come over as soon as you’re up.’ He laughs, though I know he means it. 'Getting to spend a whole day with you seems like a rarity, so I want to make the most of it.'

My breath catches as I take in Joss's bare-faced honesty; that he's assured enough in his feelings about me to admit he wants us to spend every second of that Sunday together, and also willing to accept I might be scheduled away from him for a lot of our free time.

'I will,' I say, relieved that after this weekend, when the launch is over and I've selfied and schmoozed my way out of my last official event, I'll have whole afternoons stretching into evenings, into lazy long weekends to be with Joss. As soon as I figure out how to tell Mum I quit.

Weeks of future dates unspool in my mind as we emerge from the shadows to join Hev idling by the Beetle. The woman behind the wheel jerks the handbrake up, hooks an elbow over the side of the car and pushes her sunglasses back into her hair.

'Hev, oh my gawd,' a forty-something female Joss cries. 'How's you, love?'

'All good thanks, Cheryl.' She sugars up her voice as we step a little closer to the car. Hev's being fake sweet, the way you've got to talk to adult acquaintances sometimes. 'And you?'

'Alright, Mum?' Joss says, tugging his t-shirt loose so it hangs below his crotch. He cuts his eyes at me, then throws his head down to tie up his hair, ducking his red face out of sight.

'Gooood, good. Alright, Joss, love. Hey.' Cheryl waggles her fingers at me, acknowledging me too. 'Wait, are you . . .?' I tense up, expecting to hear *Eve Fairchild's daughter*, or *from those Zara bus shelter ads that have been up forever around the city centre.* '. . . Joss's doughnut date? Almond? What an unusually lovely name, by the way. I hope you liked them! I've never baked anything ve-*gan* before.'

'Doughnut date!' Heather says in my ear, her body trembling with laughter.

'Jesus, Mum,' Joss mumbles as he climbs into the passenger side.

My laugh sags out of me like a loosed balloon, giddy with relief. 'They were amazing,' I say, bubbling that Cheryl only knows me as the girl Joss likes. That I'm Almond, I'm vegan, and I like doughnuts.

'Oh good, I'm glad. Joss has never been out with a ve-gan before. Anyway, we'd better go, traffic's a nightmare.'

'Bye,' Joss calls in a begrudgingly amused groan.

'You and Joss are going out now?' Hev squeaks out of the side of her mouth as Cheryl starts the engine.

'I have no idea,' I whisper back, then call out to Cheryl, 'It was nice meeting you.'

'And you, my lovely, take care!'

The car squeals off, taking Joss and all the sexual tension between us away. I exhale hotly, watching Heather's thumbs dot across her screen as she texts. Her eyes flick up at me.

'Lol, not Marius asking me if I'm free later after ignoring me all night at my own party.'

'The nerve.' I mock-gasp, laughing as my own phone vibrates, hoping it's Joss.

Your video *Celeste Shawcross is a SOCIOPATH* is now live!

What. The fuck?

Anxiety douses out the heat of just now. On autopilot, I abandon Heather and drift over to the bike stands, unlocking my bike and swinging my leg over it.

'You alright?' Heather asks, right behind me. 'Who was that?' My grip tightens on the handlebars. 'Okay, you're not alright. What's wrong? Who are we mad at?'

'My *idiot* of a manager who never listens to a word I say.'

Who the hell does he think he is, uploading to my channel without my consent? Knowing that deleting it now would only piss fuel onto the fire, causing more speculation, the circulation of screenshots, reuploads to accounts I don't have control of. People with notification bells on my content will have already seen it, it's too late. Celeste will respond, making up even more lies about me – or worse, telling them the truth of why I'm here at Tranquillity, having pressed Imogen for information on our sessions – giving her followers the green light to hit me with all their hate, diverting raging traffic to my socials.

Imogen wouldn't do that, would she?

I can't deal with a whole army of Anarchy troll clones writhing in my DMs.

A breath skitters up my diaphragm like a frightened bird.

'Need backup? Support?' Heather ducks down, gets in my eyeline. 'Subtle comedic relief?' She lifts my chin with her pinkie. 'Just say the word, I'm yours.'

Numbly, I nod. In through the nose, out through the mouth. I count and count, counting myself down to a steady heartbeat.

'I'm okay,' I breathe. 'Honestly I'm okay right now, thank you, Hev. You're a good friend.'

'I know,' she says, closing her hand over mine, then dinging the bell on my bike a couple times so my mouth wobbles with a smile. 'Seriously though, text me if you need anything, like, literally anything. And remember to call us before you leave for the launch tomorrow, yeah?'

'I will, believe me I will. Bye.'

Heather's goodbye gets snatched away by a surge of wind as I take off, a tingle of cold in the air as the clouds grumble closer together. I pump my legs against the pedals, riding away from Spencer's drama-baiting bullshit, letting the air whip away my panic. Standing tall over my bike, my curls stream behind me as I feel the first flecks of rain spit against my face.

I cycle so fast, I'm hurrying into Dad's flat in less than twenty minutes, out of the summer storm. A gust of wind follows me in and I see Gramma Em standing in the middle of the room, her skirt fluttering about her ankles, plucking grapes from a punnet tucked under her arm.

Gramma picks one off the vine and pops it into her mouth, lips smacking as she talks, 'Good timing! Mi just got 'ere,' she says by way of explanation, shhing Honey as she barks hello to me. 'Your father tells me you 'ave a big fancy pants ting 'appening in London tomorrow, no? So I just came to send all mi love on the way wi' you.' She chuckles, but just hearing her buttery-kind voice makes my bottom lip wobble and I burst into tears. 'Oh baby, come 'ere,' she says, unravelling her headscarf, raindrops falling off the silken material as she opens her arms out to me. 'What's a matter?'

I collapse into her, her body cushioning my fall. After a few minutes of Gramma shushing my tears and rubbing my back, with Honey licking at my hand, she unpeels me from her, wipes my eyes with her hankie then folds it in half, wets it, and scratches off the snail trail of snot on my upper lip. Her knees click as she stoops to stay in my eyeline, fixing me with those big, dark eyes of hers, brown and flecked with green like wizened, mossy tree bark, as she asks me again what's wrong.

I open my mouth to tell her about Spencer going behind my back, about Anarchy's hate having made a home in my head, to tell her *everything*, but as her balmed lips stretch into a smile, all the intrusive racist ugliness I've seen commented about Gramma over the years hacks into my thoughts. 'Monkey woman.' 'The oldest slave.' 'Windrush wog.' I almost wretch with the urge to shield my Nokia-using, bingo-playing Gramma from every act of inhumanity ever typed out on a keyboard.

So instead, I say, 'I'm just tired. Really tired.'

''S'okay. If you tired, it means you working hard. But we need to get you rested up, nuh,' she says, plopping a bunch of grapes into her mouth and handing me the punnet. She hauls some bags for life up onto the kitchen side. 'Your father fridge always empty, so mi brought this from home. First, we start fixin' food. Food nourishes the soul, and righ' now baby girl's soul could do wi' more than a likkle nourishment.'

'Where is Dad?' I ask, crouching down to give Honey my full attention, letting her nuzzle into the crook of my neck.

'Working late,' Gramma says, flicking on the main light. 'Bit depressin' in 'ere, nuh? Lemme get some . . . some music on the . . .' She holds her phone out at arm's length, squinting to make out the screen. 'On the YouTubes, yeah?' And then her face lights up as the intro to Dawn Penn's, 'You Don't Love Me', starts playing. 'Love this one,' she mumbles.

'I know.'

'No, No, Nooo,' Dawn croons, stirring up the anxiety stewing in the pit of my belly. Even Gramma can't quiet the constant static background buzz of the internet going on in my brain. 'Give it here,' I say.

Grabbing a glass off the draining board, I take Gramma's phone and place it inside, echoing the volume up a bit, like how we used to in Callie's garage, willing my mind to relax, to lean into this comfortable distraction.

If I don't look at my phone it isn't happening.

Two tins of kidney beans, long-grain rice, chickpeas, sweet potato, and plantain roll out of Gramma's other bag for life and onto the worktop, and immediately she's hollering orders.

'Drain 'dem.'

'Peel 'em up.'

'Chop it, chop it.'

'Sea-son-ing. It needs some season, hmm?'

'Wai-wait. How old you, nuh? Seventeen and yuh don't know how to use potato peeler propl y?'

I pause with the potato in my hand, ripping a strip of its skin off with my fingers before thrusting the peeler out to Gramma.

'You do it then,' I say, putting all this afternoon's hurt on to Gramma chiding me about potatoes.

'I will do it *th*en,' she says, mimicking, and I watch as her papery, love-lined hands grip tight and twist. Hands that have held mine as we walked to school, braided my hair in protective styles before bed, clapped, caressed, and called me home. Hands that have always been there and always will be, to help me up whenever I fall. No matter who's pushed me. And I know that whatever Twitterstorm awaits me tomorrow and whatever Anarchy threatens me with next, they can never take her love away from me. 'Here taste,' she says, catching me off guard as she spoons sauce into my mouth.

'Love you, Gramma,' I say, my throat thicking up as I swallow.

'What's a matter, too hot?' Gramma kisses her teeth, tasting it for herself. 'You don't eat enough of my cooking, child. Still, I love you too.'

Friday 11th Aug 18:39

Almond

So wtf was that???

What happened to: I want no part of this cancellation shit anymore?

Friday 11th Aug 22:54

Spencer

As your manager and the overseer of our brand relationship with VeGlow, I made the executive decision to . . . override your decision.

In the five hours since your latest video dropped, your YouTube channel's up 4k, your Instagram is up 6.5k and the Serenity page is up 3k. We needed to smash sales targets and that cookbook woman was stealing your moment

Almond

My moment!? They're talking about firing her from her job. Whatever 'moment' she's in, I don't want any part of it

Also MY latest video!?😂 You've had to cut and edit the thing so much because I walked out on your precious script, I don't even think I say one complete sentence!!

Eve

Look, it's not nice for anyone, darling, but this is the world we live in now and you can't deny these numbers😬

Celeste knows the game. This isn't anything she can't come back from xx

Almond

Are you for real??? Did you not hear the dirt you were making me rake up on her. Her career is over. Probably Immy's too.

Spencer

Well, then she deserved it! Am I wrong?

Tell me I'm wrong!?

Almond

Did you know he was still going to post it, mum?

Eve

No. I wouldn't go against your wishes like that . . . BUT, am I happy to see more of a buzz about the campaign, and that you're back in Twitter's good books? Yes xxxxx

. . .

You've all lost your heads with power. We're selling moisturiser ffs!!!? I backspace the message I just typed, my thumb stabbing at the delete key as I actually thrash my legs under the covers with frustration. Honey lifts her head from her paws, jostled by the movement, then pads up the bed to curl closer to me. Not a single spoonful of Gramma's sweet potato curry I ate earlier could settle my stomach or lull me into sleepy contentment like her comfort food usually does. Nor did blankets and popcorn with Dad in front of our all time so-bad-it's-good nostalgia movie,

Con Air, quiet my mind from all this unnecessary drama playing out over the internet.

I'm supposed to be getting an early night before the launch tomorrow but that's not happening. Between dealing with text exchanges of this level of fuckery and the staccato mumble of TV gunfire coming through Dad's thin walls, my mind remains utterly and angrily awake.

A news alert slides down from the top of my phone screen, notifying me that Celeste's broken her five-hour silence since my – no, *Spencer's* – response video came out. I lie rigid stiff, gripping my phone like it's about to sprout little mechanical wings and fly away.

I skim the replies to the tweet Celeste put out to inform her dwindling starlets that she's taking a digital detox for a while, burying down deeper under the covers, wanting the bed to swallow me into sleep.

Katy @katykinsdoescupcakes · 3m

Replying to @celeste_shawcrossxox Byeeeeee hun😌 The internet doesn't need to be giving money to any more closeted racists than it already is #byebitch

Mads in the Wild @lifeofanomaddison · 1m

Replying to @katykinsdoescupcakes Hardly closeted! I can't believe she had the audacity to leave this up and none of us bothered to check. Well done @thereal_almondbrown for waking us up to her bullshit

With quick, clumsy thumbs I search for Celeste on Social Blade, my stomach swirling sickly with guilt when the page loads and I see her numbers. Already, she's lost close to 100,000 subscribers. And that's only on YouTube.

My phone buzzes in my hand with notifications from followers tagging me in Tea for Two's breakdown of the drama between me and Celeste. Oh God, the last thing we need is the commentary community regurgitating content out of this.

Fuck, what if this breaks into mainstream and Celeste's whole online platform gets engulfed by the drama? It's happened before. She'll lose all her sponsors, every source of income, just like that. What if she can't pay her bills? At the beginning of all this, when we were sat at the chabudai table with Celeste making me feel like a speck of myself, I wanted her to pay, yeah, but most of all I just wanted her to learn a little kindness, to understand how her words had hurt me.

You can't fight hate with more fucking hate.

Should I tweet that? Without the swear?

No. I can't type my way back into the storm now, while Celeste's cancellation courses across the internet like a viral infection. Symptoms include: lack of empathy, misplaced sense of justice, urge to exercise intensive keyboard typing causing arthritic cramps of the fingers.

Dropping my phone, I swipe at the stress tears blotting onto my pillow. What if . . . Celeste *does* something? Real world serious. Immy had to have been drinking her mind out of some kind of trauma the other night. What if Celeste takes all this backlash out on her?

Okay, stop.

I breathe slow, close my eyes against the blue light of my phone and let my mind feel around in the dark for a sense of calm. I breathe in, breathe out, and try to let my catastrophic thoughts pass like clouds, accepting that that's all they are, bad thoughts. Not bad things that *have* happened or necessarily *will* happen. Just thoughts.

As I drift off, the only slivered silver lining I hang on to is the hope that if Celeste does get kicked off the internet, maybe she'll spend more time *with* Immy, rather than focusing on the *spectacle* of interacting with her. Maybe she'll have more time to spend on giving love rather than taking likes.

29

MY ACTIVITY TRACKER

NAME: Almond Brown

DATE: 5th/6th August

TIME	ACTIVITY	MOOD	ACCOMPLISHMENT
18:00	Cycling to Dad's flat at 100mph probs	2/10	9/10
19:00	Crying in front of Gramma	6/10	10/10
20:00	Cooking Bajan curry with Gramma + singing (badly)	7/10	10/10
21:00	Eating with Dad & Gramma	8.5/10	6/10?
22:00	Late night walk with Dad + Honey	9/10	9/10
23:00	Arguing with Mum + Spencer – can't sleep!	1/10	0/10
00:00	Sleeeeeeep ♥	10/10	10/10

TIME	ACTIVITY	MOOD	ACCOMPLISHMENT
07:00	(Nightmare about launch. My skin was photoshopped green in the ad.)	1/10	???
08:00	Couldn't go back to sleep. Watched TikToks in bed for toooooo long	4/10	-1/10
09:00	Dad up early! We walked Honey on the Downs :)	9/10	10/10
10:00	Breakky at Jemima's w/ Dad + Hon. Jerk avo toast!	10/10	7/10
11:00	Me + Dad took Gramma to the International Foodstore for goat meat ... :/	2/10	8/10
12:00	Said goodbye to Dad and Hon. Posted to story. Rode home.	6/10	8/10
13:00	Followed one of Mum's hatha yoga vids on YouTube	7/10	8.5/10
14:00	Facetime w/ Mum + Spencer for rundown of tonight's events	3/10	10/10 (Spencer was testing me)
15:00	Getting ready	2.5/10	9/10
16:00	Order Uber to the train station		
17:00	Have a lil anxious cry on the train maybe!?		
18:00	It's launch time.		

30

Late, stressed, and probably underdressed, I prop my phone up on my chest of drawers and nervously examine myself in my front-facing camera. The FaceTime dial tone chirrups away as I call through to the Tranks group.

Eyeing the lens, I wait for them to pick up, digging my hands in just above my hips, and pouting forward, trying out different poses so I can view how tonight's pictures might come out. I'm forcing it though, like twisting the stiff, plastic limbs of a Barbie doll into playing pretend.

The FaceTime dial tone *bleep-bleep-bleeps* out, with no answer. I jab at the screen to redial, because even when I think I look good I need reassurance, some real-life heart-eyed-emoji expressions. Especially tonight. A gust of wind leftover from yesterday's summer storm coughs in through the open window, hitting the back of my legs, hot like bad breath.

But I can feel it. On my bare skin.

Come on, answer, answer.

If Joss and Hev don't pick up this time I'm gonna just have to go without their big-ups; the Uber's booked for four thirty. I'll be wallowing in my insecurity all the way from the back of the Uber, onto the train's first-class carriage and into London, wondering if I've made the right decision all the way up to the sixty-ninth floor of The Shard where, as Anarchy said, all eyes will be on me.

'Fuck sake,' I mutter.

My black, pleather wrap dress is all bunched up at my waist, so I undo the belt round the middle to tie it tighter, which is of *course* the exact moment Joss answers the call. I'm holding both sides of the dress open like leathery bat wings when my mouth drops open.

'Shit, I'm sorry,' he says. 'I didn't see—'

There's a lag in the FaceTime connection and Joss freezes with a hand slapped across his face, one eye still peeking through his fingers. I whip the dress across me again, tying the belt tight, a smile shying away from my lips.

'Didn't seeEe-Ee anything.'

The picture skips forward a few frames as the call tries to stay connected, and in this freeze-frame Joss's eyes are screwed shut, his mouth stretched into a big, dumb grin, like a kid who's been allowed to stay up late to watch the 12A movie with boobs in it.

'SorRrrRRy – internet's shit.'

His voice comes through in scrambled pitches, but as his pixelated face jerks around the screen and the broken sounds of his laughter fill my bedroom, my room glows a little warmer,

Joss's voice chasing away the echoes of the empty house and the doubts that I don't look good enough. As the call tries to connect me to him, I realise that *this*, genuine human connection, and being able to put the sound of their laugh, the smell of their clothes, or the texture of their skin to the face behind a username, is what I've been needing for a long time, what the kind words of faceless strangers in comment sections could never give me.

Meeting Joss and Hev dragged my ego-shattered essence back into my body; when I met them in group therapy, I had to be real.

The call quality sharpens a little and I can see Joss's cheeks are dappled red.

'It's fine, you can look now.' I laugh, fiddling with my belt, unable to hold his stare. 'But can we not make a big deal out of this?'

'Me? Make a big deal out of virtually walking in on you nearly naked. Never.' Joss beams teasingly, laughing low as he plants his hands behind his head. 'Hi.'

'Hi,' I say. 'So, what do you think'

'Girl, wowwwww.' Heather's face pops up in a video square as she joins the call, all tits and chins because she's got her MacBook resting on her stomach. 'You look bossy as fuck, like you mean *business*.'

'Hi, Hev,' I say.

'Alright?' Heather struggles against the mound of cushions behind her as she props herself upright. 'So, go on, how'd you do it in the end? Your legs look fab, like, I'd never be able to tell.'

As the last words leave her lips, her eyes bulge wide. 'Not that if you decided to go out without covering your scars, it wouldn't be okay. I don't mean that,' she gabbles. 'You know how brave and beautiful I think—'

'Hev, seriously.' I stop her. 'I *know* what you mean.'

Joss clears his throat, clearly only just remembering why I called in the first place – and that it was their messages of encouragement that gave me the guts to go out bare-skinned tonight anyway. 'God, yeah. You look great.' He swallows.

'You didn't remember we were going tightless tonight, did you?' Hev says.

'Well, no, but only because I always think she looks beautiful. You always look beautiful, Almond.'

'Thank you,' I say, twisting to hide my face and show the camera the backs of my calves, the dress tapering in with a neat hem just above the knee. 'I had to YouTube some tutorials. Honestly, it was like I was in hair and make-up for a movie or something.'

That'll do. I won't bore them with how I palmed primer all over my legs, dabbed long-wear concealer over the scars, baked the make-up, slathered on a special body foundation – that I had to scour the internet to find a vegan version of – then dusted them with powder *and* setting spray. I know I'm not going a hundred per cent natural, maybe not even seventy per cent but it's what I feel comfortable with at the moment. Removing one layer of cover at a time. Tonight, it's the tights. One day, I hope my practice of self-love will have seeped in bone-deep, enough for me to show every last inch of my imperfect skin without a mask of cosmetic-counter cover-up, but not tonight. We're not there yet.

I peer down at my handiwork, my confidence faltering as I imagine making my entrance at the launch. From far away I reckon someone would guess I had cute freckles, skin like speckled eggshell. But close up you can see dry, broken skin, claggy with layers upon layers of make-up on top, like preschool papier mâché. The worst of my scars, the darkest and deepest that have healed badly, still look visible if you stand close enough.

'You really think they look okay?' I say, struggling with self-doubt.

When I'm met with silence, I glance up, seeing the picture's frozen again just as Heather's voice breaks through with a, 'Girrrrrrrl. YoU . . . loooOok eleven out . . . ten,'

'Legs eleven!' she cries, the video finally unfuzzing so I can see her beaming face right up close to the camera.

'Thanks, Hev,' I say, peeking at the ceiling to stop the tears in my eyes from running my mascara. 'Joss, you're still frozen so I'm assuming you're saying "Yes bitch, slay," to which I say, thank you – thank you very much. And with that' – I lean into the camera, flicking away the notification telling me Aleksander has arrived outside in his Mercedes Benz – 'I must bid you goodbye, my Uber's here.' I suck in a breath through my teeth. 'Wish me luck, love you guys.'

With Heather happy-dance-waving then hanging up, and Joss's video feed still a black square, I go to cut the call. But before

I can, a still of Joss's earnest face fills the screen, his cap balled in his hands, cloudburst eyes intensely fixed on the lens.

The connection snatches up the sound but leaves the video lagging behind. 'They're gonna love you, Hazelnut. Who wouldn't?'

I stare into his eyes, my finger poised above the red button, and smile one of those kind of smiles that feels like you've spent the whole day stretched out under the sun. Warmth shimmers down my spine.

'Bye,' I softly say, hanging up and slipping my phone into my clutch.

I do a quick bag check – keys, purse, lippy – then switch off the lights and lock up, sliding into the back of Aleksander's car.

'Almond?' he asks, blinking at me in the rear-view.

'Yes.' I smile. 'That's me.'

31

'I wasn't driving the actual train into London, okay, Spencer?' I say into my phone, ending the call as I step out of the shadowy car park and hitch myself up into the back of his car, about to continue this bullshit face-to-face. I slam the door on the bustle of people, the honking of traffic and the squelch of tyres running over the rainy street. I lean between the two headrests so I can say the rest to Spencer's face. 'I can't do anything about someone throwing themselves onto the tracks in Chippenham, can I?'

'Selfish.' He tuts, indicating to pull out of the short stay. I don't even think he means me. 'Seatbelt,' he says with a click of his fingers, pressing one to his temple, wincing at the blaring chimes of the car's safety alarm.

'You seem stressed,' I say, nonchalant.

I snap a picture of the gloomy, rain-slicked windshield, Spencer's frown lines visible even in profile as he stares out the passenger window about to cut up a black cab. I send the picture to the Tranks chat.

Almond

Just arrived in the big smoke. My chauffer's a bit of a dick.

'Whatever, I am stressed,' he snips. 'Remind me, who're you wearing again?'

'Uh.' I glance down at my second-hand H&M dress that Callie picked out for me in a Red Cross charity shop last year. 'It's vintage,' I say, its well-worn seams fitting snug and familiar on my body. I knew my adrenals were already going to be working overtime tonight, so I didn't want to add the pressure of a barely breathable corset or the faff of a stick-on bra into the mix.

How I'm wearing my clothes means more to me now than who I'm wearing.

'Hmm. So *you* not to be wearing anyone on trend.'

He's straight-up getting ignored for that. Out the window, people duck under bus shelters and scaffolding, getting out of that spitty kind of rain that spritzes you soaked. Spencer talks *at* me, jerky and stop-start like his awful driving. As I 'Mmhmm' and 'Oh, right', pretending to pay attention to who's on tonight's guestlist and which journalists' asses I'm supposed to kiss, I gaze out of the window at the people and people and people of London. Everything in everyone. Hijabs, buzzcuts, albinos, androgynous, melanin, afro, steampunk. Two boys kissing. Brown-and-white siblings, their mum with a sleeve of tattoos. Old lady with a Mohican. Man with a parrot on his shoulder. White-haired gents sharing a paper on a bench. Football lads. Mums and mums, and dads and dads. The most gorgeously, glowing lady with a big, pregnant belly, wheeling herself up the ramp of a bus. People just being people, being alive. And I'm one of them, one of us.

I duck down, run my hands over my legs like I've got magic in my fingers, goosebumps prickling the backs of my arms as a nervous jolt of excitement zips through me. I'm about to be my real self in public, the hyper-public that is influencer world. Granted, Mum and Spencer won't be thrilled that I've chosen the biggest night of their careers for me to go full peacock on them, but I'm ready for people to meet *me*. If the last couple of weeks have taught me anything, it's that it feels infinitely worse to lie for a living than to be yourself and give less of a fuck about what people think. I hold an imaginary interview in my head with one of the journalist names Spencer was hurling at me a minute ago, Harper Atkins, imagining leaning down into her little voice recorder like, *Yes, it's true. I, Almond Brown, am also a farting, flawed, annoying, vile little human being just like the rest of you.*

'Hello?' Spencer drones over his shoulder, cutting my internal exclusive short and bringing me back into the stuffy car. 'We're here.'

As I slip down off the backseat and step out into the courtyard in front of The Shard, Spencer drops his car keys into the open palm of the valet who does not look happy to be dressed head to toe in a velvet suit of VeGlow's signature colour. Egg yolk yellow. I glance up the matching yellow carpet, sparsely lined with photographers and a handful of fans, and feel my posture plunge as the glimmer of my confidence dims slightly.

Biding time before I have to face everyone, I check my phone.

Electra Lyons

Just wanted to say good luck for tonight. You've got this! Just smile and wave boys, smile and wave. I know you can plow through all the bullshit xxxxxxxx

Omg *plough

Glimmer back in full glam, I quickly reply with a string of heart emojis, aware that people know I've arrived, and Spencer won't be distracted with schmoozing the paparazzi for too long. I bare my teeth at the valet in a *Yikes* face, to which he chuckles, tossing Spencer's keys in the air, just as a gut-curdling, 'WE LOVE YOU,' scares the absolute shit out of me, making the valet chuckle some more. I'm about to ask Spencer where the hell Mum is, because shouldn't we be pictured arriving together and all that, but he's already off, sashaying up the yellow carpet.

Okay, let's go. Robot mode *On*. I slink one leg across the other as I walk, my face blank because, guess what, I don't wanna be here and I'm not giving any of these leech people a smile, even if I *am* technically working for VeGlow right now. That's the best thing about being in this business; it's perfectly acceptable for you to walk around with a face like a slapped arse – encouraged even.

A few paces in front of me, Spencer whirls around to show off his pastel purple Prada two-piece to the dwindling crowd. His expression mirrors mine – lips zipped tight, apathetic, looking a little constipated. I must've missed some subtle silent communication in that spin though, because he whips his head over his shoulder, eyes blitzing at me, and darts a look over to a group of girls leaning against the barriers. *En-gage-ment*, I realise his eyes are screaming at me. Obediently, I strut over to the gaggle of girls, all gasps and giggles as I turn my extra special, superfan smile on for them.

I wave. 'Heyyyyy.' Dead inside.

I try to swallow the bitterness I feel towards Mum, Spencer, the industry, and even these probably lovely people for bringing me here, so exposed and scrutinised, when where I want to be is curled up in my comfys watching TV with Joss in his parent-free house.

Ohmigod-she's-here-it's-her-that's-Almond-Brown-I-love-you-can-we-get-a-selfie?

For the next few minutes I pose for selfies, blinking manically, teeth fixed in place, wondering if any of my body make-up got smudged getting out of the car, but not wanting to look down to draw attention to it.

'Sorry ladies, theydies and gaydies!' Screwing his own smile onto his face, Spencer leans down to my level. 'Get to the tabloids,' he says. Making it look playful, he *shoves* me towards a group of men, looking either too creepily excited to be here or so bored it's goddamn rude. No in between. 'And *what* is that splattered all over your legs, is that dirt?'

My heart shrivels up and drops into my stomach. After all the layers of make-up, encouragement, patience and self-love I applied to myself today, Spencer Dorsey says I look like dirt and instantly I feel like dirt.

‘I’ll see you upstairs,’ he hisses.

After posing for the professionals and being dazedly shunted through The Shard’s airport-tight security, pausing between pat-downs to sing Happy Birthday through FaceTime to a security guard’s cousin, I take tentative steps across the marbled floor, wondering where Spencer went. Inside it’s eerily still, the arctic blast of aircon tingling against my skin.

I steady myself against a thick marble pillar and take my phone out of my clutch, expecting to see a text to tell me he’s gone to the bathroom and to wait there, but he’s not here digitally either. I lift a flute of champagne off a tray held by another yolky-suited man, double-pressing the call button and hoping the lift arrives before he realises I only *look* eighteen.

‘Er, miss,’ he stutters, just as the doors ping open. ‘Can I see your—’

‘Cheers!’ I beam, jumping into the lift and jabbing my finger into the panel of buttons.

The doors shut with a *sklunk* and I’m closed in on all sides by an army of my endless mirrored selves. Raising the glass of champagne to my lips, I tip it down my throat in one go, warm fizz dissolving through me. On the sixty-eighth floor, I step out of the lift and follow a rustic trail of wildflowers towards the buzz of soulless house music and the empty babbling of people from the industry pretending not to despise one another.

‘Over there,’ a woman with an iPad demands, herding me through an assault course of photo ops that have been set up in the entrance.

First, I'm photographed in front of a white backdrop with VeGlow's tagline printed across it in a blocky, garish font. '100% Vegan. 100% Plastic free. 100% Glowing.' As I turn, the words sear on the backs of my eyelids, imprinted there by the blinding camera flash.

'Okay, now side-on.'

I need more champagne.

Turning to my left so they can get me in profile, I lock eyes with a massive cardboard cut-out me. I stare into my own unblinking eyes, seeing an airbrushed, basic stranger. My flawless skin's had the pigment drained out of it, almost so I could 'pass' as white.

'Good. Moody, pensive, I like it. Keep doing that,' the photographer says.

My eyes flick to Mum's cardboard clone, posed with her hands on her hips, adjacent to cardboard me.

Thrown by the paper doll versions of us, I stumble and smile my way through the next photo op, on the outside influencing my ass off, but on the inside struck numb by mine and my cut-out's starkest difference: our skin. Hers flawless, mine very much flawed but uncannily covered. Suddenly, I'm acutely aware of the flashbulb illuminating even the faintest of my scars or any slight mismatch of my cover-up job.

'Okay, that'll do. I think we've got all we need.' The iPad woman strides over to me, her pale face looming in front of the studio lights, legs posed in an upside-down V shape as she thrusts her chin up and lowers her gaze, eyelashes batting in thought. 'Hmm,' she says, scrutinising my legs. With one last rove of her eyes up and down my body, she pulls out her phone and starts tapping away at it, staring at me straight-faced. 'Did Paisley approve this . . . outfit?'

'Um, no?' I cross one leg over the other, trying and failing to minimise their exposure. 'I don't think so.'

'Hmm. The photos will be sent to your manager for approval within twenty-four hours. We'll need you again later to pose with Eve Fairchild.'

'You mean my mum?' I snort. 'Where is she anyway?'

But my sarcasm falls on deaf, white-gold studded ears as she turns on her heel and flutters off without answering. Rude.

I sigh out the breath clenched in my sucked-in gut, sending a rush of blood round my ears that pulses with the background beat of house music. I lift a champagne flute off a tray as a server glides past and slink into a darkened corner by the cloakroom, sifting through the crowd of influentials, trying to find Mum, the only constant in all this contrived chaos. Or even Imogen. Which is silly because, as *if* Celeste would let her own daughter support us after we cost them nearly half a million followers. Naively, I kind of thought maybe Immy would sneak along anyway, in spite of her mum, just to be my friend. I think we're both trying to be that for each other. Flicking through Immy's storyless socials though, I realise she's gone radio silent.

Settling into my inconspicuous corner, I look up, scanning for Mum again, when my phone buzzes in my hand.

Hev

How's it going??? Blinded anyone yet?

(by your beauty obv, don't get done for GBH)

Almond

Not great. Not as awful as I imagined though. I know they're not but it feels like everyone's looking at me

Hev

If they are it's because it's your event!! Andddd because you're:

She sends a screenshot of the dictionary definition of beautiful, highlighting its list of synonyms, which reels a smile out of me.

Hev

All of the above.

Enjoy it, soak it up. This could be your last ME event before you get tf out of iPhone la la land

Anyway how is it??

Almond

Honestly, I'm embarrassed to be here. All this ridiculousness for some jizzed up moisturiser

Don't let my mum put my follower count on my headstone if I die of shame xox

Hev

Tell me they do not put jizz in it!?

Almond

*JAZZED omfg

As I put my phone away finally, I get a glimpse of Mum across the room in the centre of a crowd that's pretending it's not a crowd. She's surrounded by hovering Z-listers – chatting and snapping in the hopes Mum'll be in the corner of their selfie or laugh at one of their overloud jokes – like a spoiled strawberry surrounded by fruit flies, in her pearly pink, silk cami dress.

Leering over her shoulder, Spencer catches my eye as I sip down the glittery warmth of my next champagne. He's probably waiting for the instant Mum's finished talking to a woman waving one of those dicto-thingys under her nose so he can whisper in her ear.

Look at Almond just standing there, just breathing, and in such bad lighting at that.

Okay, Mum's shaking hands with the journo annnnd, just as predicted, there's Spencer *immediately* puckering up to her ear, so close her diamond earrings are almost dancing on his tongue. His gaze sears down to my legs as his mouth moves, and it's like I can feel it sizzling my skin. My guess is he's seething about the turnout of the press photos because of my scars and is about to send Mum over here to apply some parental disappointment, her face falling with the gravity of what he's saying, but instead she scrambles into a recovery smile as she taps an ex *Made in Chelsea* cast member on the shoulder, getting wrapped up in a squealing, sequinned hug.

While she's distracted, Spencer marches over to me with acupuncture precision in his steps and bustles me into the cloakroom. In the quilted quiet provided by the walls of coats, the tinging glasses and cascading chatter of the party fades away, and I'm faced with Spencer's flared nostrils as he looks me up and down, adrenalin chasing the champagne bubbles through my veins.

'What. Have. You. Done?' Spencer says, his St Tropez face as crinkled up as dried orange peel. 'It didn't look so bad outside, it looked like something to be washed off, but *God*, under the lights – just look at you.' He hooks his knuckle into his mouth, shaking his head.

Wait, what!? Is he genuinely concerned?

'I'm okay, don't worry. It's the skin condition I've been seeing Dr Wallace about, the scratching when I—'

'Not *that*,' he scoffs. 'I know all about that. Who d'you think found you a psychiatrist with a background in dermatology? Hello? I mean what on earth possessed you to do a *leg reveal*' – he air quotes – 'tonight!? Of all nights! When you're launching a *skin perfecting cream*. Are you serious? Are you actually serious with me, right now?'

'But I'm getting better, and I just thought—'

'Zip. No, no,' he chuckles, miming locking his lips like some trashy soap villain. I think he's actually gone insane. 'I don't *care* what you thought. I care that Harper Atkins from *Glam* magazine has been waiting to interview you for ten minutes now, and all her questions are going to be wondering if this is some sort of side-effect of Serenity or something – I can't even pay off the press to shop out the scars because there'll be fan photos.'

Spencer paces past a wall of faux fur and suit jackets, talking entirely to himself now as I stand, bearing the inferno of shame that's engulfing my body. My fingers twitch at my sides. 'We're going to have to go down the social experiment route. Come clean and say that you've been struggling with this for a while but that we hid it from the public until today because it was all part of the campaign, mock up some kind of before-and-after photos. Okay, I can make this work.'

'But there isn't an *after* yet? They're still healing.'

'As if that matters? Do you actually believe that Kim K's ass looks that way from shapewear alone? Reality can be what we want it to be, sweetie.'

And with that, the little seed of self-love that these last few weeks have planted within me gets yanked up from the root, my self-esteem decayed into worm dirt in its place. I try to cultivate some of Hev's sunshine from earlier, or the way Joss made me feel wanted, but as Spencer reads aloud the Notes App draft he's typing for my supposed social experiment announcement, all I feel is blackest night. I shiver.

'Right, I'll finalise a script tomorrow and pray that Paisley approves. Give me your phone. I'll have to lay the groundwork now, put out some vague tweets that'll get people talking. And anyway, *someone's* got to be promoting this product.' He sighs, placing a finger in his bum-crack chin dimple. 'You know, it's funny. You'd think anyone who'd just become brand ambassador of the biggest vegan-whatever beauty brand would be tweeting non-stop about it like it's their job. Oh wait, it *is* your job. Your only job. And once again I'm forced to step in and save your ungrateful ass. What do I always say? En-gage . . .'

'. . . Ment,' I finish, numb to the slip of a tear down my cheek. I think of Mum and how much this means to her, how hard she's worked, snakes of guilt and shame writhing in my gut. 'Do you need me to talk to anyone? Harper something?'

'That's the spirit,' Spencer snarls, my phone clacking against his phone as he drops it into his jacket pocket. 'But no. I prefer it when you don't do the talking anyway. I'll fob Harper off with your mother, hint that she's seeing some ITV gameshow host or something. I think we've seen more than enough of you.' His eyes pointedly bungy jump down my legs, thigh to ankle then back again. He takes a step towards me, his aftershave a sting in the back of my throat. 'So, congrats, you've got the rest of the night off. You'll get your phone back when I've finished doing your job for you, okay?'

Saying nothing, I sink to the floor, covered by coat sleeves and designer cuffs as Spencer spins on his heel and leaves me alone and on fire. The thought that I'm cities away from Joss and the night I could've been having with him, where I'd be accepted, touched, and held with love, make-upless, naked in every way that's meaningful, seems to draw the ghostly hanging coats closer around me. With a sob, I thrash out, clawing my hand across them for something to snare. My nails hit against something stashed in a jacket, making a cool, metallic clunk. Hoping for a minibar bottle, I swat through the rich-people pockets until I hear the clunk again and slip my hand into the lining of an Armani suit jacket. Spencer's words slither around my skull as I pull out a whole hip flask full of slish-slosh sounds and— oops, there goes its cold metal kiss on my lips. I gulp. Wince.

Fuck, what is this? Whiskey?

I throw some more back, waiting to feel its smooth numbness.

32

Hiccup. 'So, what do you think? Is this still just a talking stage? Should we get together?' I ask, desperate for Nevaeh's opinion on me and Joss after basically dissecting my heart in front of her as she touched up her make-up in the bathroom.

The toilet flushes and Nevaeh struts out of the cubicle, a finger holding one nostril closed as she sniffs up with Dyson standard suction through the other one.

Standing beside me at the sinks, she dusts white powder off her cupid's bow and asks me, 'How old are you again?'

The elbow propping me up slips into the basin and it's like I watch myself in a superzoom slow-mo bash my face against the mirror. My reflection's all droopy-lidded and slack-jawed. A sack of sad.

'Okay, ow?' I scoff, fake laughing so she doesn't think that actually *really* fucking hurt. 'How old d'you think I am?'

I clear my throat, embarrassed by my slurred speech, though

I can't stop my tongue stirring the words around my mouth into a thick, stringy stew.

Nevaeh studies me in the mirror a long time as she glazes her lips with gold carat gloss.

'Too young to be here, mixed up in this shit,' she says after a dramatic pause, with a satisfying pop of her lips. God, she's sexy. And cool. She looks like influencing and money is the exact kind of shit *she* should be mixed up in. She's like nineties Naomi Campbell, except millennial and midsize.

'So, what d'you think? Am I being too trusting? I *really*, really like him though.'

'I don't know, babe. But look, I'm going on to someplace else now, so you'll have to make a new bathroom friend.' *Another one?* Nevaeh's already my second.

The girl before was a better listener.

Oh my God, did I just say that out loud!?

Eyes flicking up from her phone, she stares at me with this stilted sense of maternity, thumbs still tapping out a text like they're possessed. She sighs. 'Right, you and this Josh boy. Honestly, I just think people act dumb when they're all up in their feelings. That's you. And your boy too – he's probably as confused and scared as you are to get involved with someone like you.'

'Someone like me?'

'Someone famous. Someone who everyone else already has a piece of. Trust me, this life really shows you who's in it for the real thing and who's just clout-chasing, okay.' Placing her cheek on mine, she soullessly smacks her lips at my ear. 'Mwah. I'm going now. It was nice meeting you, babe.'

'Bye, Nevaeh, bye – thanks for everything . . . babe?' What's left in this dude's hip flask tinkles against the metal as I wave her out of the toilets. 'Wait, we already met?' I mumble as she disappears through the swing door.

I shrug, wincing as I drip the last few fiery drops of whiskey down my throat.

Now what?

No phone and I'm all out of alcohol. Trudging into a cubicle, I bang down the toilet seat and sit on it, cupping my chin in my hands. Well, this is boring. How long was I talking to Nevaeh? And what was that girl's name before her? Hannah? Hayley? No *Harper.* She was nice, listening *so* intently to everything I said. I drum my nails against the sides of the cubicle, realising I literally have no concept of what time it is right now. Wait, didn't Nevaeh say she was leaving for an after-party? Like *leaving?* How long have I been MIA, bathroom drinking from a stolen hip flask at my own launch party? Oh, God.

I stumble out of the cubicle and feel my way along the cool tiles to the swing door, my fingertips just grazing it when someone pushes through from the other side.

'Oh gosh, sorry. Hello?' Mum's face appears in the gap between the door and the wall. 'Jesus, Almond,' she hisses, letting her airy-fairy interview voice float right out the window when she realises it's only me. 'I've been looking for you everywhere.'

'Yet the toilets are the last place you look?'

'Well, I didn't expect you to be *hiding* in here . . .' She trails off, fanning herself, flustered. Her eyes narrow at me over her nails. 'Are you a bit squiffy, darling?'

'I'll be honest with you, Mum,' I say, lurching towards her. 'I'm a lot squiffy.'

'Okay, come on. We're getting out of here,' she mumbles, linking her arm through mine as she confirms the Uber pick-up point on her phone. I note the spontaneous physical contact, how she doesn't even flinch when my chin nearly smudges make-up onto her white blazer, her un-sucked-in stomach, and I narrow my eyes right back at her.

'Mum? Are *you* a bit squiffy?'

Holding her hand up to pinch her thumb and forefinger together, I notice that pale band of skin where her wedding ring used to be again, as she squeaks into my ear, 'Teeny-weeny-incy-wincy-wee bit, yeah.'

We laugh, barging out of the swing door and through the dimly lit, emptying event space. There're only a few people left: guests loudly saying their goodbyes, exchanging details – 'my people will call your people!' – and staff, dressed in those God-awful yellow suits, cleaning up the place.

'So, how was the party?' I whisper. 'Bit early to be over, isn't it?'

Mum sighs. 'A boring success, I think.' The tip of her coffin-shaped acrylic jabs the lift's call button. 'Paisley didn't even bother making an appearance, but the product's going to sell, that's the main thing. And what's all this about you staging some sort of social experiment? I thought we left that kind of content in the 2010s.'

'Spencer's idea,' I say, shivering with self-consciousness all over again, grateful that Mum's actually way more drunk than a teeny-weeny-incy-wincy-wee bit – *too* drunk to properly take in the ravaged extent of my excoriation, the make-up barely concealing any of it now. She probably still thinks my legs look like the reference photos we sent Dr Wallace months ago when my problems only manifested themselves as a nettly, red rash on the backs of my knees, a kitten scratch on the shin.

'Where is he anyway?' I ask, standing on tiptoe to look over Mum's head. 'Please tell me I don't have to endure a two-hour long train journey with that Parma-violet-looking prick.'

'He looked dreadful, didn't he?' Mum guffaws, the lift dinging as the doors open. They close, and it's just me and Mum and the million mirrored versions of us trapped in the lift. 'But no, he's meeting a Tinder match at a bar in Shoreditch, so it's just me and you riding first class, baby.'

'Cool,' I say, avoiding eye contact, shying into the corner of the lift as Mum flicks through clips people have posted from tonight. Suddenly, remembering Spencer's reaction, my mind exaggerating the scene with finger pointing and chest-rumbling cackles, I'm not so sure I'm ready for Mum to see my scars. But I *am* ready to expose that nasty tongue-twisting leech for the fake friend I always knew he was. 'Mum, about Spencer ...'

In the back of the Uber, I relay the cloakroom confrontation and end up having to convince Mum not to fire our so-called manager over the phone while she's four porn-star martinis deep.

'What a horrible overreaction. I'm so sorry I wasn't there,' Mum's saying, backspacing on the paragraph I just stopped her typing out to Spencer. 'The pictures would've been fine. You've been seeing Dr Wallace for three months now and your scars weren't that bad to begin with anyway, darling. Let me see.'

My kneecaps press painfully together as Mum hovers her torch over my shins.

'Oh, Almond.' Mum sits back, her face drawn with distress, and for a second I expect it to morph into disgust the way Spencer's had, but she just shakes her head, reaching across to take my hand. 'Why didn't you *tell* me?'

'I couldn't. I didn't want to worry you, and you've been so busy with the campaign and it's so important to you. I just . . . I kept thinking I'd feel better soon – which I do – and it would go away and nobody would even notice.'

'Oh my God,' Mum sighs out, barely audible. 'And I didn't.' She unbuckles her seatbelt and switches to the middle seat, tucking my head onto her shoulder. 'You must've been in so much pain,' she says, more to herself.

'It's okay, Mum. I'm okay now. I seriously am getting better. The Tranquillity sessions really are helping,' I say, thinking mostly of Joss and Heather.

'Okay. I'm going to see if I can get you in for some more dermatology treatments with Dr Wallace.'

I nod. Lulled by the rise and fall of Mum's chest, I blink in and out of sleep as the lights of London flicker by the window on our way to Paddington. We thank our driver, then swagger through the station in our full – if a bit faded – launch-night glam, grabbing avo baguettes from a vending machine. When the train screeches to a halt in a gust of oily black fumes, we scamper to the other end of the platform for the first-class carriage, collapsing back in our seats, breathless.

'Here's your phone by the way,' Mum says, skidding it onto the little fold-out tray I've opened up a bag of crisps on.

'Ta.' I go to unlock it, but the screen stays black, the battery dead. 'Cheers then, Spence,' I say, looking sideways at Mum, splayed in the window seat as I worry at a pouch of lip skin between my teeth, psyching myself up to say the thing I *need* to say before all the courage I've guzzled back tonight sobers out of me. These past few weeks I've seen snatches of *my* mum, pre-2019 before hustle culture took her, and before 2020 when we all got locked inside and hyperfocused on how the outside world perceives us. I know the way I feel about this whole mess of being an influential figure echoes within her somewhere too. 'Mum?'

'Mmhmm?'

'Can I ask you something?'

'Shoot,' Mum says, her own reflection glassy in her pupils as she watches herself boomerang across her phone screen. For once I'm glad she isn't looking at me.

'Why'd you do it?' I find myself whispering. 'You know, all the social media stuff. Why'd you even start?'

Locking her phone, Mum stuffs the last hunk of her baguette

into her mouth and stares out the window, chewing slowly, scrunching the wrapper up into a tiny, crackly ball of plastic. I wait, watching her in the window, an itch skittering up the back of my neck. After a minute, she inhales sharply through her nose and faces me as a dark rush of trees hurtles past.

'Did I ever tell you what I wanted to be when I grew up?' she asks, folding her arms like she's made a Big Decision in her head.

'Nope. What?'

'A midwife.'

'You!?' I shovel a handful of crisps into my gob, laughing. 'As if. You can't even watch *Casualty* without heaving.'

'Oh shh. I even completed my first year at uni, you know. With a distinction.' She turns her bottom lip out and tugs on her blazer collar, playing at being smug. I giggle but I'm actually kind of shocked. Proud even?

'So, what happened? Why are you delivering ASOS discounts now instead of babies?'

Mum smiles sadly, goes quiet for a minute, and all I can hear is the rattle of the tracks and the tinny trickle of trap music coming from some guy's headphones a few rows in front.

'Mum got cancer,' she says eventually. 'Your grandmother. Hazel.'

Hazel? Mum never mentions her, the grandmother I never got to meet. I only know her as my mum's mum and my middle namesake, but that's it. She died before I was born and Mum never talks about her. Maybe I'm about to find out why.

'So you dropped out?' I ask, one eyebrow creeping up.

'I had to – there was no one else to look after her. My dad died when I was three and I'm an only child, like you. Like your dad.' Her fingers feather lightly across her collarbone as she gazes out the window again, and I can see from her reflection she's faraway in thought. 'Me and your dad, we kind of found each other not long after that, became our own family. I was nineteen, your nan was in remission, and your dad and me, we'd just got our first flat – God, it was this poky, little box in Easton. But I was happy, darling, free. And after everything with Mum the first time round – all the hospital stays, the endless hours of chemo, even that bleachy hospital *smell* – I kind of didn't want to go back to midwifery.'

'I don't blame you,' I murmur, sucked into the story. I tuck my feet up under me, curling into Mum's side.

'Moving to the flat in Easton was lonely, though,' Mum says, crunching a crisp. 'Your dad was doing his carpentry apprenticeship and I was stuck at home, scouring the paper for job ads every day. Actually, my first-ever video was a sort of jokey, sarcastic virtual CV that I uploaded to Myspace.' Mum cringes, screwing her eyes tight and pouty frowning. 'Unlisted now, of course.'

'That bad it's unlisted? You're definitely showing me.'

'Oh, it's probably still out there somewhere. Once something's on the internet, it doesn't belong to you any more, does it?' Her gaze, deep with nostalgia, washes over me, and she swallows, speaking quieter now. 'I don't know how or why but that video just blew up. And this was before going viral was a *thing* that happens every day. And then I had all these people messaging me asking for updates and advice videos, and the more requests and views I got, the more I started watching videos of other people and commenting on their stuff. It was therapeutic, darling. I had a community where nobody knew me, nobody wanted to ask me how Mum was doing or how I was *coping*.' She shudders. 'Hate that word. Online I could just be the funny girl who made that CV video. So I filmed some more, just Q&As and tag videos at first, but I poured my all into them and people *liked* me. As I got more followers, I started blogging, then vlogging.' She bows her head, a curtain of blonde feathery bangs hiding her face. 'You know the rest.'

'Yeah. I never knew it was because Hazel – I mean Grandma, got ill.' I nod slowly. 'And, okay, this sounds like I'm starting a fight, but I'm not. I just need to know . . . why I had to be a part of it. If *you* loved it so much for you, how did I come into it? Why . . .' *Oh for fuck's sake, just say it!* 'Why did you want this for me?'

'I . . . oh, Almond,' Mum gasps, pinching her nose to hold in a sob. 'Give me a minute.'

Listening to Mum sniffle and dig around in her bag for a tissue, I wish I could cram the question back into my mouth. I just had to go and ruin it didn't I, us getting along, being friends.

When she opens her mouth to speak, an announcement comes over the tannoy.

'You know what,' I say, cutting in while her breath's still snatched. 'We don't have to talk about it. We can just pretend I never said anything, and—'

Mum shakes her head, smooths her thumb over my knuckles and I know she has to say it now, before the moment's gone.

'There's a reason there aren't any pictures of Hazel in the house, why I don't often visit her grave.' Her eyes flick up to the roof of the carriage to stop the tears in her eyes from falling. 'I was never hungry, never cold. And she loved me. She was a good mum.' She pauses, her eyes searching the ceiling like she's choosing her words extra carefully. 'But she was old-fashioned. Conservative and stuck in her ways.'

Digging my heels up into the seat, I wrap my arms around my knees, wanting to bury into myself, to muffle out what Mum's about to say because I can already guess what's coming.

'She kicked me out,' Mum whispers. 'Put her only daughter on the streets for falling in love.'

She looks down, won't say the rest. So I say it for her.

'Because dad was black.'

Nodding, Mum blows her nose into a biodegradable VeGlow napkin. 'She said she didn't have any problem with people of colour – that's not the way she worded it back then, but we won't go there – but she didn't want me getting involved with *one of them*.' Mum does air quotes as if I won't know *she's* not the one chatting that outdated shit. As she does, I grab her hand and fold her fingers into mine. Between quiet sobs she tries to get the next part out. 'Because she said ... she said it wouldn't be fair on any children we'd have. *Half-castes*. She thought bringing biracial children into the world would be cruel because they wouldn't get treated the same as white kids, wouldn't have the same opportunities, would be ... ugly.' Mum's head drops and she takes in a few long, trembling breaths. 'It's like she'd already decided their lives wouldn't be worth living before they'd even had a chance to try living it.'

The train clatters towards home as the story of how my mum, *this* mum, came to be plays out in my head. My mind conjures an image of Hazel from the small, square passport photo I found in the top drawer of Mum's bedside table years ago, her harsh, drawn together brows just visible under a straight-edged fringe, her hair fine and auburn like Mum's is naturally. Thin-lipped and neat-nosed, irises like lily pads. I always thought she looked hauntingly beautiful and that I wished I'd known her.

Now I picture this woman calling my dad the N-word and forcing my mum out of her home, alone with no family left.

No wonder Mum let herself be adopted by strangers online.

'My life matters,' I say eventually, lifting my chin up, because Mum's truth doesn't shrink me or shame me down. It makes me proud. Because I'm here, because I'm doing it, because I'm *me* in all my mixedness magic. And no matter how many copycat therealalmondbrown, or almondhazelbrownofficial accounts crop up, or how many times someone's catfished with my photo on dating apps, or shared, downloaded, reuploaded my face for likes, or has a weird folder of screenshots of me on their phone, I'll always be me, existing in my own little slice of life.

Mum nods, as if she can hear my thoughts. 'Exactly. If only she could've seen what a beautiful, bold, brilliant daughter I'd have. And I guess I just wanted the rest of the world to see that too.' She smooths a hand over my forehead, whirling one of my curls round her finger and tucking it behind my ear. 'You know why I snuck her name in as your middle name? So that a little part of her would always be with you, through all your successes, all your wins. So you could prove her wrong, just by being.'

'Love you, Mum,' I say as I fall into her. Mid burying my face into her shoulder, I gasp, remembering she's wearing a *white* blazer.

'What?' she says, double chinning as she follows my horrified stare to her shoulder pad now covered with the Neapolitan smear of my foundation, blush, and highlight. 'Oh, bugger. Never mind, I'll get it dry-cleaned. I love you too, darling.'

And she hugs me back just as tight.

Two blubbery, bleary-eyed hot messes, we spend the rest of the journey bundled together, scrolling through the *VeGlowXEveAlmond* hashtag, zooming in on accidental photobombs and reading people's cringey Instagram captions to each other. We never do this any more, sit and talk like friends. Mum's usually silently tapping away at her phone, micromanaging, compartmentalising, not really here. This is better. Infinitely better.

'Sending this pic off to NASA, because I'm a star,' she reads out another caption, sniggering into my hair.

I know – and probably always knew in the tiniest cupboards of my heart – that I'd never get back the old Mum, who I pined for by rewatching earlier vlogs of the woman with frizzy, sunny hair, who shopped exclusively high street and shared her thrifty finds online, who couldn't tell you the difference between a down dog and an up dog. She's gone and that's okay. People change. New doesn't have to mean bad. This new Mum's alright. Not perfect, but anyone who looks like they are? Definitely pretending. I have to accept that this is who she is now and that Mum's just being herself – her name-dropping, forehead-injecting, incense-burning self – and I love her.

'Hey, there aren't any pictures of us on this hashtag, darling, and it was *our* event.' Mum stretches her arm up over the seat as we smile towards the ceiling. 'Sayyyy shitshow.'

Laughter spit-splutters out my mouth as the flash goes off.

'Sorry,' I mutter, composing my face, ready to take another one. But Mum's arm's already down, no pinching, zooming, or distorting.

'I like this one.'

In the picture, Mum's gazing sideways at me and laughter's actually crinkled at the corners of her eyes, despite the efforts of her Botox. Her skin's streaked with teary mascara, and she's open-mouthed smiling, not pouting. My eyes are squinted shut from laughing too, lipstick-chinned with a paint splatter of eyeshadow all over my lids.

On autopilot, I say, 'God, I look awful. Don't you want to take another one?'

'Not at all. You look happy, darling,' Mum says, smiling. 'You know what. I think I want to keep this one just for me.'

33

Darling,
Am heading to hot yoga – need to restore my energy. Alcohol always lowers my frequency. I'm popping by the farmers' market on the way home. Will bring back fresh berries for brunch. Have left some cucumber water and painkillers on your bedside table in case you have a sore head this morning. Don't go back to sleep after reading this!! You'll feel worse later. Try a sun salutation.
Love, Mum xoxo

34

Downing the pint of water Mum's left on my bedside table, I read her note again, eyes skimming over the silky flicks of her handwriting. I don't think I even remember the last time I saw anything handwritten by Mum other than her signature. Even all her Christmas cards are ordered online and typed out.

I sink back into my pillows, late morning sunshine pouring through the window, and I stretch out into it, pointing the tips of my toes and throwing my arms up above my head, my muscles yawning with tired satisfaction. Shielding my eyes from the sun, I laugh out loud as it hits me; I'm free. I get to quit being thereal_almondbrown. I haven't told anybody that yet, but I know I can now. After our chat last night, I genuinely think Mum will let me terminate my contract with Spencer and give up the #ad life without any resentment, maybe even with a little bit of encouragement. The realisation feels like drinking ice-cold orange juice, fresh, exhilarating; a plunge into a pool on a hot day.

Grinning, I grab my phone to message Joss that I'm awake and will be over in the next hour, but I'm met with an unresponsive black screen. I must've forgotten to put it on charge after we got home last night. I fumble among the pile of clothes on the floor for the end of my charger, thinking about Mum's advice about morning yoga. Buoyed up by these glorious Sunday vibes, I get up and clear a space in the middle of the floor. Mum always begins her routines with a mountain pose, so I stand up and relax into it, focusing on my breathing, placing my palms together at my third eye before bowing my head down into a forward fold and wrapping my arms round the backs of my calves. It feels like diving into a pool of white paint. Blank, soothing calm.

After practising my own version of a sun salutation, I collapse back into bed and grab my phone as it wakes up, thumbs tapping the screen impatiently as I wait for it to ask me for my password. Immediately my phone shivers with notifications, my blanket of calm being whipped out from underneath me as I see that familiar crooked username over and over.

anRkey_InCel51

Surprise bitch, bet you thought you'd seen the last of me, right???

I throw my phone onto the pillow, not moving, not breathing as I watch message after message from Anarchy pile up on the screen. They ping in from all through the night into the early hours, and I wait for the incessant vibrating to stop before scrolling all the way to the top of Anarchy's one-sided conversation.

How naive could I have been? Thinking they'd be satisfied with just that one-time payment and then forget all about me, moving on to bully their next victim into being extorted.

anRkey_InCel51

Don't think I've been sitting here twiddling my thumbs either. I've been watching you.

Ever the ungrateful famewhore. You have over three million followers and you barely post!? So entitled and undeserving.

As a token of my ingratitude, I've been working on a little launch night surprise for you.

Here's an exlusive preview

Breaking out in a cold sweat under my duvet, I tremble as I scroll to a stop at Anarchy's next message, staring at the video file. My brain intrusively shoves that doctored image Anarchy already blackmailed me with to the forefront of my mind, panicking at the prospect of a faked, full feature porno. No, no, *no*. Like, *how*? What editing software or app would allow that? I stare at my phone in horror. There's no thumbnail or title for the video, no way to prepare myself for what I'm about to see.

So, I press play.

The scene takes place in an obvious hotel room – swirly

carpet, blank walls – with an older man, naked and erect, sitting at the end of a large bed, his chest hair grey, head hair black. He pats the space on the bed between his thighs, which makes me zip mine together, cross them and squeeze tight, my body reacting like there's a physical threat even though I'm sitting alone in my room.

On screen, the actress struts one leg in front of the camera, then the other, her skin silkily shaved and slathered with oil, unblemished, no scars, which sends a waterfall of relief tumbling through me because it's *not* me – which is ridiculous because *of course* it's not me. Yet as the girl walks a little further and the tops of her thighs come into the frame, then her butt, the scoop of her lower back, finally revealing the ends of long, curly, chocolate-coloured hair just like mine, I feel reality sieving from my mind.

She can't be me.

The camera pans up *my* hair spiralling down the girl's back, and when the guy that looks old enough to be her granddad says, 'Give us a twirl,' a nauseous, paralysing fear pummels me in the gut. Because it's my face that looks over the girl's shoulder as she teases the camera. *My* lips that blow a kiss to the lens. I gag.

Her body shape's similar to mine, but not a perfect match – her nipples a little smaller, higher, her belly less wobbly – not that any of that matters because nobody's seen me naked anyway. How will anyone know that's not my vagina? The girl walks the rest of the way to the bed and straddles her scene partner, slowly grinding her hips.

anRkey_InCel51

Now everyone else will see you as the same desperate, whoring, corporate sex slave that I do.

I can't watch the rest. Eyes squeezed shut, a tear slips down my cheek as the girl's breathy moaning ramps up along with the squeak of the bed springs.

A raw, feral scream rips its way up my throat as I hurl my phone across the room. Cheek pressed against my mattress, I draw my knees up to my chest and cry, sobs being dragged out from within this deep, echoing hole I realise has always been in me. A vast, dark cavern that's remained hollow no matter how much money, or likes, or *stuff* was thrown into it. Defeated, I stop trying to claw my way out of the emptiness and instead, I let it swallow me.

I don't know how long I lie there, but when I drag myself up off the bed, the sheet's smeared with blood, my nails having eaten into my skin in half-moon slices. I don't feel anything though I know it should hurt. I stand, pick up my phone, a lightning bolt of cracked glass going through it, and force myself to read through the rest of Anarchy's unhinged ramblings.

anRkey_InCel51

Hope you liked your X-rated debut. You're a pro, a natural.

It's like you were born to sell yourself, don't you think?

anRkey_InCel51

HELLO???!!!!11!?!??!1

Bet you're wondering what I get out of making my little masterpiece. Apart from the joy of humiliating you that is.

DO NOT ignore me

I scroll through maybe about a hundred and fifty messages, some of them just made up of a single word or a run of exclamation marks.

anRkey_InCel51

Clearly your TOO BUSY, TOO IMPRTANT to talk to me righ now!!! So I'll just leave my demands here for whenever you decide to get back to diong your 'JOB'

First I want you to delete your account.S EVERYTHING gone. No more @almondhazelanything

I skim down to the next message, letting out a strangled gasp.

anRkey_InCel51

And I need more money. £12,800. Use the same email adddress. anarchyanderson@protonmail.com

You have until midday tomorrowo. That's when 'Amateur Almond's Anal Debut' is scheduled to be uploaded.

Do not fuck with me. I'll know if you go to police.

Midday!? It's 11.48, *fuck*. I swipe through to my online banking app, stomach shrivelling when I see there's still no 'advanced' payment from VeGlow sitting in there collecting interest. There's only what's left over from the monthly allowance Mum pays me out of the AdSense money. £139.68.

Oh my God, *Mum*. Maybe I could ask Mum. Tell her it's for a new bag? Valentino? D&G?

No, she'd never believe I'd want to waste that kind of money on anything designer. What can I say it's for? Puffy-eyed, I look around my room, searching for something expensive enough and necessary enough that I can break and ask her to replace right away. But I don't *have* anything that urgently replaceable enough.

I close my eyes and breathe deep, trying to think, and when I open them again I'm staring right at my answer. Kent. Oxford Brooks. Bath Spa. The spines of all the prospectuses of universities I was pretending to consider stacked on my desk. I'll tell her the money's for a university course. Mum can't say no to that. Quickly, I leaf through the booklet on top of the pile in case she asks me about this imaginary course I'm about to be super-hyped about. Fuck, it's 11.51, I don't have time for this. Radio broadcasting, that'll do.

MUM CALLING . . .

Or maybe I should do what I should've done a long time ago and just *tell her* about Anarchy, because I can't deal with this on my own anymore. She picks up on the first ring, the call connecting into silence.

'Hello?' I pull the phone away from my ear, checking to see she hasn't hung up, that the signal's fine, and it is, but still there's only Mum's clipped breathing on the other end. Who answers the phone without saying hello? Why isn't she saying anything? 'Mum?' Nothing. 'Hello? Can you hear me?'

There's a pop of her gloss as her lips peel apart. 'You haven't checked Twitter then?'

Beer fear chugs its way around my body, hopping up my nerves and settling like sludge in my stomach, a tang of vomit in the back of my mouth. This time it's me that doesn't talk.

Mum daintily clears her throat. 'This is all some hypocritical bullshit, really.' Oh no. I think I said that. The memory's underwater-warbled, but I know Mum's quoting me. 'Like, yeah, they've slapped the word vegan on it and there's a cute pic of a bunny on the side so of course you know a million per cent not one single animal was hurt in the process – hmm, okay then, hun – but it's still made of plastic, still overpriced elitist shite that only the dummy, yummy mummies will buy.'

Oh my God. I grasp my phone with both hands, squirming against the gunky black tongue of anxiety that's flicking in and out of my ear as it whispers what I already know, *You did a bad thing.*

'This is my favourite part, listen,' Mum says, hollowly. 'It'll sell 'cuz it's got our name on it, yeah, but VeGlow know they're milking the influencer teat dry with this one.'

I grip my throat, unable to breathe. I can't speak, not that anything I could possibly say right now would fix this. A memory rear-ends the back of my brain in a collision of guilt and shame. Last night, the bathroom buddy I met before Nevaeh, it must've been—

'Harper Atkins, page six of *Glamour* magazine today. Ringing any bells?'

'Mum,' I choke out, tears dripping into my mouth. 'I'm so sorry. I—'

'I don't want to hear it, Almond. I mean, really, do you hate me that much? You resent me so much for putting you on the internet when you were little that you're hell-bent on ruining me completely, is that it?'

'It wasn't me … talking,' I gasp, trying to scrape air into my lungs.

'Oh, so it's all lies is it?' Mum cuts. 'You didn't say any of that to Harper, then? It's all a misprint?'

'No, I mean, I didn't know what I was saying, I was—'

'Oh, I know what you were. You were drunk.'

'So were you!' I sob, angry and confused, feeling betrayed out of our tipsy train ride home last night, and stupid for thinking things might be better now.

'I'm forty years old, for crying out loud! Since when have you started getting yourself in such a state anyway? Oh, I know. Since you've been staying round your Dad's every weekend.'

'It's not his fault,' I choke out.

'You're seventeen, Almond. *Seventeen.* It's time you acted like it.'

'I would,' I scream. 'If you'd just let me!'

On the other end of the receiver, Mum's breathing hotly, the blare of car horns and the hiss of bus exhausts loud in the background.

'Where are you?' I whisper.

'On my way to Spencer's.' She sighs, all the fight sparked out of her, leaving just the stale air of disappointment. 'Don't worry, he's still fired – or will be – but Paisley's called a Zoom meeting, though I don't know why she's calling it that, it's obviously a firing. The product will be pulled off shelves, the posters ripped down. Everything deleted. Nine months of work just—' Her voice squeaks off and she sniffs, the traffic hum growing fainter.

She must be at Spencer's apartment building already. I have to ask her now.

'I'm s-so sorry, Mum. But I need to ask you something – there's someone . . . I don't know what to do, I need . . .'

My throat's caving in, trapping the words.

'What?' Mum sighs. 'Almond, calm down. Look, don't cry like that, darling.'

'D-don't be nice to me. I don't deserve it.'

'Just breathe, in for five, out for five. Tell me what you're trying to say. Quickly though, I'm about to go up to the penthouse. I need to at least *try* to salvage some professional relationship with VeGlow.'

'Can't you just come home?' I beg.

'What did you say?' Her voices crackles. 'I'm in the lift, signals not great—'

The line goes dead, and when I throw my phone onto the bed, the time stares back at me coldly, alone in the middle of the screen.

11.59.

35

'Hey, this is Hev, leave a message, or don't. I probably won't listen to it anyway. Who calls people these days?'

Dad

Baby, I'm at work. Can't pick up now. I'm working all Sunday to earn some extra annual leave so we can go away somewhere this year. Turning my phone off now tho, boss just caught me. Talk soon xxx

'The person you are calling – *Joss* – is currently unavailable. Please leave a message or try again later.'

Callie

Message Not Sent

This person isn't receiving messages at this time

'Oh, I'm sorry, this is Nina, you've come through to reception because your grandma isn't in her room right now. It's Sunday Funday in the dayroom from noon. Can I take a message?'

36

I'm on BBC's *News at One*.

The woman from *Points West* with honey highlights and a peony-pink trouser suit presses her palms to the desk. She solemnly shakes her head beside a green-screened still of me, cropped from the shoulders up, taken from Amateur Almond's Anal Debut. My face, mapped onto a porn star's head, is frozen in a yawny O of pleasure.

They've spun the story into a cautionary tale about how posting provocative content can attract the attention of manipulative members of the porn industry who scour socials for young, impressionable, fame-hangry girls to exploit.

'Someone stole my face!' I shout at the TV, my blood-rushed pulse reverberating in my bones. I'm shaking all over, unable to cope with the knowledge that this image is being broadcast into millions of people's homes. Into their living rooms, on 4K TVs as big as eighty-five inches, no longer confined to a phone screen.

Honey Highlights finishes her hot take on the issue. '... the important lesson I hope our younger viewers learn from this unfortunate incident is that once you post something on the internet, it's no longer yours. You belong to the world wide web.' As my eyes fill with tears, she steeples her fingers, the absolute *picture* of judgement.

I toast the TV and crack the seal of a bottle of vodka I know cost nearly a hundred quid, watching the flecks of twenty-three carat gold inside swirl as I swig from it, gulping, dribbling the vile liquid down my chin a bit, then wiping it on my duvet, flakes of gold coming off on my bloodstained sheets.

'Cheers.' I take another gulp, probably a tenner's worth.

I wonder how many bottles of this it would've taken to pay off Anarchy.

'Now, onto our next story. How you can use your smartphone to cut supermarket queues ...'

I mute the TV, instinctively grabbing my phone, the screen smashed and the back dented from when I threw it at the wall earlier. I run my finger across the zigzag of broken glass, a shard of black puncturing my fingertip. A bubble of blood. Through the splinters, I make out that the battery's warning me it's on ten per cent and I've got four missed calls from Joss. I'm squinting to read the previews of his texts when a new call buzzes through from him.

'Hello?'

'Almond, hey. What's going on?' His tone's laid down thick like concrete, making me squirm self-consciously knowing he's seen Anarchy's video. 'Are you okay? Hello?'

The vodka scorches down my throat, anaesthetising what I suspect this phone call to be – Joss stating he doesn't want anything to do with me any more. Because even if he doesn't believe the video, thanks to his mistrusting, fake-news bias, this will all be too much, my life too invasive and publicly owned for him to be a part of.

'I'm not actually, no. The video – it's totally fake, it's not me—'

'I know it's not,' he says, firm, defending, as if he's insulted I thought he'd think otherwise. 'Even if I hadn't met you and gotten to know you, and . . .'

I tense, both hands gripping my phone, desperate to know what he stopped himself from saying. 'What?'

'Nothing. I'd just know that wasn't you, from the sheer amount of *you* there already is on the internet.' A laugh, awkward and not *his* laugh strangles off into a sigh. 'Obviously it's fake but . . .'

'But what? What's that supposed to mean?' The vodka upchucks assumptions out of my mouth, the ones that have been festering in the pit of my stomach since the video broke and the whole world decided it needed to voice their opinion on me. 'That all this time I was asking for something like this? Because I posed in bikinis and wore a lot of make-up?' By now my words are clumped and knotted with sobs. 'It's not fair. Why would someone do this?'

'That's not what I meant at all,' he says quietly. 'And I don't know who the *fuck* would do this.' He inhales sharply and I hear a distant thump on the other end of the line. 'What's your address? I'm coming—'

'Joss?'

My phone falls from my ear, a black-screened dead weight in need of a battery replacement. *Fuck*.

My vision reels towards my laptop, closed acute at the foot of my bed. I yank it open and towards me, feeling untethered without my phone, realising when I stare at the Facebook search bar that Joss has no social media presence, no way for me to contact him. Another searing gulp of vodka. My mouse drifts towards the next tab, its notification number ticking upwards at a dramatically faster rate. Pulling the duvet up over my head like a hoodie, I click into Twitter, where my literal asshole is a trending topic.

1 · Trending
#AnalAlmond
13.9k Tweets

Imogen Shawcross @immy_sc2004 · 1m Hey, my lovelies. I'm sharing this to highlight that Almond Brown is not the girl we all thought she was, and I hope that this will make people reconsider the allegations she's made against my mum @celeste_shawcrossxox. While I am all for sex positivity, I do not think this content is appropriate [1/2]

Imogen Shawcross @immy_sc2004 · 35s for Almond's demographic. I also think this change to graphic sexual content isn't helpful for female content creators who are already sexualised daily and battling against society's expectations of us. Almond, I wish you well but honestly, this – is not it xxxx [2/2]

I angrily wipe away tears, staring as Imogen's likes flicker into the hundreds in seconds. I can't believe that she thinks *I think* that hardcore porn is suitable for my audience with an average age of fourteen. Why would she broadcast this to the internet without even considering texting me and asking me for the facts? Unlike all the other people shouting their opinion into the anonymous void – not thinking of the consequences of their words, whether I'll read them and how they might make me feel – Imogen has my phone number, she's been to my house! And the political stance of these tweets will encourage hundreds of replies and debates, dragging this out even longer.

I thought she was a friend. A precarious, unpractised, mutual-follower friend at that. But a friend who wouldn't do this to me.

I lose half an hour, maybe more, reading through the hashtag, needing to know what people are saying about me and dousing the hurt with more mouthfuls of vodka.

Stephanieee @steph-sophia-halls · 1m Known #AnalAlmond since school. We all saw this coming!!! How is anyone AT ALL shocked when she was getting bikini waxes at 12 yrs old!? Baby slut graduatedddd

I'm not even shocked. Steph has been *waiting* for this one.

Letitia @bacon_letishtomato · 2m Yet another insta thot cashing in on her body. Kmt!!!! #AnalAlmond

Milk Two Sugars @milk2sugarteachannel · 2m The tea is a'brewin over in our editing suite rn guys. We're working on a 3 part tea series unpacking the #AnalAlmond scandal and all the beef that went down with @celeste_shawcrossxox

Karen L. Grosvenor @karenlouise_grosvenor · 10m No wonder young girls have no respect for their bodies anymore when THESE are their role models #endoffeminism #AnalAlmond

Miss Mary M @magdalenequeen · 11m GIRLLLLL GET IT!!! #AnalAlmond is living!!!!! End sex work stigma y'all!👅

T @Treyvon_B_Michaels · 13m Why u let some ol white dude wreck u like that #AnalAlmond ????? Dem goods is damaged now 😔

Lucy Lou @lilLucyLouise · 19m @eve-s-fairchild you should be ashamed of yourself. This is the result of you exposing your daughter to social media from such a young age without her consent. She was always going to go down this path. #evefairchildiscancelled #AnalAlmond [1/13]

Big B @robert6969bradford · 25m 👀 Wait til her daddy see this #AnalAlmond

I'm Ava! @ava_arianafan2010 · 26m WE LOVE YOU ALMOND! Don't listen to the haters, I'll always be your number 1 fan no matter what💕 #AnalAlmond Only using this gross hashtag so the haters see this 🖕🖕🖕

Kyle @fukwitmyglock · 33m Ebony slut was asking for it. Lil bitch bout to get raped #AnalAlmond

I wince as I lift the bottle of vodka, only a quarter of its liquid left, the gold flecks dancing inside the glass like falling stars towards my lips. I take a gulp, my mind dizzying away from that last tweet, that awful wound of a word that felt like a slash between my legs when I read it.

He can't get me in here. The world can't get me in here. Inside this bottle.

The LED sear from the laptop aches my eyes.

Next tab, YouTube. The mouse whirls-twirls-swirls as I refresh.

Oh, it's me – I'm featured on the homepage. Tea for Two are the first drama channel to comment on the deepfake, though they're not calling it that, their new upload thumbnailed by a badly pixelated screenshot from Anarchy's video. I skip through it, crushing the right arrow of my keyboard, trying to decide whether these people actually believe this is real, or they're being wilfully ignorant for more views. Clearly their team's done some digging; their sources were able to confirm the identity of the man in the video. Veteran porn actor, Björn Hammer, declined to comment on the situation. Probably because like me, he *knows* this never happened, *knows* there'll be no repercussions, only free publicity and notoriety once this whole thing is proven to be a hoax.

I copy-paste his name, waste a few minutes googling him.

Björn Hammer wiki
Björn Hammer young
Björn Hammer wife

I strike out, the laptop smacking to the floor, and then I'm pressed back into my bed by the weight of my drunkenness, blinking at the ceiling swirls as the tweets, comments, threads and hearts climb the walls of my bedroom, falling down on me like the vodka gold. Except they don't warm my insides up, they cut into me, crush my bones.

Fresh tears sting down my cheeks. My brain spins behind the backs of my eyes, dizzy and numb, leaden and weightless all at the same time. But still, it's not enough. I want voiceless, numbing darkness.

I don't want to die.

I don't think so.

I just want to go to sleep for a really long time and wake up when the world's forgotten all about me.

My head flops to the side, cheek sticking against something slimy-cold. A puddle of puke on my pillow. I threw up? When did I throw up? My eyes laze along its splattered trail to my bedside table, the vomit on my meds.

Pens and pills and lipstick lids clatter to the floor as I fumble for the packet.

'Side'ffects include sickness, drowsiness and excessssive tiredness,' I read off the side of the packet of Sertraline. 'Oh.'

The cardboard crumples because my hands are too big, as I wrestle to get the blister pack out. Drowsiness. Tiredness. That's all I want. To sleep off the spinning room and the hate splintering through the walls from the outside. The news segments, the think-piece columns, the @s, the opinions, the accusations. I'll just sleep it off. When I wake up they'll have moved onto something new. All be gone. By the low light of my laptop glow, I push two pills, three pills out of the pack, the foil spitting them into my palm, a cluster of powdery, mini moons.

I stare at them,

counting them in breaths of five,

my hand moving closer to my lips.

One, two, three, four, five. One-two-three-four-five. Onetwothreefourfive—

*

And then the soft burr of a video call sounds out of my laptop speakers.

Stone-limbed and faint, I drag the laptop back onto the bed, accept the call.

'Almond? Oh my God, I got you.' Heather, her brief smile strangled with concern. I drop the pills, letting them roll loose into my bedsheets. Behind Hev the background shakes and swerves, fences, bushes, concrete and sky. 'Almond? Hey, it's okay, I'm coming, alright.' She's out of breath, running, the stomp of her boots on the concrete in rhythm to the heartbeat in my ears.

'Hev?' I say, though I know it's her. My thoughts aren't catching up. Seeing her, I know I should feel relieved, saved, but Heather's is just one loving face in an abyss of thousands of faceless voices who hate me, think I'm disgusting. Suddenly soupy, my mind slow, body fast and pulsing, my hands rove across cotton and fluff, searching for the lost pills so I can carry on and forget.

'Yeah, listen to me. I'm on my way and everything's gonna be okay, alright? Joss called me – I'm on my way to get him now and then we'll be with you. Hey, look at me, what are you doing?' I'm plucking at pillows, lifting blankets, looking for the pills. My eyes flick to the screen and Heather's face closes in as she draws to a stop, the camera diving down as she rests with her hands on her knees. 'I thought – I don't know what I thought. I was messaging you and you weren't answering and— fuck.' She takes a deep breath, her voice cracking. 'Hey.'

'Hey,' I say, distracted. I find one. A pill. Drop it into the vodka bottle.

'Talk to me. What . . . what are you doing?'

Another. Splashing into the vodka, like pennies in a wishing well. Then another. To silence the voices, cut their power.

'Almond, stop. What are those?' Hev's running again, her forehead damp, cheeks puce.

I make some wishes.

I wish Anarchy was a happy person,

that they felt they didn't have to make the video.

I wish Callie was still my friend.

I pinch up the powder of a crushed pill, sprinkle the dust down the neck of the bottle. Find another one.

I wish I'd kissed Joss the moment I met him.

'Oh my God. *Stop* it, okay? Look at me.'

I wish Honey were with me now.

'Can you hear me?'

I wish I'd met Heather years ago.

Actually, I wish my parents had never met at all.

'Almond, do not drink that!'

I wish thereal_almondbrown had never existed.

I lift the bottle, watching the sediment of white pennies and the drifting scraps of gold swirl and tilt, tip. The ocean in the bottom of a wishing well. And I am a ship in a storm that wants to dash me against the rocks, ruin me then take pictures of the wreckage. I'm going to find my quiet treasure, sparkling there in the depths of the ocean. I try, but it's too heavy. Tipping, tilting, the ocean spilling. Drenched.

'Almond!'

Drowning down, down into the dark.

Eyes closed, body unmovable. Molasses trapped. I feel a hand grip the fleshy part of my arm, hold my body against theirs to prop me up. I smell vanilla musk shampoo and the domestic notes of a familiar home I've slept in, eaten in, walked home from school to before, and know that I am safe.

I'm moved to the floor. Clothes are dragged off and over my body, my head fitted through new, loose ones by gentle hands. A breeze blows in from an open window.

With some effort I push into the faraway part of my mind, searching for some kind of something to remember. Behind my lids, I wade through desperate, blunted images. Carats of gold swimming through liquor; the three-quarters of it I drank. The Sertraline and its desired side-effect. More than tiredness. Inky, black oblivion. I just wanted to sleep. And sleep.

Or was there something more? Did I really want to—

No. I just wanted to make it all go away for a while.

Footsteps fade, while I spin and spin on the bed, trying to keep my eyes open, to pin the ceiling in place. And then the nutty, roasted tang of strong coffee wafts towards me. A thumb strokes my cheek.

'Almond? Can you talk to me?'

Callie.

Everything sighs, the moulded stickiness melting away from my muscles as she rouses me out of half-consciousness, her voice making my room feel like less of an echoing hole I can't climb out of.

'You're here?' I murmur, her stricken face circling in my vision.

'I'm here.' Her voice winds up tight, reedy with the effort of not crying. 'Where I should've always been. Oh my God.' Her bracelets jangle as she buries her face in her hands, their dainty touches erupting pain signals at my temples. 'I came as soon as I realised what was happening online. Like, what the fuck? I can't believe it, I'm so sorry. Here, drink this.' Callie hands me a steaming mug of black coffee and places a huge bottle she's filled with ice water on my lap. 'And a lot of this.'

'I . . . I feel sick.'

'I know. And you are gonna be sick at some point, I'm sorry, but I'll be here, I've got you.' Her hands wrap around mine as she helps guide the coffee mug to my lips, the bitter warmth of it inching me out of my fug.

'Hww . . .' I start again, willing my words to walk in a straight line. 'How'd you get in?'

'Climbed over the back fence. And don't tell me you've forgotten how many times we had to mash up that decorative rock to get your spare key.'

I try to laugh but my stomach lurches, and I lunge for the plastic bowl Callie's placed at my feet. As she's rubbing my back, my curls held back in her fist, the doorbell goes, chiming again, and again, making my skull pound inwards.

Lip bitten, glancing from me to the door, she says, 'I'll be right back. Don't move, just drink some water if you can. Two secs, okay.'

I clutch the bottle and try to sip from it but miss my mouth, waterfalling half of it down my chest. My head lolls back, eyes being pulled closed, and suddenly there's a scuffle of shoes on the stairs. Voices wavered with panic. My name, and someone's crying. I blink and there's Callie shhing Joss and Heather in the doorway. Joss, his t-shirt sticking to his chest, gasping for breath. I see his lips breathe out the words *'thank fuck'* as our eyes lock and Heather barges towards me, mascara inked down her cheeks in oily streaks.

'You didn't drink any of it, did you?' she sobs. Heather reaches over my head and finds the spilled-out vodka bottle, crouching to get in my eyeline. 'Almond, for real. We need to know if you drank any?'

Limp-necked, I shake my head, trying so hard to be here and tell them I'm okay. I reach out to wipe away Heather's tear tracks, but my hand falls slack at my side.

'What is that?' Callie's acrylic taps the base of the bottle, where the pills have all but dissolved into white motes of moondust floating amongst the gold.

'Her antidepressants,' Joss says, coming all the way into the room. He picks up the spent foil by the side of my bed, tracing the pushed-out cavities, then grabs my hand. 'She's still conscious. I don't think she actually took any.'

'Spilled it,' I manage to say.

He nods. 'But I think we should get her to a hospital anyway.'

The room blunders with people hauling me up, clothes being thrown into a bag, keys and phones found, the question of Uber or ambulance blurted, and then I'm bundled into Joss's arms, his hands keeping all of me together as I'm carried down the stairs. Away from the internet's dissection of me, their words like scalpels, slivering strips of skin off me until I am nothing, away from—

'Anarchy,' I mumble.

'What did she say?' Callie hurries to my side while Heather taps at her phone. 'Tell me again, what?'

'My phone. Anarchy.'

'Okay? Like chaos. None of that matters now—'

'A person.'

Callie nods slow like she doesn't quite understand yet. 'A person *called* Anarchy? Is that who did this?' Her eyes widen as she lights up my phone. 'You know where the video came from . . .'

Everything else fades. With my head held against Joss's chest, I hear his heartbeat swell and pulse, ebbing into a faraway echo, like I'm listening through a shell to my ear. As my eyes close and my friends' voices hush and soothe, I let the nothingness cradle me in its velvet-warm blackness. The world, gone away.

Sleep.

37

Sun laps over my face – deep, day-long, evening sun – making it so I don't even have to think about opening my eyes, they just do, fluttering open like how it is in the movies.

I can't see out the window properly, so I still don't know where I am, which hospital I'm at, but I can see the sky. It's beautiful, ironed smooth with no clouds, no planes, nothing. Just blue. The room looks private, stupid fancy with oil paintings on the wall, a mini fridge hum, and three plush, claw-footed armchairs placed around the bed, one of which Dad's dropped asleep in, snoring softly.

'Dad,' I whisper. He doesn't stir. 'Da—' I cut myself off.

What am I doing? Waking him up when I have no idea how I'm going to explain all of this yet. But instead of letting my thoughts spiral into the what-ifs and what's-going-to-happens, I sink myself deeper into the bed's memory foam and steer my mind back to the present, to the little things I can control.

I lie there, listening to the smoker's wheeze of Dad's deep breathing, counting the stitches in the ivory embroidery on the corner of my bedsheet, grateful for the stillness, being able to see the sky, the bright white room dappled with sunlight. Callie, Joss and Heather. That my friends were able to find me and get me help. At peace with only the sound of our breathing.

A door closes at the end of the corridor, a polite thank you is said, and then the familiar squidgy clunk of Mum's Chloé boots approaches. I'm not sure why but I screw my eyes tight shut, yanking the covers all the way up under my nose.

Squeak-scuff. She stops dead in her tracks. I squint one eye open and through the brush of my eyelashes, I see Mum, her cheeks ruddy, coverage patchy where she's probably tissued off mascara streaks. Hesitantly, I open my eyes all the way and we *see* each other.

The heart monitor bleeps. Birds chitter outside the window.

'Sorry,' I say, small and quiet like a kid.

'*You're* sorry?' Mum's face draws back in disbelief, her lip wobbling as she walks towards me. 'You've got nothing to be sorry about,' she gasps. '*I'm* sorry. So, so sorry, darling,' she says, hands clasped at her chest. I watch her eyes brim with tears. 'I don't . . .' Her voice shudders to a halt.

As she pours out a lifetime's worth of apologies through her tears, I take her hands in mine. Dad's awake and sitting behind her now, a hand on her shoulder, his own eyes watery. The sight of them both breaking makes me cry too, and I cry and cry, gripping Mum's hands.

'It wasn't me,' I finally catch my breath enough to say. 'The video that got leaked. The ... porn. I've never even—'

'I know. We know.' Mum lets out a rasping sigh.

'Of course we know,' Dad says solemnly. 'Did you think we wouldn't believe you, baby?'

I nod slow, shrug. 'I should've told you as soon as they— as soon as *Anarchy* started asking for money.' I close my eyes and feel a swell of fresh tears behind my lids. 'Their username is anarchy-underscore-incel-fifty-one. They blackmailed me.'

'Oh, darling, we know. Callie showed us the messages.' I flash back to the house, my whispered admission as Callie unlocked my phone. Mum grabs a fistful of her hair and forcefully sweeps it off her face. 'What a vile, cruel, sadistic thing to do.' She sighs, her throat sharpening it into a frustrated growl at the end. 'I wish you felt you could tell us, darling. I'd do anything to go back and not step foot in that elevator, to stay on the phone with you. I was so obsessed with this *stupid* campaign.'

'Stop apologising,' I mumble. 'It's okay.'

Is it okay with Mum, though? I think of the last conversation we had over the phone, how even then, taking care of the brand felt more important than taking care of me. But if I'd told her the truth of what was happening, do I think she'd have come home? Of course. I know she would've. So, maybe it's not totally okay yet, but it will be. We've both got some things we need to work on in our relationship. Communication for one. Honesty. Trust.

Dad kneads the back of his neck. 'This whole thing ain't right. Whoever this Anarchy motherfu—' Sucking in a breath through his teeth, he propels himself up off the bed, feet pounding the floor as he socks a fist into his palm. 'I tell you, I'll kill him. You have *got* to tell me these things, baby. I know why you didn't.' For a millisecond his eyes cut to Mum. 'I get it, I do, but if we'd have known we could've helped you sooner.'

I look between my parents as I choose my words carefully, not wanting to hurt either of them with what I'm about to say. 'Dad, if I told you about every single hate comment or creepy message I got, you wouldn't be able to sleep at night. It's endless.'

Mum's fingers brush shakily across her collarbone, her gaze lingering on the ECG monitor, the tube feeding into the back of my hand, her eyes widening like it's taken her all this time to realise that it's actually *me*, her daughter, in those fake-ass photos on her feed, in the gossip forums tearing apart my every decision, in the public comments from men twice my age graphically detailing what they'd do to me if they had the chance. The rape threats, death threats, upskirt shots, troll accounts, *whore, slut—*

'Breathe,' Mum says, making me realise the tremble in my bones. She inhales deep with me, nodding her head as she swoops a hand down her torso, reminding me to breathe into my belly. 'Joe, maybe you should sit down. There's nothing we can do about finding this person right now, okay.' Mum lets out a cleansing breath, as if it's taking everything for her not to get up and start pacing with him too. 'First thing tomorrow, we're going to the police.'

'The police?' I forget for a second that the worst has

already happened, that there's nothing Anarchy's holding over me any more.

'Yes. We've got to make a complaint,' Mum says. 'If only to stop them from doing this to someone else.'

'I know. It's just, what if they don't believe me that it's fake?'

'Almond, they will. These are law enforcers, trained to deal with cybercrime. And even if that video were real, it was still posted without your consent. Which is against the law,' she says, her face pressed with concern.

Seriously nodding, Dad grips the bedframe so tight I hear his knuckles crack. 'They're gonna get him, don't you worry.'

'Okay. Tomorrow.' I nod, trying but failing to suppress a yawn. 'When can we go home?'

Mum sighs out a soft laugh, dragging her hand through her hair. 'Soon. We're just waiting for the doctor to come round and formally discharge you. And to remove the tube.' She touches the plaster covering the hole where the drip's been inserted. 'You were put on an IV and flushed with fluids while you were out.'

'I didn't take anything,' I say quickly, not ready to unpack what it means that in my lowest moment I mixed a cocktail of hard liquor and Sertraline together and almost drank it, unsure whether Callie and the others have told them about it.

'We know you didn't,' Dad says, massaging his temples. 'First thing they did was a substance screening to see if there was anything in your blood besides alcohol. Your friends said it was just a lot of vodka, but it's hospital procedure anyway.'

I say a silent thank you to Joss, Hev, and Callie that they

decided not to tell my parents about the antidepressants. That's something I need to come to terms with on my own and discuss with Dr Wallace. As I am now, I know I never wanted anything else to happen but for me to quiet the fallout from the video, and to stop my head from feeling like imploding. The seriousness of the consequences didn't even occur to me. Just like how I didn't recognise the effect drinking was having on my mental health either, while my medicated brain struggled to balance the increase of serotonin from the Sertraline with the depressants in the alcohol. What was I *doing?*

'How're you feeling?' Dad says when it's been quiet for a bit.

'Tired,' I say. 'I'm just really tired.'

After swinging by Dad's flat to pick up Honey, who clambered onto my lap in the back seat and hasn't moved an inch from me since, we arrive back at the house in Clifton.

In the hallway, Dad catches me in a strong hug, his hand getting lost in my unbrushed hair, lips taut as he lands a kiss at my temple, Mum offering me a wobbly smile over his shoulder. Honey pads up the stairs after me and lies on the bathroom tiles as I shower, nose between her paws, her droopy eyelids fighting sleep, like she knows I'm fragile, something to guard. Her nose is at my heels twenty minutes later when, blanched clean, in freshly washed pyjamas, the ends of my hair still damp, I tiptoe downstairs and back into five years ago, it feels like.

Mum sits at the marble table, face creased in concentration against the glare of her laptop. She's wearing her reading glasses, bundled in her sherpa dressing gown, feet tucked up under her bum. Behind her, Dad's standing in front of the cooker, headphones on, flipping, sifting, and stirring various pots on the stove, hands switching tasks like some culinary DJ.

My double-socked footsteps go unnoticed against the hardwood and as I go to take the seat next to Mum, the scrape of the chair yanks her out of the white wall of text she's reading, a hand flying to her chest.

'You scared me, darling,' she says, and as she cups my chin, staring into me, I know she's referring to more than me making her jump. 'Really scared me,' she whispers, extending a hand across the table, palm up.

'I know,' I say, laying my hand in hers.

With the other, she runs the dainty white gold E back and forth along its thin chain round her neck. 'I was just reading up on the legislation around deepfakes.' She sighs, tracing the E across her bottom lip. 'And I've written a statement on your behalf, explaining that you'll be taking a complete break from social media for a while. That is what you want isn't it, darling?'

'It is, yeah.' I swallow. 'Thank you for writing it. Just don't put a time limit on it. I don't know when or ... if I'll be back.'

'That's okay.' She drops the necklace so it rests in the hollow of her collarbone.

'Is it? I don't have to do it any more?'

'I want you to do whatever makes you happy, and it's clear that all this' – she gestures at her laptop like she's shooing it away – 'hasn't for a long time.' Gently tugging me by the hand until I'm up and lowering into her lap, she cradles me, drying my eyes with the sleeve of her dressing gown, as I'm overwhelmed by the weightlessness of finally hearing her say those words, deciding to put my happiness first. 'It's okay, it's all okay.'

We eat roti and rice by candlelight, in the living room off trays on our laps like we used to. Honey lies like a hot-water bottle across my feet. Our talking is hushed, careful and kind, tenderly brushing over the rawness of our family wound.

Just before ten, I hand over my phone so mum can print out the message history between me and Anarchy, ready to go to the police tomorrow, and say goodnight to my parents, walking up to my room with Honey never straying from my side. Of course, Mum accepts unquestionably that Honey has to stay with me tonight; there wasn't even a discussion. My body spooned around the curve of Honey's spine, I breathe her in, trying to comfort my mind away from chasing unanswerable questions.

A while later I hear the door creak open, see Mum and Dad's shadows cast tall against the wall, and listen to them decide that I'm asleep.

The bed sinks as Mum sits down at the foot of it, and then there's this human kind of silence of a patting palm on fabric as my dad comforts her while she cries, her breaths hitched, quick with emotion.

'Look at her, Joe.' I feel an exposing whisp of air around my calves as Mum pulls back the duvet, her thumb delicately dot-to-dotting my scars. 'How could I not know how much she was suffering? A social experiment,' she mutters. 'Another thing that twat, Spencer, lied to me about.'

'Neither of us knew,' he says, and I see his shadow on the wall shaking its head.

They lapse into silence, their footsteps shuffling out onto the landing.

'Did I do this?' Mum says eventually. 'Letting the whole world walk into our lives and make themselves at home. All the perverts, paparazzi, and Piers Morgans of the world.'

'I can't get into that with you again, not now. All I know is that whatever your intentions, you didn't want *this*.'

Pondering silence for a while, arms crossed then uncrossed, a sigh.

'She is going to be alright, isn't she?' Mum whispers.

'She's gonna be just fine. Even if that prick, Piers, puts up a couple of tweets about her.'

'He is a prick.'

It goes quiet again, until I hear that spitty, forbidden kind of laughter of two old friends, laughing even harder because they know they shouldn't be.

'Fuck sake,' Mum soppily giggles, and I think she's crying a bit too.

It's sometime after that that I slip into a peaceful sleep, lullabied by the sound of my parents' laughter.

38

When we get back from the police station it's still mid-Monday morning. I pack myself into the corner of my bed where the walls meet in a nest of cushions, listening to Mum's muffled voice downstairs, ringing round to cancel the brand deals that weren't legally binding, and postponing the ones that were.

'Sorry, girl, not for you,' I say, feeling Honey's tail thump against my leg as I tear open the bar of chocolate I woke up to earlier, resting on top of a serving bowl full of Herbavive samples to balance out the sugar.

I fold the Post-it note scrawled with 'Love, Mum' and tuck it in my beside drawer.

After necking one of the bottles, I break off a giant piece of chocolate, skittering chocolate curls between the keys of my laptop, and take a deep breath. Because despite *everything*, I'm unable to keep from googling myself. You can't undo years of conditioning in one catastrophic cancellation.

There's been a shift on social media from outright hate to 'a conversation'. But despite the fact that articles like 'Ten Signs the Video You're Watching is a Deepfake' and 'Why the World Owes Almond Brown an Apology' are circulating, and I'm now being treated as a cautionary tale for how advancing technologies like deepfakes can be used to ruin reputations, people are still torn. They're either supporting me and arguing for freedom of expression, advocating for the right to privacy no matter who you are, or condemning me for self-exploitation, or my mum for allowing underage bikini pictures of me on the internet, deemed 'Pure paedo bait' as cliveyboy_01 put it. I flick through comments and posts urgently before snapping off another square of chocolate and X-ing out of Twitter, satisfied that I'm at least being believed, defended even. That Anarchy hasn't won.

For now though, I'm done. Not permanently deleting but signing out. Twenty-four hours later and the world sees fit to tick my trauma off their list of relevancies for the week, their social-justice duties done. They won't be thinking about how I've just spent the last two hours in a police station.

In the stuffy little police interview room, I recounted my story with Mum and Dad either side of me, providing all the receipts in a wad of print-outs, and agreeing to enter my phone into evidence too. It was while the officers ran through the charges Anarchy would be dealt with if found that I accepted I'm probably never going to get an apology or a reason why out of all of this, even if the police do track down the person behind anRkey_InCel51. And I remind myself again that I have to be okay with that; I don't need to tie this act to a first name and a last name, to a motive, to be able to heal.

I'm closing my laptop and zipping it away into its case when there's a soft knock on the door. Mum's leaning in the doorway, bossing it from the waist up, hair blowed big and bouncy, her features sharpened by an elegant fox-eye flick, wearing a white balloon-sleeved shirt. But below that she's wearing wash-day pyjama bottoms and slipper socks, only willing to smart up the half of her that's visible over Zoom.

'Morning, darling. How you doing?'

At the sound of Mum's voice, Honey flops her head over the side of the mattress, nose poking out from under the duvet.

We laugh. 'Good, weirdly,' I say. 'I don't even miss my phone, like one little bit.'

'I'm glad.' Mum comes to kneel at the side of my bed, tickling Honey's belly, sending her leg into blissful spasm. 'Why do I feel like I'm going to be seeing a lot more of you, huh?' she says, laughing as she dodges a chin lick.

'Mum? Mum.' I wait to go on until she looks at me. 'Give me one good reason why she can't stay? And don't give me the diarrhoea-gate excuse again. Why didn't you want her around, really?'

Mum sighs. 'Because,' she says, slightly defensively. 'It was always you, Joe and Honey, loving life in your little trio, and then me on the outside. I guess – *selfishly* – I just wanted a chance to have you all to myself. I know,' she says, before I can argue that it was actually always me, Dad, and Honey, versus Mum and her six million followers, not the other way around. 'I haven't been handling the separation well, and that particular decision was very childish of me. I'm sorry I've not been as *Mum* enough as I needed to be. Bloody hell, I should've signed myself up to those Tranquillity sessions right along with you.' Honey darts a look between us, then back again, and our laughter makes her tail hammer happily against the mattress. 'Hindsight, darling. Anyway, I came up here to tell you you've got a visitor. A very handsome one.' Mum winks her slick-shadowed eye.

'*Mum.*' The space between my hips stirs with silky butterfly wings, because the only *he* that would visit me is Joss. 'He'll have been waiting downstairs for ages now.'

'Alright, alright, I didn't know if you were up for seeing anyone just yet, so I said I'd come see how you were first. Shall I tell him to come back another time?'

'No,' I say, too quickly, which makes Mum press her lips against a smug smile.

'I'll send him up then,' she says, as Honey stretches her front paws to the floor and drags herself out of bed, looking expectantly up at Mum. 'Very handsome,' I hear her mutter as she leaves. 'You hungry, Hon? Come on, let's see what I can find . . .'

Last night as I lay awake without a phone to distract me, I let myself think about Joss. No longer withering away over the opinions of strangers, I considered the one opinion that might matter to me the most. The phone call we had when I was drowning myself numb yesterday, when we were supposed to be camped out at his house all day, alone together, came back to me in warbled ebbs. I remembered he thought the video was fake – of course he would, it's Joss – but I got the impression he still wouldn't want anything to do with me, mistrustful and aloof as he is, knowing that anytime he could wake up to a girlfriend on the Pornhub homepage. I know I didn't give him a chance to explain, in the hypersensitive, disoriented state that I was in, so maybe I need to now.

'Hi.'

My head snaps up. As the door closes behind him, silence ricochets out from the click of its hinges. Joss stands awkwardly at the foot of my bed. It's obvious he doesn't know what to do with his hands – shoved in, then out of his pockets, gripping the bedframe, raking at his hair – or where to look, *how* to look at me.

'Hey.' We lock eyes and it's like suddenly the room's filled with every unsaid want and need, all our chanced touches, every text exchange flitting back and forth from our phones. 'You *do* know it wasn't me, right?' I blurt out. 'In the video.'

In an instant, he leaps over the bedframe, landing cross-legged at the end of my bed. 'Of *course* I do. I tried to tell you that, but I made it worse, didn't say what I actually meant to say. I'm an idiot, Almond, and I'm sorry. I didn't mean to hurt you.'

'You're not. Everything was hurting yesterday. I just wasn't sober enough or *well* enough to hear you out.'

He shuffles a little closer, the space between us palpable, vibrating like when you try to force two repelling magnets together.

I let out an exasperated sigh as we both speak at the same time.

'I've been wanting to talk to you.'

'Maybe we should say where we're both at—'

I shake my head, half-laughing at the romcomness of it all. 'You go.'

Joss clears his throat overly loud. I wait, my heartbeat a hummingbird in my chest. 'I'll be honest. I had no idea who you were before we met.' His nails rasp against the underside of his hair. 'But after that first Tranks session Hev told me all about you. She showed me your Instagram, the vlogs, the interviews' – I cringe, watching him list the fragments of me scattered across the internet – 'and suddenly I was faced with like, the entire history of the girl I wanted to get to know. I already knew things about you I'd imagined asking you on our first date – which would've been at Fresio's along the harbour, seeing as I knew it was your favourite restaurant from a vlog.' He rolls his eyes. 'I could've probably even guessed your order.'

I raise my eyebrow in a challenge, still clinging on to the idea of us, despite the heavy ache of where I think this conversation's going. 'Go on, then.'

'Butternut gnocchi with tender stem broccoli and a side plate of chips.'

'You forgot vegan aioli, but okay. Can I say something?' I swallow my smile, trying to figure out how to put the juxtaposition of my two selves into words. 'The thing is, internet me isn't even … me, and half the time I was just paid to pretend I liked all that stuff anyway. There are still parts of me you don't know, that I kept for myself, offline. I think I kind of lost them for a bit and I knew I wanted to be at a place where I could share *the whole* of me with you. And I think I'm ready to do that now?' I throw my gaze up to the ceiling, willing myself not to cry. 'Do you think we can start over?'

'Yes.' Joss buries his face in his hands and laughs through his fingers. 'See, this is why I hate the world. We were so busy trying to connect through these things' – he tosses his phone into the air then tennis slams it with his palm into a lump of duvet – 'that we were completely miscommunicating. I am *never* going back on social media.'

'I don't want you to.'

'Even just dipping my toe back into that cesspool when I logged in to look you up for myself got me scared that I wouldn't be enough. Because I don't wear the right brands and I don't get TikTok.'

He shrugs self-deprecatingly as I put a finger to his lips.

'You have no idea how much more than enough that makes you,' I say, my smile pouring out like tired sunshine.

Laughing, Joss leans in and gets his fingers tangled in my curls trying to be all cute by tucking my hair behind my ear. I laugh too, scooting down the bed to meet him in the middle, my thighs either side of his waist. My lips brush against his as his hands meet round the middle of my back. I don't know who kisses who first, but it starts off gentle, like a question, my hand sliding up the nape of his neck into his hair, his gripping me into him, and then the answer, told in hungry urgency, his tongue pushing between my lips.

I gasp out of the kiss, glancing around me with the irrational – or actually *completely fucking rational* given the last twenty-four hours – fear of being watched. A little breathless, I collapse back on the bed.

'So, where are we going on our first actual date then?' I say, bringing us back to coy casualness, what with my Mum being downstairs.

'How about … Vietnamese food on a rooftop terrace somewhere?'

'Sounds good. Different,' I say, glowing. 'Different is good.'

'So, what are you doing today?' he says, stretching his arm around me. 'Hev's wondering if she can come and see you tonight, by the way. She demanded I ask.'

'Cool, let's order food or something, tell her sixish. That is, if you're not working?' I burrow into the crook of his armpit, furling my legs up to my chest, foetal, to fit on his lap.

'I quit.' He nods at my dropped jaw. 'Yeah, it was making me miserable, and I was missing out on spending time with you – and Hev, and all the other things I actually enjoy about life.' He shrugs. 'So what if it takes me another year to save up for uni, or I have to work part-time while I'm studying. I've got a couple grand saved up now, and I'm thinking I want to do something fun with at least some of it. Maybe take a look at the pyramids, see if I can figure out how the hell they got there.'

'Aliens. Hundred per cent,' I say, twisting to flare my eyes conspiratorially at him. Through a laugh, he kisses me, and I decide to map out my own future for once, throwing out what *I* want to the universe, instead of having my universe boxed up into a scheduled calendar, centred around hallmark holidays. Against his lips, I say, 'Is that a solo expedition you're thinking of doing, or would you be up for getting a second opinion on those pyramids?'

'For real? You'd want to come?'

'Yeah. I've been thinking about getting out and seeing the world, and now that I *can*, I'm not sure I want to do it alone.'

For the next hour we google ourselves into the world's creepiest dark tourism destinations, planning hypothetical itineraries for our trip if we had infinite money, laughing and imagining, my world brightening and broadening beyond a screen, knowing I won't be running away from my problems like I'd initially planned to.

Instead, I'll be running *into* something new. With Joss.

I feel his phone in his pocket vibrate against my hip.

After looking for a second, he says, 'For you.'

Callie

Hey Joss, hope everything's ok . . . How's Almond doing?? I'm guessing her phone ain't in action for a bit but if you're with her could you please let her know that I'd really love to see her if she's up for it? And can you tell her that I miss her

Joss

Hey it's me – I miss you so ducking much too. Come over to my mum's about 6. I'm having some people over that I really want you to meet x

Joss

Technically you've already met. Hence you having this number, but I mean properly and not in a crisis . . .

Callie

I'll be there xxx

Joss moves through my room with careful curiosity while we wait for the others to arrive, dusting off trinkets from my inside life: the photograph on my bedside table of two-year-old me perched on Gramma's knee as she braids my hair; the Polaroids tacked to my mirror of Callie and I as chubby, cherub-curled babies, before my hair grew out all the strawberry blonde I was born with. He asks and we talk about my childhood hobbies and favourite books, as I introduce him to myself, bit by bit, like it's supposed to be.

At exactly one minute past six, a tiger-print-parachute-panted hip swings into the doorframe.

'Hey,' Hev says, poking her head round the door. The ends of her hair are freshly dip-dyed a pastel violet and the sting of peroxide still faintly clings to her as she throws herself at me in a hug. 'Don't you ever do that to me again, okay?' She sniffs once.

'Never,' I say, shaking my head. 'I'm so sorry, Hev. You shouldn't have had to see me like that.'

'No, no, not that.' She tick-tocks her finger. 'You don't have to apologise, even if you did scare the absolute shit out of me. I'm a ride or die, and I'm sure it's not gonna be the last time I'll be holding your hair back in an Uber. I'm talking about all that running I had to do when I couldn't get a hold of you, even on your laptop – get yourself a new phone *please*. My thighs suffered third degree burns trying to get to you,' she says, airing out her parachute pants. 'Chafe city, population me.'

Through gasps of laughter, I try to apologise but Heather's intent on cushioning all my anxious guilt with hugs and comfortably worn clichés.

Not even a minute later Callie steps into view, toeing the threshold with a brand-new pair of chunky New Balance I haven't seen before, hesitating, our reunion hazy and not a hundred per cent yet. For some reason I home in on the trainers, thinking about all the mundane life-happenings as well as the Big Stuff we've missed out on telling each other all summer. I wonder what her new job's like, how much of her first month's pay she swindled on her shoes, and if her dad's mad because trainers should never cost more than thirty pounds in his opinion.

I inflate with a deep breath like one of those confetti balloons, multicoloured emotions flitting around inside me. I'm relieved-scared-nervous-ecstatic and bursting that she's here. I face my oldest and – up until a couple of weeks ago – only friend. Inching towards me, her eyes wide and glitzy with tears, she lets out a relieved snort of laughter.

'Are you laughing? Why're you laughing?' I say, though laughter's trembling in my voice too, my emotions tumbling into each other, slightly hysterical thinking about the situation that's brought us all together.

Shaking her head, Callie breaks, her bottom lip wobbling as she splutters out, 'I'm so sorry the world thought you did anal with an old man.' Her voice buckles. 'And I'm sorry for everything else too.'

'Oh my God.' We fall into each other, my cheek pressing against her scalp. I close my eyes and breathe her in, wheezing with laughter and tears. 'Fuck, I've missed you. I'm sorry too, for *every*thing. Especially for how shitty it made you feel seeing my pictures saved on Theo's phone—'

'*Don't.* None of that was on you. I should've laid blame all on that utter clown. Don't even say his name,' she mumbles, her breath on my collarbone tickling familiarly from when I've held her like this a hundred times before, felt her tears wet my skin, the lapse and sway of her body as we drunkenly danced to end-of-night music at some party. 'And like, deep down, I knew that him doing the nasty over your Insta pics had nothing to do with my *beautiful*' – Callie pulls back, standing on tiptoe to press her forehead against mine – 'twenty outta ten queen just posting up pictures because she was feeling herself or because it was part of her job. Of course I knew that. I just didn't want to admit that it *wasn't* about you, because it meant admitting that ... it was about me being second best.'

'You will never be anything but first, Callie. You're *my* first. Always,' I say, wiping away her tears. 'Fuck him.'

She nods. 'Fuck him.'

'Don't know what you're talking about but yeah, fuck him,' Heather says.

We all eye Joss expectantly. 'Yeah, okay, fuck that guy.' He laughs. 'Nice to officially meet you, Callie.'

'Oh, hi! Wait, I have to ask, are you the mystery shadow man Almond was holding hands with in that pic she posted a couple weeks ago . . .' She trails off, tongue to the roof of her mouth, realising she's been caught. 'Okay, yes, I was stalking you even when we weren't talking. Obviously.'

'I'm Joss. This is—'

'I'm Heather,' Hev says, refusing to be introduced by anyone but herself.

Callie smiles big, shaking Joss's outstretched hand. 'My man's formal. I like it.'

I laugh, my gaze lingering on each of them, knowing they'll click instantly, my mind planning up the last lighter nights of summer with barbecues, beach trips, picnics and wild swims with the three of them. My friends, who've heard me cry, seen me puke, bare-faced and bleeding, who know my flaws and insecurities, and still love every handwritten page of me, not just the front cover.

September

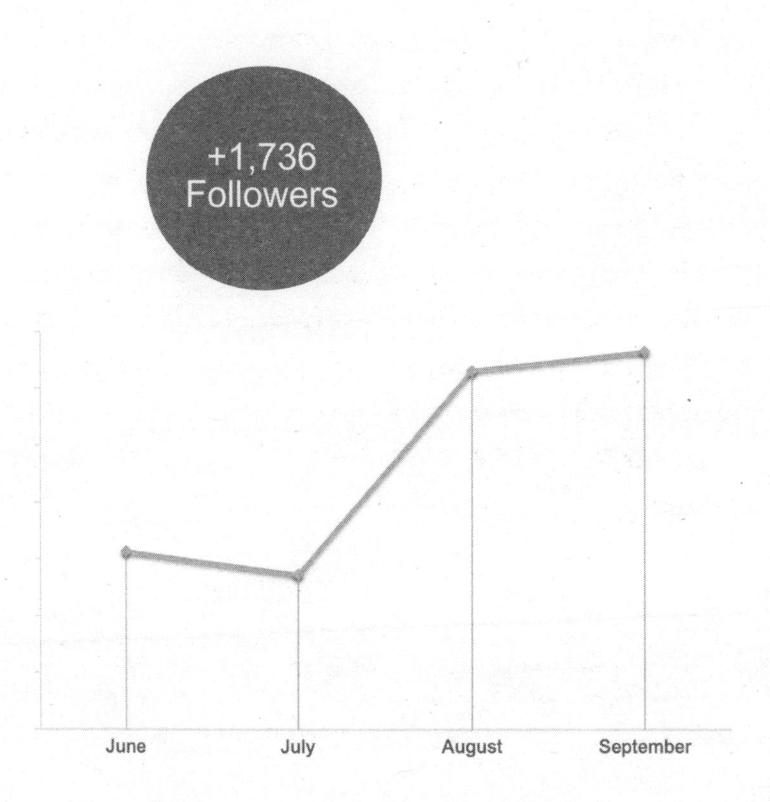

39

I stare up at the sign for Blank Space Studios, the recording studio I reached out to at the end of last month after pitching my podcast idea to Electra over Zoom.

Electra finally came through with her big secret announcement, in a fate-twisting, path-affirming moment, a week after the deepfake dropped. After my internet exit, I couldn't let go of the thought of my abandoned platform, and the things I still had to say, especially when the articles and the blogposts weren't addressing the real internal problems of the industry. By the Saturday I had a name, I had topics of conversation, and a co-host, and then Electra aligned all my manifestations by announcing she was starting up her own female-led production company. Electrafied.

When I told her about the concept over Zoom, though our eye contact was connected by satellites and servers, I knew Electra really *saw* what I wanted for this project. She wouldn't exploit me like Spencer did, overwork, or oversell; Electra had been on the other side of this contract, and that's also why I asked her to be the first guest on the podcast.

I go inside, taking in what our deposit and three months' rent bought us, with money that came *straight* out of my VeGlow advance that I'm glad to be putting to good, hope-fulfilling use. I finally got it the day after my eighteenth, which was celebrated low-key, without costumes, just me, my parents, Gramma and Honey, Callie, Hev and Joss, eating slices of Gramma's famous hummingbird cake outside in the sunshine.

Apparently, Serenity's raking in millions, though we're not seeing a single penny of it. After Mum respected my wishes and cancelled our *joint* contract as VeGlow's brand ambassadors, we forfeited our rights to the product's profit. Still, Mum's doing just fine with her new management and has even landed a segment on *This Morning* giving advice to concerned technophobe Gen-Z parents calling in.

Cheeks puffed with pride, I grab the brown-paper envelope inside our mail slot and shake out the key to our studio, a fob attached with the working title of our podcast – Influential – on it. Excitement shoots up my spine, like a zipper being pulled up slick fast, as I take a photo of the key dangling off my finger and send it to the new family group chat. Mum responds in 0.0036 seconds.

Mum

Eeek! It's showtime!! Not that you need it, but I'm sending all the luck in the world to you!❤

Dad

It's official @Eve . . . our baby's all grown up. I'm so proud of you, Almond. Now let the world hear what you've got to say xxxx

I clutch the phone to my chest, so grateful for this level of communication and open-heartedness between them now. They're not getting back together and, honestly, I don't think I'd want them to; we're finally functioning so much better as a family than we ever did before the separation. But this is healthy, this is progress.

Riding high on parental pride, I pocket the key then bound up the stairs two at a time, hyped to get first pick of the spinny chairs in the studio. Room six is on the fourth floor in the renovated attic space, so I'm panting a bit as I climb the top step into a bright, skylit corridor and – stop dead in my tracks.

Is that . . . Imogen? She's standing at the end of the hallway, forehead pressed against the floor-to-ceiling window, her fingers pattering against the glass, pinkie to thumb, thumb to pinkie.

'Immy?' I say, taking tentative steps towards her. It's been almost a month since I last saw Imogen, since she told me she didn't want the feud between me and her mum to come between us, before she forgot all that a couple of days later and tweeted Anarchy's video into mass politically charged virality. She never showed up to the last two Tranks sessions, and I've been wanting to reach out to find out why, but I guess I hadn't healed enough for that yet. And now she's here.

Immy faces me, sweeping all her hair over one shoulder and twisting it taut with both hands, turning and turning, like she's wringing out a dishcloth.

'Hi,' she says, struggling to sustain eye contact with me.

Her hair's still glossy like Barbie's, her highlight still glimmering, and her nails still shiny with mint-green shellac, no chips. Yet despite her flawless finish, the concealer can't hide the hollowing of sleepless nights under her eyes.

'What're you doing here?'

'I don't know, really,' she says, drawing the sleeves of her candyfloss-pink cardigan over her fists. 'This didn't feel like something I could do over text, but now I've come, and . . . seeing you, I feel like I shouldn't have. You look so happy.' She blots at a tear with the cuff of her cardi. 'I feel absolutely vile about the things I said on Twitter, Almond. I won't give you an excuse because there isn't one, but I'm so sorry. It was self-absorbed, shallow, and embarrassing, actually, all for a few extra likes. I tried to delete the tweets but it was too late. People were already sharing screenshots like seeing someone with a bigger following validating their opinion made them feel justified in hating you.'

'Why?' I breathe in through my nose, focusing on pressing the pads of my fingers together, hoping the pressure subsides the urge to itch, like Dr Wallace suggested. It's one of our new coping strategies I'm trying out. 'Like, I think I know why, I want to understand, but I thought we were friends. You could've called me.'

'We are . . . or were. I know you probably can't stand me

now.' Picking at a loose thread on her cardigan, she spills her words fast, like an unravelling. 'But I had Mum in my ear saying that Fast-Off were dropping me as a client, and all her upcoming sponsors were backing out. She was so devastated, crying all the time, that I thought we were going to lose the house or something. So, when I realised the backlash to the video was spiralling into a hate campaign against you – it's fucked up, but I saw it as a way to lessen some of the negativity towards my mum.' Dainty, silent tears fall from Imogen's eyes as I join her at the window. 'I just want her back, you know. I tried to tell her we'd be alright, that we didn't need the brand deals and all that, but it's like nothing else makes her happy.'

'Hey, it's okay,' I say, any resentment I had dissipating as I slip my arm around her shoulder. Because I know she's not just talking about before this internet drama began. I know more than anyone what it's like to lose your mum to the instant gratification of Instagram, feeling like your love can't compete with the likes of a thousand strangers. 'We're fine, I get it. I'm sorry for my part in all this too, and about your mum. I know how shitty that feels, trust me.'

I don't know how long we stand, sun-soaked, looking out over our city, its bricks glowed gold by summer's last afternoon. The weather's supposed to change from tomorrow. I peer through the windows across the street into student accommodation, yoga studios, kombucha shops, gin bars, and plant nurseries disguised as old, Victorian houses, observing a brief glimpse of the lives of the people coming and going, people who have whole inner worlds of their own, and moments that have perhaps been deliberately chosen and webbed across their own social media accounts for people to peek into.

I'm about to ask Imogen what she wants to do with the rest of her life when the whoosh-slam of the heavy front door echoes up the stairs, a clattering of footsteps growing louder. At the third floor, I hear Joss's stompy-big feet, Heather practising our podcast name in different pitches of the *X-Factor* voice, and Callie giggling, getting her to go again. My team. When they see me standing with Imogen they falter, their steam evaporating at the top of the stairs.

'You okay?' Joss asks, making it to me in three strides. He crooks his arm around my neck, wetting my temple with a hard-lipped kiss.

'Completely. All good. We were just talking,' I say, taking his hand.

Hev sidles over next, looking sheepish. 'I have a confession,' she says, sliding her heart-shaped glasses back into her hair. 'I told Imogen where we'd be today. I know, I know, but she said she wanted to apologise, and I thought – if it goes tits up and you don't wanna hear what she has to say, you'd be surrounded by us, not that I thought that would happen anyway. Also, I'm thinking, Imogen . . . next guest?'

I point my finger at Hev sucking in a wry smile. Because Hev would've known how the unresolved rift between me and Immy was gnawing at the back of my mind, so she brought us together to sort it, intuitively knowing it's what we both wanted. As for Immy being our next guest, I couldn't think of anyone better. From what she's just told me, it's clear Immy's feeling disenchanted from the La La Land of lies and Photoshop and is rethinking her life as an influencer. Maybe being on the podcast could actually *help* her work through all this.

Imogen wipes her eyes expertly, without smudging any make-up. 'Next guest? What is it exactly that you guys are doing?'

While Heather fills Imogen in on the premise for the podcast, and Joss busies himself stacking some of the bags of laptops, spare equipment, and snacks by the door, Callie threads her arm behind me.

'Your dad told my dad that you're going to be on the radio by the way.'

'Oh, yeah?' I catch a strand of Callie's hair that's fallen on the wrong side of her parting and smooth it back down. 'You wouldn't believe the amount of times I've told him it's a podcast.'

'He's mad proud of you, you know.'

We melt together, taking in the view, her arm around my waist, my head tilting to touch hers. 'I love living here,' I murmur, just for something to say.

'Me too. I don't want to leave. Now that I've found an actual flat share – in *Lewisham*, like all them miles away, all this uni stuff seems a bit too real. How will I cope going from living a bus ride away from you to a whole motorway?'

I laugh through my nose, closing my eyes against the warmth of the sun crowning out from behind a cloud. 'We've got FaceTime. The internet's not completely toxic,' I say. 'Plus, I know you won't be able to stay away from Jemima's plantain chips for more than two weeks tops. And I'll be up visiting you all the time, girl.'

'Promise?' Cal says, getting a little teary.

'Promise,' I say, snagging her pinkie with mine. 'Right, why're we still out here anyway – let's go see our new *studio*, team.'

Sliding the key out of my back pocket, I hold my breath as Callie, Joss, Hev and Imogen gather close, just as eager as I am to see inside.

'Ooh, I'm so proud,' Hev says, hugging me from behind.

I unlock us into a spacious studio, where sun pours through the skylight. In the middle of the room there's a table shaped like a splodge of paint, curves that dip in and out, and four swivel chairs with mismatched upholstery pulled up to it. Spiking out of the centre is some robot-arm-looking thing, with mics as thick as telescopes jutting out towards each of the seats.

'This is sick,' Joss says, letting himself into where the mixer's splayed out on a desk behind a glass screen. I beam at him on the other side of the glass and look down at the buttons on switches on sliders on dials.

'I'm so excited,' I say, slipping in beside him and resisting the urge to press every lit-up thing in sight. 'Thanks for doing this with me.'

After twenty minutes of swivelling dangle-legged on the chairs and getting our laptop situations set up in front of our mics, Joss, Callie and Imogen settle in the sound booth as Hev and I record the promo for the first episode while we wait for our guest to dial in.

Electra's ten minutes early, calling just before 6 a.m. LA time, professionally slaying in an apple-green power suit and her hair in a sleek chignon. After a quick catch-up and run-down of our interview topics, I spin the laptop around to introduce her to everyone in the studio.

'Hey!' she cries.

'Electra, this is my friend and co-host Heather, who you've sort of virtually met through emails.' Hev gives a double-handed wave to the camera. 'And we've actually got some audience members today – that's my best friend Callie, and that's Imogen Shawcross, who perhaps might make an appearance on the show next week, and lastly that's our sound engineer Joss, who just so happens to be my . . . boyfriend.' The word feels secure, grounded, a root keeping my head from getting lost amongst the dark stars again. I smile over at him, his hair swept half-up, secured by a hairband I know he probably borrowed from me. Smiling, he squints against the sun.

Electra slaps both hands to her cheeks. 'Oh my God, *what?* Why haven't I heard anything about this? Are you guys public?'

'Um, in the sense that we hold hands in public, yeah? But I'm done sharing every single aspect of my life online. I just want to focus on the podcast.'

'Good. Idea,' Electra says, clapping for emphasis. 'Speaking of . . .'

I get out my notes, waiting for Joss to count me in before reading aloud the intro I decided to script just this once. I guess it's more of a statement actually, addressing not only everything that happened with the deepfake but everything that's always been happening to me and thousands of other girls made to feel like they weren't enough.

Firstly, I felt I owed my followers an apology. My followers never had a name; they weren't my Nutties or my Brownies, and they definitely didn't become my Sugared Almonds, which Mum and Spencer pushed so hard for in the early days. So, I just start with, 'Hey guys,' and tell them that I'm sorry. For a lot of things.

I'm sorry that I lied to them about what I looked like, from the filters that pinched my features into delicate, doll-like disproportions, to the thick, black tights I wore over my legs, hiding the damage I was doing to myself and how unhappy I was. For the fake smiles and stoppering all my hurt inside until it soured into the resentment I ended up feeling towards them. I tell them I'm sorry that I took them for granted, that I didn't make more of an effort to respond to their messages or share the projects they were working on to a wider audience. That I didn't appreciate all the people who magicked me into their insanely talented artwork, or handwrote me long, soulful letters.

Mostly I'm sorry that I didn't use my platform for anything but pretending.

Before introducing Heather as my co-host, I take the time to introduce myself properly, stressing that all this time, I wish they'd either known me as *me* or didn't know me at all, but that with this podcast, I hope I can change that.

*

'... So, did you ever experience feelings of jealousy?' Hev says.

While it's not my turn to talk, I quickly text Joss under the table.

Almond

How long have we been recording??

Joss

Coming up on 40 mins. You're doing great

On the other side of the soundproof glass, next to Callie and Imogen, both totally transfixed by Electra, Joss smiles at me, hands held over his headphones because I guess he's seen pictures of producers posing like that in music videos or something. I stifle a laugh and go back to giving the conversation my full attention.

'Of course I did. I was jealous of Almond, Cece, Bella, all of them. Even friends I'd had for years became competition.' Elbows on the desk in front of her, we watch the screen as Electra speaks over her clasped hands, knotted at her chin. 'Even when I got to ten million, I felt like I still wasn't getting it, or like they knew something I didn't because they all seemed so happy doing it,' she says. 'But I think it's important for all of us to start admitting that we feel like that, because really, being jealous of the internet is like being jealous of the solar system. It's a cringey metaphor but we're all still pretty, shiny, fucking powerful stars.'

'No, it's true, it's a good metaphor,' I say through laughter. 'I think the jealousy comes from us all being products of a society that bases *so* much worth on appearance, and then we created this online space that perpetuates unattainable beauty standards that we can't keep up with. None of us.'

Hev deeply nods, really feeling it. 'Mmhmm.'

'Take me for example. When I developed excoriation disorder, I couldn't even keep up with my own beauty standards from older posts. So I lied. Faked it because I'd *already* made it, and I couldn't bear having people find out I was ... less than how I looked in the photos.'

'You know you're more, right?' Hev interjects.

'I do know that now, yeah,' I say, 'thanks to you and all the other people in the support group I was secretly attending this summer, because I felt I even had to keep *that* a secret. It's called Teen Tranquillity for anybody who thinks they're ready to seek help. I'll leave a link in the show notes for this episode. They have a bunch of free resources on their website too, like crisis numbers and self-referral forms that could be really helpful.'

Nods and *mmhmms* all round.

'See, if I didn't know you and I was still just watching from afar in that really bizarre relationship of follower to person-who-has-followers – if I just saw what you were posting, I'd have thought you were having an amazing summer. The internet isn't real,' Heather says, leaning into her microphone.

'There are corners of it that are, like the one I hope this podcast ends up in,' Electra laughs. 'But no, for the most part, it's total unreality and we have to stop comparing ourselves to one another.'

'Exactly,' I say. 'Because that picture you just scrolled past is only a tiny glimpse into a whole life that holds fears, hopes, hurt, and a whole history they don't have to share with everyone. I think if I want people to take anything away from this first episode, it's remember there's a real-life person at the other end of that message you just sent. Even though their bosses make it seem like that person's some kind of flawless, perfect prototype of a human or something, I can guarantee that they're still a girl who looks in the mirror some days and cries too.'

I fling wide the Blank Space front door, followed out by Joss, Hev, Callie and Immy, and we're instantly smothered by a blanket of sunshine. I stretch my bare arms up into the warmth, feeling like a phone at full battery, at a hundred per cent but still plugged in. Immy thanks us, asking if she can think about our offer to come on the show next week, her toes turned in, still nervous about going against Celeste's ten-year business model for her.

'You guys were amazing,' she says. 'Seriously.'

Across the road, the purr of an idle engine revs up into a roar and I look over to see a soft-top car with Celeste behind the wheel, hiding underneath a wide-brimmed straw hat and sunnies. Immy flinches as she leans into the horn, blaring it twice. I stare across the road at her, not feeling anything but sadness for this woman whose evident traumas manifested in the lashed-out, ugly words of her past splashed across the internet for everyone to see. Insecurity, jealousy, self-hatred reflected onto others. Even her own daughter.

'Call me whenever things are shitty at home. Or you can just call me whenever – things don't exclusively have to be shitty when we speak.' I tell Imogen.

We crowd around her in a group hug, hoping that the feeling of belonging will follow her home, waving her off as she slips into Celeste's car.

'What's everyone doing now?' Hev asks as she cranes her neck back, letting the sun pour over her.

'Definitely not going home yet,' Joss says. 'It's too nice, and we should be celebrating.'

'I'm down,' Callie says, peeling her jacket off her shoulders.

'Come on, I know the best place.' I cut through the circle, dragging Joss by the hand as we lead our friends up towards Brandon Hill, the scene of our first proper date, where we ate Deliveroo Vietnamese food on a picnic blanket, fending off our dogs trying to steal forkfuls of bún chay before they could reach our mouths.

'Are you trying to kill me?' Callie gasps, grasping her thighs. 'Girl, this is some mad leg work.'

'Tell me about it,' Hev says, stripping her top off and lunging the rest of the way up Brandon Hill in a holographic bralette.

'I know it's a struggle, but it'll be worth it in the end,' I pant. 'Joss, piggyback me?'

'Are you trying to kill *me*?' he says, just ahead of us.

'Just trust me,' I say, making it to the top where Joss is holding the gate open for us.

I pick a spot on the hill where the grass isn't so itchy and overgrown, nervously glancing around at groups of Bristolians, rainbowed up in their bucket hats, parachute pants, and dungaree dresses, dotted about on the green like patches of wildflowers.

Okay, let's do this.

Face sun-up, I whip my flares down rip-the-plaster-off fast before I can change my mind, planting my hands on my hips as I stand in front of my friends in a pair of skimpy cycling shorts. I clear my throat, watching as Joss lowers his sunglasses to the end of his nose, his gaze lingering.

'What d'you think?'

Hev wolf whistles, like, as hollowly loud as Thomas the fucking Tank, turning the heads of some students, but only for a moment. Because nobody cares. They don't care about me or my scars – they're too busy enjoying the sun.

'You're healing.' Joss leans forward and kisses the rough of my knee, his fingers tracing my fading scars.

'I know! Mum's been helping with all her lotions and potions. I mean, she *has* been the CEO of self-care for over a decade now, so it makes sense she'd be good at this shit.'

'You seem so much happier, girl. I'm proud.' Callie squints up at me.

'I'm feeling pretty proud too.' I mime hurling because this is so Netflix category: Teen. 'But nah, for real I am. Can we get a photo? I want to remember today.'

I set a timer, prop my phone up against the trunk of a tree, then scramble back to the others lying on their fronts, tufts of grass tickling their chins.

'Hey, before the first episode of Influential goes out, you should update your Instagram,' Callie says. 'You still have that leech, Spencer, on there as your PR guy.'

'I'll do it later,' I gabble as the flash indicates the self-timer's almost up. 'Quick, look!'

We smile as the shutter goes off.

'Go on, just delete that manipulative piece of shit from your existence. Here, I'll do it for you,' Hev says, gimme-gimmeying with her fingers.

'No way, I want that satisfaction. I'll do it in a minute.' The four of us shift onto our backs, faces glowing golden from the sun, and as I take my friends' hands, I think about how lucky I am to have found my way here, into this moment, with these people. And that is enough. 'I just want to be here right now.'

Acknowledgements

Thank you to my agent, Jessica Hare, who saw something in me and my writing that I'd never allowed myself to believe could be true before. I am so grateful for your kindness, unflappability, and unwavering support.

Thank you to my incredible powerhouse of an editor, Alice Swan, whose sharp-eyed reads, shared bafflement with influencer culture and ability to realise each character's potential shaped these pages into the story I really wanted to tell. And thank you to Ama Badu for your caring and honest insights, and for loving Almond just as much as I do. To everyone else at Faber who magicked (and by magicked, I mean worked very bloody hard on) my manuscript into an irl book, *thank you*, especially to Natasha Brown, Leah Thaxton and Emma Eldridge.

Mar Bertran, thank you for bringing Almond to life with your beautiful illustration, and for getting her curls just right.

To everybody I met on Bath Spa's Writing for Young People MA and had the pleasure of creating, growing, and trying to write a novel in the face of a global pandemic with, thank you for housing my writing while I found my voice. Special thanks to my mentor, Lucy Christopher, to Steve Voake and CJ Skuse, and to David Almond for unknowingly opening the door in my mind for Almond Brown to walk through during a lecture one day. And to Ryan Lynch, thank you for becoming more than just a scheduled friend, for your endless honesty and encouragement, and for mirroring my Capricorn energy.

My girls – thank you. To my schoolground soulmates, Adele, Georgia, Jenna and Ria, thank you for being there then and being there now, always, (usually with wine, an archive of noughties music videos, and frozen pizza). Also, to Molly, my sweetest and most light-filled cheerleader, my loves – Alice, Zoey, Gemma and all my Bunn huns.

Mum, thank you for being my constant and confidant, and for instilling a love of reading in me as a kid. Dad, for your steadfast pride in all I do. Paul, for the generous love you have for us all. And Nicki, for always lending an ear, a hand and your huge heart. To Shea, Ellis, Esme, and Svea, I'm the luckiest big sister alive to get to watch you all stumble into adulthood; thanks for all the laughs and the love. And to the rest of my extended family, the Mannings', Hegartys and Sages, I could write a whole library about how much I love all of you, but sadly I don't have the shelf space.

To Barney, thank you for giving me the world. For the kind of contentment I'd never known was possible. For knowing my doubts before I've even spoken them out loud and silencing them with fierce courage. I love you. And to our son . . . I cannot wait to meet you.